PERSEUS SPUR

Voyager

PERSEUS SPUR

An Adventure of the Rampart Worlds

JULIAN MAY

HarperCollins*Publishers*

Voyager
An Imprint of HarperCollins*Publishers*
77–85 Fulham Palace Road,
Hammersmith, London W6 8JB

The *Voyager* World Wide Web site address is
http://www.harpercollins.co.uk/voyager

Published by Voyager 1998
1 3 5 7 9 8 6 4 2

A catalogue record for this book
is available from the British Library

ISBN 0 00 224623 6

Set in Linotype PostScript Janson by
Rowland Phototypesetting Ltd
Bury St Edmunds, Suffolk

Printed and bound in Great Britain by
Caledonian International Book Manufacturing Ltd, Glasgow

PERSEUS SPUR

Chapter 1

It's a given: if the Hundred Concerns are determined to destroy you, fighting back is hopeless. But I was a proud and pigheaded man. I never doubted that I'd be vindicated because justice and righteousness were on my side; so I fought. And of course I lost.

When my final appeal to the ICS disciplinary tribunal was denied and I was Thrown Away, some important part of my personality shattered, plunging me beyond despair into a deadly apathy. Joanna was gone by then and I'd managed to alienate most of my family, my few remaining friends, and the handful of colleagues at the Secretariat who had stood by me during the scandal. I had no money left, no possibility of earning an honest livelihood, and as a Throwaway, I was eligible for only the most meagre public assistance. My spiritless inertia made even the obvious solution impossible.

Finally, the only one who ever believed that I was not guilty as charged, my older sister Eve, offered to pay my passage to a planet in the Perseus Spur, a perfect T-1 world where subsistence living was feasible and human predation at a minimum. I said: Why not? It made sense for me to keep decently out of the way until I found the courage to do what most people seemed to expect of me.

Improbably, I kept on living. Odder still, justice and righteousness did ultimately prevail. It took a while.

But I'm still convinced that the Hundred Concerns would never have come tumbling down, changing the course of human civilization in our galaxy and defeating the Haluk invasion, if the sea monster hadn't eaten my house.

*   *   *

1

The aftermath of a big storm had left the skies of Kedge-Lockaby overcast and windy that morning, hiding the comets and turning the normally gin-clear waters of the Brillig Reef murky with stirred-up sediment. The five sport-divers who had hired me and *Pernio*, my ageing submersible, for a holocam outing were noisily disappointed. Their names were Clive Leighton, Mario Volta, Oleg Bransky, Toku Matsudo, and Bron Elgar. They were a demanding and uncongenial bunch, a referral from an expensive hotel on the Big Beach.

All of them were fit and under forty. All were outfitted with the most sophisticated and expensive cameras and diving gear. All except the one named Bron (who was very quiet and in some indefinable way seemed to be the leader of the pack) were charter members of the "been there, done that" club of smartasses. Clive, Mario, Oleg, and Toku described themselves curtly as Rampart Starcorp executives, and I assumed that close-mouthed Bron was another one, perhaps their boss. Even under the best of circumstances the quintet would have been difficult. On a below-par diving day like that one promised to be, they were a total shuck.

My first mate, Kofi Rutherford, and I worked our buns off trying to please, but we bombed every time. We led a tour through the famous castle corals with their normally hilarious mome rath colonies – and the damned critters sulked in their holes. We moved on to my guaranteed crowd-pleaser, the underwater forest of multi-coloured slithy toves – but their beauty was dimmed by the excessive amount of crud in the water. The albino borogoves drooped wanly and didn't sing a note. With the divers getting glummer and glummer, I tried to demonstrate the firecracker defensive behaviour of the brillig spongids at considerable risk to my own neck. Kofi coaxed a very pissed-off bandersnatch dodecapod partly out of its shell by offering himself as bait.

The clients kept their cameras going, but they were not impressed.

At the noon break, the diver named Bron was uncommunicative, while the other four complained that the buffet spread I had provided was not up to their gourmet standards. Furthermore, they groused, my watersleds were clunkers, my sub's head was out of toilet paper, and perhaps the trip should be cancelled and their card accounts credited.

I smiled a whole lot and pointed out that the charter agreement they had signed clearly stated that my fee was nonrefundable. But hey – things would be much better when we moved on to this great new location I had in mind. With luck, we'd even see the fabulously rare giant cometworms!

I drove *Pernio* to the Isle of Rum-ti-Foo, where dramatic underwater cliffs, eroded lava formations, and rippling white laceweed usually made a striking backdrop for abundant schools of attractive piscoids. The water was a lot clearer when we went back down, but the cometworms were unfortunately still out to lunch, and so were the other spectacular varieties of marine life. All we encountered were small groups of cluckers, flame-vipers, and glass scorpions – common species that the divers had already bagged back in the tourist-trappy pools at the Big Beach. At 1500 hours they decided they'd had enough, reboarded the sub, and ordered me to return to port as soon as possible.

Was I really surprised when *Pernio*'s temperamental MFGS chose that golden moment to crash?

I spent nearly an hour trying to fix the thing while the fuming sports peered over my shoulder and made unhelpful suggestions. Finally admitting defeat, I announced that since we were incapable of navigating underwater, I would have to crank up the sub's flybridge and drive us back to Eyebrow Cay on the surface. The exasperated clients demanded to be flown off the boat at my expense, but I politely referred them again to our charter agreement, Clause 7, where they had acknowledged that all activity aboard a Throwaway-owned vessel was undertaken at their own risk.

Then Bron said he'd pay for the lift-out. Double, if necessary. The other four perked up. But when I called Eyebrow's little skyport no local hoppercraft were available. The island's two rattletrap jetboat taxis were also engaged, so the sports were stuck with *Pernio* and a tedious seventy-kilometre slog home through rough seas.

The delay meant that they would miss the 1720 express shuttle back to Manukura on the Big Beach; and if we didn't get into port before the last shuttle flight at 1845, they'd be forced to spend the night at one of Eyebrow Cay's spartan guesthouses. The men were staying at the Nikko Luxor, the best hotel on Kedge-Lockaby, and were in no mood for roughing it.

I smiled some more and told them I'd do my doodly damnedest to make knots. Then I ordered Kofi to break out the champagne that I keep aboard for special celebrations and disasters. He led the passengers below to the glasswall cabin, the snotty foursome still bitching bitterly and taciturn Bron looking like he'd swallowed a bad pup-oyster. I stayed topside on the extruded bridge, brooding, hoping nobody got too seasick.

Some submersibles move decently on the surface, but old *Pernio* isn't one of them. She wallows, especially in the kind of ugly chop we had that day, and she is very slow. Feeling none too swift myself, I wondered how much it was going to cost to repair the broken Magnetic Field Guidance System. It was newer than the sub but still twenty years obsolete, and I doubted that even my handy pal Oren Vinyard would be able to find parts for it. I also wondered if the unhappy clients would bad-mouth me to the tour booker back at the Luxor, insuring that Cap'n Helly's Dive Charters would be purged from their referral dbase.

I had long since kissed goodbye any hope of a decent tip.

Kofi came up after about ten minutes and we were able to talk privately for the first time since setting out that morning.

'They calm down any?' I asked without much hope.

He grinned at me. 'The bubbly helped. Nobody's queasy. Better than that, the storm must have disturbed the thermocline. We just passed into Blue Gut, and what d'you know? An upwelling of abyssal water brought up a swarm of ruby prawns doing their mating dance. Prettiest goddamn sight you could ask for. All of the clients except Brother Bron grabbed their corders and started shooting their tiny brains out. Acing the rubies – even through the window – will give them something to brag about back at Manukura. No way anybody can tell they didn't make a wet shoot.'

Kofi Rutherford was an embezzling accountant from Cush, hiding out from the enforcers of Omnivore Concern. Whenever I needed an extra hand, he helped out. Unfortunately for him, his ill-gotten fortune in negotiables had been ripped off in turn during a Qastt pirate boarding while his getaway starliner was en route from the Orion Arm to Kedge-Lockaby. So he couldn't buy a new identity as he'd originally planned and ended up in the low-rent Out Islands instead of in a posh villa on the leeward coast of the Big Beach. He had a smaller submersible of his own called *Black Coffee*, presently undergoing major repairs after an encounter with an uncharted shoal near the Devil's Teakettle.

I said, 'So old Bron is the only one still cheesed off . . . Funny, when they came to my place this morning, I had the feeling I'd met that joker before.'

Kofi only grunted at that. Past lives are not an acceptable topic of light conversation among the Kedgeree Throwaway community. Moving easily on the rolling sub's yielding, rubbery skin, he went to the aft dorsal flat where the diving equipment had been left in a heap, pulled a freshwater line out of its housing, and began to hose down the gear.

On an impulse, I queried the bridge computer, calling up the mystery client's full name and particulars as he had given them that morning. Bronson Elgar: Suite 1631 at the Nikko Luxor, Manukura. He was not a middle-management exec like the other four, as I had automatically assumed. Instead of a Rampart corporate card he carried a personal niobium Amex – which means Be Very Nice to Me, I Have Unlimited Credit. The only address he had given was Chesapeake Holdings SC, an e-site on Earth. I queried CorpInfoNet about the outfit and got NO DATA AVAILABLE.

Right. Chesapeake was a front for one of the big Concerns. They might as well have put up a 3D sign.

Bronson Elgar's name was completely unfamiliar, as was his general appearance – brownish hair, nonremarkable coarse features, medium height, husky build. Only his exceptionally close-set eyes, dark blue and opaque as small capped lenses (and maybe iridoplasticized to thwart standard CHW identification procedures), struck a memory chord. I was certain that I'd felt those eyes drilling into me before, undoubtedly on Earth, maybe in the capital.

Maybe in another face.

He wasn't a blast from the past from ICS, and I doubted that I

5

knew him from any of the other Commonwealth regulatory agencies or CCID liaison in Toronto. That left the mug base – but my mnemonic flicker didn't suggest that the guy was a crook, either.

Damn. Who was he? And why did my long-junked professional instincts seem to be telling me it was important to know?

The sky cleared, too late to do any good, and Kedge-Lockaby's comets came out to play, chalk squiggles and scrawls among puffy fair-weather cumulus clouds. The sun headed for its plunge beneath the horizon just as we passed through Eyebrow Cay's surf-pounded ring reef into the calm green lagoon. Kofi, who'd mostly kept quiet throughout the return voyage, had finished packing the rinsed equipment into the owners' individual mesh-topped bags. He sat astern on the flat, one leg hooked around a stanchion, and read the evening news on a magslate. He was dressed in salt-bleached dungarees, a singlet with blue and white stripes, and a flat-crowned straw hat he claimed to have won in a crap game from a banana-boat loader in Grugru City. I wore torn chino pants, oversized mirror sunglasses, and a light salty crust on my moderately impressive naked torso.

The clients had refused to come up and view what was turning into a gorgeous purple and amber sunset, but tipsy laughter echoed from below. When I sent Kofi to check on them he reported that they had demolished not only the three bottles of cheap champagne but also my medicinal fifth of Jack Daniel's sourmash Tennessee sippin' whiskey. They'd taken great pictures of the big glowing red crustaceoids through the underwater window. Also contributing to the mellower mood was the fact that we weren't going to miss the 1845 shuttle after all.

Pernio chugged around the golden limestone promontory we call Cheddar Head, where fingerwood trees were writhing picturesquely in the breeze. As we headed for the harbour I peered idly landward toward the little cove where I lived. What I saw made me squawk in disbelief and grab the oculars from the console of the fly-bridge. Enhanced survey of the shore confirmed what the eyeball scan had adumbrated.

6

'Oh, *shit!*'

'What, man, what?' Kofi exclaimed.

'Look for yourself.' I tossed him the ocs and then burst into helpless laughter. 'The end of a perfect day.'

'Lord God, Helly! It's a beached sea-toad, right in front of your place. Biggest I've ever seen! Mother's gotta be twelve, thirteen metres across.'

'Gone,' I gasped, between bouts of crazy cackling. 'Sweet Jesus! Totally gone.'

'Son of a bitch.' Kofi's voice was soft with awe as he studied the stupefying scene. 'I think you're right. If that don't pucker the butt! But whoever heard of a sea-toad coming inside the reef? They never leave deep water.'

I'd finally stopped laughing. 'This one did. And it ate my house.'

I hadn't yet got around to wondering why.

When I first came to Kedge-Lockaby in 2229 I was in no condition to appreciate its natural charms. It was enough that K-L was a freesoil planet none of the Concerns or Starcorps cared a damn about, where nobody asked a down-and-outer nosy questions and the living was easy. Best of all, the place was fourteen thousand light-years away from Earth, Interstellar Commerce Secretariat headquarters, and my father.

After I began to take cognizance of my surroundings, I discovered a pretty, mostly ocean-covered world with one large moon, having a superfluity of comets in its solar system that had inhibited extensive exploitation even after the broom technology was perfected. There was a single continent that Kedgerees called the Big Beach, along with skeins of volcanic islands and gorgeous low-lying atolls strewn through equatorial latitudes. The only sizeable municipality was Manukura, the capital. No Indigenous Sapients had evolved on the planet to complicate human colonization. The lesser biota was genome-compatible and inoffensive, with a few conspicuous exceptions. The winds blew briskly all year round, delighting sail-boarders, and the shallower portions of the sea were a sport-diver's paradise.

7

Like most of the other Perseus worlds, Kedge-Lockaby used to belong to Galapharma AC, colossus of the drug Concerns and chop-licking rival of Rampart Starcorp. Even though K-L had no significant biotech assets, Gala had developed it as an executive retreat and playground for stakeholders assigned to more rugged worlds of theirs in Zone 23. About half a century ago, when the big Concern got tired of fighting off the Qastt and Haluk – and also erroneously thought it had drained the zone of significant resources – Galapharma let Kedge-Lockaby go wildcat along with their other Spur worlds. This serious mistake eventually opened the way for Rampart's great expansion.

My sister Eve, who was Rampart's Chief Transport and Distribution Officer, had once told me it would not have been cost-effective for the Starcorp to put in a development claim for K-L, so the little world remained freesoil. Tourists came in modest numbers to loll on the luminous seashores, make holovids of the weird and wonderful marine critters, and gape at the extraordinary comets that decorated the sky. Others who found the planet appealing included congenital loafers without means, artistic disciples of Paul Gauguin, romantics afflicted with beachcomberitis, sailing nuts, and burnt-out cases like me.

Unlike the affluent holidaymakers, the riffraff often settled in to stay.

On Kedge-Lockaby, even the rawest newcomer could survive on a shoestring. All you had to do was throw up a grass shack on the shore, catch fish analogues and molluscoids in the waters outside the front door to keep body and soul together, and peddle the surplus to seaside resort hotels for booze or drug money.

For over a year I lived that way, using the nom-de-beach Helmut Icicle. Most people just called me Helly. I'm kind of an old-fashioned guy, not much into recreational pharmaceuticals or buzz-heading, and my anodyne of choice was rotgut Danaëan whiskey. I drifted along, snorkelling and scuba-diving with borrowed gear when I wasn't lost in a self-pitying ethanol torpor. From time to time I would aim a sailboard straight out to sea, determined to quit futzing around and *do* it.

But I never did. After a while I admitted to myself that I probably never would.

My big sister's bailiwick, Tyrins, was a scant six light-years away from K-L, and her spies must have told her about my slow emergence from the swamps of alcoholic nonentity. One day a StelEx messenger came to my squalid seaside hovel, confirmed that I was the ne'er-do-well known as Helmut Icicle, and handed me an envelope. Inside was a draft payable to a local marine broker and a note that said:

Dear Asa,

Happy birthday. It's all yours, and I don't give a rat's ass whether you want it or not. The boat outfit will give you piloting lessons and keep you powered up for a year. After that, you're on your own.

Love you.

Eve

I was indeed thirty-six years old, by Earth reckoning, although at that low point in my life I probably looked closer to fifty. The vintage Mawson submersible my compassionate sister had bought for me was somewhat older than that but still in good shape – and as Eve had planned, it intrigued the hell out of me and proved an irresistible temptation to sobriety. I named the boat *Pernio* (meaning frostbite) in an ironic tribute to my estranged clan, easily learned how to operate it, and undertook an extended tour of Kedge-Lockaby's underwater magnificences.

Somewhere along the way, I rediscovered sanity, a fair state of bodily well being, and even fun. Among the vacation visitors to the planet were friendly and needy ladies who looked me over, weren't too repelled by what they saw, and went riding with me in my little old submarine. Some of them also wanted to hire the boat for sport-diving jaunts with their friends. This was a scary idea, dangerously akin to earning a living, but at last I agreed. If I wasn't going to snuff myself, I figured I might as well party.

It wasn't long before the other charter-sub skippers of Manukura, jealous sonsabitches all, threatened to blow the whistle on my rump operation and/or run me off the Big Beach. I cut them off at the knees by getting a commercial licence, a laughably simple matter on a wildcat planet, and painting *Pernio* a vivid buttercup yellow.

The new hue, plus a third-hand stereo system stocked with appropriate pop classics by the Beatles, Jimmy Buffet, and the Junkanoo Jokesters drove the female vacationers into raptures of nostalgia and insured full bookings for the season.

My accelerating slide uphill toward respectability made me uneasy in more ways than one. Kedge-Lockaby was a long way from Earth, but there was always a chance that one of the visitors would recognize me. Nevertheless I would probably have stayed in Manukura indefinitely, anonymous and unnoticed, if it hadn't been for Superintendent Jake Silver, the head of Kedge-Lockaby's tiny Public Security Force. He found out who I really was when I filed an iris-print at his office along with my application for permanent-resident status.

Jake was an ageing, pot-bellied, pragmatic sort of cop with an air of melancholic disillusion, doing the best he could with minimal resources on a backwater planet far from the centre of the Commonwealth. He kept my secret, only now and again picking what was left of my brains when some matter involving Concern sharp practice crossed his desk. I gave him my grudging co-operation for as long as I lived on the Big Beach because I suspected that he was another man who'd been shafted somewhere along the line and tossed into the discard. All the same, it was a relief when I finally earned enough credit to be able to move to Eyebrow Cay in the Out Islands, far away from Jake's well-meaning attempts to make a new man of me and restore my citizenship.

Who needed it? I'd spent nearly a third of my life trying to stem the tide of commercialized corruption in the Human Commonwealth of Worlds and accomplished next to nothing. Every year the elected government got more feeble and the Hundred Concerns got stronger, tightening their grip on the galactic economy. Within another decade, Big Business would control every aspect of human civilization, eliminating the last remnants of political opposition as efficiently as it had eliminated me.

Fuck 'em all. Throwaway status suited me just fine.

On Eyebrow Cay, a couple of thousand kilometres west of the Big Beach, I hired *Pernio* out to the more venturesome sport-divers and completed my rehabilitation. The skippers of the local mosquito fleet and the other island denizens were a laid-back lot, and I forged genuine friendships for the first time.

I lived on the sub until I could afford to buy cheapo domiciliary modules, then built myself a neat little house with a really handsome bathroom and kitchen. Its front porch had a beautiful view of the water and invisible screening to keep the jellybugs and stinkmoths at bay. I wove mats for the floors and painted sincere, klutzy seascapes for the walls. Piece by piece, I assembled chef-quality cooking equipment, learned how to use it, and achieved a state of domestic competence that would have astounded long-suffering Joanna.

At night, when the stars of the Perseus Spur winked and twinkled amid the comets, I would sit on the porch in my handmade wicker chair sipping my allocated single highball of the day, now made with genuine bootleg terrestrial corn squeezings, and look for the bright, nearby star that shone on Tyrins, Eve's planet. Sometimes I'd make a stab at finding as many of the other sixty-three Rampart World suns as I could, brooding over what my life might have been if I'd done as my father had demanded, instead of following my own stubborn aspirations and ending up consummately screwed.

The damned sea monster with the perverted appetite started me on the road to finding out.

Chapter 2

I gave Kofi the helm and frantically started punching the phone, trying to raise my neighbour, Mimo Bermudez, to find out what had happened. Unlike most of the shady residents of Eyebrow Cay, Bermudez was a fully enfranchised citizen of the Commonwealth of Human Worlds and a man of considerable substance. He did not advertise the fact. His modest thatch-roofed bungalow, a few hundred metres down the beach from where my own house had once stood, seemed untouched by monsters.

After a few minutes he answered and I said, 'It's Helly. I'm just offshore in *Pernio*, heading in. What in the name of God is going on?' I thumbed the speaker so Kofi would be able to hear.

'I – I was gonna call you.' The old man's usually formal diction was frazzled. 'Right after Oren and I finished this pitcher of margaritas.'

'I could use one myself. Tell me about it.'

'The toad came up out of the sea with no warning at all. About half an hour ago. It – it just licked your house off the stilts and devoured it. Like crunching up a nacho! Nothing Oren or I could do.'

'Is the brute dead? I didn't see any movement through the ocs.'

'I zapped it with my Claus-Gewitter. Helly, what can I say? That beautiful place you worked so hard to build! All of your things! Of course you're welcome to stay with me for as long as you like.'

'Yeah. I may take you up on that.' Something that I hadn't experienced for a long time began stirring deep inside me. 'Listen, Mimo. You guys spread the bad news yet?'

'No. We were waiting for the margaritas to take hold.'

'Well, I'd like you to keep this to yourselves until I get there.'

'If you say so, *amigo*. I presume you have your reasons.'

'Yes.'

'Oren thinks we might be able to salvage some of your things if we open up the beast before the corrosive stomach liquids do too much damage. We'll need a heavy-duty cutter and a winch, and probably some protective garb and other stuff. Shall I call Sal?'

'I'll take care of that. But I can sure use a hand if – if –'

I fell silent as a crazy certainty exploded in my mind like a skyrocket. Suddenly I knew what could have caused the sea-toad to behave in such a bizarre way.

'Mimo, let me talk to Oren for a second.'

I brushed aside the commiserations of Oren Vinyard, another Throwaway friend, and asked him to nip over to his place and fetch a certain piece of equipment, if he had it available.

'I can cobble one together in five minutes once my bloody hands stop shaking,' Oren said. 'But why in the world do you need it?'

'Indulge the whim of a homeless man,' I told him. 'I'll be there as soon as I can.' I put the handset into my back pocket and met Kofi's eyes.

'Damn shame, Helly. I'll help with the salvage, too. Of all the shitty freak accidents–'

'If it was,' I muttered. The small hot knot of anger that had kindled north of my solar plexus was starting to spread, tensing my muscles and quickening my heart.

'What d'you mean – *if?*' Kofi's mahogany face was sceptical. 'You think somebody sent the toadster an engraved invitation?'

I only grunted, took back the wheel, and didn't say another word until we tied up at my slip. With Kofi's boat hauled for repairs, *Pernio* was the only sub at the docks, a yellow shark shape in the midst of a motley crowd of sailing dinghies, catboats, fore-and-aft-rig fishermen, and fusion-motor trawlers belonging to the locals. A few yachts owned by transients were moored at the public dock. Gumercindo Hucklebury, the marina owner, was pumping jewel-fuel into Glasha Romanova's classic wooden fishing smack, *Katopua*. She had on a microscopic scarlet bikini. We exchanged waves. A few male tourists hung around the quay admiring Glasha and watching Seedy McGready mend his nets. Two windsurfers were tinkering with their disassembled sailboards. A little old lady was studying flyspecked souvenir items in the window at Mulholland's Mercantile. A honeymoon couple lounged on the deck in front of Jinj & Peachy's Bed & Breakfast, looking at the sunset.

My five sports, who hadn't been told anything about the sea-toad disaster, came topside, gathered their things, and trooped down *Pernio*'s gangplank.

Bronson Elgar had changed into a crisply pressed black jumpsuit with a natty silk scarf at the neck. He bared his teeth in a tight smile. 'See you again, maybe, Cap'n Helly.' His colourless voice rang no gongs, nor did his walk as he sauntered away, carrying his heavy gear without effort. The only striking thing about him was the odd set of his eyes – the main facial feature that a superficial genplas makeover can't alter.

He'd done it, all right.

And his mocking little promise meant that he'd come back and finish the job some day. Seething with renascent fury, I watched Elgar climb into Kofi's van. If only *Pernio* had arrived in port a quarter hour later, and the five men had missed the last air shuttle! But there was no way I could detain him now while I checked out my suspicions, short of locking him (and the other four, who might be accessories and were certainly witnesses) in the sub and fomenting a calamitous flap. The sports were all well-heeled citizens and I was nobody. It was Kofi's job to drive clients to the hopper pad, only a kilometre away. He whispered that he'd meet me at the site of my late abode after he put the men on their flight. When his van was gone I cast *Pernio* off again and mooched across the harbour basin to Sal Faustino's boatyard.

I found her at supper in her open-air kitchen shack, dressed in a paint-splattered coverall and devouring a great bowl of *frutti di mare*. She dropped her fork with a howl of dismay when I told her my bad news. Her sublimated maternal instincts kicked in and she clapped me to her pneumatic bosom, crooning comfort, cursing my misfortune, and demanding to know what she could do to help. I pulled free of her embrace with some effort. I'm no middleweight, but Sal's square form outweighs mine by over ten kilos of solid muscle. She is the best marine engineer in the Out Islands, with a heart sweeter than rozkoz, a temper to melt diamond drill-bits, and an outstanding arrest warrant for manslaughter on Farallon-Zander.

I said, 'Can you let me borrow some halide lamps, a port-a-winch, an antigrav toter, and a Randall torch? Mimo and Oren and Kofi are ready to help me open the toad up and save what we can. We could also use some envirosuits and a couple of Scott Air-Paks. The critter's guts will be awash with hydrochloric acid and God knows what else.'

'Take anything, boy! The hazmat soakers, too, if you want 'em. How about I come over myself with the tugboat, help you tow the remains out to sea?'

'I'd appreciate that. Give us a few hours to salvage whatever hasn't been digested.'

And also let me check out my suspicions.

Sal took hold of my face, pulled it down, and planted a wet smack on my forehead. 'Don't you fret, Helly. Eyebrow Cay takes care of its own. I'll organize a gang to rebuild your house, scrounge up furniture and whatever else you need. Count on it.'

I thanked her sincerely. The flip side of free, easygoing Kedge-Lockaby is that nobody in authority would give a good goddamn about my little catastrophe. Any relief would have to come from the charity of my friends.

After I had loaded the necessary salvage items into *Pernio* I puttered over to my cove. En route I used the phone to get in touch with Jake Silver. 'Do me a big favour,' I said, 'and find out whatever you can about one Bronson Elgar, guest at the Nikko Luxor. He'll be returning to the Big Beach starport within the half hour.'

'Why should I?' The Superintendent was ever gracious.

'Because I think he just tried to kill me.'

'Kill who?' the tired voice inquired with testy irony. 'The fish-flickin' fool who calls himself Helmut Icicle . . . or the picture that's turned to the wall in a certain stately hacienda back on Earth?'

'Take your choice.'

'Tell me about this attempted homicide.'

When I did, Jake broke into derisive chortles.

'Enjoy yourself, Superintendent,' I said. 'Then remember who showed you how to deal with those redskin sharpshooters from

15

Infinitum Concern who were ready to take over the Kedgeree Kasino last year. If that pair had clinched the deal, the budgets of half the schools on K-L would've gone down in flames.'

'Yeah, yeah. But if this Elgar is staying at the Luxor, he's nobody to play games with. He could even be connected. I'm not laying my department open to Concern intervention. Especially not for the likes of you, Hell-Butt.'

'I'm not asking you to collar him. Just discreetly run his name and his credit card code through the sifter. This is no joke, dammit!'

Jake gave a conciliatory growl. 'I'll do what I can and get back to you.'

I brought the sub as close to the beach as I dared, set out a couple of anchors, and went ashore in the inflatable. The stranded monster was the size of a small warehouse, a glistening mound in the dusk. Inland, the snapped-off pilings that had formerly held my house stuck up from the sand like broken teeth. The porch steps were still there, leading nowhere. There was slimy mucus all over the place and a pungent stench filled the air. I recalled that sea-toads liked to give their captured prey a preliminary spritz of corrosive, enzyme-laden saliva.

Mimo Bermudez was waiting, his seamy Don Quixote face contorted by indignation and his white hair flying in all directions like an electrified sheepdog. He handed me a large mug of tequila and citrus and clapped me on the shoulder in silent sympathy. His full name is Guillermo Javier Bermudez Obregon, and he is a long-retired, long-widowed transport captain who likes to soak up rays on the beach and sip tropical distillations while plugged into trans-galactic soccer games. He keeps his astrogational skills honed by flying contraband from Earth and the Concern planets into Perseus Spur worlds. He is also my closest friend on K-L.

We stood side by side in the fading sunset, staring up at the revolting corpse of the sea-toad. Its clawed flippers, over two metres long, had dug broad trenches in the sand as the animal hauled itself onshore. Delicate knob-studded antennae on jointed stalks were almost retracted back into the creature's warty, barnacloid-encrusted head. The protruding eyes, big as watermelons and uncomfortably human in structure, were wide open and glassy in death. Just above them were two oozing burn-holes a centimetre wide. Captain Bermudez – handy in repelling interstellar highjackers – had neatly drilled both brains with shots from a photon beamer. The thing's incredible mouth, through which two subs the size of *Pernio* could have cruised abreast, was held slightly open by the crumpled mast and sponsons of Mimo's red Hobie catamaran. I had been re-rigging the little boat for him in the area behind my house, and the toad must have snapped it up for dessert. Maybe it thought the poor cat was a deformed ruby prawn, its legitimate nocturnal prey.

'You want to give me the whole story?' I asked.

'Oren and I were taking it easy in hammocks on my verandah. I was linked into Uruguay versus Vonnegut-Two and he was listening to my Charlie Barnet collection. There was a *jumongo* splash. I fell out of my hammock. The creature was there, as you see it now, half out of the water. I lay like a paralytic and watched while its tongue-tentacles took hold of your home and swallowed it. Oren was screaming like a madman. He said it would come for us next. At last my senile brain rebooted. I ran into the house, grabbed a long gun, and shot the damned thing dead. Oren puked his guts out and I nearly lost it myself.'

'Christ.'

Mimo lifted his bony shoulders in a fatalistic shrug. 'Thank him for your deliverance. As I recall, the vomeropalatine bone in the roof of the sea-toad's mouth is studded with hundreds of sharp spikes the size of baseball bats. You would have surely died inside your crushed house if you had come home at the usual time.'

'Yes,' I agreed quietly.

A clapped-out old Toyota four-wheeler swung off the marl road and rattled down the beach toward us. Oren Vinyard was at the wheel, looking as though he'd just stuck his head under the tap. Water dripped from his fair hair and his face was still greenish. 'I got the ultrasound detector. Where shall I set it up?'

Oren's ramshackle dwelling is crammed with defunct and sporadically operational high-tech gadgets. These are scavenged from Big Beach sources by impoverished Dumpster-divers, who are paid a pittance by Oren for each piece of junk. The stuff is shipped back to the islands as ballast in the holds of local fishing boats, and Oren repairs and sells what he can and survives on the proceeds. He was born in a British hamlet called Nether Wallop ('Not to be confused with Middle Wallop or Over Wallop'), and once upon a time he was a top energen physicist for Sheltok Concern on Erytheia. His wife came down with Percival's syndrome and Sheltok's CMO refused to authorize an expensive experimental treatment. After she died, mild little Oren punched the Concern medical evaluator to a bloody pulp and fatally fritzed the fusion generator prototype his unit had been working on. He served his prison term, paid his whopping fine, was Thrown Away, and ended up on Kedge-Lockaby with the rest of us flotsam-and-jetsamites.

'Get close to the toad,' I told him, 'and do the sweep pronto. I think there's a sonic generator inside this beast – if it hasn't already melted into slag. Look for emissions above 120 kilohertz.'

Oren powered up a dirty black box with a tiny dingus on top, poked a few of its control pads, and aimed it at the dead monster.

'Ah. There you are, Helly! Intermittent modulation at 122 to 131, with complex harmonics at higher frequencies. You want to hear it? Let me bring the noise down into human auditory range.' He tickled the controls again.

Kofi Rutherford came trotting up just as the black box let off a series of ear-splitting stuttering whoops. A flock of elvis-birds exploded out of the nearby mint palms, wailing like singed cats. Mimo Bermudez flinched. Oren turned the gain down hastily.

'What the hell was that?' Kofi yelped.

'The sea-toad's dinnerbell,' I said. The box warbled on, pianissimo. 'What we're hearing is the song of some kind of large and undoubtedly very tasty marine lifeform, being broadcast from a portable transmitter now in the toad's tummy. I had a hunch that was the way the critter got lured ashore. See those knobby things above the eyes? Antennae for hunting pelagic prey – the kind that floats on the surface and gives off ultrasonic music. Like giant peacock eels or pink elephant slugs.'

'And somebody put the transmitter in your house?' Oren said in disbelief.

'Probably this morning. Timed to sound off at an appointed hour when I should have been home. Only I wasn't.'

Kofi nodded grimly. 'Had to be one of the sports. Maybe the one who looked bogus to you.'

'They were the only strangers in my place all week,' I agreed, 'plugging in their credit cards while I checked out their dive gear.'

Mimo Bermudez cleared his throat with tactful diffidence. 'Helly, please don't misunderstand. But this seems to me a most chancy and inefficient way of committing murder. Why wasn't the transmitter set to broadcast later, at night, when you would certainly be home in bed? For that matter, why would any competent killer consider this charade with the sea-toad at all, rather than disposing of you in a more discreet and workmanlike fashion?'

'The toads only hunt for pelagic prey during daylight,' I said. 'At night they go after ruby prawns and other quarry deep underwater, using different sensory equipment. The ultrasonic call would be useless after dark. As to the why . . .' I trailed off.

'It is none of our business, of course,' Mimo said. 'Forgive me for mentioning it.' The other two made reassuring comments and began setting up the spotlights.

I said, 'I haven't a clue why someone would want me dead. I'm no danger to anybody. Not any more.'

They stared at me, and I experienced an overwhelming desire to pour it all out. Anger was still on a slow boil inside me, an emotion that I hadn't felt since I first realized that the frame-up was going to stick. Then, I'd raged against the great companies that had financed humanity's colonization of the stars, trampling or sweeping aside anyone who dared oppose them. Until the end, I had refused to accept that it could happen to me.

Now it seemed that my foes weren't content simply to remove me from the gameboard. They wanted to obliterate me altogether.

Or was my death intended to serve another purpose?

I posed a question to my friends. 'What would have happened if I'd died in the gulped house – a poor shmuck of a charter-boat skipper on an obscure little planet, wiped out in such a flat-out ridiculous way?'

'The Tabloid Web would have leapt on the story,' Oren Vinyard said promptly, 'and spread it from K-L to the Sagittarius Whorl.

Absurd demise is always good for a gasp and a giggle amongst the jaded masses.'

I said, 'And the tale would have been all the more juicy if the webstringer at Manukura learned my real name from some anonymous source before sending the story out.'

My pals again regarded me with silent speculation. They'd never ask the question, but I almost answered it anyway. If I had, I might have started to unravel the mystery right that minute. Unfortunately, the phone in my pocket buzzed. I excused myself and stepped away.

It was Jake Silver calling back from the cop shop on the Big Beach. 'Bronson Elgar is somebody very special,' the weary voice said. 'His ID is ex-census-database. I had a devil of a time tracing his personal card, but I finally called in a marker from an old crony in ECID and got it. Elgar's bills are paid from a numbered account by CreditEuro Bancorp.'

'That's the financial arm of Galapharma.'

'Whatever. Your suspect never returned to his suite at the Luxor. His four buds – who claim they were only casual acquaintances, by the way – last saw him going off for a drink with a woman in a red uniform who met their hop-shuttle flight at the starport. The description matches the livery of the comet-broom crew. I checked, and GAL-6236T's tender was in for supplies. It's presently on the way back to the mothership, and your alleged assailant is probably aboard.'

'God! I forgot that the broom system still operates under the original Galapharma contract. That means Commonwealth law enforcement has no jurisdiction over any of the broom vessels.'

'Not without a heavyweight warrant,' Jake agreed. 'Your homicidal toad-wrangler is home free.'

'If somebody found a way to bring Elgar back, would you be able to hold him?'

'Not on a complaint by a Throwaway.'

'Then I guess that's all, folks.'

'Seems like,' Jake said. He broke the connection.

I looked at the dead telephone in my hand, then stowed it away with an odd sense of relief. The small conflagration in my guts eased and began to peter out. For all my sassy backchat to Jake, I was glad that it had become impossible for me to pursue my attacker – ashamed to be glad, but glad nonetheless. Big Business had swung at me again and missed. I was safe until the next time . . . but I could worry about that some other day.

I returned to the others. Oren worked with the cutting torch's power supply and Kofi loudly disputed some technical point with him while pulling on one of the envirosuits. Mimo sat a little way apart on a piece of driftwood, smoking one of the high-tariff Cuban cigars he regularly smuggles into the Spur. I hunkered down beside him and told him in a low voice how Elgar had escaped, together with my suspicion that he was an agent of Galapharma. 'With luck, they won't try another hit now that I'm alerted.'

Captain Bermudez smoothed his frowzy hair with a long brown hand. His eyes in their wrinkled pouches glittered as madly as the Man of La Mancha's. 'My Javelin starship is yours, Helly,' he said softly, 'and my decrepit piloting skills also, if you wish to go in pursuit of this Bronson Elgar.'

'Don't be ridiculous,' I muttered. 'The bastard's long gone. End of story.'

'I know a way we could catch the tender before she reaches the broom mothership. Elgar and his pilot will never suspect they're being chased until it's too late.' He explained while he studied the cylinder of contraband Earth-grown tobacco, smiling in what might have been fond reminiscence. 'And we could board them quite easily! My ship has mechanical excursion suits, fully powered and with weaponry interfaces. I'm certain that the tender is only minimally armed, whereas my Javelin –'

'Absolutely not!' I hissed. 'Why should you get mixed up in my private crock of shit?'

He tilted his head and lifted his shoulders in comical irony. 'Perhaps smuggling has lost some of its savour. You know I haven't been off K-L in weeks.'

A harsh little yap that might have been a laugh forced its way out of me. 'You don't even know who I really am.'

'I know that you're my friend and that you need help badly. It suffices.'

Kofi and Oren were still arguing about the equipment, paying no attention to Mimo and me. I spoke in a whisper through clenched teeth. 'I'm Asahel Frost. Old Simon's youngest son. The family black sheep who refused to become an officer of Rampart Starcorp.'

'Ah. I remember! You joined the ICS instead. And then –'

'I had a lot of silly ideas about exposing the corruption of the Amalgamated Concerns and breaking their grip on the Commonwealth. I thought my background would give me a unique advantage, and so it did. I turned into Supercop – crusader against corporate villainy. When I started cutting too close to the bone, the Concerns didn't dare kill me out of hand. Instead they arranged to have me framed for malfeasance and disenfranchised. Now it seems as though they want to finish me off. God knows why.'

'But surely you see that this makes it even more vital that we pursue this corporate assassin! To restore your good name and citizenship as well as to expose Elgar's backers.'

'I won't let you endanger your life.'

'I do it on every contraband run I make from the Orion Arm into the Perseus Spur. *No me importa dos cojones.*'

'You can't risk the Javelin.'

'Pah! Do you think I have only one starship?'

Kofi and Oren, dressed now in slick white plastic and wearing Air-Paks, were prowling around the flank of the toad, apparently deciding where to make the first incision. Out to sea, the calm lagoon waters were darkening while the comets overhead glowed brighter, omens in the gloaming.

The old starman's voice became an insidious wheedle. 'If you won't let me join you in the pursuit, then fly the Javelin yourself. Her name is *La Chispa*. That's Mexican slang for a brazen woman. She's a real sweetheart.' He began to elaborate on his bold plan.

I said, 'No.'

'Do you mean you're unqualified to pilot a starship?'

'It's impossible, dammit!'

'Nonsense. I've known you for nearly two years, Helly. Watched while your soul-wounds healed over and turned to scars. You're a strong man once again, and whole.'

He was wrong. 'You don't understand, Mimo.'

He puffed smoke at a stinkmoth. The carrion-loving insectiles had discovered the reeking toad carcass and were gathering for the festivities. 'Nail the *hideputa*,' the old man urged me. 'Force Elgar to talk. When you have the truth, either stuff him out *Chispa*'s airlock or send him back to his principal with a message of your own. Otherwise another killer will come. You know that.'

I said nothing.

'You can have your pick of my portable arms collection for the on-board confrontation. We'll take my hoppercraft to the Beach. I'll call ahead and have the Javelin readied. There will be no formalities with the Port Authority.' A sly wink. 'For me, there never are.'

I remained silent, knuckling my brow like a man trying to banish an excruciating hangover or some appalling temptation, actually weighing the pros and cons of the audacious scheme. It could work. I had never been an official interrogator, but I knew that if I got my hands on Elgar I could probably turn him inside out like a sock. But finding out why he was sent would be only a first step. Going on from there was the prospect that made my balls shrink, made the fear-demon whisper: *Let it be. You can't win. Only a madman would start it all over again . . .*

After a while I said to Mimo, 'Okay.'

He smiled beatifically. 'Come to my house. Take a quick shower and get some fresh clothes from my malle-armoire. There's plenty of time.'

I went over to where my other friends were at work. The glow of the lamps illuminated a great cloud of orbiting moths. Kofi had opened the monstrous body with the cutting torch and Oren was using a fish-gaff as an improvised flensing tool, peeling back the toad's rubbery hide.

'I'm going to Manukura on urgent business,' I called out. 'I might be gone for some time.'

Kofi straightened. I didn't need to see the expression on his masked face. 'No problem. You go on, do what you gotta do, leave this pile of crap for me and Oren to take care of.'

'Do your best to find that ultrasound transmitter,' I said. 'It's the only real evidence we have that the toad attack was a set-up.

Never mind the rest of my stuff. It's toast. Sal Faustino said she'd bring the tugboat around later to tow away the carcass.'

'Don't worry,' Oren said. 'By the time you get back, the whole mess will be taken care of.'

I didn't have the heart to contradict him.

Chapter 3

The Javelin starship named *La Chispa* was a marvellous vessel, much larger than I had expected, with a bridge worthy of a Commonwealth Zone Patrol cutter and a hold large enough for nearly fifty kilotons of cargo. Its computer voice was warmly feminine, addressing me first in Spanish, then switching resignedly to English with a piquant Hispanic accent when it realized that I was not Captain Bermudez.

Mimo had often invited me to join him on one of his extralegal jaunts to Earth or other worlds of the Orion Arm, but I'd never accepted. Frankly, I was afraid to leave my sanctuary and risk damaging the fragile new identity I had built for myself.

That was understandable. What I didn't understand was why I was leaving now – and why my entering *Chispa*'s bridge and settling down in the command seat didn't deliver a chilling reality jolt instead of inspiring me to start whistling through my teeth as the computer and I worked through the lift-off checklist.

The song was the John Williams 'Superman Theme' rip-off of Richard Strauss's *Death and Transfiguration* leitmotiv.

Supercop lives?

Or was my unconscious reminding me that I was already dead, with transfiguration way overdue?

To hell with it.

It had been nearly six years since I had piloted a starship. ICS Divisional Chief Inspectors don't have to do their own driving. During the hop from the island to Manukura with Mimo I had expressed reservations about the upcoming stunt on a strictly practical basis; but he only laughed and assured me that the Javelin had SLD and ULD systems that an idiot child could operate.

I knew it wouldn't be that easy. But as he described the ship's goodies in more detail, I decided I could at least muddle through the primary astrogational punch-up leading to the intercept. You never forget the basics. Later on, when things got livelier and I had to do close-in manoeuvring, I could use the cerebral command headset.

As Mimo had promised, I was able to lift off from Manukura without filing a flight plan or even feeding my escape vector into traffic control. K-L's starport was small and its operation underfunded and casual. Frequent solar flares made landside EM scans of local interplanetary space difficult and often inaccurate. Nobody in the tower really cared which ships flitted in or out, provided that they weren't Qastt or Haluk, and didn't smash into orbiting rubble and force the Port Authority to write up tedious accident reports.

Comet-broom tender GAL–6236T hadn't filed a flight plan either, but there was only one place it could go – to its mothership, which my computer located in an orbit five hundred and ninety-seven million kilometres from Kedge-Lockaby, over on the other side of the sun. Since the tender was not a starship, it would have to travel home to its mommy using conventional sublight inertialess drive, while *Chispa*, with ultraluminal capability, had zippier options.

I was going to nab my prey by making a hyperspatial microleap.

Outward bound through restricted space at mandatory one-tenth SLD velocity, I had a striking view of sea-girt Kedge-Lockaby. The abyssal plains and submarine valleys were deepest indigo blue, while the sunken continental masses were blotched with overlapping circular basins of cobalt, turquoise and varying tints of green – scars of the huge primeval comets that had not only pockmarked the little world but also left it with an overgenerous cloak of water.

The outer atmospheric reaches shimmered with an endless bombardment of micrometeoroids, those dust-sized bits of rock, metal, and simple organic compounds that are the ashes of defunct comets. At this point in its history, the Kedgeree solar system had very little large-scale asteroidal material left over from condensation of its primordial nebula. Few of the space rocks that remained were large enough to survive passage through the planetary atmosphere or pose a danger to cruising spacecraft carrying conventional shields.

The comets, of course, were something else – or would have been, without the broom.

While I waited for *Chispa* to power up to full subluminal auto I ordered a bland reconstituted supper of saffron rice, grilled galloid, and rozkoz-blue flan that I hoped would lie easy on my turbulent stomach. A couple of Carta Blanca beers helped relax me. I ate slowly and watched the scenery on the main viewer, thinking about the wretched sea-toad and my friends' salvage hopes. Realistically, almost none of my possessions would have escaped the beast's invincible gastric juices unscathed. Except for my crippled sub, I was probably wiped out.

It made any decision about my future easier . . .

Whoever had tried to engineer my demise had been exceptionally well-acquainted with the obscure fauna of Kedge-Lockaby. Ever since the cosseting of amateur divers became my bread and butter, I had made it my business to check out those marine creatures most apt to appeal to visiting thrillseekers. The sea-toad was an uncommon sort of monster. Its life cycle had never been studied and filed in the public database by Commonwealth exobiologists, who still scrabbled for funds to inventory the lifeforms of freesoil planets in the populous Orion Arm – never mind the godforsaken Perseus boondocks. Only a handful of us Out Islanders, professional fishermen and divers, knew how the toad tracked its musical food.

Had one of my friends or acquaintances on Eyebrow Cay conspired to set me up? Perhaps. But there was another way my assailant might have found the information necessary to bait his trap: he could have read it in the dead-files of K-L's previous tenant, Galapharma AC.

I had no doubt that the mammoth drug Concern had once compiled a dossier on my designated predator. A century ago, when Gala exploration teams first cruised Zone 23 of the Milky Way and claimed Kedge-Lockaby, they would have inventoried every living thing on the planet that might have furnished a valuable new product – an antibiotic, a genetic engineering vector, a cosmetic, a heretofore undiscovered source of pharmaceutical excitement for bored middle-class humanity.

(But Galapharma had unaccountably missed rozkoz when they combed Seriphos, so the confection more delicious than chocolate had founded the fortunes of the Frost family!)

Even today, when Gala's old exobiology files were still top secret, it was theoretically possible for a determined outsider to hack into them and study the sea-toad's life history. But was it probable, when there were so many easier ways of stopping my clock?

Unless Galapharma itself had planned my grotesque death . . .

Three years ago in 2229, when my ruin had been so artfully contrived that there was not a single clue left to hint at the perpetrator, I had concluded that there were two categories of evildoer with a motive for destroying me – the most obvious being crooks with a grudge. Every enforcement official leaves human wreckage in his wake, embittered individuals who blame the catcher when they're forced to pay the price for their crimes. There were hundreds of commercial-sector felons who would have loved to slice and dice my ass back then, but almost all of them were either in prison or Thrown Away at the time of my frame-up. Of those remaining at large and enfranchised, none had seemed to command the resources and clout necessary to concoct such an elaborate conspiracy.

A more probable candidate for my nemesis was one of the Hundred Concerns.

Homerun, the Japanese heavy-industry behemoth, and the great Franco-American starship conglomerate, Bodascon, had both been under investigation for criminal violations by my division of the Interstellar Commerce Secretariat at the time I was discredited. Both had managed to get the probes quashed once I was out of the picture. Then, I had been virtually certain that one of them had been responsible for my downfall.

But neither Homerun nor Bodascon had anything to fear from me now, and my death as 'message' made no sense in relation to either of those two Concerns.

The threads of evidence pointing to Galapharma suggested a whole new scenario.

Jake Silver's information about Bronson Elgar's source of financing – plus the fact that the assassin had fled offworld on a spacecraft owned by Gala – made it plausible that Elgar might be in the pay of that Concern. Further cogitation (yes, I know I was slow on the uptake) now hinted at a whale of a potential motive behind the attack.

The toad incident *was* supposed to be a message, and the intended recipient was my father.

Damn you to hell, Simon! Was it all aimed at you and Rampart from the beginning? *Did you know it?* Did you let me go down rather than cave in to the devouring colossus?

I pushed aside the rozkoz-flavoured dessert, suddenly taken with nausea, and called up two fingers of Pedro Domecq. I swallowed the brandy in a single belt and wiped stinging water from my eyes.

On the viewer, Kedge-Lockaby and its moon had become thin crescents almost lost in a blazing kaleidoscope of comets. There were hundreds of them, glowing brush strokes on the star-spangled firmament, their proper motion imperceptible to the human eye. The comets were large and small, coloured white, blue, greenish, and yellow. Their tails – some stumpy, others streaming across my entire field of vision – were variously curved, straight, knotted, multiple, corkscrew, fanned, or broken. All of the tails pointed away from the spotty sun, whether the comet was on approach or in retreat, as though the orbiting objects were medieval courtiers forbidden to turn their backs on a poxy-faced monarch. One four-tailed specimen had an uncanny resemblance to a swastika. Another seemed to wear an elaborate spiked collar of light. A few were mere fuzzy balls, lacking trains of glowing dust or plasma. The heads of others were encased in gauzy helmets, concentric envelopes of ionized gas shaped by the solar magnetic field. A particularly fantastic comet looked like a string of incandescent beads wrapped in twisted scarves and furbelows of golden mist. It was probably on its last go-around, shattered into pieces and doomed to fall into the sun or impact one of the gas-giant planets in the outer reaches of the solar system.

None of those chunks of beautiful dirty ice posed any danger to Kedge-Lockaby. If a comet had been on a collision course with the planet, the broom's great computerized telescope array would have fingered it while it was still over half a billion kilometres away. A small robocraft called a spiker, one of several controlled by the mothership, would then fly up and zap the errant iceberg in a calculated pattern, producing jets of superheated steam that would thrust it into a safer orbit. If spiking didn't work, the threatening comet could be vaporized by a small antimatter bomb delivered by a manned extirpation vessel – a costly and fortunately infrequent expedient. Broom systems were common enough among the human-colonized planets of the Orion Arm, but K-L was the only Perseus Spur world that had one.

I had no idea why this particular broom was still operated by a Concern. Maybe there was some loophole in the original Commonwealth lease that didn't oblige Galapharma to turn over the system when it surrendered the unprofitable world. That would have left CHW with hard choices. It could abandon K-L to cometary bombardment, necessitating human evacuation, or install a new broom of its own at prohibitive cost, or contract the sweeping to Gala, on Gala's terms.

Obviously, the Commonwealth had done the latter – and incidentally provided Elgar with an escape route.

I doubted very much that the hit man had originally planned to leave Kedge-Lockaby on the broom tender. The next commercial starliner outward bound from the planet was a Hyperion flight scheduled to lift off at 2530 hours on the day after tomorrow. If I had been killed by the sea-toad according to plan, that departure would have suited Bronson Elgar's needs perfectly. Only my unexpected survival – and the possibility that I might use my friendship with Jake Silver to stir up a nasty ruckus – made it imperative for Elgar to get off the planet as soon as possible.

He might have tried to hire a private starship for his escape, phoning the starport from the shuttle. But there were very few noncommercial ultraluminal vessels docked at Manukura, and their owners were wealthy vacationers, hardly types to respond favourably to a proposition from a poorly documented stranger who might be a pirate's shill. Freighter captains would be even less likely to accept such a passenger, for the same reason. The broom tender would have been Elgar's only option.

The question of whether its crew knew what kind of hitchhiker they'd taken aboard was still open. The killer could have simply bribed his way on board. In about fourteen hours the vessel would reach its mothership, leaving ample time for the Hyperion starliner to make an unscheduled stop there – provided that the broom commander agreed to permit such an extraordinary action. More bribery might have turned the trick.

On the other hand, the entire getaway would have been dead easy to arrange if the mystery passenger was a Galapharma agent.

Chispa's powerful sensors easily located the subluminal drive signature of GAL–6236T, even though its two-hour head start placed it some seventy-seven million kilometres distant. The tender travelled the most economical course to its destination at rated cruising velocity, encouraging me to believe that Elgar had no notion he might be followed. Keeping him in the dark was the first priority of the pursuit plan Mimo and I had concocted.

So I didn't head out directly after GAL–6236T. Instead I had set a reciprocal course taking *Chispa* in the exact opposite direction. My intention was to reach a position far enough from Kedge-Lockaby so that I would not disrupt electromagnetic systems on its surface when I made my hyperspatial leap, yet close enough to the planet so that it would eclipse the dazzling EM pulse of my ultraluminal crossover from the rinky-dink sensors of the tender. Emerging from the hype at a suitable intercept point and making the snatch without alerting the prey would be much trickier, however, unless I found an appropriate comet to conceal my exit flash at the other end.

I had to strike from ambush, from behind a relatively large object. Mimo had warned me that my astrogational skills were too amateurish for me to attempt popping out of hyperspace close to the tiny, elusive target represented by the broom tender. I was certain to be disoriented during the critical moments after the jump, when inertial dampening took place and the sublight engines re-engaged. Meanwhile the tender would slam up its heavy force-shield and go into evasive manoeuvres a microsecond after its sensors registered my suspicious 'piratical' exit pulse. An experienced space marauder might be able to match sublight velocities and get its quarry under the guns almost instantaneously. I hadn't a prayer. Hot pursuit was no option, either. Even though *Chispa* had superior subluminal drive capability and armament, the last thing I wanted was a running battle with the tender. Bluffing its captain into surrendering Bronson Elgar was one thing; a dogfight with a possibly innocent vessel that might send an SOS to Commonwealth Zone Patrol was a different, and unacceptable, kettle of fish.

In going after Elgar myself, I was gambling that he – and his backers, whoever they were – would do anything to avoid attracting the attention of CCID. If I snatched the assassin without harming the tender or its crew, the incident would doubtless never be reported to the authorities. A skipper who had taken a bribe to transport an unauthorized passenger wouldn't jeopardize himself by reporting the abduction. On the other hand, if Galapharma had put a contract out on me, the big Concern wouldn't dare admit that Bron was their button man.

Either way, his ass belonged to me.

Performing an accurate hyperspatial microleap is difficult under the best of conditions – rather like an Olympic-class broadjumper attempting a flea-hop precisely one millimetre in length. Doing it within the gravity well of a star is tougher still, requiring virtuoso computing and a barrel of luck. Mimo had assured me that pirates and certain smugglers carried out the manoeuvre all the time, which was why *Chispa* had such a superior navigation system. If I picked a largish comet for my target, I should have no trouble. Microleaping was a unique experience, Mimo said, one I would find memorable.

I did the preliminary hyperspace vector calculations, then asked the computer to scour the ephemeris for a cometary stalking-horse to suit my purposes. It gave me several choices, but the no-contest winner was comet 2231–001-Z1, a relatively huge mother thirty-six kilometres in diameter, just entering its perihelion swing and boiling off two tails and a bright plasma hood. The broom tender would have its closest encounter with Z1 in 2.39 hours, passing it at a distance of four hundred and eighty-six thousand kilometres.

If I emerged successfully behind this great snowball, then charged out of the sun at full subluminal velocity, I could confront GAL–6236T within thirty-six seconds. That was good enough. The tender's sensors, dulled by the ionization of the comet and the spotty solar orb behind it, would never lock onto *Chispa*'s sublight drive signature or spot her visually in time to confirm a threat and flee.

I entered Z1's orbital stats into the nav computer and asked for more data about its physical characteristics. What next popped onto the display made me frown. Z1 was a long-period near-virgin from the outer Kuiper Cloud of the system. Its enormous orbit took it close to the sun every nine million years. The nucleus, which was extremely active, was formed of dihydrogen oxide and exotic ices, with a thin crust of miscellaneous organic molecules. Z1 had an enormous knotted tail of ice and dust, a plasma tail, and at least three concentric ion hoods within its great coma. Made itchy by the sunspots, it was emitting significant amounts of x-radiation.

Shit.

In order to balance safety with subterfuge, I was going to have to analyse that x-glow – and do a damned accurate job of it – before finalizing my exit point. I had to emerge from the hype near enough for the comet to eclipse my flash; but if I dropped out too close to the simmering icy mountain, there was a chance that even a well-shielded ship like *Chispa* might end up with permanently blinded sensors. If that happened I'd be forced to fly the starship by the seat of my pants, without a hope of engaging my prey and boarding.

Hell, I'd be lucky to get back to K-L alive.

Whistling the 'Superman Theme' just a tad off-key, I summoned a large pot of coffee from the galley and got to work on the x-spectrum analysis. It took an ungodly amount of time, but at last I obtained an auspicious positional resultant, fed it into the navigator, and locked up the plot. I'd allowed half an hour at the other end of the leap to suit up and prepare for the actual attack, which now left me about twenty-five minutes to spare before ULD engagement.

I used the time practising my marksmanship on jettisoned containers of food and drink. Zapping away incompetently, I depleted *Chispa*'s provision stores considerably before I decided I'd pretty well got the hang of the brain-interface gunnery system. At least I knew how not to blast the tender out of the ether inadvertently, while sending cannon shots across her bows and ordering her to stand and deliver.

Finally it was time to get going. I started the two-minute auto countdown for the leap, and as I waited I magnified the crescent images of Kedge-Lockaby and its attendant Moon of Manukura and just stared at them, remembering the good stuff and the good people.

The computer cooed: *Initiating solar-proximity ULD manoeuvre in five seconds. Four. Three . . .*

I ignored the countdown, expecting nothing more than the usual 'stretched stars' effect of ultraluminal travel, truncated to an eye-blink by the minimum 1 ross pseudovelocity I had programmed. I had forgotten Mimo's remark about a microleap near a star being a memorable experience.

When it happened, I couldn't help howling.

There was the familiar blinding flash of hyperspatial entry. But then the viewer seemed to show *Chispa* hurtling directly toward K-L on a collision course. The blue-and-white sickle swelled with monstrous speed. Screaming, I knew I'd done something hopelessly, fatally wrong.

We weren't ultraluminal in hyperspace at all. We were travelling below light speed in the normal continuum, and the racing starship with me inside was going to impact smack in the middle of the night side of the planet –

We went through Kedge-Lockaby as though it were smoke and continued on our sunward course, accelerating but still apparently moving much slower than we should have been. The comets had seemingly vanished but the stars and the fast-approaching solar orb remained, shining in an odd flat-black sky. I stopped yelling, only to gasp out an astonished curse as I realized that the stars were pulsing like novae about to explode. Then the speckled sun seemed to lurch, and an instant later began to waltz and whirl impossibly about the firmament, drawing fiery loops that became tighter and tighter while its light changed from white to orange to green to an impossible dazzling violet.

Then *Chispa* whizzed past the giddy spinning anomaly and only the crazy stars were left throbbing on the viewscreen. Slumping back in my seat with relief, I realized that the lightshow must be an artefact of the sun's gravity, wildly distorting the hyperspatial continuum and subjectively 'prolonging' my brief trip. *Chispa* was actually travelling at over a billion kilometres an hour.

Memorable.

Another burst of light blinded me as the ship exited the hype. Inertial dampening was imperceptible, accomplished in about two seconds. I drew in a breath before my vision cleared. Ignoring the main viewscreen, which now only showed the speckled sun with a thick overlay of brilliant golden sparkles, I checked the control console before me. The shields were still up and all sensors were operational. The x-radiation and ionization levels were within acceptable range. The icons of the position monitor indicated that I had emerged at precisely the co-ordinates I had calculated, five hundred kilometres from the cometary nucleus in a matched solar orbit, with the bulk of the comet between *Chispa* and the trundling broom tender, and the sun in line with all three of us.

So far, so good. Now for a look at the iceberg itself. I toggled the aft sensors, since the comet lay behind me and slightly to the left, and 2231–001-Z1 came onscreen.

Chispa was so close to the comet that the filmy double tail could not be seen. Even the hoodlike envelopes of the corona were invisible, lost in the pixie-dust glitter of the inner coma. I had expected the sunlit nucleus to be chunky and irregular in shape, resembling close-up images of other comets I'd studied in long-ago astronomy classes back at the University of Arizona on Earth. But I'd forgotten that Z1 was a near-virgin, making its latest pass around the sun after lurking for nine million years in the outer reaches of Kedge-Lockaby's solar system. It was no misshapen clinker but rather a nearly perfect sphere, turning very slowly as I watched, mesmerized.

The surface was reddish black, a thin cindery crust of polymerized organic material punctuated with countless holes and crevices like an enormous sponge. From the orifices luminous jets spewed at me, straight as a die and glowing with rainbow splendour, fountains of mingled water-ice crystals, dust, and gases sublimed from the comet's frozen interior by the heat of the sun. To me, Z1 looked almost like a celestial sea-urchin with hundreds of luminous spines radiating from its sunlit side, an eerie and beautiful simulacrum of life.

I gave *Chispa* a minuscule noodge with the AG thrusters, emerging from behind the comet, and picked up the broom tender, which was presently some eight million kilometres distant. It had not changed course so I assumed it had not seen my exit flash and spooked. The odds were good that Z1's electromagnetic hyperactivity would conceal whatever small-scale manoeuvring *Chispa* now did within the inner coma.

I had 24.55 minutes in which to prepare my ambush.

Chapter 4

Romping through interplanetary space in a mechanical excursion suit is not my favourite activity, but there was no other way I'd be able to abduct Bronson Elgar from the tender. The more efficient ship-to-ship docking manoeuvre customarily used by Qastt and human pirates (and smugglers) would not have been a prudent option unless I first disabled my quarry's engines. Unfortunately, only a primo gunner could manage the trick without also breaching the hull and killing the tender's occupants, and I didn't qualify. I'd be lucky to do a decent job firing bluff shots as I'd planned.

I linked the cerebral command headset into navigation and made certain that all the peripheral-vision displays were functioning. The lower data crawl-strip, evanescent little yellow letters that blurred if you tried to look at them directly, said: 19 MINUTES TO TARGET INTERCEPT INITIATION.

Right. I visited the captain's head, relieved myself of some of the coffee I'd drunk, then trudged off to the excursion bay to don armour for the joust.

I prepped two units, doing a special job on the one intended for my prisoner, which I tethered to my own suit with a six-metre steel flex on a zing reel. After I had disabled the internal command and monitoring systems of Elgar's suit, switching its controls to the computer in my own unit, the number-two piece of space armour became nothing more than an elaborate man-can. Its occupant would be incapable of independent movement or even environmental adjustment. I figured that final modification might come in handy later, when I had the bastard safely aboard *Chispa* and started to interrogate him . . .

Almost ready. I fastened a pair of Kagi blue-ray blasters to the shoulder mounts of my own suit and made certain that the brainboard hooked them into my optic nerves. Then I exchanged my clothes for the techno-longjohns of the armour, climbed inside, braced myself, and powered up. Things grabbed, stabbed, and engaged. The suit computer announced that the abominable machine was supporting my life and showed me prideful displays to prove it. I responded with an obscenity.

I loathe the way excursion-suit plumbing insults my family jewels. I find servo augmentation of my human musculature to be creepy. I dislike hearing my own breathing – to say nothing of pops and squeaks from my sinuses and inner ears and the gurgles of my gastrointestinal tract. The wondrous gadgetry that virtually transforms a human being into a miniature spaceship has a certain small-boy fun factor; but it can't compensate for the attendant claustrophobia and divorce from normal human sensation.

To my mind, excursion suits suck.

Nevertheless, on that day I was going to learn to love mine.

I wriggled and shrugged and made myself as comfortable as possible. I sampled the helmet's quartet of sipping tubes, which typically provide water, insipid electrolitically balanced faux juice, high-calorie vanilla soyshake, and proteinoid gunk that tastes like off-brand peanut butter. Thanks to Captain Bermudez, the refreshment reservoirs of *Chispa*'s suits had a better menu. Besides the water, there was non-alcoholic piña colada, a decent cognac that I couldn't quite identify, and a spicy paste of refried beans.

The lower crawl-strip now said: 3 MINUTES TO TARGET INTERCEPT INITIATION. The navigation data displays reassured me that my starship was poised to pounce just as soon as the broom tender came within the designated striking zone of 486,029 kilometres.

The computer spoke up: *Target in scan range.*

I told it, 'Confirm target ID.' A cartoonish diagram bloomed before my eyes. Bingo! The identification was positive for GAL–6236T. I said, 'Cancel icon.' The little vision winked out.

The computer said: *Target vector deviates point oh-two-six percent from stored parameters. Do you wish to make a correction?*

'Affirm. Feed precise target vector to ship navigation plot. Power up ship actinic cannons. Merge ship proper situation display and suit targeting grid. Maintain ship full defensive shields. Open ship broadband hail. Adjust com wattage input to range plus-minus one kilometre.'

The excursion bay where I stood waiting seemed to vanish. My eyes became the eyes of *La Chispa*, seeing what she saw. The cometary nucleus seemed to drift further upward and then recede as the starship dropped into position for its waylaying sprint.

Initiating interception manoeuvre now.

We roared off at max subluminal. The crawl counted down the thirty-six seconds to intercept. *Chispa* came up from behind the tender, swooped and rolled, matched vectors, and ended up hovering nose-to-nose with the other ship, precisely two hundred metres away.

I'd done it. To the skipper of GAL–6236T, the Javelin would have seemed to appear out of nowhere.

Zap zap zap zap! Four actinic blasts framed the quarry in the classic piratical challenge and I called out a minimally powered hail.

'Attention GAL tender. This is a hostile intercept and you are a locked-on target. Do not attempt to change vector, do not erect class-three force-shield, do not attempt to transmit alarm or I will shoot to inflict serious damage. Acknowledge your surrender, audio only, on Channel 233 with input wattage no more than ·25.'

I waited, letting the tender scan me. *Chispa*'s configuration would be evident to the prey's optical sensors, but her transponder ID and external designations, illegally suppressed by the tap of a pad once I had left Kedge-Lockaby restricted space, would not be.

The response came in an outraged contralto. 'What the hell do you think you're doing, bandit? We're carrying groceries, for chrissake!'

I said, 'Identify yourself.'

'This is Captain Demetria Panayiotou, master of GAL–6236T.'

'We can do this short and sweet or long and ugly, Captain Demetria. Believe me – I'll fire on your vessel and disable or destroy it if I have to. I'd rather not. All I want is your passenger, the man who calls himself Bronson Elgar.'

'Are you out of your friggin' mind?'

Tempted to reply in the affirmative, I controlled myself. 'Captain, is Bronson Elgar on your bridge, able to overhear this transmission?'

There was a pause, then: 'No.'

'Make certain that he doesn't hear it.'

'Explain.'

'No explanation is necessary. I demand, you comply. Then I go away and you forget that the passenger ever boarded at Manukura. Here's how we'll work it: You yourself – and nobody else – will take Elgar to your cargo-loading bay. I'll come over and collect him there. If you have to coerce the bastard at gunpoint, it's okay with me. I'd even recommend it as a safety precaution if you value your ship and your life. He might try to self-destruct and take you with him.'

'That's ridiculous! The man is a Galapharma executive on urgent Concern business. He carries documentation to prove it –'

'You have a very nice voice, Captain Demetria, but I don't have time to debate Elgar's status with you. He's an assassin, a paid hit-man. Back on Kedge-Lockaby, he tried to murder me. I'm going to take him in charge and hand him over to the authorities on Kedge-Lockaby.'

Eventually.

'Planetary law has no jurisdiction –'

I cut her off. 'That's enough!' I bracketed the tender with another brace of cannon shots. 'Now listen to me. I intend to cross over to your vessel in an excursion unit and bring a second suit along for the prisoner. I'll be outfitted with personal armament and my crew will keep you targeted with my ship's guns until I return safely with Bronson Elgar. I'll give you two minutes to decide whether to comply. After that –'

'I don't need two minutes,' she snapped. 'Come ahead, bandit. He's all yours.'

It seemed to go slick as a whistle.

I exited *Chispa*, towing the other suit of armour behind me, and soared across the void to the homely red ship with the stylized galactic-spiral **G** logo on its flank. The comet, now over half a million kilometres away, was fully visible on my left and breathtakingly beautiful. Z1's golden coma had three 'onionskin' hoods, the enormous curved dust tail was silver, and the rippling ion tail shone blue with red wisps.

I gave it a mechanically augmented salute in passing. Then I helped myself to a generous swig of cognac to raise my anxiety threshold.

The tender's airlock gaped wide as I approached. The meteoroid force-field winked out momentarily and I pushed inside, landing with a tooth-jarring thud in the artificial gravity. I clumped a few paces away from the second suit, unreeling the attached cable. The airlock chamber's outer hatch rolled shut, a ruby light blinked, and an illuminated sign announced that repressurization was in progress.

I found myself holding my breath at the same time that I swivelled my shoulder guns to bear upon the inner hatch. The caution light went out, the interlocking leaves of the hatch slid apart, and I exhaled with relief.

The bluff had worked. Elgar stood in an aisle space of the densely packed cargo bay, hands clasped on top of his head. He wore the same black jumpsuit he'd worn on *Pernio* and his face was as dour and unreadable as ever. Behind him was a grey-haired woman with a nose like the Statue of Liberty's, dressed in a uniform of crimson trimmed with black. She prodded Elgar in the small of the back with the nozzle of a Claus-Gewitter photon beamer. He stepped forward reluctantly.

'Is this your alleged hired killer, bandit?'

'The very same, Captain,' said I through the suit annunciator, twiddling the Kagi guns so that their little servo motors buzzed ominously. I used the brainboard to pop open the second suit. 'Elgar, strip off and climb into that armour.'

The opaque dark blue eyes narrowed. 'Where's my IM garment?'

'Oops,' I said, letting satisfaction colour my voice. 'Forgot it. Afraid you'll have to go in buck naked.'

He didn't utter another word as he removed his clothes and gingerly fitted himself into the excursion unit. I'd set the interior temp at a brisk 10°C.

Captain Demetria studied my own armoured form with a wintry smile. 'You did a hyperspatial microleap from K-L? I'm impressed.'

'A tradition among us bandits. Did Elgar transmit any subspace messages while he was on board your ship?'

'Ask him yourself.'

I cut off the annunciator and spoke to my prisoner on the suit intercom. 'Did you?'

'Fuck a duck.'

'Difficult in armour. Are you all settled in and comfy?'

He spoke evenly. 'You know I'm not, you sadistic jizzwad. I'm half freezing to death.'

'Mercy me. I forgot to tell you that my computer controls your environmentals and I'm having a few problems with signal feed. Well, maybe things will heat up for you once we're landside again on K-L.'

'Are you stupid enough to think the K-L cops will hold me?'

'I really don't give a doodly damn what they do with you after you tell me everything I want to know. And you *will* tell me, Bron, if you ever want to get out of that tin chilly bin.'

I spoke to the tender's skipper over the annunciator. 'You can cycle the airlock now, Captain Demetria. I'll be out of your hair in a nanojif. Bon voyage – but don't even think about changing your vector. Keep on trucking toward your mothership per sked, and I'll refrain from amputating your pretty tail.'

She gave a contemptuous snort at my lame innuendo. The inner airlock hatch closed and the outer one opened immediately. She'd spitefully shut off the gravity and my prisoner and I were blown out like spat melon seeds with the quick decompression, twirling merrily in the void ass over teakettle with the cable leash connecting us like a couple of bolo balls.

Well, I'd asked for it.

Elgar was cursing non-stop. I straightened us out and set off for *Chispa*, towing him on the tether. I travelled backwards so I could keep the prisoner targeted in case Captain Demetria misbehaved.

'Shut up and hang in there,' I told Elgar, 'and remember my epaulettes can shoot large holes in you if the tender tries anything funny. Food and drink are available from your helmet sippers when you feel thirsty or peckish. But if I were you I'd go easy on the *fritos refritos* in the food tube – at least until your suit ventilation problems are resolved.'

'I suppose oxygen deprivation is next on your agenda, laughing boy.'

'Nooo . . . not until we've gone as far as we can with hypothermia and cruder forms of distress. Of course, you could just answer my questions and spare yourself. Did Galapharma send you to kill me as part of some scheme involving Simon Frost and Rampart Starcorp?'

Silence.

I sighed. 'Who the devil are you, anyway? You've changed your face, but I know I've seen you before, on Earth.'

More silence.

'Did we meet at some regulatory confab in Geneva? Or at an ICS corporate security briefing in Toronto? I have the distinct feeling that you're not just an independent contractor or a third-string corporate goon. You're special, aren't you? Why did Galapharma send the likes of you to do the wipe-out personally?'

Nothing.

'You know, it was sheer bad luck that gutted your game, Bron. I should have been easy to kill. My being able to come after you was equally flukey.'

More nothing.

'On the other hand, your bosses have miscalculated badly if they think my death will cause Rampart to cave in to a hostile takeover or some other acquisition manoeuvre. Simon Frost doesn't give a damn about me.'

'You're wrong,' Bronson Elgar finally said, 'not that it makes any difference.'

'Why do you say that? My father's hated me for years because I defied him and wouldn't agree to work in the family store. After my frame-up, he decided I was criminally incompetent and a moral coward as well.'

43

'You *are* a coward, Cap'n Helly,' Elgar said softly. 'In the ICS, you were nothing but a candy-ass bureaucrat – not a real copper. When the shit came down you went to pieces.'

'True,' I admitted. 'Everybody's got a breaking point. You may want to speculate what yours might be.'

'You won't torture me, limp-dick,' he sneered, 'any more than you would have shot up the comet-broom tender. I tried to tell that stupid cunt of a skipper you were faking her out, but she wouldn't listen.'

The conversation was wandering in a direction I didn't much like. I had certainly been bluffing about destroying the broom tender. How far I was actually willing to go to get information from Elgar was a matter I hadn't seriously addressed. Still, tough talk was cheap.

'We'll be taking a nice roundabout route back to K-L,' I told him, 'me in the nice warm command bridge eating recon rare fillet steak and you chained in a garbage hold open to deep space sucking Mexican bean-dip while your hands and feet freeze black. You can decide for yourself what kind of a lily-livered wuss I am.'

He shut up after that and so did I. I guess both of us were weighing our options.

We were about halfway to *Chispa* when a tremendous burst of white light came from somewhere behind me.

For a terrible instant I thought that the Javelin had somehow come under attack. Then I realized that the silent explosion was a hyperspatial exit flash. Another starship had joined the party.

I spun my suit around. *Chispa* was still there but the starry sky behind her was obliterated by a massive shape that my ship-sensor feed pegged at over eleven kilometres overall length. It was the weirdest starship I had ever seen in my life, resembling nothing so much as a gleaming warty acorn pierced laterally by an ornate dagger. The upper surface of the knobbed main structure was surmounted by a shining sapphire dome, and a myriad of glittering blue ports studded the curving intricacies of the 'hilt'. The ship was not human and much too large and sophisticated to be Qastt. In the Perseus Spur, that seemed to leave only one other possibility.

'Haluk?' My voice was scarcely more than a shocked whisper. 'You sent a distress call from the tender ... and a *Haluk* vessel responded?'

The immense starship disgorged a ladybug-shaped gig with two blue headlights like eyes, which sped purposefully toward us.

'They would have picked me up at the broom mothership tomorrow,' Elgar said. 'It was no big deal asking the Haluk commander to put the pedal to the metal in an emergency and come to the rescue at maximum ross.'

I still hadn't taken it in. 'Galapharma ... working with the Haluk?'

Bronson Elgar chuckled. 'Boggles your puny mind, does it? But it's only a matter of good business, mutually beneficial.'

I was struck speechless by the manifest lunacy of the notion. Humans who first explored the Perseus Spur learned early on that it was impossible to make binding treaties with the unrelentingly hostile Haluk or even traffic with them in a civilized manner. They are an allomorphic race whose ethics are as mutable as their bodily form – fierce, envious, and deeply afraid of humanity. Only the limitations of their peculiar physiology, and the fact that their technology is inferior to ours, had prevented them from waging a war of expulsion when human exploiters penetrated their territory in the farthest reaches of the Spur. We dealt with the Haluk only when we had no other choice, and then only from a position of overwhelming strength.

Yet here they were, apparently at the beck and call of Galapharma's enigmatic hatchet man. And their starship didn't look all that 'inferior' either – at least not in my none-too-expert evaluation.

'Now what?' I asked the cosmos at large. The enormity of the situation had thrown me on my beam ends. My Brit pal Oren Vinyard would have called me well and truly gobsmacked.

'Well,' Bronson Elgar remarked dryly, 'I suppose you could finish me off before the Haluk gig picks us up. Just pop my helmet seal. Get instant revenge for your munched-up house, maybe piss off my principals a little.'

I said nothing. Didn't kill him, either.

45

He laughed at me. 'No? I figured it wasn't your style . . . Don't even think of firing on the Haluk starship with your cannons. It's shielded up the wide wazoo with improved defensive fields. And if you target the gig, the aliens will blast your little crate to subatomic soot, and you and I and the crew of the broom tender will die in the shock wave.'

'Scragging you wouldn't bother them?'

Elgar said, 'Plenty more when I came from, Cap'n Helly. If I were you, I'd surrender.'

So I did, knowing I was a dead man but curious to see how the assassin would orchestrate my termination the second time around. I figured he still had to send an unforgettable message to my father, but what could possibly be more bizarre than being eaten by a sea-monster?

They marooned me on the backside of the comet.

Bronson Elgar used a Haluk holocam to make a video while two aliens spreadeagled and pegged me down over one of the smaller sublimatory jet orifices on the 'night' surface of Z1. He and his associates had other business, so they weren't able to wait around for the comedy's finale in two hours' time, when rotation of the comet nucleus would carry me into sunlight, activating my jet. As the icy interior warmed, the hole I plugged and others around it would erupt with incandescent gases, x-rays, and steam at a velocity of approximately two thousand nine hundred kilometres per hour. The excursion suit would not be able to save me. My armourclad form would be hurled into space and I would suffer massive radiation trauma. Bleeding from every orifice, skin hideously inflamed, wracked with vomiting and unending pain, I would endure until my air supply ran out or I strangled in my own puke.

So many times I'd toyed fearlessly with the notion of ending my life! But always doing it the easy way, snuffing myself tidily like a candleflame, flying away, fading into negation. I'd managed to keep my mouth shut while Elgar and the Haluk tied me down, but my self-control cracked when they went away and I lay alone and helpless, facing the actuality of a messy, agonizing death.

Self-pitying tears coursed down my cheeks. To keep from screaming I nursed away desperately at the cognac sipper in my suit, staring at the colourful wisps of plasma and sparkling ice crystals of Z_1's inner coma through bleary eyes.

After a while all things passed away into infinite night.

Chapter 5

My last conscious thought was of my friend Captain Guillermo Bermudez. I wanted to tell him how sorry I was that the Haluk bastards had destroyed his lovely *Chispa* before casting me away on the comet to die. In my imagination I heard the old man chuckle and utter his familiar disclaimer: *No me importa dos cojones* – it doesn't matter two balls' worth.

I whispered, 'So long, pal. Nice knowing you.'

He replied, *No seas capullo, muchacho.* Which means: Don't be stupid, kid. Then he said, 'Are you awake, Helly?'

I said, 'Of course not. I'm dead.'

'Nonsense. Open your eyes.'

I did. He was bending over me, his grizzled hair an einsteinian bird's nest, dark eyes twinkling in their wrinkles, an unlit cigarillo clamped in his cosmetically enhanced teeth. He had on a white linen shirt with an embroidered yoke, and a dark blue Jaffé windbreaker. Above him was a lumi-ceiling with half the tiles burnt out. Behind his right shoulder stood a redheaded woman wearing a pale blue medic's coat. She had a diagnosticon hanging on a lanyard around her neck and a name-tag that read DR FIONULLA BATCHELDER – CYTOPLASMIC MEDICINE.

I asked the inevitable questions. 'Where am I? What happened?'

'You're in Manukura Community Hospital, Mr Helmut Icicle,' the doctor said, giving my pseudonym an ironic inflection. 'You've just successfully completed a three-week course of dynamic stasis gene therapy –'

I croaked, 'Three *weeks*?'

'– that restored tissue and chromosomal material damaged by x-radiation and intense ionic flux. As to what happened, I think

48

you'd better ask your friend, here. Captain Bermudez brought you to us and he's paying your tab – but he's refused to give us any particulars about the source of your injuries.'

'An accident in space,' Mimo said. 'The details are immaterial.'

I hoisted myself up. 'You sneaky old bootlegger. You followed me!'

He clasped me in a bony *abrazo*. 'And a good thing, you bungling *cagon de mierdas*, or you'd be strumming a harp off-key instead of lolling in bed bankrupting me with the exorbitant cost of your medical care.' He let me go and I flopped back helplessly onto the mattress. He said, 'Can you prop the patient up a bit, doctor?'

'Of course.' She tapped a control-pad on the bed's headboard. The ageing mechanism shuddered and wheezed a little, then uplifted me so that I was supported at a forty-five-degree angle. I discovered that I was wearing one of those hospital gowns that fasten behind the neck and leave your buns bare. A neatly mended sheet and a threadbare blanket covered me to the midsection. I was nice and warm. My upper left arm was fitted with a medicuff armlet, and my seagoing tan had unaccountably faded, leaving my skin almost as white as chalk.

Dr Batchelder did a fast once-over with her diagnosticon, prodding my half-shrouded form with brisk efficiency. 'You'll do. How do you feel?'

'Pretty good,' I admitted. 'Very confused. A little woozy and stiff in the joints.' I had been wriggling my fingers and moving my arms and legs. Everything worked. I tried to sort the wild flurry of thoughts capering in my brain: I wasn't dead. I wasn't adrift in the tail of comet Z1, barfing my dissolving guts into the helmet of my space armour. Somehow, Mimo had saved me.

'Your dizziness will pass,' the doctor said. 'The physical weakness is a side effect of the dystasis treatment that will wear off in about two weeks as you get up and about. You should feel well enough for very moderate exercise sessions in three or four days. Until then, bed rest alternated with brief sessions of slow walking.'

'Then I'm all right? I'm cured?'

'We even repaired your liver – and its general pathology had very little to do with your escapade in space. You can leave here tomorrow and complete your convalescence at home. You'll have to wear the medicuff armlet for ten days. It administers necessary medication and you can also use it if you need a stimulant, relief from pain, or help in sleeping. The radiation injuries to your non-germinal body cells were only moderate, thanks to your armour, and genen procedures have healed them completely. It will take somewhat longer for your sperm DNA to normalize. I wouldn't advise you to father a child for at least six months.'

Mimo guffawed. 'His many female admirers will be devastated.'

The doctor rolled her eyes toward heaven. 'The patient is allowed visitors for half an hour only today, Captain Bermudez, and there are others waiting.' She pointed a finger at him. 'Remember: don't light that cigar!'

She whirled out of the room and closed the door. For the first time I noticed that the place was hip-deep in vases of tropical flowers. The window, with salt-stained panes and curtains that were a trifle faded, had a nice view of the evening sea with the Moon of Manukura rising in romantic splendour. The bedstand and clothes locker were old but freshly painted apple green. Mimo had sprung for one of the best private rooms in the Big Beach's overburdened little hospital.

'Other visitors?' I queried.

'Friends from Eyebrow Cay,' Mimo said. 'When they heard you were coming out of the tank today, they forced me to ferry them here for the occasion. They've already spent several hours in a nearby pub celebrating your safe recovery.'

'Well . . . Jeez.' Some sort of a pang passed through me. Mostly surprise.

'Shall I call them in?'

'Maybe you'd better tell me how I got off the goddamn comet first.'

He shrugged, rolling the cigarillo from one side of his mouth to the other, and pulled up a white plastic chair.

'After you took off in *La Chispa*, I went back to the island. Kofi and Oren had finished with the toad. They managed to save three ceramic flowerpots, a few pieces of stoneware table crockery, your porcelain toilet and hot tub (minus the plumbing), and a platinum neck-chain threaded through two gold wedding rings. Those are in my safe, at home. My red catamaran is repairable, amazingly enough. Unfortunately, the supersonic generator planted by your would-be murderer had melted away to an unidentifiable blob by the time Kofi and Oren located it.'

'It doesn't matter. Without Elgar himself, the evidence is useless.'

Mimo nodded sombre agreement. 'Sal and her tugboat towed away the toad carcass. The boys washed down the beach with hazardous material neutralizer and then went home. I sat on my verandah and drank strong coffee and began to have very serious regrets about urging you to go after Bronson Elgar. My senile *machismo* had overcome common sense. I decided that the interception scheme was foolhardy to the point of madness. Only an exceptionally large comet, located in an ideal position, would suffice to conceal the flash of *Chispa*'s microleap from the tender you pursued. I feared that the odds of your finding such a comet, and executing the delicate manoeuvres required for concealment, were impossibly long.'

'Thanks all to hell for the vote of confidence.'

'Try to understand my feelings, *compadre*. I knew in my heart that you would not turn back even if you failed to find a big comet. Your mood was both fatalistic and reckless. I believed you would leap behind an inadequate smaller comet rather than let Bronson Elgar escape, and if you did, the tender's crew would surely detect your presence. Elgar would know at once who was following him. He would order the tender's captain to erect class-three defensive shields. You would be forced to pursue and pound your target with actinic blasts for a dangerously long period of time before the shields collapsed and the ship surrendered.'

I didn't bother to correct his misconceptions. 'Why a dangerously long time? I could still catch the tender before it reached its mama.'

'Helly, my friend, I confess I had forgotten one vitally important fact! *The broom mothership has ultraluminal capability to enable it to move between solar systems.* It could have come to the tender's aid. And while it is not armed itself, the auxiliary robocraft called spikers that it carries are fitted with powerful cannons capable of boring through *Chispa*'s strongest defensive shields.'

'Oh.'

'Yes. Sitting there on my verandah, I became convinced I had sent you to your death. There was only one thing I could do: stop you if I could. By then, nearly an hour and a half had gone by since your departure. I knew it might already be too late, but I raced for the hopper and returned to the starport at top speed. My second starship, a new Bodascon Y660 cutter named *El Plomazo*, with twice the sublight speed and three times the armament of *Chispa*, was ready for lift-off. Ordinarily these vessels are sold only to Zone Patrol squadrons and high executives of the Hundred Concerns, but I . . . recently obtained one.'

'You never can tell when a thing like that might come in handy.'

He made an airy gesture. 'Once offworld, I used *Plomazo*'s exquisitely responsive sensor equipment to search for you. I located the broom tender easily, even though it had already passed beyond the sun. But there was no trace of *Chispa*.'

'By then I was hiding behind the comet,' I said. 'And it was plenty big enough.'

He nodded. 'I discovered that for myself when I examined the ephemeris. Comet 2231–001–Z1 was your only logical choice for the ambush, and my calculations showed that the tender had not yet reached the appropriate intercept point. What joy! I decided that my worries had been meaningless and I now had every confidence that you would succeed. Nevertheless, I decided to watch the encounter from K-L orbit to ensure that all went well. Visual observation was impossible at that distance, of course. But I picked up your subluminal-drive signature when you were about halfway through your attack charge. Then *Chispa* matched velocities with her prey and I knew you had won.'

'Until the Haluk made the scene,' I muttered.

'Imagine my amazement! My horror! At first I thought the EM flash belonged to the broom mothership, coming to the rescue of its tender. But analysis of the drive trace revealed at once that the fuel was Haluk and the vessel itself of unprecedented configuration – larger and more elaborate than any of those I am familiar with. I hesitated only for a moment, then executed a wham-bam microleap of my own. (Forgive my immodesty, but I'm an old hand at such things, and the calculations took no time at all.) I exited behind the comet and in line with the sun, as you had done, trusting that the Haluk starship was too busy to notice me. Then I shut down all my ship's systems except environmental and sensory, engaged a certain dissimulator field that has been newly developed, and became a virtual orbiting chunk of debris – a satellite of comet Z1 – watching as you were marooned. I saw poor *Chispa* blown to bits. I had to wait until the big Haluk ship re-entered hyperspace and the broom tender was well out of sensor range, then I rescued you and brought you home. Your injuries were only moderate, since the jet had not yet attained full eruption – but another half hour on the cometary surface . . .' He shrugged.

I said, 'Thank you, Mimo.'

He said, *'Por nada.'*

After that the gang trooped in and there was happy bedlam. Kofi was there with Oren, and so were Sal Faustino, Seedy McGready, Glasha Romanov, Billy Mulholland, Gumercindo Huckelbury and Jinj and Peachy Tallhorse. I discovered that my friends had been busy while I was zonked out and afloat, getting my irradiated DNA put back together. Seedy, Goom and Kofi were erecting a new shack for me, a little smaller than the old place but capable of expansion. They showed me a holo of the work in progress. Sal and Billy had hit up everybody on Eyebrow Cay for furniture and domestic appurtenances. Glasha and the twins had passed the hat and twisted arms for a clothing and food fund. Oren had even managed to repair *Pernio*'s busted MFGS.

'You're gonna be back on line in a couple more weeks, sweetie,' said Sal Faustino, giving me one of her juicy kisses. The other three women had already had their wicked way with me. 'The medics say they'll toss you out of here tomorrow. All you have to do after that is rest up and eat and do something about that fishbelly inverse tan you're wearing.'

'I think it's cute,' said the lovely Glasha.

'You guys,' I said. My vision had somehow become a mite blurred.

'We won't stay any longer,' Mimo said. 'You take it easy.' He herded the others out the door and closed it.

I relaxed and helped myself to a drink of water from the bedside carafe. Then I cranked up the bed a bit higher. In a minute or two, I was going to try to stand up. I felt pretty fair, except for my growling stomach. The last real food it had encountered was the refried bean paste in *Chispa*'s space armour. The twins had brought me a little basket of pitless black cherries, a rare luxury that had to be imported from Yakima-Two. I ate a few, wondered what the hospital menu might have on offer, and decided to kick up a monumental stink if they tried to fob me off with invalid's slop. I wanted something substantial. A cheeseburger. Fried onion rings. Jojo potatoes. Meanwhile, I'd have the cherries for an appetizer . . .

The door opened again and all thoughts of eating were erased from my mind. Superintendent Jake Silver slouched in, looking sweaty, untidy, and put upon. He said, 'Might have known you'd survive, Hell-Butt.'

I groaned. 'Oh God, it's Kedgeree Kop! Don't tell me you're here for an official statement.'

'From a Throwaway? Don't make me laugh.'

'Then what the devil *do* you want?'

'Don't get your fundament in a furore. Here's a little get-well present for you.' He fished in his tunic pocket, pulled out a much-folded piece of paper, and handed it over. Then he grabbed a big handful of the cherries without asking, started chomping, and surveyed the collection of flowers. 'Very pretty. I'd've sent some, but the florist was fresh out of skunk lilies and pissweed.'

The paper had four names and addresses on it: the domiciles of record for Clive Leighton, Mario Volta, Oleg Bransky, and Tokuro Matsudo. Leighton lived on Seriphos. The other three were from Hadrach, Plusia-Prime and Tyrins.

'What's this?' I asked.

'Clues, numskull,' Jake said, turning back to me with his mouth full, 'as any competent cop would know without asking. What you do with the information is none of my business. The individuals are probably just what they said they were: innocent vacationers who'd never laid eyes on Bronson Elgar before. Or maybe not.'

Damn straight, maybe not. But Jake's unexpected gesture assumed that I was going after Elgar and whoever had hired him. How much did Jake know, anyhow? Mimo would never have revealed details of my ill-starred venture into space piracy and neither would the comet-broom commander. On the other hand, the story of the sea-toad eating my house was probably K-L's Chuckle of the Month.

'Well, thanks,' I said grudgingly. I put the note under my pillow. 'But actually, I was planning to forget all about the unfortunate incident. Go back to Eyebrow Cay and resume my career as fish voyeur.'

'Somehow, I doubt that. Toads are one thing. Comets are something else.'

Rats. 'Who told you?'

Jake gobbled up the last of the cherries and heaved a regretful sigh as he deep-sixed the empty plastic basket into the recycling bin. 'Been years since I had any of these. Delicious.'

I was halfway out of the bed. 'Who told you, Jake?'

But he didn't answer the question directly. 'You've got one last visitor. I'll have to go outside and fetch him from my cruiser. He wouldn't stay in the hospital waiting room. Afraid your tacky friends might recognize him.'

He went out, leaving me furious and worried. My only hope of being left in peace was for Elgar & Co to think I was dead. The fact that I was alive today was pretty good evidence that the assassin didn't know I'd been rescued. I knew I could depend on my Throwaway buddies to help me sink back into anonymity, but Jake and this other mystery visitor were another matter. If my survival became common knowledge among the enfranchised, the word would eventually find its way to Elgar's backers.

Then I'd have to leave Kedge-Lockaby. Find another wildcat planet. Build a new fake identity and start all over again, hoping Galapharma's spies wouldn't track me down.

I lay back wearily and let my eyes close. Tomorrow. I'd think about it tomorrow . . .

The door opened and I heard heavy footsteps. Someone came in, closed the door, and approached my bed. To hell with him, whoever he was. I could pretend I was asleep–

He said, 'Asahel. We have to talk.'

I knew that voice. The sound of it hit me like a punch in the belly. I opened my eyes. A tall man stood at my bedside, dressed in immaculate tan Western wear and improbably holding his broad-brimmed Stetson hat in both hands.

The rough-hewn trailboss face was my own – modified by forty-eight additional hard years of life and a modicum of genen rejuvenation. High forehead, hair the colour of breadcrust with an exaggerated widow's peak, pale brows above sceptical hooded eyes of cold green with an inner ring of amber around the pupil, thin-bridged nose, mouth habitually downturned so as not to give away the fact that the infrequent smile could charm and bedazzle.

I said, 'Hello, Simon. So Galapharma delivered the message.'

My father blinked, his customary understated indication of acute astonishment. His voice was harsh, with only a touch of Western twang. 'A holovid dime and a printed note appeared mysteriously on the desk in my study at the Sky Ranch in Arizona. The holo showed a man in space excursion armour lashed down on the surface of some sort of celestial object. The note said: "One dead, one on hold, three at risk unless you fold".'

'Atrocious doggerel,' I said. 'The poker analogy seems to indicate a certain familiarity with your life-style.'

One on hold?

'The note went on to say that your corpse was to be found in the vicinity of a comet in the Kedge-Lockaby system. The armour's emergency beacon would serve as a guide to the remains.'

'A considerate touch. I'm surprised you didn't just dismiss the whole thing as a hoax. Or ignore it on general principles.'

'I'd been thinking about you recently, Asa. Last September, Eve was at the Sky Ranch for a family conference. She said you'd been . . . coming along well.'

I gave a noncommittal murmur. No doubt she'd had another go at trying to patch up the rift between Simon and me and got nowhere. Good old Eve.

'I contacted the head of Kedge-Lockaby's CID and demanded an inquiry into your alleged death.' Simon's lips tightened in distaste. 'A certain Superintendent Jacob Silver said that you were more or less alive, being treated for radiation trauma. He told me the day you were scheduled to be released from the dystasis tank but refused to give me any more details, the insolent shit.'

'Unimpressed by Rampart's Lord High Plunderbunder, eh?' I flashed him my own version of the family grin, the one Joanna used to say would melt a glacier. It hadn't a hope in hell of thawing Simon Frost. He only stared at me, frowning. I couldn't tell if he was pissed off or perplexed.

'So you came,' I prompted him.

'At maximum ross on the *Mogollon Rim*. Twenty days.'

'Eve would have flown over from Tyrins to check me out if you'd asked her.'

'I tried to.' He clammed up again. His gaze shifted for an instant and his prominent Adam's apple bobbed up and down in his corded neck as he swallowed. More portentous silence. Then he sat down heavily in the bedside chair.

'I called Eve's office from Earth. And her personal assistant tried to give me the runaround. Me!' The *lèse majesté* of it all made me smile for an instant, but my amusement evaporated as he continued. 'All he'd say was that Eve was unavailable. I finally told the stupid galoot I'd personally tear out his sweetbreads and fry 'em in bacon grease if he didn't explain. That's when he admitted that she had disappeared.'

Another phantom wallop jolted my innards. So Eve was the one 'on hold' – whatever that meant! And my older brother Dan, my sister Beth, and my mother were presumably the 'three at risk' unless Simon capitulated to whatever pressure was being exerted on him. For the first time I noticed that my father's features were not truly impassive. Behind the masterful glare lurked an emotion I had never seen in him before.

Fear.

'When did Eve go missing?' I asked him.

'In mid-January, by Earth reckoning. Thirty days ago – nine days before your run-in with the comet. I finally got hold of Tyrins External Security, but they referred me to Zared on Seriphos. He said Eve told her staff that she was taking some time off, supposedly to recuperate from overwork. She never returned. The manager of the secluded little Tyrins resort where she'd booked a cabin said she personally cancelled the booking via videophone. Eve had stayed there before and the manager knows her. She didn't give any hint of why she'd changed her plans or where she might be going. Zared claims that Rampart security agents turned Tyrins upside down but failed to find any trace of her. They're still looking. The investigation has been quietly extended to the other Spur worlds, including the freesoil planets.'

'What about the Commonwealth police? Have they been notified?'

'Zared didn't bring in Zone Patrol for fear of Eve's disappearance being leaked to the media. He thought that might compromise our ongoing efforts to be granted Concern status and leave us wide open to ... our business rivals. When I asked him why he hadn't told *me* earlier that Eve had vanished, the imbecile claimed he was just finalizing the investigation report and would have sent it on within a few days. Zared seems convinced that Eve's gone to ground for some personal reason of her own and she'll surface when she's damned good and ready. I call that complete horse puckey!'

'Did you tell Zed or Rampart ExSec about the mystery message?'

'Not yet.'

I wondered why. I also wondered whether Bronson Elgar had made a stopover on my sister's planet before coming to Kedge-Lockaby. 'Well, what do you intend to do now?'

Simon studied me with an oddly speculative expression. He was silent for some moments, then said suddenly, 'Matt Gregoire, Eve's Chief of Fleet Security, will be meeting with Rampart's Board of Directors on Seriphos day after tomorrow for a confidential debriefing on the disappearance. I want you to join us, Asahel. Help us find Eve.'

'You're joking!'

But he rarely joked, and his face had abruptly regained its invincible confidence. He checked the Rolex Scheduler on his wrist, got up, and started for the door. 'Come to my suite at the Nikko Luxor tomorrow. Breakfast at 0730 hours, then we'll fly to Seriphos together in the *Mogollon Rim*.'

'No,' I said, lowering my bare feet to the floor and sitting on the edge of the bed. 'I've got other plans.' I'd investigate my sister's disappearance, all right – but I'd do it unencumbered by Simon,

Rampart Starcorp, or anyone else.

When I tried to rise the room began spinning. I tottered like a mesquite tree undermined by a desert flash flood and dropped back, cursing.

My father returned to my bedside. He flipped open the draggled sheets, picked up both my legs, swivelled me around on my butt, and forced me to lie down. Then he covered me up, hit the bed control, and rendered me horizontal. 'You're supposed to rest. Your pal Jake Silver said so.'

'Stop ordering me around!' I struggled to get up again. 'I'm not one of your Rampart stooges, and I'll be damned if I waste my time at this corporate confab of yours.' Sudden weakness sandbagged me. I flopped back onto the thin pillow. 'Maybe Eve finally got sick and tired of your bulldozery and Cousin Zed's fusspot shilly-shallying and just packed it in.'

'You know she wouldn't do that.'

Yes, I knew. I was just rattling my father's chain. Eve was as indomitable and loyal to Rampart as Simon himself, but without his ruthlessness or contempt for human frailty.

And she was 'on hold'.

Bending over me, Simon forced the words out. 'Please come to Seriphos, Asahel. Your professional experience could be invaluable to this investigation.'

I threw it at him without warning. 'Galapharma's engineering a takeover attempt on Rampart. Right? And you suspect they're mind-fucking you by abducting Eve and trying to kill me.'

A brief nod. 'There's more to it than that, but you're on target.'

'Do you know about the Haluk connection?'

'What?'

'Not so loud.' I peered up at him with sour satisfaction. He was no longer making any effort to hide his dismay.

'Are you serious? What Haluk connection?'

'I could be mistaken.' He was ready to persist in the questioning, but I shook my head tiredly. 'Not now. We can talk about it later. I feel lousy. You'd better go.'

'Asahel, at least come to the board meeting. Please.'

I refused to look at him. 'Why?'

'Because I need you. You may be the only one who can save your sister from the bastards who have her – you, with your ICS background, your knowledge of Concern skulduggery. Rampart has been in a state of managerial crisis for nearly two years. Eve's disappearance renders us more vulnerable than any of the others realize. I want you to listen to what Gregoire and Ollie Schneider, our Vice President for Confidential Services, have to say about the situation on Tyrins. I'll also see that you're completely briefed on the Galapharma takeover bid and the internal problems. Give us whatever advice you can. Help us find Eve. Then turn your back on us and go back to your island, if you still insist.'

He was very persuasive, damn him. It was unthinkable that I not do everything in my power to find my sister. If Galapharma was behind Eve's disappearance, as both of us suspected, the job of locating her would be easier if I knew as much as possible about the conflict between the family Starcorp and the big Concern.

Another notion came tiptoeing into my mind. I pulled myself up on my elbows. 'Do any of the other Rampart directors know about the attempts on my life?'

Simon looked surprised. 'There was more than one?'

I sighed. 'Just answer the question.'

'Nobody else knows. Not even Daniel.' He was referring to my older brother, Chief Corporate Counsel and Syndic of Rampart. 'I did tell him about Eve's disappearance. He flew with me to Seriphos on the *Mogollon Rim*. I left him in Vetivarum to organize the meeting and came to K-L yesterday for your roll-out. Nobody but the *Rim*'s pilot knows I'm here.'

'Do you intend to tell the board members that I'm attending the meeting?'

'No. I didn't even decide to invite you until – until I got here.' The hooded eyelids lowered. His mouth became an obstinate line and it was clear that he was not going to say anything else on the subject. I was forced to consider the amazing idea that Bronson Elgar might have been right in his extraordinary judgement of my father's feelings toward me.

Unless Simon was trying to manipulate me as he'd manipulated so many others . . . but I'd already made up my mind to go to the

Rampart board meeting by then, for Eve's sake.

'All right,' I said. 'Forget about doing breakfast and toting me along on the *Mogollon Rim*. I'll get to Seriphos under my own steam and arrange my own accommodation. Schedule the meeting for 1300 hours at Rampart Central, day after tomorrow. Don't tell anyone I'm coming.'

Simon nodded curtly. His anxiety had receded and I had no doubt that he felt he was in control once again. He had compromised his iron principles by pleading with me; now that I had agreed, there would be no thanks.

I said, 'Give me your personal phone code.'

He took out a card and placed it on the bedstand. 'Asa . . .'

I deliberately turned away from him and closed my eyes. 'Go away and leave me alone.'

After a while I heard the door close. When I sat up there was only a little vertigo. The telephone was in the bedstand drawer. I punched Mimo's code, caught him in Nordhoff's Raiatea Bar with the gang, and asked another great favour of him: a ride to Seriphos. Without hesitating, he agreed.

Clive Leighton, one of the sport-divers, lived on that planet. With luck, I might wring something useful out of him before the board meeting.

I lay back again and went peacefully to sleep.

Chapter 6

Mimo Bermudez and I took off for Seriphos as soon as I was discharged from the hospital late the following morning. The trip from K-L to Vetivarum, the planet's capital, took a little over two hours at a sizzling 60 ross, ULD max for *El Plomazo* – The Bullet – and for virtually any other ship in the galaxy. No protests of mine could discourage my friend from demonstrating the awesome capabilities of his expensive new toy. When we reached the Seriphos system he switched to subluminal drive and began juking around like a bat out of hell, performing inertialess vacubatics at engine redline velocity (a hundred million kilometres per hour) and showing off the ship's guns by demolishing blameless little asteroids.

I suppressed my queasiness – which might have been attributable to my invalid status, but was more likely apprehension over things to come – and expressed admiration for his skills, while tactfully pointing out that time was a-wasting. I had important business to transact on Seriphos before meeting with the Rampart board members tomorrow. Besides, *Plomazo* was getting low on fuel.

Then I made a mistake. 'But don't worry about that, Mimo. I intend to see that you're reimbursed for this trip's costs – and my hospital expenses and the loss of your other ship as well.'

'That's not necessary,' he said.

'My father can afford it.'

'I would rather not.'

'For God's sake, be reasonable! At least let me get you compensation for *La Chispa*.'

'It was I who sent you out in her! Should I accept a reward for saving a life I myself had endangered?'

'I'm still going to see that you get a new starship,' I muttered mulishly.

At that, Mimo lost his temper in a way I had never seen before, cursing me out in eloquent Spanish that my own knowledge of Arizona-Mex couldn't half follow. When he wound down, I managed a lame apology. 'I didn't mean to insult you.'

'But you do, damn you! You were gratified by the charity of *los pobres del arrecife* who rebuilt your house, gathered furniture and food for you, but my generosity is unacceptable! Is it because I break stupid laws? Do you fear that one day I'll ask something from you in return that would affront your tender conscience? Or is it that I'm rich like your father, and the only good gifts are those that come from raggedy-ass Throwaways like yourself?'

'Don't be silly. You're the best friend I have on K-L. I don't give a flying fuck how you make your money. But –'

'Helly, there's a little-known virtue called magnificence: an unostentatious liberality of expenditure in doing good. You would deny me the practice of it. *¡Mierda!* I should have left you on the comet.'

I took a deep breath and said in careful Spanish, 'I have behaved like an imbecile, and you are in truth magnificent, Don Guillermo. Thanks for all of the good gifts, but especially for that of your friendship.'

His English reply was a mollified growl. 'We will say no more about payment – at least of the monetary sort! I was touched that you were willing to confide your great secret to me, back there on the beach at Kedge-Lockaby. I also confess that I find this predicament of yours fascinating, with a far greater potential for amusement than the other activities I've indulged in lately. If you truly wish to compensate me, then let me help you in whatever way may be most useful. Keep me in your confidence. You won't regret it.'

I said, 'It's a deal . . . up to a point.'

'*¡Claro!* That goes without saying. My offer includes taking you anywhere in the galaxy. But you will forgive me if from now on I do the piloting myself.'

*   *   *

63

I had been to Seriphos only once before, when I was a child. The planet is a limited T–1 with two major continents. The larger, wrapped around the equator like an enormous rusty scab, is geologically ancient and worn down almost to sea level. Tangled, almost impenetrable salt marshes fringe the muddy shore, and the hot arid interior is almost totally devoid of vegetation and inimical to higher forms of life. Only insectiles and the flying animals that prey on them survive there. The north polar continent is more user-friendly – if you like jagged glacier-crowned volcanoes, roaring torrents, hot springs, boiling mudpots, and precipitous valleys almost entirely devoid of level ground.

The local Indigenous Sapients sensibly built most of their permanent settlements along the deeply indented seashore or on the river deltas of North Continent. The invaders of Galapharma AC followed suit, evicting the Insaps from the most inviting locales and terraforming them for the human colonists brought in to exploit the world's natural resources. When the Concern abandoned Seriphos the scattered company towns reverted to temperate jungle, being considered cursed – for good reason – by the native peoples.

Rampart's recolonization plan (which proved so successful that it was replicated on the Starcorp's other Spur worlds) minimized the number of outlying human communities and concentrated most of the Earthlings in a single conurbation, the city of Vetivarum and its satellite townships and spaceport. Situated on a spectacularly beautiful bay, it eventually became the largest human settlement in the Perseus Spur, the centre of Rampart's planetary operations.

Plomazo wowed the ground crew at Vetivarum Starport's General Astrogation terminal. They had never seen her snazzy like before. The port agent who attended to our brief landing formalities seemed well acquainted with Captain Bermudez and gave us an obsequious welcome. My friend slipped him a small package, which the official tucked without comment into an inner jacket pocket. We were not asked for corporate passports or any other identification.

The two of us took a short walk to the rent-a-car parking lot to pick up our hired ground transport. I suggested that we travel as inconspicuously as possible, but Mimo ordered a Jaguar four-seater convertible with a heather metalflake paint job and goldplate trim. I did persuade him to leave up the black lamé top.

We headed into the city through heavy late-afternoon commuter traffic. Mimo was at the wheel, driving manually with careless expertise. He had programmed his favourite sentimental Latin ballads on the car stereo.

'Now, Helly! What about this important business of yours?'

I hesitated. I had intended to drop the old man off at our hotel and deal with Clive Leighton alone, but even the brief stroll at the spaceport had brought on an ominous fatigue. I was still a sickie and the person I intended to interview was in excellent physical shape. To get what I wanted, I'd probably need back-up.

'Jake Silver gave me four addresses when he visited me in the hospital. They belong to the young Rampart executives who accompanied Bronson Elgar on the diving trip. It's possible that these guys have no connection with Elgar, but I intend to check them out. One of the men lives here in Vetivarum. I'm going to go shake his tree and hope something useful falls out.'

'Ah.' Mimo's tone was dubious.

'Ordinarily, I wouldn't hesitate to tackle the job by myself, but I'm not in the best of shape yet, so I'll need a little help. A frightener.'

'I don't think I shall volunteer.' Mimo gave a self-deprecating chuckle. 'At first glance I'm lovably eccentric, not intimidating. It takes time for people to learn to fear me ... No, you require a specialist. Let me think. I have many friends on Seriphos.'

'The muscle will receive a substantial fee, payable by Rampart. We'll tell him up front who I really am, and that the job could be dicey if Elgar shows up.'

Mimo considered for a moment, gave a judicious nod, and picked up the car phone. After he finished a cryptic conversation he said to me, 'I think we've got our man: the son of an old business associate. He should be completely dependable – and discreet.'

We drove to a gym near the Vetivarum waterfront called Sluggo's. I stayed in the car while Mimo went inside. He returned almost immediately accompanied by a placid-faced mountain of male flesh, aged somewhere in his early twenties. He was at least

65

two hundred centimetres tall, with a torso shaped like a meaty inverted triangle. His blond hair was pulled back in a tight ponytail and he was attired in a grey velveteen tracksuit adorned with tasteful blue stripes. He wore gunboat-sized Nike athletic shoes. Around his neck, which was roughly the circumference of my upper thigh, was one of those myostimulator collars that provides extra oomph to the large muscles whenever the wearer flexes his sternocleidomastoids.

Mimo introduced Ivor Jenkins. The young man gave me a sunny smile and shook my hand gently through the open car window. His voice was soft and cultured. 'I understand your requirements, Citizen Frost. Your financial terms are very generous. I'll endeavour to give satisfaction.'

'Call me Helly,' I said. 'There's an off chance that the job could be dangerous. Not the guy we're going to roust, but the people behind him. They might come after you later.'

Ivor Jenkins shrugged. 'Then I'll deal with them – and bill you.'

I grinned at him. 'Ivor, I like you. What's your usual gig?'

'Physical fitness coach. I find it rather humdrum. Your assignment will be a welcome break in the quotidian ennui.'

Heavens to Betsy! A literate Goliath. 'Climb in,' I said. He shoehorned himself into the back of the Jag and its suspension groaned.

Primed with the address Jake Silver had obtained for me, the car's computer took us to the gated foothills community where Clive Leighton, Associate Legal Analyst and sometime sport-diver, lived. We arrived a little after 2100 hours, local time. The high-latitude sun was still brightly shining in a buttermilk sky.

A live human security guard came out of the kiosk at the entrance to the compound. Mimo told him that we were offworld friends of Leighton. We didn't want to be announced because the visit was a big surprise. As a token of appreciation for the gateman's co-operation in the jest, the old smuggler handed over another of his little surprise packages.

The guard, who wore the uniform of Rampart External Security, looked over the expensive car and Mimo's Izod sportswear and glowing green tsavorite pinkie ring. He took in my scannerproof sunglasses and snappy sweatshirt proclaiming OK CORRAL – TOMB-STONE, ARIZONA, and young Ivor's cherubic bulk. The car stereo warbled 'Solamente Una Vez'. Finally the guard pocketed the package and hit the gate-opener pad.

'Prob'ly find your pal barbecuin' out back of his place. Barbecuin' fool, young Clive. Expectin' another guest in half an hour. Female.'

We drove through pleasant streets lined with the most conventional sort of executive dwellings. Many of them had lawns of terrestrial grass and gardens with flowering rose bushes and azaleas. If you ignored the alien trees with their scaly trunks and droopy foliage of blood-clot red or goose-turd green, you could almost imagine you were in Topeka, or some other banal Middle American city. But then you spotted the uniformed Insap gardeners and groundskeepers – skinny ruddy-skinned beings with large heads, a central compound-eye cluster, and grasping beetlesque mouthparts on their inscrutable faces – and you knew you weren't in Kansas any more, Toto.

Leighton's place was an attractive bi-level of mortared dark stone, one of four in a wooded cul-de-sac. Mimo parked on the shady side of the turnaround. Something small, black and furry flew out of a blood-clot tree, glided across the Jag's gleaming bonnet, and dropped a faecal souvenir that barely missed its target.

'I'll wait,' the old man said, unwrapping a fresh cigar. 'I'd only be in the way. Besides, if we leave the car here unguarded, these *criaturas cagones* will make a filthy mess of it.'

I told Ivor Jenkins to follow me as quietly as possible. 'If the guy gives me any trouble, you get me out of it. If he refuses to co-operate, your job is to adjust his attitude. Got that?'

The young athlete smiled sweetly and nodded.

We slipped into the big back garden, which seemed to serve all four houses, keeping hidden among the rhododendrons and exotic fern analogues. The rear of Leighton's place was clearly visible; the other houses were partially obscured by trees. There was no sign of our subject, but the scene was set for an *al fresco* dinner for two. In a shrubby niche roofed by a sparkling force-umbrella to thwart picnic-pooping critters stood a table covered with a red-and-white checked cloth. It held place settings of maroon stoneware, crystal wineglasses, silver, a water carafe, a bowl of salad, sauceboats of dressing, and a cutting board with French bread and a crock of butter. Silvanian champagne was chilling in a quaint wooden bucket, and a bottle of what looked like embargoed vintage burgundy waited to be uncorked. Sexy saxophone jazz came softly from speakers hidden in the bushes.

At first I didn't recognize the barbecue grill, situated some six metres away from the table and downhill in a paved area surrounded by a wrought-iron fence. The squatty cone of blackened rock was waist high and topped with a shiny pyroceramic gridiron. A pulsating red glow shone from within the cone's aperture, which was a metre or so wide. There was a tiny plume of smoke, and the air above the grill wavered and shimmered with intense heat. I realized then that the outdoor cooker was a natural fumarole, a geological feature that I recalled was common on the northern continent of Seriphos.

Clive Leighton emerged from the back door of his home after a few minutes and began meal preparations on a rustic stand next to the table. The legal analyst had brought a tray full of makings: a couple of deep purple Yakangus steaks, skewers with baby aubergine and squashlets wrapped in bacon, monster mushrooms stuffed with something, thickly sliced blue onions, a quartered pineapple, a bottle of rozkoz syrup, olive oil, and a collection of spices.

Leighton was a man of less than medium height, but broad-shouldered and fit. He wore an azure silk shirt with balloon sleeves, fawn slacks, a white chef's apron, and an honest-to-God pair of blue suede shoes. The careful styling of his chestnut-brown thatch almost disguised his very large ears. As he began to crack peppercorns in a marble mortar, I crept up noiselessly behind him and tapped him on the back. He turned around with a welcoming smile, expecting his lady, and gave a great start when he found me looming over him.

'Who the bloody hell are *you*?' he demanded in a nasal drawl.

I suppose I was medium unrecognizable. My cadaverous pallor had been slightly alleviated by the ship's tanner during the trip from K-L, but I was still a wan shadow of my normal bronzed self. My hair, which I had worn almost shoulder-length in the islands, had been mowed short in a buzz-cut for my sojourn in dystasis. Huge mirrored sun goggles covered most of my upper face.

I summoned the no-nonsense tone that cops use to intimidate lowlifes. 'Leighton, you've got something I need: the holovid you made on your diving session at Eyebrow Cay. I'm willing to pay whatever you ask for a copy of it.'

'Not fucking likely,' he sneered. 'Who the devil d'you think you are? Sod off before I call security.' He reached for his back pocket.

I motioned for Ivor to step forward from the concealing greenery and the executive's puppy-brown eyes bulged with alarm. I said, 'We're not leaving without the holo data-dime, Clive. I hope you'll be reasonable. If you refuse, my friend and I are going to do whatever it takes to change your mind.'

He dropped the mortar and pestle on the lawn and shuffled backwards away from us. 'Wait a mo'! You – you're that boat bum from K-L! But you were supposed to be –'

'To be what?' I said. 'Dead? Is that what Elgar told you?'

Suddenly Leighton bolted, taking off at top speed toward the house.

'Get him,' I ordered Ivor. But the giant had anticipated me. His bionic-stimulated muscles made him faster than I would ever have expected. He overtook Clive Leighton almost at once, seized him by the back of the belt with a ham-sized paw, hoisted him high, and whirled him around a couple of times in an aeroplane spin. The Rampart exec's blue suede shoes pedalled the air and he uttered a thin screech.

'Be quiet,' I said, 'or my associate will break some of your bones.'

Ivor did something that must have been painful and Clive's scream started falsetto and slid down the scale into a rough moan. He went limp. A dark stain spread around the fly of his fawn slacks. He gasped, 'Don't hurt me! Please don't hurt me!'

I told Ivor, 'Put him down.'

The muscle complied, retaining a firm grip on his captive's neck. 'This man has micturated in his underpants.' Ivor's nose wrinkled fastidiously.

'Then let's get our little errand over with,' I said, 'so he can clean himself up before his guest arrives. Into the house.'

Ivor frogmarched Clive Leighton along and I opened the back door, hoping that none of the neighbours had witnessed the strong-arm exhibition. We came into a superbly appointed kitchen. The stove was La Cornue, the pots and pans were Calphalon, the counters and cabinets gleamed with black enamel, brushed steel and ivory tile. It was the domain of a serious and very affluent amateur cook. Recalling the fate of my own cherished kitchen, I decided that whether or not Clive Leighton was guilty of criminal conspiracy, I hated his yuppoid guts.

'Where do you keep your holovid files?' I said.

Clive seemed to be regaining his courage. 'Why should I tell you?'

'To avoid painful damage to your person.'

A sudden grin of triumph. 'Gotcha! Now let me tell *you* something, Cap'n Helly Bloody Throwaway from Kedge-Lockaby! Surveillance cams have tracked us ever since we climbed up the back steps, and you just screwed yourself royally by threatening me with bodily harm. The cam records are in Rampart's central data depository downtown. Tell this ape to let me go!'

I shook my head. 'Clive, Clive, Clive. We both know that the surveillance records won't be accessed unless you file a complaint – or turn up missing or dead. Right?'

The triumphant look changed to one of wariness.

'So I'll just have to make sure that none of those contingencies prevail. Now where's the holovid dime?'

'Go to hell!'

I turned to Ivor. 'Encourage him just a bit more.'

An enormous hand encircled Clive's throat and began to tighten. Ivor supported the sagging body as the legal analyst gurgled thickly and his face turned puce.

'That'll do,' I said to the giant. 'Turn him loose.'

Leighton leaned against his splendid Sub-Zero refrigerator, gagging and gulping air.

I said, 'Clive, you stink. I'd really like to get this over and done with as quickly as possible. You aren't going to report us to Rampart Security. I'll tell you why in just a few minutes. You *are* going to co-operate – else my associate is going to work you over. He won't

70

break your bones or choke you any more. Those little ploys were only to get your attention. Do you see that collar on my friend's neck? Normally, it's used to temporarily increase muscle strength. But it can do other things, too. Have you ever heard of tetany? It's a violent spasm of the muscles accompanied by excruciating pain. The collar can bend your spine like a pretzel. Shall we try it on you for size?'

Clive said, 'You swine!'

I repeated, 'Where is the holovid dime?'

The reply was almost inaudible. 'In the library. Upstairs.'

He would have a library.

We ascended, Clive leading the way, and entered a large, rather messy room. There were shelves of genuine paged books as well as dedicated magslates, e-books and hundreds of data-storage containers. Clive sullenly pointed to a cluttered table. Almost lost amidst the empty Diet Coke and beer chillinders, dirty coffee cups, printouts and bottles of Maalox and Zintrin was a red plastic box. I opened it and found a neat collection of coded 1.5 cm disklets in tylar envelopes.

'Find me the dime you recorded on Kedge-Lockaby,' I said.

Clive propped himself against the table, glowering at me. Finally he took the filecase, spoke to it, and handed over the tiny envelope that had popped into the eject tray.

The holocamera sat on a shelf with other technotoys. I inserted the dime into the instrument, set it for internal view, fast forward, audio off, and looked into the eyepiece. I hoped to hell I'd find what I was looking for. If I didn't, I'd have to waste time going after the other three sport-divers – each resident on a different planet – trusting that they wouldn't find out I was gunning for them and destroy the evidence before I could get my hands on it.

At first I thought I was out of luck with Clive Leighton's holo. The object of my search was notably camera-shy, except when the faceplate of his diving equipment obscured his features as he swam among the fishies. But finally I came to the scene where the drunken young executives, belowdecks in *Pernio*, celebrated after making successful shots of the dancing ruby prawns. Clive had panned his camera unsteadily over his companions. Three of the men were smirking and grimacing and the fourth, only briefly glimpsed, was as impassive as granite. I froze the stone face, zoomed in on it, and smiled in satisfaction.

I had my mug shot of Bronson Elgar.

Unless he changed his features again, I'd be able to find the assassin if he was on any of the Spur Worlds. And with luck, a forensic anthropologist might even get a positive ID through bone structure.

I lowered the holocam. After extracting the data-dime I returned it to its envelope and tucked it into my wallet. Clive Leighton watched me, exuding pure hate. He seemed about to say something nasty but shut his mouth when Ivor laid an admonitory paw on his shoulder.

I now began to feel distinctly debilitated, so I found the relevant control pad on my medicuff armlet and gave it a prod. The subcutaneous vaporizer shot stimulant into me, but unfortunately the perk-up wasn't immediate. I looked around. A straight chair heaped with slates and prints stood beside the desk. I dumped the stuff on the floor and sat down, motioning Ivor to unhand the prisoner.

'I'm still not sure whether you're part of the conspiracy against Rampart or not,' I said to Clive. I was careful not to mention Galapharma. 'If you are, I hope you realize that your life isn't worth a bootful of warm piss – as the cowpokes would say in my old hometown of Phoenix, Arizona.'

'I don't know what you're talking about,' the legal analyst growled.

'Did Bronson Elgar tell you and your three friends that I was killed on the comet?'

'Comet? What comet?'

I wagged my head sadly at his obstinacy. 'You poor bastard. When Bron finds out that I'm still alive – and that you caved in and gave me a dime with his image – he's going to go ballistic. He knows I'll use that picture to run him down. You've managed to endanger the whole conspiracy against Rampart, Clive. I wouldn't want to be in your pretty blue shoes.'

'You're insane! I don't know anything about Elgar. I never even met the man until the day of the dive. And I've got nothing to do with any conspiracy. I'm completely loyal to Rampart.' He had retreated to a corner of the room, as far away from Ivor and me as he could get. He adjusted the twisted chef's apron to hide his damp crotch.

'How about your diving buddies?' I said. 'Are they loyal, too?'

'You're damned right they are! All of us are Rampart stakeholders. We'd be crazy to do anything to harm the Starcorp.'

I looked at him thoughtfully. 'Maybe you're innocent after all. On the other hand, perhaps you four were forced to go along on the trip in order to prove yourselves to Elgar's backers. To make your first bones.'

'What's *that* supposed to mean?'

'A reference to ancient history. Over two hundred years ago, members of Sicilian organized crime gangs had to demonstrate their commitment to the group by killing one of its enemies – a gesture of good faith that was also self-incriminating.'

'What utter rot! Who's supposed to be behind this alleged conspiracy of yours?'

I ignored his question. 'Did Elgar give you a cover story to justify my murder? Did he even bother to tell you how a down-and-out charterboat skipper could threaten the big scheme?'

'You're out of your mind! You've no proof of any of these wild allegations.'

'How about my word,' I suggested, 'against yours?'

'That's rich! Who'd ever believe a Throwaway with no civil rights?'

'The Chairman and CEO of Rampart might. Simon Frost.'

Clive Leighton burst into near-hysterical laughter. 'Now I know you're a flaming nut case!'

'Tell him who I am, Ivor,' I said.

The huge young man smiled benignly. 'This is Asahel Frost. He's old Simon's youngest son.'

'That's ... preposterous.' The haughty accent faltered into a whine.

'No,' I corrected him. 'It's something else altogether. It's why you aren't going to lodge any complaints with Rampart Security, and why you're going to tell me everything I want to know.'

Inside Clive's lawyerly mind, jigsaw puzzle pieces were clicking ominously into place. A hunted expression passed fleetingly over his features, and at that moment I was certain of two things. He *was* an active participant in whatever chicanery was going down –

And he was going to crack.

'Let me verify my identity,' I said in friendly Good Cop style.

Throwaways have no credentials. But there was an impressive computer on a stand by the desk, so I called up *The New York Times* for 12 October 2229. I printed the front page, walked over to the cowering analyst, thrust the page under his nose, and took off my sunglasses.

My portrait was in living colour. I had more hair then, a brave smile, and hollow, hopeless eyes. The adjacent headline said: *REVIEW BOARD RECOMMENDS ULTIMATE CEN-SURE FOR ACCUSED ICS OFFICIAL.*

Clive Leighton took the print and read the article, horrified gaze flicking back and forth between it and my face. 'It – it says here that Simon Frost repudiated you.'

'We kissed and made up.'

'Oh?' He managed to be archly sceptical.

'My father is here on Seriphos,' I said. 'Tomorrow there'll be a meeting of Rampart's Board of Directors. He and I will both be there. The agenda deals with the conspiracy.'

'You can't prove I'm disloyal!'

'Maybe not,' I said. 'But an interstellar corporation is hardly a court of law, is it? If the chairman is convinced of your guilt, you're buggered, Clive. And I'll convince him. You can count on it.'

We stared at each other for a silent beat. Then I added, in a kindly fashion, 'Of course, if you were to go with me voluntarily to the board meeting and tell all, I could persuade my father to be lenient. Instead of nuking your double-crossing posterior, he might let you emigrate to a wildcat world in the Sagittarius Whorl where Bronson Elgar and his masters will never find you. We could give you a new ID, set you up in a small business –'

Ivor said brightly, 'Maybe you could open an espresso stand. Never have too many of those.'

Clive Leighton winced. He was just about hooked. 'Tell the

Board of Directors . . . what?'

'Everything – including the names of other conspirators known to you and the organization behind the plot. We'd use psychoprobe machines for verification afterward, of course.'

The door-chime rang and a female voice cooed over the intercom: 'Cliveykins, it's me!'

'Oh, my God,' he moaned. 'Lois is here! What am I going to do?'

'Never mind her. Tell me who recruited you and your three friends for the big scam. Was it Bronson Elgar? Someone in Rampart itself?'

Ding-dong. 'Clive, dear? Are you there?'

'Speak up!' I suddenly took hold of his silk shirt with both hands and yanked him toward me. I was a lot bigger than he was, and he had no idea that I was almost ready to keel over from accumulated stress and decrepitude. The stench of his urine mingled with the acrid adrenalin odour of renewed terror. 'What was your role supposed to be – infiltration of Rampart for general espionage and data-theft, or something more active? Like sabotage?'

Ding-dong! 'Darling, is something wrong?'

'I was . . . we were . . .' He shook his head and mouthed a despairing obscenity.

'The organization behind the conspiracy!' I barked. 'Is it one of the Hundred Concerns? Answer me!' I shook him like a doll.

'Stop it! For God's sake! I can't think straight. We were never specifically told who the principal was, although I had my suspicions. The recruiting . . . there's so much to explain. And Lois –'

'Send her away.'

'I can't! Look at me, for Christ's sake!'

'Then I'll do it.'

'No! She'll know something's wrong if you try to put her off. Tonight we were going to . . . she and I are very close.'

Ivor snickered. The bell went *ding-dong* a whole lot. Lois was beginning to sound irritated.

'Please,' he begged. Tears were glazing his eyes. 'We've got to let her in. She might call security, or go round back and try to enter the house through the kitchen. I'll tell you everything I know tomorrow. I swear it. Tomorrow . . .'

I cursed mentally and tried to decide what to do. I wasn't thinking too straight myself. Finally: 'All right. But God help you if you change your mind about co-operating! Now listen to me, Clivey-kins. My friend here is going to stay overnight and keep an eye on you. His name is Ivor. He'll make certain you don't do anything silly. I'll pick you up at noon tomorrow and take you to the board meeting.'

'Yes. Yes. Anything!'

I said to Ivor, 'Go answer the door and pretend to be the new houseman. Tell the lady –' I turned to Clive. 'What's her full name?'

'Lois Swann-Hepplewhite,' he said listlessly.

'Tell her that Citizen Leighton has been unavoidably detained by an important business matter, but he'll be out in the garden with her shortly.'

'I'll pour her some champagne and finish coating the pepper steak,' said the young Hercules. 'And I'd better uncork that nice bottle of Chambertin. It really needs time to breathe.' He went off.

A belated thought struck me. I said to Clive, 'Give me your telephone.' He pulled it out of his back pocket and handed it over.

'How many more phone units in the house?' I asked.

'Six, seven, I don't remember.'

'Never mind. I'm going to disconnect your whole system from the satcom net. I know you wouldn't dream of making any compromising calls between now and tomorrow, but let's make certain of it, shall we?'

I sat down at the computer, summoned up half-forgotten techniques that had once been part of my ICS investigatory arsenal, and after about three minutes' work rendered the Leighton establishment electronically incommunicado. He watched me without interest. When I finished and rose to go, I spoke to him very gently. 'Clive, I'm your only chance. You do realize that, don't you?'

He hesitated, not meeting my eyes, then nodded.

'Good. Now go change your pants, have a stiff drink, and get ready to be a gracious host.'

Chapter 7

The Jaguar rolled smoothly along the elevated expressway, heading back into the city centre and the hotel. The sky behind the mountains had turned purple and the sea was silver with pointy black islands dotting the mouth of Vetivarum Bay. On the stereo, Nat King Cole was singing 'Adios, Mariquita Linda'. Mimo commented on the beauty of the scene and I responded with a dispirited mumble.

Slumped back against the reclined leather seat, I gave myself another hit from the medicuff. I felt atrocious – weak as a beached jellyfish, short of breath, and aching in every extremity, including my thick head. I'd done the best I could with Clive Leighton, but I couldn't escape the conviction that I'd botched the job. I had serious misgivings about the wisdom of leaving a sharpie like Leighton in Ivor's inexperienced care. I knew I should not have postponed Clive's interrogation, regardless of my own frailty. I'd also forgotten that the girlfriend might have brought a phone in her purse.

Ask Mimo to turn back? Not a chance.

God, how I wished I were back on Kedge-Lockaby, convalescing in my new little house and being pampered by my friends! I wished I had told my father to go to hell. I wished I could forget about Rampart's corporate machinations and Bronson Elgar and just live my quiet Throwaway life again.

Believe me – I'd have been gone in a cloud of sour owlshit if it hadn't been for my sister Eve.

Mimo had continued to chatter away while I indulged in self-pitying mopery. I snapped out of it as I heard him say, 'You could do worse than hire Ivor for the duration of your stay on Seriphos.'

'As what? A male nurse?' I was only half kidding.

77

'He's an excellent bodyguard,' Mimo said. 'A valued associate recommended him very highly, and you said he did well.'

'I'm in no danger. If Elgar suspected I was still alive, he could have killed me easily while I was in dystasis back on K-L by just sneaking into the ICU and pulling the plug.'

'I was thinking of Clive Leighton, not Elgar. Even with his comsys out and Ivor guarding him, he might still manage to contact some other member of the cabal here on Seriphos who –'

I didn't want to hear this. 'The chance of some local tracking me down and trying to blow me away tonight is vanishingly small. Besides, Leighton has nothing to gain by sending someone after me. For all he knows, I've already told Simon or Cousin Zed about his own starring role in tomorrow's show-and-tell. Clive's terrified. He knows his only hope of avoiding disenfranchisement is to cooperate with me. And he will.'

'I'm not sure I agree with your logic,' Mimo said. 'Frightened men sometimes do rash things.'

'Not this one.'

He persisted. 'It would have been more prudent to take Leighton and the woman into custody. We could have recorded his incriminating statement immediately.'

'Whose custody?' I asked wearily. 'Ours? You think we should have kidnapped both of them, shlepped them along to the hotel or your starship, and played babysitter till tomorrow?'

'You could have used your father's authority and had them locked up by Rampart security.'

'Rampart security,' I said bleakly, 'could be part of the larger problem ... And any statement we recorded privately would be legally uncertified and useless as evidence. The Rampart Board will only believe Leighton if he talks to them freely in person and then checks out on the truth machines. Don't worry – the guy won't send anybody after me and he won't try to do a flit. Where would he go? The conspiracy won't protect him. They'd be more likely to vaporize his ass.'

'But –'

I wiped sick perspiration from my brow. 'That's enough. The matter's closed.'

The old man fell silent and I tried to nap during the rest of the drive, lulled by Nat Cole's mellow Spanish warbling.

We checked in at the Ritz-Carlton Vetivarum, a neo-Babylonian pile complete with hanging gardens, mosaic floors, and red jasper pillars with gilded capitals. The flunkies at the front desk were so overjoyed to welcome Captain Bermudez to their expensive establishment once again that I expected them to kiss the hem of his garment and strew his path with rose petals. Nobody said a word when I registered as Helmut Icicle and declined to submit an iris-print ID. I was still wearing the scannerproof sunglasses.

Our bags had already been sent in from the starport. As we stood waiting for the transporter that would carry us to our suites Mimo invited me to dinner. I pleaded mortal fatigue, at which he nodded in understanding. 'You must rest, of course. Meanwhile, perhaps I could make a few discreet inquiries –'

'Absolutely not! You have to promise not to go poking around in this mess by yourself. Don't misunderstand me. I'm grateful for all your help. But I've got to do this investigation my way, even if I bumble and fumble. If it's any consolation, I intend to tell my father the same thing.'

'Then perhaps I'll just look up a certain lady of my acquaintance.' He winked. 'We might go to the casino, then find other ways to entertain ourselves.'

I went to my suite, stripped off my clothes and tossed them into the valet, then had a hot shower. The palatial bathroom, like the one on *El Plomazo*, was equipped with a tanning unit. I took a double treatment of melanin enhancer, which turned my skin slightly darker than my stubbly hair, and ended up looking surfer-fit on the outside even though I was still a bucket of guano within.

A royal-blue silk robe was part of the bedroom decor. I put it on and ordered supper from room service. During the voyage to Seriphos with Mimo, I'd found out the hard way that my digestion hadn't yet caught up with my appetite, so I contented myself with zikel Meunière, spinach soufflé, baby peas and carrots, and rozkoz-gold cocoa. When the dumbwaiter pinged a few minutes later I took out the tray of food and carried it to a table on the balcony where I could dine overlooking the lights of the city. The coves

and promontories and heights of sprawling Vetivarum were decorated with twinkling pinpricks of colour. Nearly half a million
human beings lived here, employed in Rampart Central, in the
extensive rozkoz production facilities, and in the service industries
that modern civilization demands.

A faint aroma of the peerless confection floated on the cool
evening breeze from one of the rozkoz factories. I ate slowly,
remembering my first day on the planet so many years ago: the
steaming mudpools surrounding the spore collection depot, the
native worker with his unreadable alien face and incongruous
human voice (courtesy of the general translator), and my first taste
of rozkoz-gold.

Above all I thought of my Uncle Ethan, the real founder of
Rampart, dead now for five years. When reminiscence palled and
I finished what I could manage of the food, I gave myself a sedative
shot from the medicuff, flopped onto the kingsized bed, and slept
like a dead man.

I was sent to Seriphos when I was thirteen, chockful of adolescent
angst, contrariety, and grief over the impending divorce of my
mother, Katje Vanderpost, from Simon. Neither of my parents
wanted me underfoot during the inconvenient summer break before
I returned to boarding school, so I was dispatched offworld to my
godparents, Ethan Frost and Emma Bradbury, who lived in the
Perseus Spur. It was high time, Simon told me, that I visited the
part of the galaxy where I would be working throughout most of
my adult life.

Aunt Emma was a frequent visitor to Earth, but I hardly
remembered Uncle Ethan, whose reputation had made him a demi-
god to the younger generation of the Frost family. He had not
travelled to the home world for many years. My father, who was
happier coping with the complex political and financial aspects of
the business, then served as Rampart's Board Chairman and Syndic,
the Starcorp's official liaison to the Commonwealth legislature in
Toronto. Simon's relationship to Ethan was peculiar, a combination
of sincere respect and covert envy of his older brother's business

acumen and unflagging drive. Ethan was the Starcorp's President and Chief Executive Officer from its inception in 2183 until his death in 2227. He was responsible for the discovery of rozkoz, which set the stage for Rampart's meteoric growth. He was also the one who had masterminded Rampart's expansion into the sixty-three other Spur worlds that comprised the corporate empire.

I was sure that my father had sent me to Seriphos hoping that Ethan's influence would counteract the rebellious tendencies I was already beginning to display. I was a bright kid with a tender social conscience and fancied myself a keen amateur historian and cultural anthropologist. My juvenile researches had convinced me that the commercialization of the stars superseded the Jewish Holocaust, the African Plague, the Great Seattle Earthquake and the Martian Meteor Impact as the premier human disaster of all time. I had just begun to agonize over what I was going to do about it.

My uncle was waiting for me at the arrival gate in Vetivarum Starport, which amazed me because I knew what a busy and important man the Rampart President was. Yet there he stood, alone, dressed in a none-too-clean blue corporate coverall, with a broad smile and an outstretched hand ready to shake mine after I hastily put down my encumbering carry-on case. After the greeting, he retrieved my other bags and carried them himself as he led me into the subway connecting to the private hoppercraft garage.

I was also startled to realize what a small man Ethan was – only five or six centimetres taller than I, and I was a *kid*. His grey-green eyes were so deeply hooded that they almost seemed oriental. He was fifty-nine years old at the time, but his face was nearly unlined. He had a narrow, beaky nose and a sandy gunfighter moustache, and he wore his hair combed over his forehead in a short fringe – perhaps to minimize the sharp widow's peak that characterized so many of the Frost family's men.

'You mind if we make a little detour before heading to the house?' Ethan asked – as if any objection I might make was worth taking into consideration. 'Something at one of the spore collection depots I need to check out personally. You know anything about the production of rozkoz?'

'I've read about it, of course. Seen holovids –'

'All showing nice, sanitary factories, I bet. The plants growing in stainless steel drums, tended and harvested robotically. Well, there's a bit more to it than that. I think you'll be interested.'

Uncle Ethan's hopper was an impressive machine with the corporation's crenellated castle wall logo on the door. He entered the destination into the navigation unit, then sat back and pointed out landmarks to me as we flew a programmed course out of the conurbation and into the precipitous wilderness in which the facility was situated.

I had visited numbers of planets in the Orion Arm, many of them notably weird and picturesque, and I had expected the Rampart worlds of the remote Perseus Spur to be especially bizarre. But this part of Seriphos seemed to be a rather conventional blend of the geothermal areas of New Zealand and the Canadian Rockies, distinctive only because of the alien vegetation and the moderate vulcanism. Away from the temperate coast where humans made their homes and natives had permanent villages, the North Continent consisted mainly of steep mountains, with the lower slopes and valleys clothed in reddish or dull green foliage and the eminences thickly plastered with snow and ice. No roads led into the interior, but there was a webwork of faint trails at lower elevations that my uncle said were the work of the Zmundigaim Insaps. None of their camps were visible from the air.

'Asa – how are things at home?' Ethan asked bluntly.

I shrugged. 'Civilized, I suppose. Simon spends most of his time at the Sky Ranch when he's not in Toronto doing Syndic lobbying. Mom lives in the corporate apartment complex in Phoenix and does her charity work and goes to cocktail parties and dinners given by closet Reversionists. My sister Beth cries a lot. Dan's too busy with work to come to any family affairs. Eve's finishing her business administration studies at the university and does the best she can to be with me and Beth, but you can tell the divorce thing has got her down.'

'And how do you feel?'

I took a breath. 'I don't know how Mom put up with Simon for as long as she did. He doesn't really give a hoot about any of us –'

'He does, in his own way,' Ethan said.

'His way stinks,' I said. And then I shut up for the rest of the trip.

After an hour or so the hoppercraft descended into a steep valley carved by a brawling torrent. The righthand slope was conventional mountain country, thinly vegetated weathered rock. The left side held a series of peculiar geothermal terraces framed with lush growth. The gently steaming stepped ponds looked as though they held different colours of bubbling paint – pink, teal blue, greenish yellow, and terra cotta. As we landed on a small pad beside a medium-sized building crowned with antennae, a geyser erupted from one of the higher pools, spraying the landscape with rosy mud-mist.

'There are thousands of depots like this scattered through the North Continent interior,' Ethan said. 'Insap tribes collect the koz spores by hand and bring them in. One part of the depot is a company store stocked with all kinds of goods that the natives favour. They can also order special items from a catalogue.'

The door of the depot opened and a single aborigine emerged. The Zmundi wore a general translator lavaliere pinned to its Rampart coverall. It was very tall and thin, of roughly humanoid form, with smooth reddish skin. Its rounded head was bald, with a cluster of gemlike compound eyes at the centre of the bulbous forehead above four small nostrils. The wide mouth bore clasping mandibles like those of an insect. Its hands, which seemed made of chiton or some other hard material rather than flesh, had six articulated digits of uneven length. The Zmundi's unshod feet made it seem as though the being walked on tiptoe on three stout claws or stubby hooves.

'I am Lmuzu,' it said. The mandibles buzzed and vibrated slightly when it spoke. 'Welcome to Depot G-349, Ethanfrost and companion.' It was strange to hear the perfectly articulated human voice come from such an alien creature. Since the translator provided a baritone timbre, I presumed that the Insap was a male.

'Greetings and good health to you, Lmuzu,' said my uncle, speaking carefully to accommodate the translator. 'This is my nephew, Asahel Frost, who has come to live with me for a little while. Why have you summoned me in this special manner? Is there some trouble?'

'Not at all, Ethanfrost. It may even be a matter for rejoicing. Please follow me.'

He turned and beckoned for us to enter the building. Inside it was very warm, probably over forty degrees. We passed through the trading post area into a test laboratory/storage chamber. The place was filled with equipment interconnected by a tangle of technical plumbing. At the rear was a neat stack of hexagonal storage modules that I presumed were filled with koz spores. Over against the right wall stood a compact lab bench with smaller testing instruments.

Lmuzu opened a grey incubation cabinet and took out a lidded culture dish. Something that looked like crinkly peach-tinted lichen was growing inside.

'Gzonfalu of the Mlaka Clan brought in a sample of an unknown variety of koz last sixday, saying that the clan's women were very excited by its properties. He had travelled over three hundred of your kilometres in order to bring the specimen to my attention.'

Ethan peered at it intently. 'Interesting!'

Lmuzu's translator gave off an unnerving ha-ha-ha. 'The rozkoz made by the Mlaka women from this stuff was even more interesting.' He set aside the culture dish and picked up a little round basket that seemed to have been woven of red and white grass. Inside were pale orange crystals, like rock candy. 'I have prepared a human-style recipe.'

Ethan ate one. His eyebrows shot up. 'Hey! That's really different – but good.'

'Ha-ha-ha,' laughed Lmuzu. 'Very good! Perhaps as good as rozkoz-blue, no? You can call it rozkoz-gold.'

'If it tests out.' Ethan turned to me. 'Would you like to try it, Asa?'

I nodded bravely, accepted one of the small crystals, and put it into my mouth. The exquisite flavour made me exclaim out loud. 'Wow! It's like regular rozkoz, but with – with –' I broke off in confusion. 'I don't know. But I like it.'

'We'll call this first human taste test a success,' Ethan said heartily. He ordered the native technician to pack up the culture dish, the basket, and the jar containing the new spores in an armoured dispatch case. Then: 'Lmuzu, I thank you for calling this to my attention. For the time being, you and your people must say nothing about rozkoz-gold to any other human. Is that understood?'

The Zmundi said, 'Yes, Ethanfrost.'

'Who knows? The koz variant may turn out to be worthless after all, or impossible to culture in bulk.' Ethan eyeballed the case's lock and it clicked emphatically. We said goodbye and took off in the hopper.

When we were airborne my uncle said, 'I suppose you know that rozkoz production still depends upon the natives gathering koz spores. After two or three generations, the plant's reproduction fails under laboratory conditions for unknown reasons. There must be some natural factor in the mudpools we've failed to duplicate in our factories.'

'Is that why rozkoz is only produced on Seriphos?'

'Yes. The flavouring principle itself can be made artificially, of course, but it lacks the subtlety and smoothness of the genuine stuff. We've set up thousands of small collection depots at the principal geothermal areas where Zmundigaim collectors bring in the spores. Each batch is tested for contamination by the native technician in charge of the depot before being stockpiled for shipment to the factories in Vetivarum.'

'Is it unusual to find mutant strains?'

'It's happened seven times in the twenty-five years Rampart has exploited the resource. Six of the mutations turned out to be useless commercially for various reasons. The seventh was the blockbuster flavour variant we call rozkoz-blue. Boosted corporate profits by fifteen per cent.'

'Did the Insaps who found the blue stuff get a bonus or anything?'

Ethan looked at me askance. 'No.'

'It figures,' I muttered. My tone was just short of impertinence, but my uncle didn't take offence as Simon would have.

'The human lab workers who cultured the new strain and refined and tested it didn't get a special reward, either. Why should they? They're employees, not Rampart stakeholders.'

'But the Zmundigaim are different. It's their world!'

'So?'

85

'Maybe they ought to be stakeholders. Did you ever think of that, Uncle Ethan? Rampart has earned billions from rozkoz and its other xenocommodities, but all the Perseus Spur Insaps got was *dependency*. Their culture has been changed forever because of human interference.' I stared out the hopper window at a towering volcano belching grey ash into the stratosphere. 'I think it's wrong . . . and I'm not the only one.'

'Would you like to see the Zmundigaim producing rozkoz themselves and selling it to humanity?'

'Yes,' I said, with righteous defiance.

'But they wouldn't be able to do that without our continuing help.'

'Then why can't we just give them that help? They're intelligent. They could learn to operate the factories.'

'That's not the way interstellar entrepreneurship works. We don't operate as charitable institutions. Do you seriously think we should give away everything we've worked for to natives who are still basically at the hunter-gatherer level of society?'

'Not everything. I'm not an idiot. But if Insaps were actual stakeholders –'

'A stakeholder is a direct participant in corporate management, Asa. A highly educated, sophisticated being whose life is intimately involved in the high-tech workplace. Not a single Indigenous Sapient race in the Perseus Spur could fill those criteria. The Qastt might qualify if they weren't so self-centred and devious. The Haluk might qualify if they weren't so relentlessly xenophobic. Nobody else.'

But I persisted. 'That Zmundi back at the collection depot seemed to have the potential to be more than a button-pusher. People like him could surely advance to a high level of civilization if we didn't deny them education and technology as a matter of policy.'

'The Zmundigaim wouldn't make it unless they were willing to change their lives in a drastic fashion. Give up their nomadic habits and live permanently in cities. Go to school for years. Organize their days by the clock. Change their clan-based political structure. Engage in social and economic planning. Live like *humans*. Do you think that Lmuzu and his people want to do that at this stage in their evolution?'

'I don't know,' I admitted.

'Well, I do,' Ethan said. 'And the answer is *no*.'

'Maybe on Seriphos. But how about the other inhabited worlds that humanity has colonized and exploited? In the Orion Arm, the Hundred Concerns use the preindustrial alien races as slave labour, or treat them like hostile savages if they decline to co-operate with the commercialization of their worlds. Maybe Rampart isn't quite as bad as the others, but –'

'So you're a Reversionist like your mother,' Ethan said mildly. 'You think the Commonwealth should force human companies to abandon planets having pretechnological Insap populations – or else accept the natives as full stakeholders in every commercial operation.'

'Yes! That's exactly what I think. Go ahead and laugh if you want.'

'I won't do that, Asa. I won't even lecture you on what would happen to our human economy if we followed the Reversionist Guiding Principles – or remind you that the Commonwealth doesn't have the power to force Big Business to do much of *anything*. I will point out to you that Rampart's colonial policies are among the most humane and liberal in the galaxy. And not for altruistic reasons, either, but for practical ones! I'll also state my belief that you and the adult Reversionists propose a simplistic solution to a fiendishly complex problem.' He paused for breath, frowning. 'Maybe a little story would get my point across. Do you know how I discovered rozkoz?'

'I thought you just . . . did.'

'Not quite,' he said, and told me about it.

When Galapharma AC retreated from the Perseus Spur in 2176 [Ethan said], the native populations saw their fortunes take a disastrous nosedive. Concern policy had denied the natives higher education and advanced technology, while at the same time permitting them to become addicted to the luxuries of human culture. But now Big Business had sailed off into the sunset, taking most of its goodies with it. Things looked grim. No more modern tools to cut wood or break stone. No more fusion stoves to cook on. No more heaters to warm the hut or Glo Lites to keep it brightly lit after sundown. No more telsats that let you keep in touch with relatives in the next valley. No more Danaëan beer!

Even the Qastt pirates fell on hard times without human ships to plunder. Only the Haluk were glad Galapharma was gone.

The commercial vacuum was so dire that most of the Spur peoples were eager to welcome the human wildcat entrepreneurs who entered the Zone after Gala's retreat. The first group of Earthling grubstakers who came here to Seriphos were pretty typical of the new wave of independent exploiters. Their little company was undercapitalized and inexperienced. They re-opened the planet's shasha-bark farms and platinum mines and got them back into production; but in the end they were defeated by the same problems that had driven out Galapharma Amalgamated Concern. The money-strapped newcomers paid native workers even less than Galapharma had and refused to compromise on local customs that seemed counterproductive. So the Zmundigaim slowed production to a ruinous level. Even worse, the company couldn't afford heavy armament for its transport vessels, and attacks by Qastt pirates during the long trips back to Orion Arm market worlds finally made it impossible to turn a profit.

The situation on most of the other Spur planets was similarly discouraging. The Commonwealth did its best to help the struggling freesoil human colonies, but it lacked the resources to patrol the Perseus region effectively and provide basic services. By 2183, CHW seriously considered withdrawing from Zone 23 altogether.

Along came the Rampart Interstellar Corporation. We were young and we were brash and we had what we thought was a completely new management philosophy – conceived by Yours Truly! I figured that we had a good chance of succeeding where Galapharma and the freelance outfits had failed.

The Starcorp founders and managing directors were my brother Simon and I, and our Arizona U college buddy Dirk Vanderpost, whose inheritance provided most of the company's start-up capital.

We were backed by seventeen stakeholders – engineers, technicians and computer wonks – who didn't work for a salary but for a share of the profits, if any.

Our outfit arrived on Seriphos in a freighter named *Rio Tonto*. She was an old ship, but we'd armed her to the teeth with high-powered actinic cannons to fend off the Qastt. Her cargo consisted of the most efficient mining and processing equipment that we were able to obtain. My grand notion, which was completely contrary to 'cost effective' Concern practice throughout the Orion and Sagittarius regions of the galaxy, was really rather simple: Rampart was going to treat the Insap workers of Seriphos like real people instead of backward savages.

We set up shop at a promising abandoned platinum mine, and a few very cautious Zmundi miners, trained years before by Galapharma, applied for work. I told them Rampart would pay human-equivalent wages to those who worked as hard as human beings, and proportional salaries to the less efficient. I also told the natives that they'd work only seven hours each day instead of the obligatory twelve they had endured under Gala and the late gang of wildcatters. And instead of restricting the workers to barracks for five days and allowing them only a single day off at home, as had been the usual practice, I let them commute to nearby temporary villages each night. Most important of all, I agreed that the Zmundigaim would not be forced to work the mines during the harsh North Continent winter. Instead we'd shut down for the season and the people would be allowed to migrate en masse to the coast, as had been their immemorial custom before the arrival of humanity.

I have to tell you, Asa, that your father didn't have too much faith in my scheme. Simon conceded that the Zmundi people were smarter than a lot of other aborigines, but he also pointed out that everybody knew they were basically lazy and undependable.

I said, 'Maybe – but the Zmundigaim also desperately want the kind of consumer goods that human credit buys, so it's worth the gamble.'

A bunch more native miners applied for work and we started producing PeeTee. And what d'you think happened?

Even with the seasonal delay, my 'inefficient' operations plan was a humongous success. The Insaps worked their tails off and old *Rio Tonto* was loaded with platinum ingots in only half the time we'd estimated – eleven months. The profits were going to be outstanding.

According to plan, Rampart got ready to leave Seriphos.

On the night before the ship was scheduled to lift off for Calapuyo in the Orion Arm, the closest market for the PeeTee, a deputation of Zmundi elders came to Rampart's headquarters at the mineworkings. All of us humans were having a farewell party and things were a trifle raucous, but I took the aliens into my office to find out what they wanted.

The headwoman was named Gminkzu. She put on the general translator and said, 'You have treated us with honour and respect, Ethanfrost. Our clan has prospered because of your coming. For this reason all Zmundigaim will look forward to your return to Seriphos.'

I thanked her, but told her that Rampart was planning to pull up stakes and move on to the planet Hadrach, a T-2 about fifty-five light-years away. I tried to explain that the Seriphos operation was intended from the start to be both a test of my novel operations theory and a means of making some fast money that would enable Rampart to upgrade its equipment and take in more stakeholders. On Hadrach, where the environment and native population were admittedly not so congenial to humanity, we'd mine and process scandium, an element essential to antimatter fuel generation that was worth three hundred times as much as platinum. I didn't bother to tell her that the EssCee was not only lucrative but also a sure attention-getter among Earthside bancorps that we hoped to cajole into financing Rampart's expansion.

Gminkzu was badly disappointed. She said, 'We beseech you to stay, Ethanfrost! Besides the platinum, our world has other products coveted by humanity. The old shasha-bark plantations, which yielded a valued medicine to Galapharma Concern, would require only fertilization, pruning, and restoration of the fog-mite barriers. There are also fine gemstones in the gravel of the River Naral –'

'I'm sorry,' I said. 'A giant outfit like Galapharma would be able to make use of those resources, but we're too small to make them pay.'

Gminkzu clacked her mandibles, expressing heartfelt regrets. Then, as a special mark of esteem, she presented me with a farewell gift, a box of delicacies resembling crystallized sugar, flavoured with a 'magic food' that the Zmundigaim had kept secret from the hated Galapharma invaders.

'Its name,' she said, 'is rozkoz. When we prepare rozkoz for ourselves we mix it with the aromatic resin of the kmulu bush. But we know that humans do not esteem the resin, having feeble mouthparts, so we have mixed your rozkoz with ababa honey. We hope you will enjoy it. Rozkoz gladdens both the mouth and the mind.'

Then Gminkzu and the elders went away. I took the box of exotic candy into the party, and Dirk Vanderpost and Karl Nazarian dared me to eat some of it. I took a little nibble, and you can imagine my reaction. Other volunteer tasters were similarly thrown for a loop, and the entire boxful of rozkoz would have been gobbled up in five minutes flat by the crew if I hadn't snatched it away. I ignored the howls of disappointment and locked it in the ship's safe.

Then I said, 'You damn drunken fools! Don't you know what this *is*?'

Gunter Eckert said, 'Better than chocolate, for sure.'

'It's our jackpot!' I told them. 'The lolly-bomb! The big break!'

Simon figured it out too and said, 'Tan my hide, I think the little pipsqueak's right.'

Next morning, when our chemist was sober enough to operate the organic analyser, she tested rozkoz and found that it contained an artful blend of twelve previously unknown alkaloids and esters. It surely does gladden the mouth and mind, as any human who's ever tasted it will agree, it has no harmful side-effects when consumed in moderation, and its usefulness as a flavouring is limited only by the ingenuity of the confectionery cook.

The rest [Ethan concluded] is history.

*   *   *

I remained on Seriphos for another two months until my parents' divorce was final, frolicking discreetly with my cousins John, Hannah and Mariah, who were all in their teens. Zared, Ethan's oldest child at twenty-two, had already mounted the lowest rung on the Rampart corporate ladder, as had my own older brother Daniel. I toured the offices of Rampart Central with Cousin Zed, whom I soon classified as a total dork, meditated upon my own future, and decided once and for all that I'd never work for Rampart. Not if my life depended upon it.

I wanted something diametrically opposed to interstellar Big Business, and I didn't hesitate to let my father know it. Simon squelched my juvenile idealism brutally by telling me that I could either study xenocommerce and corporation law with a view to entering Rampart, or forego a higher education altogether and spend the rest of my life shovelling horse manure at the Sky Ranch – since he'd personally make sure nobody else ever hired me.

I pretended to cave in, went to the University of Arizona and Harvard, and did the family proud.

On the day I earned my JD degree, I told Simon and Ethan and the other relatives gathered at the celebration that I had been accepted by the Interstellar Commerce Secretariat as a special agent in the Corporate Fraud Department. Ethan wished me good luck. My father looked at me for a few silent moments, then told me he never wanted to lay eyes on me again.

I told him that if Rampart behaved itself, he probably wouldn't.

Chapter 8

The hotel room vidphone purred at ten o'clock on the dot. I answered woozily, thinking it was the live wake-up call to be expected in an upscale establishment like the Ritz-Carlton. But it was Ivor Jenkins, and his rotund face on the viewer was ashen with anxiety.

'Helly! Oh, God – I've been trying to get through to you for hours. But the desk refused to disturb you until ten, and Captain Bermudez was out of his room and not answering his pocket phone.'

Still at his girlfriend's place, no doubt. 'Calm down, Ivor. What's happened?'

'Clive's gone! I've searched the house, the grounds, everywhere. His car is here. I'm calling from the gatehouse. Don't worry – the guard is out of earshot. The man says Clive didn't leave with anybody else. All I found were his shoes and I'm afraid – I'm afraid –'

I was sitting on the edge of the bed, dread rendering me more alert than any artificial stimulant could. I pressed the confidential encrypt button on the phone and its triple bleep sounded. 'Ivor, stop. From the beginning. What happened after I left the house?'

He told the story in his incongruously pedantic fashion. 'I took Citizen Swann-Hepplewhite into the garden and served her champagne. She was very much surprised when I told her that I was Clive's new houseman, so I waxed creative about how busy he was, and how Rampart was grooming him for an important new post – only she mustn't say a word about it to him or I'd be discharged. After a while Clive appeared and did the cookout. He was rather nervous, but he covered it well. He begged me to give him some privacy when I tried to assist him with the barbecuing, so I slipped away and undertook surveillance from the bushes. He and Lois consumed the food and drank all the wine, and then the two of them went into the house. To the bedroom. I stayed in the office across the hall, watching the door. A long time afterward they came out, went downstairs, and had some coffee. She kissed him goodbye and drove away. He went to bed. I pulled a chair out of the office and sat outside his door. But – but I fell asleep along about dawn, and when I looked into his bedroom he was gone. I searched the house and then the grounds, but all I found were the shoes. Blue suede shoes.'

'Where?' I said, knowing what he was going to say.

'Beside the fumarole,' said Ivor. 'It was smoking furiously. And somebody'd taken the grill off the opening . . .'

What was it the gateman had said? *A barbecuin' fool, young Clive.*

'Go home right now, Ivor,' I said. 'Call a taxi. I'll have someone take care of everything at Leighton's place. Mimo will come around and see you later today. Watch your back.'

Ivor's face was screwed up with horror. 'But what about Clive? Do you really think the poor man –'

'Get out of there!' I broke the connection with a savage jab, praying that the luckless executive had committed suicide. The alternative would be very bad news indeed.

I called Simon's personal code, cancelling the view option on the room phone. It was going to be bad enough telling him about the fiasco without having to look him in the eye as well. The great man was mighty annoyed at the interruption, being engaged in a tennis game on Cousin Zed's estate. I squelched his protests and waited until he reached a place where he could not be overheard and then engaged the encrypt.

'Simon, do you know anyone in Rampart security on Seriphos whose loyalty to you is above question?'

'Our Vice President for Confidential Services, Ollie Schneider, has my complete confidence. He's Rampart's top security officer.'

'Would you trust him with your life? With Rampart's very survival?'

'Um . . . no. I guess not. He's Zared's man, not mine. What the hell's this all about?'

94

'I need somebody with top-notch cop skills. Somebody you can vouch for personally, who can clean up a particularly nasty mess and see that no one in Rampart top management finds out about it.'

'Well, there's Karl Nazarian,' my father said. 'He was Ethan's head of security for over thirty years, prior to Ollie. He's semi-retired, in charge of Corporate Archives, but still sharp as a straight razor and smart as a Coconino coyote.'

'He could be perfect. Does he have full data access and command authority?'

'If I authorize it.'

'Then do it,' I said.

'Why?' my father demanded.

'Because I am a horse's ass,' said I, and I told him the tale of Clive Leighton, Galapharma mole, including its dismal conclusion.

Simon listened without interruption, then hissed, 'Jesus H. Christ, Asa! This time you really shat in your hat and pulled it down over your ears! Why didn't you wait –'

I broke in firmly. 'I need somebody to put a lid on this. If Nazarian agrees to do it, have him toss Leighton's place for clues to other conspirators. The guy's data files will have to be confiscated and checked out. His house should be sealed and the goddamn blue suede shoes taken away. Ultimately, we'll need a foolproof cover story for Leighton's death.'

'Hmph. Karl might just be able to do it.'

'I hope to hell you're right.' Another bright idea struck me. 'Do you think Nazarian might have old friends on Hadrach, Plusia-Prime and Tyrins who are as sneaky and trustworthy as he is?'

'He probably knows every over-the-hill security agent in the Spur. Why?'

'Stop asking why and just listen! Tell Nazarian to get on the encrypt subspace com right away, before he does anything about Leighton. Have him contact some of his old associates on those planets – people he can rely on absolutely, who won't stickle at keeping this business outside of the Rampart Central net. We have to locate three Rampart executives named Mario Volta, Oleg Bran-sky and Tokuro Matsudo. They're cronies of Clive Leighton.' I spelled the names and recited the home addresses and phone codes in case the men weren't in their offices. 'These three are to be taken into custody somehow or other and held incommunicado under suicide watch. Make arrangements for Nazarian's people to bring the executives to Seriphos on the fastest ships available – even if you have to use the *Mogollon Rim*. Absolutely no one questions the suspects but me. Got that?'

'What am I,' Simon roared, 'your friggin' errand boy?'

'You were the one who asked me to come here and get involved,' I reminded him. 'Who else can I ask to do the errands? Now repeat what I just told you.' A whole lot of cussing ensued, but when he finally simmered down, Simon reiterated the details in furious mutters. His memory was still eidetic. 'You realize it could take days to find these men?'

'It better not,' I retorted. 'And tell Nazarian we also need to track down and hold a woman named Lois Swann-Hepplewhite. No need for secrecy with her. She's Leighton's girlfriend and she lives here in Vetivarum.'

'Dammitall, Asa – you should be talking to Karl about this yourself! Let me have him call you.'

'It would only waste time. If he agrees to work with us, I'll see him right after the board meeting. I may have a whole lot more for him to do.' I thought of one more thing. 'Hold on a sec. Is your phone loaded with a blank disk? I'm going to shoot you some poop.' I got the dime out of my wallet, stuck it into the handset, and transmitted. 'Extract the face of the man in the freeze-frame close-up at Minute 343:03–07. Label him John Doe and send the data via *public* subspace com – not Rampart! – to Beatrice Mangan, BM7366-2ADM, Fenelon Falls, Ontario, Earth. She's an old friend, a chief inspector in the ICS Forensic Division, and that's her private mail code. Tell Bea that you're my father, and I'm calling in my marker and urgently need an ID on the John Doe. Explain that this individual tried to murder me –'

'You actually got the fucker's *picture?*'

'Simon, shut up. The hired gun probably had cosmetic surgery or quickie genen work. I want Bea to run a skull analysis of him through the Galapharma employee mug base, paying special attention to their internal security personnel. If she gets a positive match, have her send the man's dossier to Karl Nazarian's private mail code as soon as possible. You got that? The private code. It's imperative that we don't let any of this data get into the Rampart Central net.'

'What about having Karl find out if the sidewinder's here on Seriphos?'

'Absolutely not. I'll go after the guy in my own way and I don't want him spooked.'

'Do you intend to discuss this sorry screw-up of yours at the board meeting this afternoon?'

'I doubt it. Don't forget to notify your floor guards to admit Helmut Icicle to the hallowed premises.'

'Like squat I will!' he bellowed. 'You're my son and –'

'My name is Icicle until I decide otherwise. Now get busy.'

I hung up on him. The phone purred immediately with the belated wake-up call, and before I could even make it to the john it went off again. This time it was Mimo, anxious because of the message left by Ivor. I told him the bad news, which he received in nonjudgmental silence, and outlined the investigations I had hopefully set in motion. I warned him that he might have a whole lot of tedious work to do if Karl Nazarian didn't pan out.

He said *No importa*, and then: 'I can be at the hotel in a few minutes. Would you like me to drive you to the board meeting?'

'No, thanks. I'll take a taxi. What I would like you to do is go over to Ivor's apartment in an hour or so. Pay him. I'll reimburse you. Ask him if he's interested in a new job that might take him to Tyrins and God knows where else. Really excellent money, really hazardous duty.'

'So! You intend to begin the search for your sister immediately?'

'Maybe. Listen, Mimo, I've got to sign off and get myself pasted together. Let's meet in the hotel bar around 1830 and I'll tell you how I made out.'

'Very well. I'll see you then. Be sure to wear some impressive clothes to the Rampart board meeting. It will give you an edge.'

I laughed wanly. 'Clothes? Hadn't given it a thought.'

'Well, do so. Remember the immortal words of Epictetus: "Know first who you are, and then adorn yourself accordingly".' He broke the connection.

Huh. Easy for him to say. And who the hell *was* I, anyway, at this point in time? Divisional Chief Inspector A. E. Frost was long dead. Cap'n Helly the devil-may-care submariner was beached for the indeterminate duration. Helmut Icicle was a wounded nonentity, even though I'd pushed him up Simon's nose for spite.

I shuffled into the bathroom, took a leak, and then stared at myself in the full-length mirror. My sojourn in the dystasis tank hadn't diminished my normal muscle mass. The tan and the vaguely military haircut and the tropical squint lines around my eyes gave the lie to my actual physical condition. I looked robust, maybe even dangerous. I grimaced at my reflection and set about cleaning my teeth and saucing my armpits. I decided to leave the beard stubble.

The hotel suite's malle-armoire had a huge selection from the best stores in Vetivarum, including Bean & Abercrombie. I gave the matter a good think, then ordered a pair of poplin briar pants, lightweight Gokey snakeproof boots, a Navajo-motif Pendleton shirt, and an Australian Sidelock waxed-cotton hunting coat. I put the things on and surveyed the exotic result. Whoever he was, you might think twice before messing with him.

Precisely an hour later, as I was finishing a wimpy breakfast of poached eggs, white toast and mint tea, the concierge called to pass on a message from 'your father'. It was very short:

All four subjects have disappeared. Data sent to Earth. Inquiry proceeding via KN.

Rampart Central had changed drastically since the last time I had seen it, twenty-three years ago. The Starcorp's Perseus Spur headquarters was now housed in a three-hundred-storey snow-white ziggurat with glittering bevelled windows framed in blue and gold. It was surrounded by formal gardens and stately promenades, and it bulked above the adjacent urban structures like a manmade mountain with a base that encompassed at least ten city blocks. At the top of the great truncated pyramid was a hopperport where aircraft ceaselessly took off and landed.

Rampart limos and other imposing ground vehicles discharged their privileged passengers at the building's vaulted main entrance; but corporate traffic regulations obliged my humble taxi to drop me off in a subterranean garage. I took an escalator to the colonnaded lobby, an Art Deco extravaganza of white marble, blue glass and semi-abstract brushed-metal ornamentation. String music from some baroque composer diddled and skirled in the background while serious-faced men and women marched purposefully to what were undoubtedly important destinations. Apart from me in my anomalous hunting gear and the uniformed Rampart External Security guards, nearly everyone was attired in regulation corporate-pawn fashion mode: monochrome three-piece suits and matching roll-neck shirts in subdued colours such as navy blue, mulberry, charcoal and loden green. The only vestiges of individuality were provided by quietly patterned neck-scarves centred with pins or brooches. In this tasteful commercial environment, I stood out like a Comanche in war-paint at a Victorian garden party.

But the apparel proclaims the man, and old Mimo's advice had been right on the mark. I felt confident, mean, and ready for anything.

I ambled over to the security desk that walled off the elevator bank, where visitors were presenting coded plastic business cards to the guards in the appropriate manner. Picking the largest and toughest-looking functionary of the lot, I announced, 'Helmut Icicle to see Simon Frost.' The guard's dubious gaze raked me from head to toe and he held out his hand for my card. I waved dismissively and said, 'The old boy's expecting me. Just let him know I'm here.'

'Simon Frost is expecting you?' Give the bruiser credit; he didn't laugh out loud. 'The Chairman?'

'That's the guy,' I said airily. 'This *is* Simon's place, isn't it? Rampart Central? Don't tell me that damned cab driver dropped me off at the wrong address.'

The guard's face turned a dull red, but he wasn't going to let my yokel wit get to him. 'This is Rampart Central. May I have your card, sir?'

'Haven't got one. You just get Simon Frost on the horn, he'll tell you to unbar the gate for Helmut Icicle.'

'Would you please spell your name, sir? I'll consult the appointment computer.'

I did. And lo! Helmut Icicle's bizarre handle checked out. The guard concealed his astonishment very well as he gave me a visitor's badge. 'Your escort will be here in a few minutes, Citizen Icicle. Please wait by the Number One elevator.'

I gave him a friendly nod and complied, not bothering to correct his mistake about my social status. The corporate clones exiting and entering less prestigious lift cars did doubletakes as they caught sight of me loitering in the royal precincts, then sedulously ignored my presence. Finally the doors of Number One slid open and a formidable female emerged. She was tall and square-shouldered. Her silvery hair was worn in an uncompromising chignon and her garb was a symphony in mocha. The tiger-eye cameo pinned at her throat bore the image of the Gorgon Medusa.

'Mr Icicle? How do you do. I am Mevanery Morgan, executive secretary to Zared Frost. You're twenty minutes late for the meeting.'

I smiled winsomely and said nothing. Taut with disapproval, she motioned me to enter the elevator car. I noticed that it had only one destination floor: 299. We zoomed skyward inertialessly.

'It's been a long time since I had anything to do with Rampart,' I said in a conversational tone. 'You mind telling me who's on the board these days?'

The doors slid open and Mevanery Morgan preceded me into a hushed, blue-carpeted anteroom that had its own bank of restricted elevators. A sculpture that might have been a Braque was spotlighted on a white pedestal. One of the walls held a surrealistic painting by Rob Schouten of improbably balanced rocks in a nonterrestrial tidepool. The secretary's desk was backed by a computer console that looked as though it belonged on a starship, and on either side of it were tall doors. The one on the right had Cousin Zed's name on it and his title, President and Chief Operations Officer. Mevanery Morgan beckoned me toward the other door, which bore a golden plaque that said BOARDROOM. 'With the exception of Citizen Katje Vanderpost and First Vice President Eve Frost, all of the directors are present for today's meeting. I'm sure the Chairman will introduce them to you.'

So my mother hadn't come . . . That would make things a little easier.

I touched the Gorgon's arm to detain her when she would have opened the boardroom door. 'Wait just a moment, please. Are Eckert and Abul Hadi and Jernigan still board members?' They were old friends of the family whom I had seen occasionally at dinners and other social affairs sponsored by my mother.

'Citizen Frederick Jernigan retired last year. The other two directors are still sitting. Please! The Chairman has had to delay opening the meeting because of your tardiness.'

'Slap my wrist with a ruler,' I suggested waggishly.

She gave me a terrible look. I failed to turn to stone, whereupon she flung the door wide and announced, 'Mr Helmut Icicle.'

I walked into the boardroom. It was windowless and rather dimly lit. Simon was seated at the head of the long table, flanked by the eight directors. At each place, glowing computer screens were recessed into the dark, polished greenwood. There were carafes of water and crystal tumblers. Cousin Zed sat on Simon's right. On his left was my older brother Daniel, a humourless, ambitious man who served as Rampart's Secretary as well as its Chief Corporate Counsel and Syndic. Others I knew included Ethan's widow, Emma Bradbury, and the two charter directors Gunter Eckert and Yasser Abul Hadi. The second woman and the two men sitting on Zed's side of the table were strangers.

Simon said, 'It's about time!' There were two empty seats below Abul Hadi and he motioned me toward one of them. 'Let's get this damned show on the road.' Dan tipped me a minimal nod. If he was surprised to see me, he gave no sign of it. Zed reacted with puzzled suspicion, apparently not recognizing me. Aunt Emma murmured 'Helmut *Icicle*?' in an incredulous voice. We hadn't seen each other in over ten years.

'You know him better,' Simon said, 'as my youngest son, Asahel Frost. He's told me he prefers to keep the alias for the time being.'

There were smothered exclamations. Zed turned angrily to Simon. 'What the hell's going on? Why is he here?'

'He's going to address the board on a matter of moment,' my father said, flashing his rare, brilliant smile. 'And then I'm going to move that we make him Vice President for Special Projects.'

Chapter 9

'Now hold on just a damn minute!' I exclaimed.

Simon said, 'I call this meeting of the Rampart Interstellar Corporation Board of Directors to order ... Asahel, sit down! You'll have a chance to speak later.'

He was wearing his signature ranchman's outfit, in faded blue denim this time. Around his neck was a skinny bolo tie ornamented with a flat chunk of turquoise set in silver. His Stetson was parked on a greenwood coat tree in the corner. He turned to Dan. 'Mr Secretary, since this is an extraordinary meeting of the Rampart board, I move that we dispense with reading the minutes and proceed to the first order of business.'

Gunter Eckert said, 'I second,' and the motion was approved unanimously.

The three younger directors sitting across the table studied me with frank curiosity. Like Zed, they were in their late thirties or early forties, wearing elegant bespoke business attire that bore only a superficial resemblance to that of the lower-status drones I'd seen down in the lobby. Aunt Emma, who seemed frail and wispy, was swathed in burgundy chiffon and pearls. The two old hands, like Simon, indulged their penchant for sartorial eccentricity. Eckert had on a oatmeal-coloured silk tweed jacket with suede elbow patches and binding at the cuffs. It looked about a hundred years old and so did he. Abul Hadi wore spotless white robes and a head-cloth. His beard had gone iron-grey and his skin was an unhealthy colour. He closed his eyes and took out a string of worry-beads, fingering them below the level of the table.

'Before we go any further,' Simon said, 'I'll introduce certain members of the board who may not be familiar to our guest.' He indicated the men and woman sitting below Emma. 'Leonidas Dunne is Rampart's Chief Technical Officer. Gianliborio Rivello is our Chief Marketing Officer. Thora Scranton is one of our four Directors-at-Large. She represents the interests of Rampart small stakeholders. You remember Gunter Eckert, our Chief Financial Officer, and Yasser Abul Hadi, who used to be Chief Counsel and now serves as a Director-at-Large . . .'

I whispered, 'Glad you and Gunter are still here, Yasser.'

The sunken dark eyes opened but he didn't look at me. 'Perhaps not for long,' he murmured.

Simon said, 'The first order of business involves Galapharma Amalgamated Concern . . . As you all know, Gala has made numerous acquisition overtures to us over the past four years. We've rejected all of them. Six weeks ago their chairman, Alistair Drummond, met with me informally at the Sky Ranch in Arizona. He informed me that Gala is prepared to proceed with a hostile takeover effort unless we immediately enter into merger talks. I intend to tell him to go to hell. Does any director wish to move that we entertain the Galapharma bid?'

My brother Daniel said, 'Let me make one comment for the record. While I concur with Simon's decision to oppose the Galapharma tender offer at this time, I'm increasingly concerned by certain adverse factors that are seriously devaluing Rampart Starcorp. I intend to discuss these factors in detail at our next general board meeting in six months' time.'

Silence greeted this announcement, which sounded almost like a threat.

Simon appeared unperturbed. 'Are there any other comments . . . for the record?' When no one spoke he continued. 'The second order of business involves my intention to create a new executive position, Vice President for Special Projects, and hire my son Asahel to fill it. I so move and open the matter to discussion.'

The chagrin and disapprobation vibes were palpable. Even Dan gave me the fish-eye.

'I want you to know,' Simon went on doggedly, 'that I intend to take Asahel into my full confidence regarding Rampart's affairs – most especially including Eve's disappearance and the Galapharma offer – from this day forward. I need his advice and I'll bring him into this Starcorp one way or another, whether he likes it or not. Or *you* do!'

Thora Scranton had been whispering into the mike of her computer during the mini-diatribe. Now she said, 'I think this will enhance our decision-making on the Chairman's motion.'

Suddenly the screen at my place produced a slow-scrolling précis of my curriculum vitae, including the infamous *New York Times* article and picture of me. Everybody else got the same data and their eyes dropped to the displays. Scranton gave me a tiny apologetic shrug. She was a woman of ample figure whose plain, intelligent face was framed by ash-blonde hair.

Simon was unruffled. 'Thank you, Thora. I should have thought of that myself.'

The CV gave only a brief account of my career and professional triumphs but detailed my inglorious downfall in excruciating detail. It concluded with my voluntary exile to K-L and application for full-time resident status.

Leonidas Dunne spoke up in an easy, silken tone. The Chief Technical Officer had a ski-jump nose that reminded me of the classic comedian Bob Hope, and a pointy-toothed smile like a debonair alligator. 'Hardly the usual sort of job résumé, is it? I presume our Chairman has his reasons for proposing that Asahel Frost join us ... though I can't imagine what they might be, unless we have a sudden need for a disenfranchised White Hunter with an allergy to shaving-gel.'

Cousin Zed laughed appreciatively and so did Gianliborio Rivello. The implication of alliance wasn't lost on me.

Simon said, 'I'd like Asahel to tell us about the two recent attempts on his life, and his opinion about who might have been responsible for them.'

That got their attention.

Aunt Emma gave a little cry of shock and distress. The Gang of Three exchanged enigmatic glances. Dan's face registered a smidgen of fraternal concern. The others waited expectantly as I took my time responding, removing my mirror shades, shrugging off my hunting coat, tipping my chair back, and crossing my snake-booted feet.

'First,' I said, 'I want you to know that the only reason I'm here today is because Simon insisted. I had no idea he intended to nominate me vice president for whatever-it-is, and I certainly don't want the job. I *do* intend to investigate the disappearance of Eve Frost, using methods of my own.'

'I think that's an excellent idea,' said Abul Hadi unexpectedly. 'Schneider's inquiry certainly hasn't produced any results.'

Zed bridled. 'That's unfair, Yasser. Ollie's done the best he could, given the restraints we were forced to –'

'Asahel has the floor,' Simon said, cutting him off. The Rampart President subsided. His features were stiff with indignation.

I continued. 'The canned biography of me in the computer doesn't talk about the kind of life I've led since I was expelled from the Commerce Secretariat. Let me tell you about it. At first, I drank myself into oblivion. Whenever I managed to come up for air I thought about committing suicide, but I just didn't have the guts. The only people who cared whether I lived or died were a few Throwaway friends on Kedge-Lockaby . . . and my big sister Eve. When we were kids, Eve was the one who always took care of me. Wiped my nose and fixed my scraped knees. Swatted me and cussed me out when I misbehaved. Made me learn how to swim properly after I nearly drowned and she had to save my life. Took me camping and cross-country skiing in the North Woods when the family lived in the Toronto house. Taught me to ride a horse and prospect for minerals on our ranch in Arizona. Later on, when my life fell apart, Eve hatched a kindly little scheme that she thought might snap me out of my alcoholic depression. She bought me a boat, a sport submersible. The thing fascinated me, gave me a new interest in living. I sobered up, just as Eve hoped I would. After a while I was able to earn a living as a guide for scuba divers and underwater fishermen. Kedge-Lockaby is a nice freesoil planet. All I asked was to be left in peace there, living in a shack in the islands and skippering my sub. Instead, Galapharma AC sent a thug to murder me . . . because of Rampart.'

A storm of questions erupted. Simon called for order and I went on.

'The first attempt on my life failed out of sheer bad luck.' I gave them a sketchy account of the sea-toad incident, which left Zed and his buddies covertly smirking. 'The second try, which involved marooning me on a comet, seemed to have succeeded. So the hatchet man sent Simon a little obituary announcement, crowing over it.'

'Look at your screens,' my father said, tapping a few pads. 'Here's the message I received.' The mocking bit of doggerel appeared, along with the directions for finding my body.

'A comet?' Aunt Emma wailed. 'In outer *space*? Oh, Asa!'

I smiled at her. 'A friend rescued me.'

Thora Scranton said, 'This message seems to link your apparent death with the disappearance of Eve Frost. But there's no hint that Galapharma is responsible. Do you have any concrete evidence to support that allegation?'

'Yes. The proofs are circumstantial, but convincing. I don't intend to discuss them here today. I'm working to identify the would-be killer and confirm the Gala connection, and I'm pursuing other lines of inquiry as well.'

'What are they?' asked Gianliborio Rivello.

I shook my head.

'The board has a right to know!' The director turned to my father. 'If you insist on hiring him –'

Simon said, 'He'll report directly to me, Gianni. And *I'll* decide what to tell the board.'

Rivello sat back, glowering.

Cousin Zed addressed me in a studied neutral tone. 'I'm rather surprised that this assassin would have targeted you in an apparent attempt to pressure Simon. After all, your father did disavow you publicly. I assumed that the two of you were permanently estranged.'

'Well, you've been wrong before, Zared,' Simon said. His smile was unashamedly foxy. 'For instance – when you assumed Ethan would leave his entire stake to you, so we'd be forced to accept you as CEO.'

Zed's voice remained controlled. 'It's a position I've earned, and one I expect to fill in the future. But I'll remind you that we didn't come here today to debate my executive abilities. The point at issue is whether Rampart should entrust a sensitive and potentially damaging investigation to an outsider – a man who forfeited the public trust and disgraced the family name, a self-confessed alcoholic and mental basket case who may have fabricated these alleged attempts on his life for twisted reasons of his own. The Chairman is justifiably anxious about Galapharma's renewed pressure and the disappearance of his daughter. I suggest that he may not be in a position to judge this situation objectively –'

Simon let out an angry curse, but before he could deliver a riposte Dunne and Rivello chimed in with their own disparaging estimates of my character. A shouting match ensued, with Eckert and Abul Hadi calling vainly for calm and fair play while Aunt Emma moaned and Thora Scranton watched with clinical fascination.

I tuned out, considering a new and intriguing aspect of the overall situation.

I had heard rumours, prior to my personal debacle, that the dying President and CEO of Rampart believed that his oldest son was too unimaginative to take over the helm of the Starcorp. 'Number-crunching nerd' and 'not a lick of fire in his belly' were among the choicer pejoratives Ethan Frost was supposed to have used to describe the hapless Zared. Those personal deficiencies were acceptable in a Chief Operating Officer and even in a President – but not in the prime mover of an interstellar corporation.

According to the complex Starcorp bylaws, the CEO of Rampart (unlike lesser officers) was confirmed by a vote among stakeholders – one share, one vote. Almost from the beginning the three majority quarterstakes were held by Ethan, Simon, and my mother Katje Vanderpost, who had inherited them from her brother Dirk, the third Rampart founder who had died in 2186. The fourth quarter was held by the thousands of small stakeholders and administered by Thora Scranton. In order to prevent his oldest son's succession, Ethan had willed his wife Emma only half his stake. The other half went to Simon, insuring his control of the corporation when my mother voted with him, as she always did, in spite of their divorce.

Zed had been bitterly disappointed when Simon assumed the role of Chief Executive Officer following Ethan's demise. No doubt

Zed hoped that the passing of time would take its toll on the old man and force him to step down. But five years had gone by, Simon was eighty-four and still full of piss and vinegar, and he apparently refused to name his nephew as his corporate heir.

But if not Zed, then who?

Certainly not my older brother Daniel, who was even less of a hard-charger than Zed. Dan was a meticulous micromanager, a grind, a political type who hated the frontier hurly burly of the Perseus Spur and preferred the electric atmosphere of Toronto, where his wife, Norma Palmer, was a delegate in the Commonwealth Assembly.

My quiet, mathematically brilliant sister Bethany, who was Assistant Chief Financial Officer, was also unqualified by temperament for the job, as were Ethan's other adult children, a trio of unexceptional individuals who held sinecure executive posts at Rampart Central.

No, there was only one other Frost family member with the ability to lead the Starcorp and outwit the Concern carnosaur hoping to make a meal of it: Rampart's dynamic First Vice President and Chief Transport and Distribution Officer.

Eve.

I froze in my tilted chair, then slowly let its front legs come down to the floor. The ruckus was winding down as the focus of the arguing shifted away from me and toward certain serious management problems Rampart had endured over the past two years, and whether or not Zared's response to them had been effective.

I stared at my cousin with fresh interest. He was forty-five, a taller man than his father Ethan had been, with dark chestnut hair. His features were handsome and incisive – a knife-thin nose, prominent cheekbones, a lean, angular chin and a mouth habitually compressed in a determined line. He was far and away the most intellectually gifted of the Frost offspring, a business prodigy who had apprenticed under the Chief Financial Officer, Gunter Eckert. But Ethan's ultimate assessment of his son's character had been essentially correct. In light of the evidence now being flung about by the wrangling board members, Zared appeared to be overconservative and lacking in the vision and drive that mark an effective galactic entrepreneur.

Unless he had been deliberately acting against Rampart's best interests.

I'd never liked Zed. I liked him even less now, as I mulled over some alarming possibilities.

My brother Dan was saying, 'The Ackerman fiasco and the continuing state of paralysis in the Research Division following Yaoshuang Qiu's death are only the latest crises of leadership we've suffered. In my opinion, we also bungled the production breakdown at the genvec plant on Farallon-Zander, the Insap uprising on Osmanthus, the Mendip epizootic, and the RB-4238 contamination flap on Steilacoom. Leaving aside the matter of possibly inadequate executive response –'

'Nonsense!' Zed snapped.

Dan continued. 'We have to concede that all of these incidents seriously disrupted important lines of production, cut deeply into our earnings, and diminished public confidence in the Starcorp at a time when we'd hoped to expand and push for Concern status ... Lately, both Simon and I have begun to wonder whether the disasters were all due to bad luck.'

Rivello's saturnine features were sceptical. 'You see some sort of sinister pattern? Some overarching conspiracy instigated by Galapharma, intended to soften up Rampart for a takeover?'

'I admit I never considered it before,' Simon said, 'but in the light of Eve's disappearance and the attacks on Asahel, Galapharma involvement in the other events now seems possible – even probable.'

'I'm not convinced.' The Marketing Officer shook his head. 'The unfortunate events you mentioned can be explained without resorting to wild theorizing. Eve Frost's disappearance is an especially grave matter, but we still have no proof that it was involuntary. I admit I don't know what to make of the alleged attacks on Asahel or the peculiar message you received, but –'

Gunter Eckert said quietly, 'If we can prove to the ICS that Galapharma agents are sabotaging Rampart to devalue it, we can sue the bastards into receivership and grab their assets.'

'That,' Simon said, 'is exactly what I hope Asahel will help us to do when we make him VP Special Projects. He's had more experience ferreting out Concern shenanigans than Rampart's entire internal security force and legal department put together.'

'Your son has been discredited,' Leonidas Dunne pointed out. 'Reduced to legal nonentity. Evidence gathered by a Throwaway would be inadmissible in a Commonwealth court of law.'

'Leo, you're making the mistake a lot of folks do,' Simon retorted, 'assuming that once a person's citizenship is revoked, there's no recourse. Most of the time there isn't, because Starcorps and Concerns won't employ a Throwaway. Why should they, when there are thousands of unemployed citizens vying for every job? But exceptions have been made, Throwaways have been hired for good and sufficient reason, and I intend to make one of those exceptions here and now.'

Emma Bradbury looked thunderstruck. 'I think I understand! If we hire Asa –'

Daniel Frost finished the thought. 'As a salaried employee of an Interstellar Corporation, he would be automatically re-enfranchised as a citizen of the Commonwealth of Human Worlds.'

My reputation, however, would still stink from one end of the Milky Way to the other. In hiring me, Simon would be putting his own integrity on the line, and that of Rampart as well. Zed smacked his palm onto the computer display before him. 'I can't believe you're serious! This crazy message Simon received could be the work of some madman with a personal grudge. Or it could have been sent by Asa himself. Our business reversals can all be explained without blaming some shadowy conspiracy instigated by Galapharma. Eve's disappearance is troubling, but I say that any investigation of it should proceed under the direction of our Vice President for Confidential Services. It's ridiculous to assume that an outsider could do a better job than Ollie Schneider.'

'Are you calling me ridiculous?' Simon inquired ominously.

'Of course not. But I don't think you've thought this thing through, either. How do we know where Asa's loyalties lie? Can we be certain he'll act in Rampart's best interests – or will he be a loose cannon, following some half-assed agenda of his own? He was convicted of falsifying data, failing to protect the life of a witness in his custody and perjury, for God's sake!'

'It was a set-up,' I said quietly. 'And I intend to prove that, too – after I find Eve.'

Simon said to me, 'Then you *will* accept the post?'

I paused, ready to refuse again; but the logic of acceptance was inescapable. As an insider I could make use of Rampart's immense resources, compel co-operation from employees who might have knowledge of my sister's fate. Operating on my own, even with the help of Mimo and his useful underworld associates, I'd have to claw my way uphill with my fingernails, fending off Zed and his minions at every turn as well as sidestepping Galapharma's cut-throats.

And maybe the Haluk as well. I asked Simon, 'Will you give me carte blanche if I agree to undertake the investigation?'

'Yes.'

'And I report only to you?'

'Yes.'

'Then I'll accept if the board approves.'

Simon said, 'To repeat: I move that Asahel Frost be appointed Vice President for Special Projects, with his first brief being a confidential inquiry into the disappearance of Eve Frost.'

My brother Dan said, 'I second the motion and call for a show of hands. All in favour?'

Simon and Dan promptly voted for me, and after a moment's bemused hesitation, so did Gunter Eckert and Yasser Abul Hadi. I choked back a groan of disappointment. Well, I'd stick with Plan A after all and go it alone.

Dan said, 'Those opposed?'

Zed muttered, 'This is a travesty.' His hand shot up. Aunt Emma, sending an apologetic moue my way, voted with her son. Dunne and Rivello made it a foursome. They all looked expectantly at Thora Scranton.

She said, 'I abstain, lacking sufficient data to make an informed decision.'

'A stalemate?' I exclaimed in disbelief.

Simon said calmly, 'In the case of a tied vote I invoke Clause 17b of the Rampart Corporate By-Laws. I hold the proxies of absent board members Katje Vanderpost and Eve Frost, and I cast their votes in favour of the motion and declare it carried.'

'My acceptance,' I said, before anyone else could speak, 'is absolutely conditional upon confidentiality. The members of this board must agree to keep my true identity secret until I choose to reveal it. I won't have a galactic media circus impeding my work.'

Simon said, 'Is there any member who has a problem with this?'

Dan broke the smouldering silence. 'Mr Chairman, we're ready for the next order of business. It involves personal reports on the Eve Frost investigation from the Vice President for Confidential Services and the Chief of Fleet Security.'

He touched a pad on his personal terminal. The voice of Mevanery Morgan said, 'Yes, sir?'

'Please ask Oliver Schneider and Matilde Gregoire to join us.' He pronounced the unusual proper name mah-*teeld*.

The door opened. The Vice President was a sombre bulldog of a man in his early fifties, wearing corporate mufti. The Fleet Security Chief, whose job description entailed coping with ass-busting starship captains, frenetic shipping executives and galactic buccaneers, was a young woman.

But not the amazon I might have expected.

Matilde Gregoire was the perfect embodiment of an old Latin ballad (Mimo had played the Nat King Cole version on the car stereo) that celebrated *ojos negros, piel canela* – black eyes, cinnamon skin. Her short curly hair was the colour of strong coffee. She had a small tip-tilted nose and an upper lip ever so slightly retroussé. The blue-and-silver uniform she wore outlined her slim, small-breasted figure. She was not very tall. It was impossible to tell her age. Her flawless complexion suggested eighteen, but the eyes that swept in cool assessment over the boardroom occupants belonged to a woman who was much older.

One of her arched brows rose a disbelieving millimetre as she briefly met my gaze, and I knew she'd made me.

Simon didn't bother with any preliminary remarks or introductions. All he said was, 'Please present your reports. You first, Matt.'

Matilde Gregoire declined a seat and chose to address us standing at the foot of the table. Her voice was deep and husky, charged with the sort of mesmerizing authority that makes the best actors unforgettable. Her manner was easy, full of self-confidence, entirely professional. She spoke for nearly an hour, occasionally consulting a computer notebook and transposing data from it to the terminals at the table, presenting a cogent summary of the co-ordinated efforts of Fleet Security and the special ExSec task force sent to Tyrins from Rampart Central by Schneider. I was impressed by the fact that the Vice President had left Gregoire in charge of the main investigation, rather than taking control himself.

To an ex-agent like me, the minutiae of her report were fascinating and an affirmation of her own competence. She was a good one, all right, and she'd covered the ground as well as anyone could. The male animal in me also enjoyed contemplating Matt Gregoire as an *objet d'art* – with any more interesting considerations regretfully postponed until I was off the sick-list.

When Gregoire concluded, Schneider rose from his seat and discussed the search operations being conducted on other Spur worlds by Rampart's External Security Force. The hunt had been severely limited by Zared's directive not to identify Eve as the missing person, in order to avoid tipping off the ever-curious media.

It was Schneider's considered opinion that my sister might very well have dropped out of sight voluntarily. She was a qualified starship pilot and Tyrins was the busiest port in the Perseus Spur. In addition to acting as the hub for all Rampart traffic in Zone 23, it served CHW Zone Patrol, innumerable private vessels, most of the independent transports fuelling for the Orion transit, and God knew how many smugglers and human pirates. It would have been relatively easy for Eve to leave Tyrins – or be taken from it – without a trace.

As he wound down, Schneider said, 'Are there any questions?'

'Where do you go from here?' Simon asked tiredly.

'Chief Gregoire will redouble our efforts on Tyrins, while I expand the wider-scale search on the other Perseus worlds and into the Orion Arm. But you should understand that our investigations will be hamstrung unless you rescind the secrecy directive and permit ExSec to identify Eve Frost to local planetary authorities and Zone CID. We've been able to keep her disappearance secret thus far, but it's only a matter of time before it leaks out.'

'Or she surfaces,' Zed muttered, 'and asks what all the fuss was about.'

Simon ignored him. 'Ollie, I want to thank you and Matt for coming here today and briefing us. From here on in, I'm transferring complete responsibility for this investigation to our new alpha-level Department for Special Projects and its Vice President, Helmut Icicle. Please give his agents your complete co-operation.'

Schneider's bulldog jaw dropped open as if he were about to protest. But he caught himself and said only, 'Very well, Chairman. Will that be all?'

Simon nodded and the two security officers rose to leave.

I called out, 'Stay a moment, please, Chief Gregoire.' She turned and waited. Schneider went out, closing the door behind him. I said to my father: 'Carte blanche?'

He growled, 'Yes, goddammit!'

'Then I'd like to ask Matilde Gregoire to be my principal associate for the Eve Frost investigation. And Karl Nazarian to be Number Two.'

Zed broke in anxiously, 'But, Simon – Ollie Schneider has to be slotted in somehow!'

I rose from my seat and put my coat on. 'Sorry. I'm fresh out of slots.'

Disapproving murmurs came from Rivello and Dunne. Even my brother Dan looked dubious.

My father said, 'Will you agree to this arrangement, Matt? Karl Nazarian has already accepted. I realize that the set-up is totally unorthodox and will require some drastic reshuffling in your offices back on Tyrins, but . . . I also know that you and Eve are close friends. Help us find her.'

Matilde Gregoire had been staring at me in blank disbelief from the moment that I proposed her as my associate. Now the lovely cinnamon skin of her cheeks took on a resentful flush and she said, 'Chairman, am I to understand that *this* is the man now in charge of the investigation? This is Helmut Icicle?'

Through gritted teeth, Simon said, 'He is.' When she remained silent, he added in a low, pleading voice, 'Matt, please work with him. For Eve's sake.'

Since the beginning of the briefings, Yasser Abul Hadi had seemed to be dozing, his head bowed. Now he suddenly spoke up as the Fleet Security Chief continued to hesitate, his voice full of urgency. 'I beg you to do this, Chief Gregoire. He is the best man for the job. Maybe the only one who can do it. He'll explain why.'

She had to force the words out. 'Very well, then, I accept. But only for Eve's sake.'

'Thank you,' said Simon. He sat back, seeming suddenly withdrawn and shrunken.

There were more murmurings. Thora Scranton and Gunter Eckert appeared to be pleased. Aunt Emma was puzzled. Dunne and Rivello exchanged looks of frank disgust, and Dan gazed stolidly at the table, toying with a silver computer stylomike. Zared had the appearance of a dapper volcano about to erupt.

I politely asked Gregoire to come along with me and headed for the door. As I opened it, letting her precede me, I turned and said, 'We'll talk tonight, Simon, or maybe tomorrow. Be available.'

Somebody gasped at the saucy effrontery of it all. I left the boardroom and closed the door, truncating a sudden tirade from Zed.

The redoubtable Mevanery Morgan eyed me sardonically from her command post. 'Is the meeting over, Mr Icicle?'

'Only for the two of us. I've been appointed Vice President for Special Projects. Please call Karl Nazarian of Corporate Archives and say Chief Gregoire and I would like to confer with him immediately.'

The secretary hesitated only an instant, then whirled about in her swivel chair and addressed the computer. Gregoire had distanced herself from me and was putting her electronic notebook into a shoulder bag. She said, 'You don't waste much time, do you?'

'With luck, I'll get around to it. Time-wasting used to be my principal occupation ... May I call you Matt? You can call me Helly.'

The briefest of smiles, chill and unfriendly, flickered over her lips. They were full, touched with a dark red gloss. She said in a nearly inaudible undertone, 'Do you intend to let me know just what's going on – aside from the obvious fact that your father is a very frightened man?'

'Soon,' I whispered. 'Did you know who I was from the beginning?'

'You'd better believe it. Felons are my business.'

'I was framed.'

'That's what they all say.'

Mevanery Morgan turned around, cutting short the *sotto voce* dialogue, and announced that Karl Nazarian was coming to collect us personally. I thanked her and she said, 'Not at all, Mr Icicle.'

'Better make that *Citizen* Icicle,' I corrected her. 'From now on.'

Chapter 10

Karl Nazarian didn't even bother to emerge from the lift that had conveyed him to Level 299. He stood inside waiting for us, an amiable expression on his jowly, eroded face. He was probably in his eighties, but his hair still had most of its colour, his eyes were sharp, and his keg-shaped body seemed sturdy. He wore a moss-green worsted suit and shirt, a black neck scarf and a heavy gold brooch in a complex ethnic design.

'Let's go to my place,' he said without ceremony. Gregoire and I entered the elevator and I waved bye-bye to Morgan the Gorgon. When the doors closed and we started down Nazarian said to me, 'Well, Asa! The last time we met, you were a zit-faced brat of thirteen, touring my security facility with Ethan – God rest him.'

'I remember. I'm surprised you do.'

He gave a rumbling laugh. 'Your father and uncle had such great plans for you in those days. Strange that you've finally come to Rampart after all – and under these sad circumstances.' He nodded to Gregoire. 'Don't tell me Simon's co-opted *you* for this rump operation, Matt.'

'So it seems,' she said without enthusiasm.

'Matt started in at Rampart as my administrative assistant when I was VP Confidential Services,' Nazarian told me. 'That was sixteen years ago. She's one of the best we have.'

'I figured that out. It's why I asked her to help.' Sixteen years! She was probably as old as I was. I tried to catch her eye, but she looked straight ahead at the lift door. It was easy to justify co-opting her assistance, but the truth was that the decision had been purely instinctive, the impulse of a crazy moment, inspired by that fabulous *piel canela* . . .

The elevator opened on the 140th floor of the ziggurat and Nazarian guided us to a transport tube that would carry us to his office at Corporate Archives. As we strode along I felt a hitch in my step, a momentary faltering of the heart, a wisp of light-headedness, and I thought: Oh, hell. Not now!

We had the transporter car to ourselves. I lowered myself care-fully into the seat and was relieved when my body seemed to resume its normal operation.

'Simon sent me a confidential note about your new organization this morning,' Nazarian said. 'I'm damned if I know what you want with an old fart like me. You better not expect me to do all-night stakeouts or go hippity-hopping around the Spur chasing kidnap suspects.'

'You're on my team because Simon says that you're completely trustworthy – and you give a damn about the Starcorp's future. There's more to this operation than Eve's abduction.'

'Hmm. How do you intend using me?'

'You'll be my Number Two. Matt is Number One. I'd like you to take charge of the operation's co-ordination and data retrieval. I intend to run a very compact ship with as few personnel as possible. You'll need to recruit five or six associates who are loyal to you and to Rampart, and who aren't afraid to resist pressure – and temptation – from high places.' I told him what kind of hefty salary to offer. He and Matt would be getting triple their present compensation, plus additional Rampart shares.

'Will our lives be in danger?' Karl Nazarian asked.

'Probably. Want to pull out?'

He grinned. 'No.'

I turned to Gregoire, taking a figurative deep breath. 'And you, Matt? My father is a cosmic arm-twister, but if you'd prefer not to be part of this organization, you're free to withdraw – no prejudice.'

She said, 'Ask me again after we've found Eve.'

The car stopped at a door with Nazarian's name on it and he thumbed the lock. We disembarked into a spacious room that seemed more of a private study than an office. To the left was a wall crowded with glowing routing displays and multicoloured device-driver telltales pertaining to the corporate archives. On the right, comfortable leather chairs and a low coffee table were grouped around an unlit fireplace with a potted fern between the andirons. The wall opposite the entry was a floor-to-ceiling artificial window with a holo of a springtime meadow on Earth featuring a grazing black stallion, a venerable tree with fresh leaves trembling in a breeze, and droves of cyclamen and asphodels blooming around a stone fence. In front of the scenic projection stood a huge blond-wood tabledesk combined with a computer console that made Mevanery Morgan's look like a pocket calculator.

Nazarian said, 'Let's sit down,' and led us to the fireplace.

I was ready for a chair. My heart had started to thump and I was beginning to feel vaguely feverish. It was plain that I'd reverted to my walking-wounded state. I held off using the medicuff for fear of undermining my authority with the troops.

Karl offered refreshments from a well-stocked drinks credenza. Gregoire asked for a Campari-soda and I gratefully accepted a cool glass of Dortmunder Kronen from a cask imprinted with a golden elephant, wondering if Mimo himself had smuggled it into the Spur. God bless real beer! It's nourishing, it bolsters sagging vitality, and it cools the hectic brow. The terrestrial brews are so much better than the local product that it's no wonder that bootleggers prosper.

Nazarian said, 'Do you know a person named Beatrice – and do you have any idea why she would use my personal ex-net code to send me a top secret dossier filched from the personnel files of a certain business rival of Rampart's?'

'It came!' I cried jubilantly. 'Good old Bea! Who's the subject?'

'His name is Quillan McGrath, and he's Galapharma AC's Deputy Chief for Internal Investigations, based at Concern HQ, Glasgow.'

'Yes! I knew I'd seen that fucker before! The Scottish Exhibition and Conference Centre in 2227. A regulatory update meeting sponsored by the ICS. He asked a question at a symposium I led.'

Nazarian went to his desk, retrieved a bound printout and tossed it to me before sitting down with us before the fireplace. 'What's your interest in this man?'

'Keeping him from trying to kill me for the third time, for

starters.' I flicked through the dossier. It included a picture of the subject with what I presumed were his original features. The makeover was extensive but they'd left the close-set, opaque blue eyes alone. Only an expert could tell that even then he'd had an iris job, doubtless with a nanoimplant capable of projecting any number of false patterns into an ID scanner.

'Do you think he might be on Seriphos?' Matt Gregoire asked.

'Maybe not yet. This man could be very important to us. He might lead us to the persons responsible for a whole lot of bad luck Rampart's had lately . . . and even bigger trouble upcoming in the future.'

'Ah.' She looked uncertain, but said nothing more.

'Karl, how much did Simon tell you this morning?'

'He was very agitated. He told me about Eve's disappearance, which I'd already heard through the corpnet grapevine. He restored my line authority and gave me some very unusual orders, which he justified by sharing suspicions about certain top executives of Rampart. That should have shocked the pants off me – except I'd already been wondering about the situation myself. Then he delivered the final zinger and told me that Rampart's survival is probably in your hands. That made me wonder whether my poor old friend had lapsed into senility. I took care of the jobs he laid on me and did some heavy cogitating.'

'What do you think now? Is Simon crazy? Am I?'

'I think you're both in a hell of a mess, boy – and so is Rampart. Beyond that, I'm reserving judgement.'

'Suppose,' I said, 'that you tell us about Simon's suspicions.' He hesitated. 'Some of this might be a nasty surprise for Matt.'

She said, 'Just answer Helly's question.'

'Helly?' Karl's right eyebrow lifted quizzically. 'Short for Helmut Icicle, I presume? Or are you officially Asahel Frost now that you've signed on with Rampart?'

'I'm a man of many monikers,' I said alliteratively. 'For good and sufficient reasons I'm using the alias for the time being, and you should, too. It might also help you dissociate me from the thirteen-year-old zit-faced brat.' I repeated my query about Simon's suspicions.

A shadow passed over the old security officer's craggy features. 'There isn't a lick of proof to support this, Helly, but Simon is afraid that your cousin Zared is actively encouraging the Galapharma hostile acquisition bid. You probably know that Zared expected to be named CEO after Ethan's death. When it didn't happen, he swallowed his resentment because he thought that Simon would step down in his favour eventually. But your father has become increasingly dissatisfied with Zared's handling of corporate operations – especially his tardy responses to certain crises we've endured over the past couple of years. This morning Simon told me he had intended to bump Zared and name Eve President and CEO at the next general board meeting.'

'I had a feeling something like that was in the wind,' I said.

Matt looked profoundly shocked. 'You think Eve's disappearance might have been engineered by Zared?'

'Simon wouldn't go so far as to accuse the President openly,' Karl said. 'But if it's a coincidence, it's a mighty convenient one.' He turned to me. 'And those three questionable middle-management execs Simon put me onto . . . they represent the first concrete evidence that a Galapharma conspiracy has penetrated Rampart itself. I'll have more information on them and on the late Clive Leighton in a day or two. The cover story for Leighton's death is already in place.'

'Good. We have to presume that the Swann-Hepplewhite woman told the others that the jig was up. All of our suspects are probably on their way back to Earth on express starships – unless they're already pushing up daisies in the canyons above Vetivarum. Any other turncoat employees or stakeholders will be especially careful to cover their tracks from here on in. By the way, I don't want Oliver Schneider or his security organization to be any part of our investigation. We don't use them, we don't scrutinize them. Simon seems to think the man is reliable, but I don't want to take any chances. If I were directing Gala's penetration of Rampart, security would be my first target. I want you to be damn sure that the people we take into our little bucket shop have no ties to Schneider.'

Karl nodded in agreement. 'I can find the researchers and operatives we'll need. Some of them might be a little long in the tooth, just like me.' He pointed to the McGrath dossier, which lay on the seat beside me. 'Is that the fellow Simon said marooned you on a comet?'

Gregoire nearly choked on her drink.

I said hastily, 'I'm sorry, Matt. We keep talking over your head. Let me tell you both how I was drawn into Rampart's crisis in the first place.'

I spun the wild yarn all over again, in considerably more detail than I had supplied to the Rampart Board of Directors. I told them about my first encounter with Bronson Elgar (I found it impossible to call him McGrath), the monster making a nosh of my house, the space chase, the Haluk starship, and the ominous message Simon had received, which seemed to imply that Eve was a prisoner of Elgar or his gang of Galapharma baddies. When I finished, Matt and Karl sat quietly for a moment digesting the data, then pronounced a single word in unison:

'*Haluk?*'

'I know it seems incredible,' I admitted. 'But there it is. Elgar – I mean, Quillan McGrath – boasted that the aliens were allied to Gala for reasons of mutual benefit. My friend Captain Guillermo Bermudez can vouch for the fact that a huge Haluk vessel of unfamiliar configuration came to the rescue when Elgar whistled. Two of the xeno bastards lashed me down on top of a cometary gas vent while he made jokes about human cannonballs.'

'What allomorphic stage were the Haluk in?' Karl asked curiously.

'The gracile humanoid, judging from their space armour and brisk movements. I couldn't tell what colour the eyes were. They kept the helmet domes opaque.'

Matt Gregoire was frowning thoughtfully. 'You know, we had an odd incident about five weeks ago with a Haluk angle. My Fleet Security people headed up the investigation rather than turning it over to ExSec Central on Eve's direct order.'

I listened with increasing excitement as she described how Qastt raiders had engaged in persistent highjacking attempts during the past three years, targeting Rampart freighters bound from the planet Cravat to the terminal at Nogawa-Krupp. I knew almost nothing about Cravat apart from its dubious status as the most remote of the Rampart Worlds. It lies near the tip of the Perseus Spur, over eighteen hundred light-years from Seriphos and nearly three hundred from Nogawa. This is not a region that the Qastt customarily infest, being uncomfortably close to the No Man's Land between the Zone 23 boundary and the Haluk planets. The Qastt alliance with the Haluk is shaky at best, based on their mutual antipathy toward humanity.

Eve had assigned Rampart's fastest, most heavily armed freighters to the Cravat run to foil the Qastt pirates, who never took a single Rampart ship. But five or six weeks ago there was a serious confrontation. The Squeakers narrowly lost the fire-fight, their damaged starship was unable to flee, and it surrendered.

'The odd thing was,' Matt said, 'when our people boarded the bandit, they found a dead Haluk. Gracile. It had committed suicide. Our crew just managed to intervene before the Qastt could destroy the body.'

I murmured, 'Jesus!'

'Eve was notified immediately, in her capacity of Chief Transport Officer. For reasons she didn't explain, she ordered the Rampart skipper to deviate from standard procedure. Instead of reporting the incident and turning the pirate over to CHW Zone Patrol, we put a prize crew aboard. They did makeshift repairs and then took the starship and the surviving Squeakers into Nogawa-Krupp. I sent a crack alien-interrogation team to try to find out why the Qastt were so interested in Cravat ships, and what the Haluk was doing aboard.'

'What did you learn?' I demanded.

'The interrogations were rigorous, but they produced only a single interesting piece of information. The Qastt were targeting specified Cravat freighters because the Haluk promised them a colossal price for the cargos.'

'Which were?'

'The planet produces scandium, a small amount of promethium, and fifteen different biologicals – only seven of which were common to all the freighters targeted. The captive Squeak crew had no idea which product the Haluk particularly fancied. They admitted that

Haluk agents had been riding along with them in hopes of scoring. If the Qastt managed to nab a Cravat transport, the Haluk on board was prepared to summon one of its own vessels immediately, transfer the loot, and pay off the bandits in unhexocton – element 168.'

'Wow!' I marvelled. Karl said, 'But what were the hot goods?'

She shrugged. 'It can't be the scandium or promethium, even though they're Cravat's most valuable exports. The Haluk colonies have an adequate supply of both elements. Cravat biologicals are unique, but apart from an elemental concentrator and a euphoric drug, they're not exceptionally pricey on the human market. It seemed obvious that the Haluk undertook to use the Qastt as middlemen, hoping to prevent us from discovering their interest in . . . whatever it is.'

'I never heard anything about this,' Karl said. 'Didn't you liaise at all with Rampart Central?'

'Of course,' Matt said. 'We submitted a full report to Schneider's office after the interrogation. But there was no follow-through.'

I gave a suspicious little snort.

Matt continued. 'Eve brought up the incident again in a conversation we had a day or so before she went on her fatal vacation. She was disturbed about Central's apparent indifference. She said they discounted the matter's importance, seemed to think it was just another example of Haluk eccentricity.'

'Why did it bother her?' I asked.

'Eve wouldn't say. Using hindsight, in view of your evidence of Haluk collusion with a Galapharma agent, I'm inclined to wonder if she had other information that she kept to herself.'

'Where's the captured Qastt ship now? On Nogawa-Krupp?'

'Impounded and scheduled for scrapping,' she said. 'As far as I know, the crew are still in the N-K slammer waiting to be ransomed and repatriated in the usual way, once insincere apologies by the Qastt Great Congress are accepted by Toronto. The Haluk Council of Nine sent a strongly worded message to CHW Secretariat for Xenoaffairs requesting that we return the suicide's body for funerary rites, but it had already been sent to Tokyo University on an express courier ship. Scientists don't often get an intact Haluk corpse to examine and they paid Rampart good money for this one. The fact that the subject was on a pirate ship didn't make the legal eagles at XS very sympathetic to the aliens' request. Tokyo has promised to return the remains to the Haluk when the research is completed.'

'Hmm. We'll have to check on the autopsy results. I don't know that much about Haluk physiology myself. And I think we'd better postpone scrapping that Qastt ship and keep a lid on its crew until we get a better notion of what's going down.' I turned to Karl. 'Can you use that computer without anyone else in Rampart following in your tracks and compromising our investigation?'

'You betcha. What's more, I can hack tracelessly into any part of the corporate net, including Confidential Services itself. Hell, I designed both the InSec and ExSec programs . . . After they stuck me on the geriatric shelf here in Archives, I didn't have all that much to do. So I spend a lot of my time cyberprowling, checking on what the younger generation is up to. What do you need?'

'For now I want two things. First, call up the cargo manifests for Cravat freighters encountering Qastt pirates during the past two years. Then access Eve's personal log and bring up anything with the key-word HALUK.'

He rose. 'First one is easy. The other is a tougher nut to crack. The logbook will be encrypted. I'll need your sister's personal code sequence unless you want to wait a couple of weeks for me to pry open the file.'

'I have the code.' Matt opened her shoulder bag, took out her notebook, and spoke to it. After a moment she handed Karl a data-dime. 'Following Eve's disappearance, I went over the more recent parts of her log looking for clues, but I found nothing obvious. She did note the Qastt-Haluk piracy incident, but I had no reason then to consider it significant.'

Karl said, 'Hang in there for a few minutes.' He went to his computer console and got to work.

Matt Gregoire sipped the Campari and said very quietly, 'Are you thinking what I'm thinking?'

'Probably. If Eve had other information that made her suspicious of the Haluk, she might very well have decided to do an unofficial snoop job on Cravat. It's possible she got caught at it.' I had another glass of the marvellous Dortmunder beer. Mercifully, the feeling of mortal weakness seemed temporarily in abeyance. I made a snap decision. 'I'll go to Cravat immediately.'

'Good idea,' Matt said. 'The planet's Fleet Security contingent is small, but I can have a fully equipped SWAT team waiting for us –'

'I won't need an assault team. I intend to look into the matter myself. Very quietly. And you won't be going. I want you here on Seriphos, Matt, directing investigations into the corporate infiltration and sabotage angles.'

'Karl can do that kind of job better than I,' she protested. 'For that matter, you could. Your background is in corporation law, for God's sake! You were a desk jockey at ICS, not a field agent – to say nothing of the fact that you're three years out of practice.'

'I'll conduct this investigation in my own way. If you can't accept that, then bail out right now. This outfit has only one boss: me.'

Her jet-black eyes blazed. 'Have you ever been to Cravat?'

'No, but –'

'I have. It's borderline S–2 – very nearly out of the human-compatible range. It takes nineteen inoculations and Class B enviro-gear for safe walkabout, unless you want to live inside your sealed hoppercraft. The small predatory lifeforms drive you nuts nipping and pouncing and the bigger ones don't give up unless you use drastic discouragement – Kagi blasters and C-Gs and gigatazers. I have a strong contact on the planet. I can arrange all the tricky logistics without alerting the wrong people.' Her voice fell to a barely audible, fierce whisper. 'I'm going, dammit! Eve is my friend. My dearest friend! If there's one chance in a million that she's being held captive somewhere in that green hell, I'm going to investigate it myself – not leave the job to a bloody bent has-been like you.'

Ouch!

I was willing to ignore the nasty truisms, but not the imputation of an intimate relationship between the two women. My masculine disappointment must have been transparent as glass when I blurted out, 'You mean you and Eve –'

127

'No,' she replied coldly. 'I love her the way you do. Like a sister . . . Not that it makes your chances any better.'

'The thought,' I lied, 'never occurred to me.' But then of course I had to ask the obligatory trolling-male question: 'Do you have someone special back on Tyrins, Matt?'

'You might say I'm wed to my job.'

According to the rules of the game, she was supposed to add: And you? She didn't, but I supplied the answer anyway. 'I was divorced after the inquiry commission dry-gulched me and left me for the blowflies.'

My attempt at colourful insouciance fell flat. She stared at me in silence for a moment, looking me up and down, taking in my fatuous White Hunter get-up and dismissing it for the ego-propping sham it was, then letting her gaze drift away in feigned indifference.

She knew that I was attracted to her, that my impulsive request for her assistance had been coloured by the oldest of ulterior motives. It must have puzzled her that my father and Yasser Abul Hadi, men she deeply respected, had concurred in my choice and pleaded with her to accept. Under ordinary circumstances, she would never have agreed to work with me. She firmly believed that I was a rogue cop, a Throwaway for cause, and a loser. Nevertheless, she'd give me her fullest professional co-operation.

Despising me all the while.

I knew that the wisest thing I could do would be to assign her to work that would keep us as far apart as possible . . . but if I had been a wise man, I'd never have left my beach-bum sanctuary on Kedge-Lockaby.

Besides, the *piel canela* was irresistible.

I said to her, 'You can come to Cravat with me if you want to.'

She smiled in triumph, showing marvellous white teeth and dimples in her cinnamon cheeks. 'Was there ever any doubt?'

Chapter 11

Karl Nazarian came back to us with printed copies and handed them over. 'Here are the Cravat cargos. The log scan will take a little longer because of the need for a subspace link to Tyrins.'

I studied the manifests. Of the seven potentially relevant bioexport products, three were pharmaceuticals used to treat obscure human ailments and two were viral genetic engineering vectors. The final pair of biologicals, significant moneymakers, were a recreational mindbender called Red Skeezix and a marine microorganism able to concentrate the rare element lutetium from juvenile water emitted by abyssal thermal vents.

Matt frowned as she scanned her copy. 'This really doesn't tell us anything. For all we know, one of these products could be the Haluk rozkoz!'

'I can research them all quickly enough,' Karl said.

'Wait,' I told him, 'till we see what Eve's diary says.'

He and I had some more beer. My head had started to throb and my throat felt like sandpaper. I still held off using the medicuff. Matt worked with her notebook, setting up a new chain of command for Fleet Security on Tyrins during her absence. Karl and I discussed some nuts-and-bolts details of administering the new department. Finally the computer said: *Search completed. Four Haluk references found, all alphanumerical transcriptions from handwriting.*

I might have known Eve was too efficient to have a verbal logbook. No matter how hard you try, you always end up dictating more words than you need. The three of us went over to look at the display, which showed an entry with the relevant word highlighted. The first was a single sentence dated four years ago:

1.6.28: **HALUK** *DNY KDNAPG 6 FRM NAKN SWN.*

'It's Eve's shorthand,' Matt said. 'It reads: "Haluk deny kidnapping six people from Nakon Sawan."' That's a newly settled S-1 Rampart world about one hundred and fifty light-years from Cravat, adjacent to the Haluk planets that lie within the Perseus Spur. I'm afraid I have no knowledge of the case.'

'We can pull up the particulars easily enough,' Karl said.

The next item was three years old:

12.8.30: CPT S WOLLONGONG RSS GIPPSLAND CRAV-NK RUN RP DRLCT **HALUK** *LFBOAT ENCNTRD [23]31.017/15.221/+40.916 (PROX CRAV SYS). D CRW = 3 GRC, 11 LEP, 2 TST. ALSO 1 D FEM HUM. ZP IR-ID EMILY BLAKE KONIGSBERG, X-RSRCHR GALA. UNCLR SHE PSGR OR CPTV. GALA DSCL KNWL HR MVMTS.*

'Well, that's an odd one,' I commented. 'A derelict Haluk lifeboat, with assorted dead crew members and an anomalous human corpse, is found near Cravat by a Rampart ship. Zone Patrol checks the woman's eyes and finds out that she was a researcher once employed by Galapharma. It's unclear whether she was a passenger or a captive of the Haluk. I suppose the last part means that Gala disclaimed any knowledge of Emily Konigsberg's movements.'

'Funny,' Matt said thoughtfully, 'that there were so many lepidodermoids aboard the lifeboat. As I understand it, that transition phase is only minimally able to perform starship crew duties. A major screw-up by the lepidos could account for the abandonment of their principal vessel. Some Haluk personnel exec must have miscalculated badly in the assignment roster.'

'I'll do a background check on Emily Konigsberg,' Karl said, 'and get everything else we have pertaining to the incident.'

The third excerpt was briefer, from late last year, and was more of a puzzler.

11.15.31: LNCH BOB B IN TRANS CRAV/ETH COMP LV. HE FND **HALUK** *LEP HUSK + 1/2ETN TST ON BKCNTRY HNT TRP NR PICKL PH. POOR DVL! WH AWF PL TO DI BUT WH HELL DOING THR? NO SUIT ETHR. BOB RPTD TO XSEC BT NO ACTN TKN.*

Matt deciphered. 'It reads: "Lunch with Bob B in transit from

Cravat to Earth on compassionate leave." That must be Robert Bascombe, Cravat's Port Traffic Manager. He more or less runs the planet. He and Eve have been pals for years. I know him and his wife Delphine. He's the contact I mentioned.'

'Go on. What does the rest of the entry say?'

'Bascombe found a Haluk lepidodermoid-phase husk plus a half-eaten testudinal-phase body while on a back-country hunting trip near Pickle Pothole. The alien wore no envirosuit when it was in the lepido phase. That's even more unusual. Eve says: "Poor devil. What an awful place to die but what the hell was it doing there? Bob reported the incident to Rampart External Security but no action was taken".'

Maybe just sloppiness or bureaucratic inertia in Central, maybe something else. No wonder Eve had assigned Fleet Security to the Qastt-Haluk piracy incident rather than leaving it to ExSec.

'What's a pickle pothole?' I asked.

'The name of a rather notorious place on Cravat,' she said, 'a deep, elongated lake of sulphurous dark water, ugly as sin but a famous haunt of dangerous big game. Macho humans like good old Bob go to Pickle to shoot things. He took me on photo safari twice. God knows why a Haluk would be in the area – especially one on the verge of the Big Change. It must have morphed into the helpless testudinal phase unexpectedly and died when one of the carnivores found it. Bad luck. The Haluk chrysalis shell is extremely tough.'

'Let's have a map,' I said to Karl.

He was way ahead of me, whispering into the computer stylomike. A chart labelled *CRAVAT – MICROCONTINENT GRANT* popped up on a second monitor screen. Grant was an isolated blob of land in the southern hemisphere, no more than six hundred kilometres wide, surrounded by sprinkles of low islands. Prompted by Karl, the zoom-frame locked onto a piece of real estate in the microcontinent's heart, magnified, and produced a three-dimensional topographic display. Pickle Pothole was gherkin-shaped, about thirty kilometres long and seven kilometres wide. It was surrounded by lesser blue features, most of them round lakes with precipitous shores. The terrain height nowhere exceeded two thousand metres, but it was horrendously irregular, a confusion of abrupt pinnacles, sharp ridges, and swampy hollows without surface watercourses.

'Eroded limestone,' Matt said. 'A couple of the larger Cravat continents have vast solfatara fields belching smoke, hydrogen sulphide, and other filthy muck that gets swept around the planet, giving it almost permanent smog and incessant acid rain. Grant and most of the other southern micros are nonvolcanic, all sedimentary rock. Geologists call the kind of country on this map karst. It's something like a giant distorted waffle – enclosed valleys of dense forest almost impossible to penetrate via surface routes. The water mostly flows underground except for the ponds and potholes.'

Northwest of Pickle, perhaps nine kilometres distant, was a site designated *NUTMEG-414 (MOTHBALLED)*. It was one of a handful of similar outposts on the microcontinent, all in a temporary state of disuse. 'Check that out,' I told Karl.

The computer obediently reported that Nutmeg-414 was a Rampart collection and processing site, closed down five years earlier after the raw materials were largely exhausted. While the place was operational, robot pickers had gathered diseased fruits of the exotic tree *Pseudomyristica denticulata* from the surrounding dense jungle. An automated on-site factory chewed up the rinds and eventually produced cultures of Vector PD32:C2, a virus useful in genetic engineering. Nutmeg-414 and nine other mothballed facilities on Grant were tentatively scheduled to be re-opened in two years, after which time the exotic plantlife would have renewed itself naturally.

Karl said to the computer, 'Describe Vector PD32:C2. Include commercial applications and production statistics.'

A mind-numbing blast of scientific jargon, combined with spreadsheets, appeared. He studied it and shook his head. 'PD32:C2 is produced at three hundred and twenty-seven active sites on eleven Cravat microcontinents. There are one hundred and seventy-eight other sites that are on hiatus. The viral vector has a very broad-spectrum transferase used principally by terraformers tinkering with the zygotes of exotic animals. Says here that it's also been proposed for use in "an experimental human germ-line manipulation procedure".'

'What do you suppose that means?' Matt said.

'Check it later,' I said. The headache was making me irritable and I could feel my physical strength seeping out of my bootheels. Damn it all to hell. I had no time for this sickie shit.

The old man was eyeing me doubtfully. 'You all right, son?'

'Fine and dandy. Bring up the last entry from Eve's log.'

It was from five and a half weeks ago, and referred in considerable detail to the Qastt pirate ship with the suicidal Haluk aboard. Eve didn't seem to show any exceptional interest in the incident, and there was no hint in the diary that she planned to undertake any unofficial investigation of her own.

'Not much to go on,' Matt commented ruefully.

'It's plenty,' I corrected her, 'when you add my Haluk encounter to the overall equation.'

Karl said, 'You're still determined to search for Eve on Cravat?'

'Matt and I will leave tomorrow, first thing. I've got a suitable starship. We'll drop in unannounced on Bascombe and get him to take us to the pothole. It's as good a place as any to start, and Bascombe himself needs to be put through the wringer. Meanwhile, you carry on here.'

'Now wait a minute!' Karl protested. 'There's got to be more to this new outfit of ours than pinning a deputy-sheriff badge on me while you and Matt go galloping off to the other end of the Spur. We've got an intelligence-gathering apparatus to set up, new personnel to approve. To say nothing of deciding ... direction our internal investigation of Rampart Central and ... should take ...'

Whoa!

Karl's voice fading. My visual input flickering. Room tilting off plumb. Something icy blooming behind my breastbone and an iron spike piercing my right temple. I clutched the edge of the computer console just in time to keep from keeling over.

Brain says: Stay upright eyes focus pain go away come again some other day shit shit shit ...

Through a blur, Matt Gregoire's face registered shocked understanding. 'Why, you're ill, Helly! You're still recovering from the dystasis treatment, aren't you? For heaven's sake, sit down.' She took one of my arms and Karl grabbed the other. They drew me back to the easy chairs at the fireplace.

'You push yourself too hard after one of those tank sessions,' Karl chided me, 'you'll find yourself back in the hospital. Maybe we ought to postpone the planning until tomorrow.'

'No, we'll do it now. Tomorrow I'm off to Cravat. Just give me a minute to regroup.' I took off my hunting coat, rolled up my left shirtsleeve, and selected a fresh fix from the medicuff. The drugs in the armlet took hold and turned me moderately bright-eyed again. Karl and Matt were silent. Their expressions said it all.

'I'm okay,' I assured them. 'The doctor back on Kedge-Lockaby said that this weakness will pass. The armlet has everything I need to keep me going.'

'On Cravat?' Matt said dubiously.

'I've got a great nurse-bodyguard. Wait till you meet him. Now, can we start making plans?'

During the next three hours we created the new Department of Special Projects. It would work completely outside Rampart's normal protocols and have its own independent communications system. Karl rustled up a crew of six savvy, well seasoned, indisputably loyal ex-security agents whom I interviewed one by one on encrypted vidphone. They agreed to report for duty tomorrow. Three of them, former Internal Security research operatives, would investigate the vanished pals of Clive Leighton and covertly probe Rampart for other Galapharma conspirators – paying special attention to Zared, Dunne, Rivello and their close associates. The other three, retired ExSec field agents, would attempt to ascertain whether sabotage had taken place. None of the new people would be privy to the Haluk angle.

Karl himself would check out the more obscure uses of Vector PD32:C2, as well as the other Cravat biocommodities. He would also compile dossiers on the six people allegedly kidnapped by Haluk, plus the deceased scientist Emily Blake Konigsberg. Two broader research projects of his involved an updated report on the Haluk themselves and their relations with the Qasst, plus a data-search for any other human residents of the Spur who might have gone missing under circumstances that implicated either alien race.

I expressly forbade Karl to undertake any further inquiry into the background or whereabouts of Quillan McGrath, alias Bronson Elgar. Now that I was actively on the trail of Galapharma maggots inside Rampart, the big Concern would have a greater motive than ever for eliminating me. The logical man to do the dirty deed was Bron, and I didn't want him scared off.

No indeedy. One of my principal duties as Vice President for Special Projects was to act as bait in my own trap.

Now that I was a citizen again and, like Matt Gregoire, a security officer at Rampart Starcorp's alpha executive level, I was what the lawyers term a *praefectus conlegius* of the Commonwealth Judiciary. It was now perfectly legal for me to take suspected lawbreakers into custody, squeeze them like lemons, and turn over the evidence gleaned through interrogation to CCID prosecutors.

If he didn't manage to kill me first, McGrath/Elgar might just be the key to destroying Galapharma Amalgamated Concern.

When our schedule of operations was complete I asked Karl and Matt to take a break and summoned Simon to a private meeting in the little conference room adjacent to Karl's office.

My father arrived looking subdued and anxious. He sat quietly as I described the new organizational set-up and the assignments, and after I'd finished he asked, 'What do you need from me?'

'Your authorization for unlimited expenditure and for Rampart employee co-operation with me and my agents.'

'Way ahead of you. You asked before, remember?' He handed me three small plastic rectangles, niobium Rampart credit cards made out in the names of Helmut Icicle, Matilde Gregoire, and Karl Nazarian. Three more cards, bright scarlet, were 'open sesame' documents endorsed by him, enjoining all Rampart employees to co-operate with me and my two top associates on pain of instant dismissal and disenfranchisement.

He said, 'Anything else?'

'Karl will need a secure location for our offices and the best computer and encrypted subspace communications equipment available.'

'He'll have it within twenty-four hours. How about starships? Additional personnel?'

'Taken care of, but the less you know about them, the better. Are you heading back to Earth right away?'

'Yes. Daniel and I have to huddle with the legal department and prepare an official response to Alistair Drummond's tender offer ... Dammit, Asa – if only Rampart had managed to get Concern status! Then Gala wouldn't be able to touch us.'

I'd forgotten that Simon had mentioned that prospect when he'd visited me in the hospital. 'Is there any hope of it being approved?'

'We've lobbied our brains out in Toronto for over two years. Every time we seem to round up enough delegate votes to get the application out of committee, some glitch hamstrings us. Delegate Kovalev, our man in ICS, resigned from the Assembly because of ill health last year. His successor turned out to be in the pocket of the Hundred Concerns.'

'Tough luck.'

'We lost another vote when Söderstrom was linked to a Reversionist group selling embargoed computer equipment to the Insaps of Wigan-Sleet. He was impeached and may end up indicted for treason ... But in a real way, we're our own worst enemy! You probably know that Rampart's earnings picture over the past few years isn't as solid as it could be, which doesn't help our push for Concern status. Over seventy more Spur worlds ripe for immediate exploitation. But we've had to rein in plans for expansion because of all the setbacks.'

'Mmm.'

'And then there's me – maybe the biggest obstacle of all! A fuckin' dinosaur clinging to the corporate leadership. Not willing to name a successor.'

It surprised me that he was aware of the problem, although it should not have. Shrewd and strong-willed as he was, Simon could never fill Ethan's boots.

I said, 'Would it help Rampart's status-upgrade case if you named Eve President and CEO?'

'So you figured that out, did you?'

'By a process of elimination. Eve's the only one suited for the job.'

'Damn right! She'd have to prove herself, of course. Clean up our messes. Get some significant new operations going. Demonstrate to the galaxy that Rampart still has plenty of gumption – that we deserve to stand up there with the best of 'em, steering the government of the Commonwealth as one of the Hundred Concerns. Eve had a lot of ideas that we talked about last fall at the Sky Ranch, some of them pretty radical, but –' He broke off, shaking his head. 'Asa, just tell me what else I can do to help you find her.'

'If you give Alistair Drummond a few crumbs of hope – schmooze the old python – it may forestall any adverse action against Eve by her captors. We've turned up some longshot clues to her whereabouts that I'm going to follow up on personally.'

His weathered face brightened. 'Tell me! Does it have anything to do with those goddamn Haluk?'

'I'm not sure. I may have the answer within a few days.'

'Call me on *Mogollon Rim*. You have my personal subspace code.'

'If we find Eve,' I said, 'you'll be the first to know. But for God's sake, don't mention the Haluk angle to anyone. Not even the family.'

'If you say so.'

'I absolutely insist! And that brings me to another crucially important matter we haven't touched on yet, one that also pertains to the family. You realize, don't you, that Mom's quarterstake is pivotal in preventing the Board of Directors from accepting a hostile Galapharma tender offer?'

'Of course. But Katje always votes the way I tell her to. She trusts my business judgement.' He scowled. 'So far.'

'You'll have to put Mom in the picture. Tell her what's been going on, including your suspicions about Zared's disloyalty, my close scrapes, the warning message you got, the possibility that Eve may have been killed. Then –'

'*On hold!*' Simon said furiously. 'That bastard said Eve was on hold, not dead! And why should I tell Katje? It would only get her riled up.'

I forged ahead, ignoring the outburst. 'Mom has to understand the seriousness of the situation: that all of her children are in deadly danger – and so is she – if she still plans to will her quarterstake to that collection of xenocharities without reserving family control of the voting rights.'

His eyes widened in dismayed comprehension. 'Oh, hell. I see what you're driving at.'

'If she dies – perhaps in some convenient accident – and her shares pass absolutely to the charities, their directors will jump at the chance to exchange Rampart stock for Galapharma's, which is more valuable. Zed controls Emma's 12.5 per cent, and he'd vote for the merger as well. Those two blocks of stock would counter your own 37.5 per cent. That would give Thora Scranton and the minor stakeholders the deciding votes. Would Thora stick with you – or go with Zed and the charities and agree to the takeover?'

'Thora would stick with *Eve*,' he said bleakly. 'She's got her doubts about my leadership. It was one of the reasons why I'd decided to step down as CEO.' He was silent for a moment. 'Do you really think Katje is in danger?'

'Your note from the hired gun said "three at risk",' I reminded him. 'Dan and Bethany are the other two, and they'll have to take strong precautions. But I think we can neutralize any threat to Mom if you convince her to change her will immediately, putting her shares into a trust benefiting the charities. The trustees can be Dan, Beth, you, Gunter Eckert and herself. With the establishment of a trust entity, any motive for killing Mom or trying to coerce her vote through threatening you or her children vanishes. Not even Galapharma would dare to murder all five trustees.'

Simon shook his head. 'Katje might not agree. Most of her so-called charities are nothing but Insap-coddling Reversionist front groups. She won't let anybody else control the money pipeline to her precious radical causes.'

But I knew the answer to that one. 'Set up the trust with Mom as sole disburser of benefits. She'll retain control of the money, but the votes will be controlled by the other four trustees.'

A smile quirked my father's thin lips. 'You know, with a set-up like that, we could even elect your sister Bethany to the Rampart Board of Directors as representative of the trust. Remove Katje! I've been trying for years to find a way of securing that quarterstake your mother inherited from Dirk. There was always a danger she wouldn't go along with me in the voting, out of spite or even some half-assed Reversionist political agenda. But if she thinks it's the only way to keep you children safe from those Galapharma maniacs –'

At that, I exploded. 'God damn you, Simon! This isn't about votes and boardroom finagling, it's about my mother's life! She matters. Eve matters. So do Dan and Beth. Apart from them, the Rampart Interstellar Corporation doesn't mean jackshit to me! Can't you get that through your thick head?'

The hooded green gaze glittered. 'What about me? Do I matter?'

'Don't push your luck,' I said.

Amazingly, he burst out laughing. 'Any other orders?'

'No.' I turned away, drained of emotion as well as stamina, lacking even the energy to hate him, wishing more than ever that I could tell him to go to hell. Every bone in my body ached. My own quotient of gumption was at minus ebb. I checked my watch. It was 1752 and I had been at Rampart Central for nearly five hours. I was sick and tired of planning and palavering, yearning for sleep the way a man lost in the desert craves cool water. But I still had to meet with Mimo to organize the perilous trip to Cravat, and confirm that Ivor Jenkins had agreed to sign on with us.

Simon and I left the conference room and went back into the main office. Matt and Karl were standing by the holo window watching the tranquil scene in silence. A chestnut mare had joined the black stallion and a long-legged colt was frolicking in the illusionary sunshine, trampling the asphodels. In the distance were mountains with snowcaps.

The former security chief eyed me with concern. 'Helly, you look beat down to the anklebones. Go get some rest before maintenance has to scrape you off the carpet.'

'I'm okay.'

Matt Gregoire said, 'Don't be a stubborn fool!'

'I'll rest tomorrow. Right now, you and I have a dinner date with a smuggler.'

'A *what*?'

'Our chauffeur to faraway places, Captain Guillermo Bermudez Obregon. You'll like him. He sings old-fashioned Mexican ballads, drives a brand new Bodascon Y660 cutter, and really knows how to use his ship's cannons.'

She looked helplessly at Simon, who merely shrugged.

Crossing to the transport entry, I pressed the call-pad and said to Karl, 'I'll talk to you before lift-off tomorrow. You know what to do. Do it.'

Karl pretended to be insulted. 'Is he always like that?' he asked my father querulously.

'Seems like. God knows where he gets it from . . . Well, us two old geezers better sit down at your computer and find this Mickey Mouse outfit a good hidey-hole. Then I think we ought to go out and get shitfaced together.'

'Good thinking,' said Karl Nazarian.

Chapter 12

It was going to take *El Plomazo* thirty-one hours to reach the planet Cravat at maximum pseudovelocity of 60 ross. I spent the first twenty-seven of those hours unconscious in my cabin, allowing my body to restore itself and enjoying sweet REMories of my Kedgeree island home, courtesy of Mimo's dream machine.

When I finally surfaced around noon ship's time on the second day out, I felt almost normal. I called Mimo on the intercom. '*¡Hola, mi capitán!* You guys have lunch yet? I'm famished.'

'That's good news,' he said. 'A hungry man is one on the mend. We'll be eating shortly. How does pasta, salad and citrumquat sorbet sound?'

'Perfect. What's a citrumquat?'

'Join us in the dining salon in half an hour and find out. Meanwhile, you might like to look over the information sent by your friend Nazarian via subspace encrypt.' I thanked him, pulled the data out of the ship's computer (unlike lost saucy *Chispa*, *El Plomazo* communicated in stern masculine accents), and made a hard copy. There were also two holovid dimes from Karl's archives with background on Cravat's natural history and the production of PD32:C2. I put them aside.

The first section of the printed report was a background summary and statement of the operation's objectives. A tidy mind, old Karl's. There was no new information on Eve's disappearance or on Clive Leighton and his buddies, although our new team was beavering away. Two of the field agents had been dispatched to Rampart worlds where Galapharma-inspired sabotage might possibly have taken place. The other four were working with

Karl in the secret lair Simon had found for our establishment in the sub-basement of the Vetivarum Public Database.

Our computer wizard was pursuing an interesting trail, attempting to decipher the highly convoluted routing of a crucial subspace-patch call made on Lois Swann-Hepplewhite's phone. In it, Clive had presumably warned his Galapharma controller to tell the missing trio of execs to flee for their lives, all is discovered. More ominously, Leighton also could have notified the molemaster of my own presence on Seriphos – not dead as presumed but very much alive, kicking ass, and flinging Simon Frost's name around in an overfamiliar manner.

A successful trace of this call was a very long shot, since it had caromed through the telecom systems of four planets like a manic pinball. The odds were slightly better that *other* Galapharma hench-folk working in Central had also used the distinctive secret routing some time within the past twenty-four weeks, reporting to their glorious leader. (After that time interval, interplanetary communications records were purged.) If this proved to be the case, portions of the peculiar pathway itself might be detected by a cybersleuth, even if the ultimate message recipient remained unidentifiable, and we might be able to finger other corporate traitors and put them under surveillance.

Of course, if the molemaster knew his stuff, he'd change the com routing regularly and the net result of our sifting would be zero. But it was worth a shot.

Another of our research operatives had ascertained that the untimely death of Rampart Chief Research Officer Yaoshuang Qiu had been attributed to a cerebral aneurysm with unseemly haste. Without Qiu's leadership, a vital division of the Starcorp had been floundering for months while Zared first named a successor who turned out to be disastrously inadequate, then procrastinated in searching for his replacement. The CRO's body had received a traditional Chinese burial on Seriphos. Our agent was arranging for a secret exhumation in an attempt to prove murder. He was also checking the background of the physician who had certified Qiu's cause of death.

Weird thing: the University of Tokyo was balking for some

reason at releasing their bioassay of the Haluk suicide's cadaver. Karl had decided to ask Simon to put the screws on personally, since Rampart was the scientific community's best source for more Perseid dissection subjects, and the Starcorp was under no obligation to sell to the highest bidder.

Two other nuggets of information gleaned by Karl himself were particularly noteworthy.

The six people allegedly kidnapped from the planet Nakon Sawan four years earlier turned out to be genetic engineers from a local terraforming installation. The only witness, an employee of the catering service returning to his quarters after a long night's carouse, claimed that he saw a single gracile Haluk prowling around the building where the abductees had been working.

Although the blood-alcohol content of the witness was 175 mg/dL (i.e. drunk as a skunk), his statement was verified under psychotronic interrogation. No other signs of Haluk presence were detected by Rampart External Security, nor was there any record of a Haluk vessel entering or exiting the planetary atmosphere. However, Nakon Sawan had been newly settled in 2228, and its meagre satellite sensor array was down for repairs on the date in question. Surprise, surprise.

CHW had forwarded Rampart's official protest on the Nakon incident to the Haluk Cluster and asked for permission to scan their eleven Spur colonies for human life-signs. The request was rejected by the Haluk Council of Nine. Zone Patrol attempted the scans anyhow, at long range, with negative results. Since evidence of Haluk involvement in the Nakon abduction was so flimsy, the matter was shelved by the authorities. Rampart had paid death benefits to the engineers' families.

Karl's second significant discovery concerned Emily Blake Konigsberg, deceased. She had been a physician and distinguished professor of xenobiology at Stanford University on Earth before being hired away by Galapharma in 2226. Her particular area of expertise was DNA mapping of Insap races of the Perseus Spur. In 2228 she had left Gala to go into what was described as 'private research'. Karl had found a mountain of data on her work at Stanford, but he ran into a blank wall trying to discover what her duties had been at Gala, and what her private research project might have involved.

The mysterious presence of her body on a derelict Haluk lifeboat drifting in space near Cravat in 2229 remained unexplained. There was no evidence that Emily Konigsberg had been abducted, nor was it illegal for an unaffiliated citizen to consort with an alien race. The powerplant malfunction that cut off the lifeboat's environmental system and killed those on board had also wiped out navigation data that might have indicated the boat's point of departure or destination.

When Haluk authorities were informed of this incident, they professed no knowledge of Konigsberg and would not speculate upon why she had been travelling on a Haluk ship. The Haluk remains were returned to their people. Konigsberg's body, as requested by her surviving brother, was transported to Earth and interred in the family plot.

Karl also sent along voluminous information on Vector PD32:C2, including the interesting fact that it had been in extensive use at the terraforming establishment on Nakon Sawan. Sales figures for PD32:C2 showed purchasers of record over the past ten years: the Commonwealth itself was the largest customer, with the fifty or sixty Concerns who maintained their own colonies making up the balance. Galapharma was one of these. Its purchases of PD32:C2 weren't excessive, given the vast scope of its operations in the Orion Arm and Sagittarius Whorl.

PD32:C2 was only one vector out of thousands of useful megacarriers on the market. The virus's particular value lay in its ability to transfer very large amounts of DNA into both the ordinary body cells and the germinal cells of higher animals. Following the procedure, the engineered individual would not only be physically altered, but would also reliably produce offspring like itself.

Karl had also researched the 'human germ-line manipulation' project utilizing PD32:C2 that had mystified us. It turned out to be a controversial joint operation sponsored by Galapharma, Carnelian and Sheltok Concerns that had never actually got off the ground. In 2226, they had sponsored preliminary research on the creation of a new Homo subspecies capable of surviving on certain heavily irradiated, notoriously inhospitable R-class planets deep within the galactic hub.

Some of these awful places were chock-full of unhexocton, unhexseptine, and other ultraheavy elements coveted by Sheltok's energy division and Carnelian's atomic chemists. Robot refineries, controlled by human workers from orbit, had proved prohibitively expensive; but highly modified humanoids living on the planetary surface could probably have produced the rare elements economically.

Minor genetic modification of humans to enhance adaptation to T-3 or S-class colonies was already a fact of life; but earlier proposals to redesign people for R-worlds had always been defeated in the Assembly on ethical considerations. The necessary genetic engineering would be so drastic that the new species could not survive on earthlike planets. Instead, they'd be condemned to permanent exile in places that made Dante's Inferno look like the beach at Waikiki.

Sheltok, Carnelian and Galapharma had been very displeased when their project was condemned by the Commonwealth Assembly. Sheltok's CEO even professed surprise at all the fuss. After all, the banished humanoids would have been very well paid . . .

I set Karl's report aside, shucked off my pyjamas, and put on a pair of jeans and my OK Corral sweatshirt, thinking about what I'd read. If my team and I could follow this improbable data trail and make a connection between Gala and the Haluk, then so could Eve. It had been imprudent of her to undertake a clandestine investigation on her own, rather than alerting officials of the Interstellar Commerce Secretariat or the Department of Xenoaffairs, but it was understandable.

She had no proof.

Eve lacked my own first-hand evidence of the link between Galapharma Concern and the aliens. If she had gone to ICS with her suspicions after Rampart External Security failed to investigate the testudinal Haluk corpse found on Cravat, the Secretariat would certainly have declined jurisdiction and passed the buck to DXA. DXA would bump the inquiry to Zone Patrol, an outfit that probably included even more paid Concern informants within its ranks than DXA. The Patrol would come galumphing into Cravat on its big flat feet with sirens wailing, and any ne'er-do-wells on the scene – alien or human – would vamoose faster than a raped ape, covering their tracks behind them.

Eve would have known that. Like me, she could also have had doubts about the loyalty of Ollie Schneider and his Rampart ExSec force. Since the issue had such explosive potential, she might not even have trusted her own Fleet Security people (or her pal, Bob Bascombe) to keep a lid on it – especially if evidence might link Galapharma or the aliens to traitors inside Rampart.

She could have decided to do a quiet preliminary check of the Pickle Pothole region herself, the one place where clues of Haluk chicanery might exist. Perhaps she'd planned to report her findings directly to Simon.

It had been a mistake. Maybe even a fatal one.

Mimo and Matt were already seated at the round messtable, waiting for me to join them for lunch.

'High time you showed up,' said Captain Bermudez. He wore a natty pearl-pink corduroy zipsuit with a blue turtleneck. Matt had on athletic track gear and her dark curls were damp. I presumed she'd been working out in the ship's gym.

'Everything going well?' I inquired. 'No villains in hot pursuit?'

'Not a one,' Mimo said. 'I put us on an aleatory course for the first few hundred light-years and did repeated scans as we zigged and zagged. Nobody chased us. By now we're so far out in the Spur tip that the chances of a bandit picking up our energy signature are minimal.'

It was the one disadvantage of using *Plomazo* for transport: there were only a handful of Y660 cutters in the Spur, and all but Mimo's belonged to Commonwealth Zone Patrol. Our hyperspatial trace was thus nearly unique, and readily identifiable to anyone who cared to search for it – not that the search would be easy. The concealing dissimulator field Mimo had used so successfully while hiding inside comet Z1 only worked in a orbital situation, in which the ship used minimal sublight drive.

'By now, Galapharma certainly knows I'm alive and aboard this ship,' I said. 'There's a possibility that they might deduce that we're headed for Cravat. Especially if Eve is being held there.'

'Our medium-heavy shields are up,' Mimo soothed me. 'Even if a hostile does spot us and mine the hyperspace trajectory, we'll get by unscathed. And they haven't a hope in hell of catching us when we drop to subluminal velocity in the Cravat system. Now sit down and stop fretting.'

Plomazo's messroom, like the rest of the new starship, combined efficiency with touches of outright opulence – justifying its designation by Mimo as a 'dining salon'. The furniture was polished garnetwood, a handsome Mexican wrought iron chandelier hung over the table, and the viewport that opened onto fire-streaked starry space was flanked by hand-woven draperies and colourful jars of ornamental cacti.

There were four place settings of casual Lenox china and sterling flatware. I said, 'Where's Ivor?'

On cue, he pushed open a swinging door and entered the salon, beaming. He wore a striped apron and carried a tray laden with food. 'I'm right here – the designated *chef de cuisine*!' He put down a big platter of pasta in redolent tomato sauce, a bowl of bean salad and four coldcups containing some frivolous dessert, then took off his apron and joined us.

I helped myself and sampled the pasta. 'This is great! A real improvement over the meals-ready-to-eat stocked on poor old *Chispa*.'

'I made the lunch from scratch,' Ivor Jenkins said. 'That's *spaghettini alla carrettiera* with fresh basil and lots of garlic.'

'He's insisted on doing the cooking during the voyage,' Mimo said. 'Matt and I have dined like royalty while you slept your life away.'

The giant youth ducked his head shyly. 'I wanted to earn my keep.'

'You'll earn it when we get to Cravat,' I said. 'Even with environmental gear, it'll be rough duty.' Ivor wasn't wearing the myostimulator collar and I made a mental note to be sure that he put it on before we tackled the playful wildlife of Pickle Pothole.

Matt said, 'I'm still opposed to working the back-country of a hazardous world like Cravat with so few people. Bob Bascombe can surely furnish us with dependable guides and a security team –'

'No,' I said. 'We're sneaking into Cravat unannounced in *Plomazo*'s gig. The starship stays in orbit with its dissimulator up and Mimo keeping an eye on things. Bascombe himself is going to take us to the Pickle Pothole area, where we'll begin the search. I don't want anybody else on the planet to know we're there.'

Matt scowled but made no further comment.

I scarfed down a big plate of pasta and advanced to the cold piscoid and kidney bean salad with crunchy red onion. Ivor had done some creative shopping back on Seriphos. The fish analogue was very tasty and the citrumquat sorbet dessert turned out to be sweet-sour and refreshing, topped with a dollop of clotted cream and a sprinkle of raspberries. As we finished up with embargoed Upper-Orinoco-blend coffee, I offered my ultimate compliment to the cook: 'Nice going, Ivor. I couldn't have done a better job on the grub myself.'

'It's something I learned to do at an early age,' Ivor said. 'My father and I had to fend for ourselves after Mummy left, and he's always been too preoccupied with business to care about cooking.'

Matt gave him a sympathetic glance. 'What does your father do for a living?'

The young man looked away, suddenly nonplussed, and I remembered how Mimo had described him as 'the son of an associate'.

Captain Guillermo Bermudez said, deliberately, 'Ivor's father is in the import-export trade, as I am, Chief Gregoire.'

'I see.' Matt sipped her contraband coffee with equanimity. 'Most Rampart employees who live in the Spur owe a debt of gratitude to people such as you and Ivor's father. Life would be drearier – and a great deal more expensive – if we were forced to buy all our little luxuries in Starcorp-approved outlets ... Don't worry, Ivor. My official duties as Fleet Security Chief have been shelved for the duration. And God knows I've bought as much ex-tariff goods as the average citizen.'

'So you *are* corruptible!' I joshed her.

'Only where French perfume and Belgian chocolates are concerned,' she retorted. 'Not insofar as neglecting to protect the lives of witnesses in my custody or falsifying evidence.'

Mimo opened his mouth to defend me. I said, 'Never mind. Matt's entitled to her opinion of me, which she's made clear from the start of our association. I don't have the inclination or the energy to rehash ancient history now.' I nodded at Karl Nazarian's report, which I'd left lying on the table. 'Have all of you had a chance to look that over?'

Ivor was clearly grateful for the change of subject. 'I haven't seen it. But perhaps you don't wish me to be privy to such sensitive material.'

I gave a snort and tossed him the print-out. 'I didn't bring you along to be chief cook and bottlewasher, Ivor. You're a full member of the team. Give this a quick run-through. I'm going to need input from all of you, trying to make sense of it.'

'I'll do my best,' he said.

'The part of the report that bothers me most concerns the possibility of Haluk involvement – both in Eve's kidnapping and in the Galapharma conspiracy. I'd like your opinions on why these aliens seem suddenly willing to put aside their longstanding xenophobia, get chummy with Gala, and perpetrate a series of crimes that could result in massive retaliation by the Commonwealth. It's obviously got something to do with genetic engineering. But what?'

'The most obvious answer,' Matt said, 'is that the Haluk may want desperately to do some radical lifeform-modification of their own. Perhaps on T-3 planets in their own cluster that they hope to colonize. I presume you know that they have a rather severe population surplus.'

'Refresh my memory,' I said. 'I really don't know much about the race at all.'

'The Haluk evolved in a smallish satellite star cluster seventeen thousand, two hundred light-years off the tip of the Spur. Their peculiar allomorphic cycle was a response to the home planet's elongated orbit that made the world excessively hot and dry and UV-irradiated for about half their year. Haluk are carbon-based oxygen breathers who use nitrogen, sulphur, and phosphorus to make proteins just as we do, and their bodies derive energy from the Krebs cycle, just like humanity. Given a choice, they prefer to live on T-2 worlds that are warmer and more arid than the T-1's that Earthlings and Squeakers favour, but they can manage very well on terrestrial worlds.'

'Sounds like they'd adore Arizona,' I muttered. 'I bet they'd get along just dandy with the Gila monsters and sidewinder rattle-snakes. Compatible temperaments, too ... Sorry, Matt. Don't let me interrupt.'

'I'll try hard not to,' she said wryly, then continued the lecture. 'The Haluk have colonized all of the genome-compatible T-1 and T-2 worlds in their own bailiwick and desperately need *Lebensraum*, but expansion into the Milky Way Galaxy had to wait until their inefficient starships were up to the task. When they finally made the leap to Spur-tip about a hundred and twenty Earth years ago, they established settlements on eleven worlds that were ideally suited and made big plans to colonize more. But they were stopped in their tracks.'

'By the Galapharma invasion of the Spur,' I noted.

'Exactly. Over a four-year period beginning in 2136, the Concern exploration fleet inventoried all the planets in Zone 23 – excluding the Haluk and Qastt worlds that had been designated off-limits by CHW under Statute 44. Gala claimed all the remaining T-1s and T-2s. Since the Haluk Council of Nine adamantly refused to enter into trade agreements with humanity, CHW told them to forget about colonizing any more worlds in our galaxy. Galapharma ExSec and Zone Patrol backed up the ruling with force ... for as long as the Spur seemed worth fighting for.'

The Haluk never dared all-out warfare with humanity over the colonization issue. They knew they didn't stand a chance of beating our superior technology. Under duress, they entered into a non-aggression agreement that was more honoured in the breach than in the observance, and continued to harass human starships and colonies when they thought they could get away with it. Like the much less numerous Qastt race, with whom they formed a thorny alliance, the Haluk officially maintained that 'uncontrollable outlaw elements' of their society were responsible for the piracy and the landside smash-and-grab raids.

When Galapharma pulled out of the Perseus Spur, the Haluk got their expansionist hopes up again – only to have them dashed by the coming of Rampart.

'But I don't see how this meshes with their new interest in genetic engineering,' I said, 'much less Bronson Elgar's claim that Gala and the Haluk are now allied for purposes of *mutual* benefit.'

'Maybe,' Mimo suggested, 'the aliens have made a deal to use human biotechnology to modify the biota of T- and S-class worlds back in their own star cluster. They could theoretically gain thousands of new worlds to conquer after turning vicious and yucky ex-genome critters benign or tasty with the help of our superior science. As a payoff, the Haluk might open all their worlds to trade with humanity. Gala could get Most Favoured Concern status.'

It still didn't make sense. 'Then why didn't the Haluk make their deal with Rampart, rather than going secretly through Gala middlemen?'

'Maybe Galapharma offered them something that Rampart doesn't have,' Matt said, 'or wouldn't sell, even if the price was right.'

'Like the Perseus Spur itself?' I said satirically.

A silence, of the variety called pregnant, fell over the table.

'Oh, come on!' I scoffed. 'Not even Gala would be that crazy. The Concerns don't own the Commonwealth yet! They can't make a treaty with a sovereign alien race. Besides, Gala's top execs have been kicking themselves ever since Rampart moved in and proved that the Spur could be economically viable. That's what their takeover bid is all about. They *want* Perseus.'

'Galapharma owns thousands of worlds in the Orion and Sagittarius sectors,' Matt said. 'It doesn't need all of the habitable Spur planets.'

'No,' Mimo agreed. 'Only the ones with the most valuable resources.' 'There are three thousand and sixteen human-compatible worlds in Zone 23,' Matt said. 'Sixty-four of them have sizeable Rampart colonies. Another two hundred or so are sparsely settled freesoil, former Gala outposts with exploitable commodities, potentially annexable by us. The rest are Rampart-dedicated under ICS mandate, but presently uninhabited by humans. Perhaps Galapharma has offered all of those worlds to the Haluk.'

Mimo lit a Romeo y Julieta Fabulosa. It smelled like spice and cedar. 'Gala could do it quite legally, you know – after acquiring Rampart. The Assembly would have no reason to disapprove if it was convinced that such a move would open vast new markets in the Haluk Cluster, as well as in populous Haluk Spur colonies. The aliens would gain not only *Lebensraum* but also a tremendous scientific leg-up as they traded raw materials for human high technology.'

'It might be the answer,' I conceded. 'But it still doesn't explain why the aliens would try to steal PD32:C2 and kidnap human scientists who know how to use it. Why take the risk if Gala is selling them its expertise?'

Ivor Jenkins had finished reading Karl's report and put it down on the table. He had listened to our discussion, frowning judiciously. Suddenly he said: 'Perhaps the Haluk aren't really interested in the modification of planetary biota at all. What if the genome the aliens want to modify is their own?'

'*¡Caracoles!*' Mimo whispered. 'Imagine how much progress humanity would have made, if we were forced to spend nearly half of every four-hundred-day year in a state of hardshell hibernation as the Haluk do!'

'Aestivation is the proper term for dormancy during a hot, dry season,' Ivor corrected him.

Mimo shrugged. '*No importa*. It's still a hell of a way to live.'

'The Assembly has persistently forbidden any major tinkering with human genes,' Matt said. 'I hardly think it would accede lightly to significant genetic alteration of another sapient species – even by that species itself. There'd be lengthy debate over the potential consequences. Approval might be doubtful.'

'Damn straight,' I said, 'given the track record of the Haluk. If their physiology became as efficient as ours, the balance of power in the galaxy might eventually be knocked into a cocked hat. Fifty years down the line, they might decide it's their manifest destiny to expand into the Orion Arm.'

Matt's expression was grave. 'Would Galapharma even consider that possibility? Or would its executives only think about the marketplace?'

'Bolster the old bottom line!' I proclaimed cynically. 'That's all any of the Hundred Concerns care about. And I don't think Rampart's all that much better –'

Brrap! Brrap! Brrap!

A skull-piercing ship's alarm went off. I nearly jumped out of my skin and Mimo bit right through his expensive cigar. He leaped to his feet and raced into the corridor leading to the bridge. I was right on his heels. Every loudspeaker in the ship broadcast the steely tones of the computer's warning:

Interception alert. Interception alert. Vessel on closing course. Tentative ID Haluk. Estimated time of arrival within photon weapon range, five minutes thirty seconds.

Chapter 13

Seated in the command seat, Mimo turned off the alarm and calmly said, 'Navigator, program random evasive action.' Then: 'Computer, explain tentative identification of approaching vessel. Is it Haluk or isn't it?'

Ultraluminal drive trace is modified Haluk, said the computer. *Conformation does not equate with any known Haluk starship.*

'Show me!' Mimo demanded.

The bandit was still too far away to pick up on full visual scan, so the main viewer produced a silhouette with dimensional indications, pseudovelocity and subspace vector. Gripping the back of Mimo's seat in frozen astonishment, I whispered, 'Hell's bells. No wonder it was able to sneak up on us!'

The icon indicated that the damned thing was moving at an impossible 63 ross. It was another dagger-pierced doojigger with knobs on, very similar to the colossal alien starship that had come to the rescue of Bronson Elgar, but only about two hundred metres long.

Our computer made the laconic observation: *Approaching vessel matching evasive manoeuvres and continuing to close. Estimated time of interception within photon weapon range, four minutes fifteen seconds.*

Mimo told it, 'Power up weapon system.'

'This can't be,' I blithered. 'The only ships that fast are Bodascon experimental jobs – not even in production yet!'

From behind me, Matt Gregoire said, 'Tell it to the bandit. And may I strongly suggest that you sit down and get out of the captain's way.'

Mimo said urgently. 'You, too, Matt . . . Ivor. Everyone be seated. Hurry!'

I relinquished my hold on Mimo's seat-back and flopped into the co-pilot chair. There is never any sensation of movement in an inertialess vehicle; but to my shocked surprise, I heard Mimo give the order: 'Full crash-harness deployment on bridge.'

My seat glommed onto me with various liquicell appendages, rendering me incapable of movement except for my eyeballs and my mouth. I swore luridly.

Estimated time of interception, three minutes.

Mimo gave calm commands. 'Enter defensive program: on my mark, erect maximum defensive shields. Enter navigation program: on same mark, exit hyperspace. Simultaneous with emergence into normal space-time continuum, override sublight drive inertial dampening sequence. Do not – repeat do not – start SLD engines or programme default vector upon exit from hyperspace. Do – repeat do – initiate default programme five hundred milliseconds after exit.'

At that, even the computer lost its cool. *Danger! Danger! This manoeuvre is not recommended! Conservation of galactic angular momentum will–*

'Cancel warning,' Mimo broke in. 'Enter weapon system program: target pursuing starship. Maintain target lock through hyperspatial transition. At earliest enabling point, fire six homing AM torpedoes at target exit co-ordinates. Computer, now state residual time to interception and begin countdown.'

Time to interception one minute fourteen seconds . . . thirteen . . . twelve . . .

I knew what Mimo intended to do. It might save us – but it was equally likely to kill us.

Scan instrumentation on the Haluk bandit would give adequate notice of our intent to drop to sublight velocity. They'd follow. The aliens might even be expecting the manoeuvre, a classic tactic for a starship eluding a swifter ULD pursuer. They'd also be confident that our vessel would re-enter the normal space-time continuum following the same virtual course it had maintained in hyperspace, SLD engines and inertial dampening field generators kicking in automatically to compensate for galactic angular momentum.

In effect, the Haluk expected us to 'hit the ground running' along the same course we'd followed going faster than light. It was the sensible thing to do. Only after full inertial dampening had taken place, a couple of seconds later, would they expect us to commence the sublight jinking and swerving that might provide a means of escape.

Hot on our tail, firing their photon cannons as they followed us into the normal continuum, the aliens expected to nail us during our brief window of damper vulnerability.

Unless, like T.S. Eliot's elusive cat Macavity, we weren't there, where they expected us to be – courtesy of the conservation of galactic angular momentum.

Angular momentum is obscure but not mysterious. Its effects are manifest in the rolling wheel, the umbrella twirled on its stick, the carousel with its spinning painted horses. Close to the axis of the thing that rotates, the movement around and around is relatively slow. Out at the edge, the movement is much swifter. Mud clings to the hub of a wheel; but out at the rim, it loses its grip and is flung away. Raindrops are easily spun off the umbrella's edge. The horses at the outside of the merry-go-round go faster than those nearer the centre.

And in our spiralling Milky Way Galaxy, the stars and other celestial objects out at the edge – in the Perseus Spur, for example – whirl around the galactic hub at a very brisk clip indeed: well over a million kilometres an hour.

So does a starship at what is simplistically termed 'full stop'. Even though it *seems* motionless relative to the dust particles and bits of interstellar debris around it, it nevertheless maintains the angular velocity of the whirling starry carousel. It obeys the constrictions of celestial mechanics and 'conserves' galactic angular momentum.

Horrible things happen to a starship dropping out of hyperspace when, for some dire reason, it fails to execute the inertial dampening program. The ship's abrupt burden of angular velocity is instantly converted to *tangential* velocity. Like a clot of mud flung from a spinning bicycle wheel, the ship flies off to hell and gone in a more or less straight line. To our pursuer, *Plomazo* would seem to roar away in a totally unexpected direction . . . unless it broke into pieces first. Even though some inertial negation remains, the manoeuvre wrenches a starship's frame brutally and tosses unsecured occupants about like sparrows in a hurricane. If ship and crew survive, they have a brief tactical advantage against a pursuing enemy.

Mimo had allowed us half a second.

Ten seconds to interception . . . nine . . . eight . . .

Just before the countdown reached one, he said, 'Mark.'

During that excruciating hyperspatial crossover, *Plomazo* screamed like a tortured animal, stressed to the brink of annihilation. We four humans lost consciousness even though our crash-harnesses generated small bubbles of enveloping force that saved us from being excessively mashed and bashed. The ship's computer, safe inside its own independent force-field, carried out the skipper's instructions.

Five hundred milliseconds winked by. Default re-entry sequencing kicked in. The uncontrolled tumbling and mortal vibration moderated, ceased, and the ship's agonized cry faded.

It all took place too quickly for human brains to process. My heart beat, my blood circulated, I breathed, made small stupid noises, and realized that we had at least survived the manoeuvre. My blinded eyes regained normal vision, but there was nothing much to see. The bridge seemed undamaged. Still in the clutches of the crash-harness, I heard the nearly inaudible sounds of normal sublight starship operation, overlaid by the moans of my companions.

With the ship's defensive shields still at maximum, the main viewscreen remained blank. The helm console indicated full stop default. We were secure again on the galactic merry-go-round, quietly adrift. Angular momentum ruled, imperceptible to us.

Mimo said, 'Cancel bridge crash-harness deployment. Lower defensive shields.'

Why not? Either we'd won or we'd lost. Let's find out.

The viewscreen revealed a scene of sinister beauty. Dozens of faint concentric rainbow shells, onionskin layers of ethereal colour, were expanding from a dark centre and fading away against the starry dark. While *Plomazo* had staggered on its wild re-entry tangent, the ship's computer faithfully followed orders, compensated for the chaotic movement as best it could, and sent a shotgun spread of homing antimatter torpedoes toward our pursuer. At least one of them must have found its quarry. The Haluk ship had vanished utterly in a burst of gamma radiation.

The damage to *Plomazo* was minimal except in the kitchen and dining salon, where unsecured cooking gear, tableware and food-stuffs had created a spectacular mess that gave new meaning to the term 'galley west'. Ivor, who claimed that he felt no after-effects from our ordeal, insisted on going aft to restore the culinary facilities. Matt asked me very politely to accompany her to the ship's lounge in order to 'review the overall situation'. Mimo stayed on the bridge to program the repair robots and re-establish our course to Cravat.

I'd already had an emergency fix from the medicuff armlet, but the aftermath of sheer terror called for additional aid and comfort. The refreshment unit menu listed grapefruit margaritas, so I called up a pitcherful and filled tall glasses for both of us. I drained mine almost without taking a breath. No salt. I hate salt with margaritas.

Our ultraluminal entry flash filled the lounge with white light for an instant. We were on our way again. I plopped down into one of the sofas arranged in front of the observation port. Matt seated herself with more dignity and sipped her drink in silence, staring at the racing stars. Minutes passed. She began casting stern, meaningful looks in my direction.

I knew what she wanted me to say.

I wasn't going to.

Finally she abandoned tact and professional courtesy and came out with it. 'Helly, we can't continue with your original plan of action. This attack by the Haluk means that we'll have to notify Commonwealth authorities immediately.'

I said, 'No.'

'But it's the only sensible course! Now that we have proof that the aliens are involved in the conspiracy against Rampart—'

'We don't have anything of the sort. *Plomazo*'s computer can produce data proving that we were chased by an unknown ship that might or might not have been Haluk. The fact is, our bandit never actually identified himself or even indicated his intent. All he did was approach us at humongous pseudovee on an interception course. And Captain Guillermo Bermudez, Rampart hireling and suspected dealer in contraband goods, blasted him out of the ether without so much as a howdy-do.'

'But ... both you and Mimo *knew* the ship was Haluk – and hostile! You can testify that it had the same configuration as the large vessel responsible for marooning you on the comet.'

'I was a Throwaway then. My earlier evidence is inadmissible. And Mimo's would be uncorroborated and automatically suspect because of his shady background. Even if we could prove the bandit's identity, we couldn't demonstrate hostile intent. The Commonwealth isn't at war with the Haluk. Officially, we're in a state of armistice, with both sides pledged to nonaggression.'

She abandoned that angle. 'You know that someone inside Rampart must have told those aliens to come after us.'

'Probably.'

'Then you must realize that it's lunacy to mount a search operation on Cravat without a decent-sized task force to back us up.'

'Not necessarily.'

'At least let me call in Zone Patrol! I can tell them that information received leads me to believe that Eve is being forcibly detained on Cravat. ZP can have a heavy cruiser there in less than four hours. Meanwhile, we can monitor the planet and make certain that no suspicious ships enter or leave.'

'No. We're not notifying the Patrol until I'm ready – until we find evidence that no one can ignore or explain away. I told you before: we're conducting this operation my way. If you don't want to participate in the ground expedition, then stay in orbit with Mimo, watching for bad guys. Ivor and I can manage.'

'Damn you, Asahel Frost! You're as pigheaded as your father.'

I gave her my best smile, then poured another margarita.

She sat there, glaring at me, but after a moment her face softened and she asked a surprising question. 'What kind of a name is Asahel, anyway?'

'Biblical. My mother told me he was one of King David's warriors. Fast on his feet. The name's been in the Frost family for five generations. Nobody seems to know why. I've always wondered whether the other Asahels hated the tag as much as I do.'

She laughed quietly. 'Try living with a name like Matilde.'

'Is it French?'

'Originally.' For the first time she seemed to lower the barrier she'd erected against me when we first met in the Rampart board-room. 'My parents came from Martinique, in the Caribbean.'

'I've heard those islands are very beautiful.'

She shrugged. 'I wouldn't know. I've never been to Earth.'

That was a surprise. Rampart's leave policy was exceptionally generous. 'Where did your parents settle?'

'Loredan. I was born there. They had a little mom-and-pop trading post on one of the lutetium-producing islands. I was sixteen, away at boarding school on the mainland, when a pirate attack on the mine escalated into a firestorm that destroyed the entire settlement. My parents died.'

'I'm sorry, Matt. Were the pirates Qastt?'

'Human. A Rampart Fleet Security cruiser blew them out of the sky. And after that . . . it seems rather like a cliché, I suppose, but when it came time to make Career Track selection, I chose Fleet.'

Before I could draw her out further, Mimo came bursting into the lounge. A broad grin lit up his face as he spotted the frosty pitcher.

'Wasting away in Margaritaville, you two? Yes! I'll join you – and then accept a very special reward in honour of my great victory.'

Matt sat up straight, her expression instantly shuttered. I cursed my old friend silently for trashing the tête-à-tête just as it had started to get interesting.

He took a small drink and began to rummage in an elaborate humidor cabinet, gabbing away happily.

'I have one last Hoyo de Monterey Particular left that I've been hoarding for nearly a year, and I intend to smoke it right now . . . Ah! Here it is.'

'Did you look around for other bandits before engaging ULD?' I asked.

'We're safe for a while. The high-resolution scan showed no other ships of any sort within thirty light-years. This sector is rather empty of inhabited systems. I think it's very likely that the Haluk we destroyed was too busy chasing us to get off a subspace squawk.'

I wasn't as confident as Mimo that our enemies would be more leery of attacking us now that we'd shown our fangs, but I figured the odds of a successful reconnaissance were still on our side – provided that we acted quickly.

'I wonder how many of those new ships the Haluk have?' Matt said.

I shrugged gloomily. 'God knows. Sixty-three ross! Jeez Louise . . .'

Mimo clipped his cigar and ignited it with an antique Zippo lighter, taking his time getting it burning just right. The scent of the precious weed was robust, almost like roasted coffee. He drew deeply and exhaled a smoke plume in the direction of the main viewscreen. Beyond the dwindling numbers of Spur-tip stars shone a scraggly swarm of tiny lights that was the Haluk Cluster, seventeen thousand, two hundred light-years away. Once upon a time, it had taken those aliens seven Earth months or more to travel to the Milky Way. Their new clippers could do it in less than twelve days.

When Mimo spoke again, some of his good humour had diminished. 'In all my travels throughout the galaxy, I have never heard even a hint of *any* alien vessel capable of such speed.'

Matt said, 'Developing and manufacturing ships like that would be especially difficult for an allomorphic race because of their inherent physical inefficiency. Perhaps that's what the genetic engineering scheme is all about – making it possible for them to work harder and longer in the techno sweatshop.'

'Hard to believe they invented those speedboats,' I commented. 'It's as though nineteenth-century Apaches suddenly produced Jeeps to chase the U.S. Cavalry.'

'Don't insult the Indians,' Matt said tartly. 'They wouldn't have needed genetic engineering to do the job. Just automotive engineering.'

'Seriously,' I said, 'do either of you know of any evidence that

Haluk colonies in the Spur have undergone drastic mobilization?'

Matt said, 'The planets have large populations, but they're really only subsistence worlds, without significant heavy industry. If unprecedented high-tech activity is going on, it's happening back in the Haluk home cluster, not around here.'

Mimo contemplated the glowing end of his cigar, then dropped a bombshell. 'My friends, I would wager you a box of these Particulares – which I would have to return to Earth to obtain – that the new Haluk engines are human-designed. Maybe even human-made.'

'Impossible!' Matt exclaimed.

'Both ships' exhaust traces contained typical Haluk fuel-element signatures,' I pointed out.

'Nevertheless! That race of *vergas* could never have made such a vast technical breakthrough on their own. They needed help. A great deal of it – and over a period of some years.'

Matt was aghast. 'Do you realize what that would imply?'

'There's another thing I am certain of,' Mimo said. 'The sophisticated Haluk starship we just destroyed and the gigantic one Helly and I encountered in the Kedge-Lockaby system could not have been built with the connivance of Galapharma alone, nor by using human outlaw vendors of astronautical components. There would have to be multiple Concern collusion at the highest levels. What if the engines came from Bodascon? They already have prototypes undergoing tests, and their interests are closely affiliated with those of Galapharma.'

It made a horrible kind of sense. The astroindustrial Concerns had to wade through morasses of CHW safety and performance regulations before introducing new starships on the human market. Selling a few spiffy prototypes to eager aliens away off in the boondocks was illegal as all hell. It might also have been immensely profitable.

'Perhaps the shipframe was contributed by Homerun,' I said. 'Fuel innovation might have been assisted by Sheltok. Metallurgy and ceramics by Carnelian . . . If you're right, Galapharma's alliance with the Haluk is only the tip of the iceberg.'

'The imbeciles!' Matt cried. 'How could they ever justify sharing the most advanced human technology with potentially hostile aliens? What the *hell* do the Concerns think they're playing at?'

'A dangerous game,' said Captain Guillermo Bermudez Obregon.

It was more dangerous than we could ever guess. But we weren't going to find that out until we reached Cravat.

Chapter 14

From space, the planet was an uninviting sight. It was slightly larger than Earth, with 1.2 gravity – high enough to make moving around tough for me in my convalescent state after years on 0.9 Kedge-Lockaby. Scores of dark miniature continents blotched the pallid sea like eczema lesions. The cloudcover, coloured khaki by smoke from sulphurous volcanic fields, was dotted with tight spirals marking the location of intense storms. Green and red auroras shone above the poles. The world had no natural moons and only four multipurpose satellites. We futzed the lone space observer with a precise EM burst before coming within range.

Mimo erected the dissimulator shields and settled *Plomazo* into a high orbit. To ground stations, cruising bandits or other starships, our camouflaged vessel would seem to be space debris. The gig that would shuttle Matt, Ivor and me to the surface was more vulnerable to conventional surface electromagnetic sensors when powered by inertialess drive; but Mimo was confident that a certain smuggler's trick he had up his sleeve would get us down undetected.

While he and Ivor did a final check of the gig and the expedition's equipment, Matt and I contacted Bob Bascombe.

The time was just after 0300 at Cravat Dome, a sealed enclave inhabited by some eight thousand souls that was the world's only permanent human settlement. The Port Traffic Manager was almost certainly asleep in bed. I tinkered with another of the satellites and patched into the planetary comsys, then Matt simply called the man on his home vidphone.

Bascombe picked up immediately. All he would have been able to see on his nightstand viewer was Matt, while she and I both watched his face in extreme close-up on the bridge's main screen.

He was about forty years old, with a pug nose and rounded cheeks that made him look younger. His eyes were puffy with sleep and his hair stuck up every whichaway. He spoke in a crabby mumble. 'Bascombe. What?'

'Bob, it's Matilde Gregoire. Fleet Security. Turn on the phone encrypt. Do it right now.'

'Mattie? . . . What's happening?' He fumbled with his handset and the reassuring triple bleep sounded.

'Are you alone, Bob? This is very important. I need your help.'

'Help?' Pause while he blinked, rubbed his little nose, got his muzzy brain back on line, and tried to muster a welcoming smile and civil tone of voice for the inconvenient VIP caller. 'Yes, I'm by myself. Delphine . . . she's gone away to Nogawa-Krupp on holiday. Hey, she'll hate to miss you. What's up, kiddo? You just arrive? Where you staying? Why'n hell didn't you let me know you were coming so we –'

She cut off the fusillade of staccato queries. 'Listen. It's vital that you follow my instructions precisely. Do you have a data disk in your phone to record?'

'Uh? Yes . . . okay, it's active. Say on!'

'First, don't tell anyone that I'm on Cravat.'

'Checko.'

'Second, you're leaving immediately on an impromptu hunting trip. Make plausible excuses to your staff. You'll be gone at least two days, maybe longer. Nobody is to contact you during that time.'

'Mattie, I think –'

'Don't interrupt. File a fictitious flight plan. Your actual destination will be on Microcontinent Grant at 43–33–02–1 South, 172–40–16–3 East. Approach by a devious route. Make sure you're not followed. After you land, contact me on Channel 677 and I'll give you further instructions. I want you to fly a fully equipped Vorlon ESC–10 hopper, the model designed to serve as a self-contained base camp.'

'That's a pretty big ship. If I tell Dome Aircraft Pool I'm just going out alone –'

'Are you Cravat's head honcho or aren't you? Get the damned hopper!'

'Understood.' He sounded wide awake now, and sadly miffed. 'No call to get p.o.'d, Mattie.'

'I'm sorry. Please forgive me for being so abrupt, but the situation is critical. Be at the rendezvous site in four hours, 0700 Planet Mean Time. Don't be late. Lives may be at stake.'

'Depend on me, kiddo.'

She held up the scarlet Open Sesame card that Simon had provided, transmitting a close-up view. 'I'm not just asking for your help out of friendship. My request is authorized at Rampart's alpha level. I have to caution you again, Bob. Don't tell anyone about the operation, or you and a lot of others may suffer some very unpleasant consequences.'

His gaze flickered. He moistened his lips. 'Is it . . . does this have anything to do with Eve Frost?'

She tensed. 'Why do you ask?'

'I'll explain when we get together.' Without warning, he suddenly punched out.

He caught us both by surprise. I said, 'Shit! Bring him back, Matt!'

She re-entered the code, but all we got was the voice-mail menu. Bob Bascombe was not answering his phone.

'Well?' Her expression was grim. 'What do you think?'

There had been a flash of strong emotion in the Port Traffic Manager's eyes, but I was almost certain that it had nothing to do with guilt or treachery. I'd seen that look on men's faces before, as they first realized that their worst suspicions were starting to come true.

'He doesn't know where Eve is,' I decided. 'But he knows *something.*'

'If he's part of the conspiracy . . .'

I thought about it. 'I can't believe that he is. Why would he have mentioned the half-eaten Haluk corpse to Eve in the first place if he knew that illegal alien activity was taking place on his planet?'

'It wouldn't make much sense. If he wanted to lure her to Cravat he would certainly have used a less ambiguous approach.'

166

Mimo's voice came over the intercom. 'The gig is ready whenever you two are.'

'I'm willing to keep our options open,' I told Matt. 'We'll take extreme precautions. After we find out what Bascombe knows about Eve, we'll decide how to proceed. We can always leave him confined in the gig while we search the area in his hopper. If the worst comes to the worst, we can signal Mimo and he can call in Zone Patrol. What do you say?'

'Let's just get on with it.' She turned away abruptly and headed aft.

We descended steeply over the frozen South Polar Ocean. The presence of a bright aurora had told crafty old Captain Bermudez that Cravat was being bombarded by a fairly solid blast of solar-wind particles. The resulting hullabaloo around the magnetic pole effectively hid us from any ground-based electronic surveillance. Flying barely above wave-top level, we continued on for five thousand, two hundred kilometres to Microcontinent Grant, which lay on the opposite side of the world from Cravat Dome. We arrived in late afternoon, local time, during a brief break in a thundering gale that was walloping the remote landmass. Skimming the trees and dodging among ridges of red and yellow limestone, we came over Pickle Pothole's deep western end and splashed down. The gig immediately sank to the bottom of the long, narrow lake.

During the low-altitude approach, our sensors had indicated that the surrounding countryside, a confusion of 'eggbox' jungle valleys, was alive with a myriad of large animals. There was no trace of human or Haluk life. If villains were in residence, they were lying doggo – at least for the moment.

And so were we.

I sat at the gig's control console with Matt and Ivor behind me and surveyed the underwater scene outside with HRMP sonar. The cloud of mud and organic detritus that we'd pushed up was dissipating rapidly. We had landed slightly slaunchwise in the midst of a tumble of rock slabs. Ribbon waterweeds several metres in length swayed in the churning currents generated by our submergence. After I determined that our position was reasonably secure, I deployed levelling gear to put us on an even keel. Then I launched one of our most versatile pieces of equipment, a tiny multifunction utility buoy no bigger than an apple, which popped up to the surface, sprouted antennas, and flashed a modulated laser pulse to *Plomazo*, informing Mimo that we had arrived safely.

When I switched the floating device to terrain-scan mode, the large monitor screen in the cockpit showed a computer-enhanced and steadied view of Pickle Pothole's turbulent surface. And something else.

Ivor Jenkins said, 'Oh, my goodness!'

I couldn't help wincing myself as I experienced a flashback to the voracious sea-toad of Kedge-Lockaby.

This thing was approximately plesiosauresque. On the screen it looked enormous, nearly as long as our twelve-metre gig, with gleaming saucer eyes and a wide-open mouth rimmed with fangs. It appeared to be steaming straight at us like some exotic Loch Ness Monster, with obvious intent to maim and mangle.

But of course we were safe on the floor of the lake, and the pesky water-beast that had mistaken the utility buoy for its next meal was actually only about eighty centimetres long. I set the instrument's defensive blaster to the lowest sting setting and let zap. Poor little Nessie reared up against the lightning-stitched black clouds and disappeared in a welter of spray.

'We come in peace,' Matt said apologetically, 'but don't get cheeky.'

I adjusted the buoy's scan range and surveyed the northern lakeshore, about two kilometres away. Our designated rendezvous with Bascombe was a small surf-pounded cove guarded by rock stacks eroded into peculiar perforated shapes. On either side of the beach loomed limestone headlands as sharp and bare as axes. To the east and west stretched broken cliffs at least three hundred metres high, riddled with caves. Waterfalls poured from some of the lowest openings.

The rendezvous was scheduled for just after sunset, local time. We were two hours early for the sake of discretion and common sense, well concealed in the water instead of attempting to camouflage the gig on land, as Bascombe might have expected. If he set the Haluk onto us, or if he brought Galapharma partisans along in the hopper, we'd have fair warning.

But I didn't seriously think Eve's pal Bob would stiff us. What did mystify me was why he'd kept information about my sister's whereabouts to himself for so long. Even though Ollie Schneider had minimized news of Eve's disappearance on orders from Cousin Zed, I was certain that the Port Traffic Manager of Cravat would have been informed. After all, he *was* the top executive of a Rampart World, even though his bailiwick had more robot workers than people. Bascombe had deduced quickly enough that we were looking for Eve when Matt spoke to him. So why hadn't he notified Rampart Central when the alarm first went out?

There was one possible answer: Eve had told him not to.

In the submerged gig, we waited and maintained surveillance together. Ivor's presence in the cockpit insured that Matt and I would share no more sweet confidences, so we passed some of the time watching the archival holovids that had been part of Karl's report. Matt had already studied both of them, but the information was new to Ivor and me.

The first show was a sort of *Appalled Armchair Tourist's Guide to Cravat* that set out to scare the shit out of you by describing abominations of the planet's geography, flora and fauna. Summed up, just about everything was out to get you. Ivor and I kept up a running commentary of blackly humorous wisecracks to distract ourselves from the shrivelling feeling in our balls, while Matt shared reminiscences of her own earlier visits to the Green Hell, which were even more bloodcurdling than the damned video. The second holovid was something completely different, a Rampart employee orientation flick describing the production of Vector PD32:C2 in over five hundred Nutmeg processing sites scattered throughout Cravat. Like most of its kind, the video was pedantic, self-congratulatory and dull. Its implications, however, were anything but boring.

I was surprised (and disturbed) to learn that the mothballed factories weren't completely shut down during the off-season, as I had assumed. Their environmental maintenance systems continued to function, as did caretaking equipment that kept the idle processing machinery in good order. Furthermore, the robot harvester units used during regular operation made periodic excursions into the jungle to gather samples of *Pseudomyristica* fruit and bring them back to the plants for analysis. On the great day that adequate numbers of rinds were once again adjudged sufficiently diseased, the news would flash to Nutmeg–1 back in Cravat Dome, an engineer would touch a pad, and production of the viral vector would resume in the reinvigorated locale.

The holovid had nothing to say on the topic of inspection procedures for mothballed facilities. Perhaps it was all done by automation – as most of the processing was – with remote data feeds assuring the absent technicians that all was well in the hinterlands. On-site inspection by live human beings might occur only at long intervals unless the computer reported a malfunction or an emergency.

When the video ended, I asked my companions the burning question.

'Do you think the Haluk could be operating one of the Grant factories, cooking up PD 32:C2 on the sly?'

'I believe it's quite possible,' Ivor said. 'Especially if they had assistance from suborned humans. Tampering with the remote data feed from the factory to Cravat Dome would be child's play for a competent computer programmer. However, it would be considerably more difficult for the Haluk to shut down the clandestine operation and go into hiding whenever human inspection teams showed up – given the hostility of the local environment.'

'Logistics and life-support would be ticklish,' Matt agreed. 'The Haluk are a bit tougher than humanity, even in the gracile phase. However, an S–2 world would represent a severe challenge. They couldn't just camp out in the jungle. But it wouldn't be practical for them to build self-contained surface bases or retire to an orbital habitat, either. Even on this thinly settled planet, they'd surely be discovered.'

While I mulled over alternative means of alien interlopery, Matt and Ivor studied a large-scale chart of the region north of Pickle Pothole where Bob Bascombe had originally found the Haluk remains. The vector-processing plant Nutmeg–414 seemed to be the only conceivable attraction for the hapless wanderer; but the site was twelve kilometres away from the scene of his death, an inconvenient distance in such rugged terrain. Eve's diary had said nothing about the deceased Haluk having transport, but in the intellectually-challenged lepidodermoid phase, the alien probably would have been unable to operate anything more complex than a tricycle. Toward the end of the allomorphic cycle it would barely be able to walk ... until it finally turned into an immobile and defenceless chrysalis and unwillingly entered the local food chain.

If the alien had been lost, separated somehow from others engaged in exploration or the secret production of Vector PD32:C2, why hadn't its associates come looking for it? They would have known their *compadre* was on the verge of the Big Change and particularly vulnerable. Even a techno-challenged race like the Haluk would surely possess warm-body scanning equipment capable of being tuned to the racial signature. But the 'poor devil' Eve had described had perished alone and unregarded, body cooled to the ambient temperature of the jungle and discoverable only by chance or through a highly dangerous ground search.

A bright idea came into my mind that might have explained both the Haluk's presence in the middle of nowhere, and a possible way for an alien operation to remain undetected. I discussed the notion with my two colleagues, who thought it had promise. Matt wondered whether Cravat had been subjected to a complete geological survey. I relayed the query to Mimo, who sent it along to Karl via subspace, and after half an hour or so we received an answer that was no answer: if such a survey existed, it was in the main dbase at Cravat Dome.

Unfortunately, there was no way to access Dome's computer from the gig (or even from *Plomazo*) without setting off an alarm. But when Bascombe arrived in the hoppercraft, we could have him pull the data and see whether I'd guessed right.

Matt and Ivor finally got hungry and left the cockpit to find something to eat. My own appetite had vanished so I stayed behind with a glass of milk and some snickerdoodle cookies, saying that I'd keep watch through the buoy's sensors.

It was quiet except for the muted hum of the gig's environmentals and occasional sounds of our hull thudding against organism-coated rocks as we rocked in the current. I decided that Pickle Pothole would have been a lousy venue for Cap'n Helly's Dive Charters. Even with the mud settled out, plankton and some peaty natural dye made the waters murky. Now and then a dull glow of lightning pulsed up at the surface. Dim illumination from cockpit instruments revealed coiling strands of weed outside and exotic piscoids swimming among them. Small lifeforms resembling slugs and barnacles crawled on the front viewport, inspecting the brand-new neighbourhood that had dropped in. No aggressive beasts showed up. Maybe Nessie Jr had spread the word.

I finished my snack and fell into a doze, rocked in the familiar cradle of the deep, until the communicator's cheep jolted me awake. But it wasn't Bascombe calling. It was Mimo again.

'Another subspace message just came from Karl Nazarian. Tokyo University finally turned over a preliminary report on the Haluk suicide's body.'

'That's nice.' Alien autopsies weren't exactly at the top of my agenda right then, and I wondered why he had bothered to call.

'It seems that Simon Frost had to grease wheels with a new research grant for Professor Shibuya and her team before they would agree to release the data. They were keeping everything top secret on instructions from the Secretariat for Xenoaffairs.'

I came awake in a hurry. 'Let me guess,' I said. 'Modified DNA in the Haluk corpus dee.'

'*Exactamente.* The individual riding on the Qastt pirate ship had a rather good motive for killing himself. If he'd been held in custody on Nogawa-Krupp for more than a few months his secret would have certainly come out. When Shibuya's people compared the body's genome to the Haluk species map, they found profound anomalies. The sequences that program the Big Change were completely altered. Verification isn't complete, but Shibuya is almost certain that the Haluk passenger would have remained more or less permanently in the gracile phase. No allomorphic cycle. No semiannual aestivation.'

'That confirms our own speculations –'

Mimo interrupted. 'There's more, the real reason why Xeno-affairs is *loco de remate*. The big news is that the dead Haluk's chromosomes had big chunks of alien DNA: ours.'

'Human!'

'No doubt of it. Shibuya won't know the precise function of the hominoid sequences until experiments are carried out. That will take at least a year. Simon is on his way back to Earth on *Mogollon Rim* and wants you to get in touch with him at once. I could patch the subspace transmission down to you.'

The last thing I needed now was a distraction like this – and having to discuss the implications of it with my father. 'Let's hold off until I have a chance to think about it.'

'Karl is afraid that Simon has linked your Haluk-Galapharma adventures with the Tokyo evidence and drawn certain con-clusions.' Mimo hesitated before continuing in almost apologetic tones. 'Helly, your father may feel you're in over your head. And he could be right.'

'There's this motto hung up inside my yellow submarine,' I said. '"Sport-divers are *always* in over their heads".'

'I know that you're very worried about Eve,' Mimo said gently. 'The primary concern in your mind is her rescue, and after that, the survival of your family's Starcorp. But you might ask yourself how your sister would react to this snowballing situation if she were in your place. Her life is of great importance; so is Rampart. But would Eve place either of them above the safety of the Human Commonwealth of Worlds?'

'Don't you go all righteous on me, *amigo!* I've already had this argument with Matt Gregoire. We won't gain a thing by panicking and turning this investigation over to Commonwealth authorities prematurely. If Simon starts pressuring you – or shows signs of jumping the corral fence and bringing in CHW on his own hook – do your damnedest to cool him down.'

'I'll try, Helly. But my best advice to you is to work as fast as you can. Your father is the least of your worries.'

Chapter 15

Bob Bascombe arrived right on the mark, just as the stormy daylight was fading, flying in to the rendezvous without any attempt at subterfuge. If there were Haluk ground observers, I hoped they would take him for just another hunter.

Ivor and I watched the monitor screen over Matt's shoulder as the Vorlon ESC-10 descended vertically out of low-hanging clouds and touched down on the beach. The hopper was only slightly smaller than our gig. No sooner had it landed than a dozen dark shapes came slinking from the shadows at the base of the cliff and began circling purposefully. Matt zoomed in on them with the light amplifier and we saw that they were a pack of formidable predators the size of bears, quadrupeds built low to the ground. Their over-sized heads had spiny crests, buzzard-like hooked beaks, and large eyes that gleamed in the fitful lightning. One of the animals attacked the undercarriage of the aircraft, gnawing a strut with slobbering frenzy. The others seemed to be cheering their pal on.

A small hatch opened on the hopper's roof and a slender jointed arm emerged and unfolded. At its tip was a cylindrical Kagi gun that swivelled about, took a bead on the chomper, and spat out a blue spark. Gigavolts of electricity coursed through the creature. It flamed hugely, its body fluids vaporized, and a shower of incandescent residue fell twinkling onto the surf-washed pebbles. The other beasts shrank back in terror and fled. Except for a few toothmarks and a patch of soot, the hopper seemed undamaged.

'Let's see if Bascombe came alone,' I said. Matt toggled the buoy's thermal scanner. The monitor showed a spectral image of the vehicle in cross-section. Its warmest parts glowed brightly green: the dual engines, the Kagi barrel, a section of the exterior bulkhead heated by the incineration of the varmint, some instrumentation in the pilot's compartment, and the unmistakable form of one adult human lifeform sitting in the command seat, a half-filled mug of hot liquid in its hand.

She switched the buoy to communication mode and selected Channel 677, short-range and voice-only. 'Bob? Come in, please.'

'I'm here, Mattie. Speak up. Your signal's pretty weak.'

'Did you follow my instructions?'

'To the letter,' he said heartily. 'Got the bus without a hitch and no one followed me. What next, kiddo?'

'I'm going to turn you over to the person in charge of the mission. He'll explain.' She detached the small hand mike and gave it to me.

'Bob, this is Asahel Frost. Eve's brother.'

'Dan! Long time no see! Welcome back to Cravat –'

'Not Daniel Frost. I'm Asahel. The other brother. *That* one.'

Silence, then: 'Oh.'

Even in the uttermost corner of the galaxy, my name was mud.

'I'm working for Rampart Starcorp now, Bob. Vice President for Special Projects. My current, extremely special project involves my sister Eve. Tell me, did she come here to Cravat?'

Another portentous chunk of empty air. When he finally spoke the words tumbled out, as though in relief. 'Yes, she was here. She came about four weeks ago, no warning, in an express freighter from Tyrins. Regularly scheduled supply ship. Sometimes they take a few passengers. She was disguised as a middle-aged woman, unrecognizable. The ship's crew had no notion who she was. Neither did Delphine and I. When Eve showed up at our apartment in Dome and peeled off the makeup, you could have knocked us over with a feather! We never dreamed –'

'Just tell me what happened.'

'She wanted survival gear, requisite inoculations, and a hoppercraft. Said she was concerned about the Haluk body I'd stumbled across near Pickle Pothole. Wanted to find out if enough tissue residue remained for a DNA sample. I thought it was possible. Only about five months had gone by. The testudinal Haluk morph is pretty well armoured. Unless a really large scavenger showed up . . .'

'And you just gave Eve what she asked for?' I didn't bother to conceal my disapproval. 'Let her go off alone into your Green Hell?'

'I *tried* to talk her out of it! First I offered to send one of my field crews to fetch the tissue sample. She told me it was a highly confidential matter. She was the only one who knew exactly what was needed. That got me curious. You know – wondering whether Haluk chrysalids might be the source of some great new antibiotic, or some such thing. I offered to go for the sample myself. She said no. I warned her what a dangerous area Pickle was, said I couldn't accept responsibility for letting her go out there on her own. She got all in a tizz-wozz then, damn near chewed my ears off. Said she was perfectly capable of handling it. You know what a temper Eve's got. I finally gave in.'

'Why didn't you report her disappearance?'

His reply was almost a shout. 'Because she *didn't* disappear, god-dammit! Before Eve left for the hopper pad, she made me and Del swear not to tell anybody about her being on Cravat. So we promised. Three days later, the hopper she'd borrowed turned up at Cravat Starport. I figured she got what she came for, then went back to Tyrins.'

My heart took a dive. Was it possible that my sister had left Cravat after all? 'Did her hopper have a fully programmable autopi-lot? Could it have been sent to the starport from some outlying location?'

'It was a Garrison-Laguna, fully equipped. You can programme one of those jobbies to dance *Swan Lake*. But why would Eve send her ship away?' When I didn't respond, he said, 'You think somebody else did? Who?'

'Just tell me what happened after you received notice from Ram-part Central ExSec that Eve had gone missing.'

'But I never did! What we got was a missing-person advisory about a woman of Eve Frost's general description. A Jane Doe, no name given. Picture looked something like Eve, but the resem-blance wasn't striking. No fuckin' way!'

He seemed to be protesting too much, and I would have pressed him further. But Matt put a warning hand on my shoulder and proceeded to calm his ruffled feathers. 'I agree with you, Bob. The picture sent out from Rampart Central was deliberately generic. Zared Frost was trying to avoid a media sensation, having ExSec keep Eve's disappearance under wraps. He thought she might have dropped out of sight temporarily for personal reasons. How did your Cravat Planetary Security Force deal with the advisory?'

'Publicized it in the usual way. No special emphasis. I first saw it on the evening news. So did my wife. I admit Del was more concerned than I was. The missing woman might have been Eve, might just as easily have been somebody else. For chrissake – it just seemed impossible that an important Rampart exec could be the subject of a Jane Doe missing-person report! But Del wasn't satisfied. She nagged me until I put in a subspace call to Eve's office on Tyrins. The secretary said Eve would get back to me. He *implied* that she was there! I never did hear from her. But she's a busy woman, and since I hadn't stated the nature of my business . . .'

'You just put the whole thing out of your mind.'

'I tried to,' he admitted unhappily. 'Del wouldn't let it rest. She pushed me to get in touch with Ollie Schneider. But I *promised* Eve, and you know how she is –'

I heaved a sigh, or maybe just tossed it lightly aside. 'Never mind, Bob. I do know.' I instructed him to wait half an hour, then home in on the buoy's signal and pick us up.

In theory, an inoculated human being can walk about on an S-2 planet bare-bod and survive the experience. Based on the holovid I'd just seen, any theoretician who tried it on Cravat would be rash, verging on the imbecilic.

So we put on Class 2 envirosuits, extremely tough and lightweight hooded coveralls of 'breathable' fabric with glove and boot extensions. An integral backpack ventilation system filtered out noxious sulphur compounds, smog particulates, deleterious micro-organisms, spores, pollen and excess humidity. Positive pressure from the ventilator kept purified air constantly flowing out of the hood's front opening, and a frame around the wearer's face provided an additional invisible ion shield against invasive small airborne life and rain. Retractable nightsight goggles with an IR option were mounted on a headset that also had an intercom unit. A flipdown visor was useful if you encountered any of the really dire conditions Cravat sometimes vouchsafed – acid hail, flocks of kamikaze hatpin bugs, even moderate amounts of fire and brimstone in the solfatara lands.

The outfits were reasonably comfortable to move around in. Even swimming was possible with the visor sealed shut and deployment of a snorkel gadget that pulled out of the ventpack. As in space armour, you ate and drank through sipper ports – although the choice of groceries and beverages was a lot broader, since you could carry any number of different ration pouches in your backpack. It was easy enough to take a leak through the suit's pee-pipe. Defecation was also possible, using awkward little disposable sacks; but if you were smart, you saved it until you returned to base camp.

We all wore wrist navigators tuned to the local navsat. Out of consideration for my enfeebled state, my pack was small and my portable weapon lightweight – a Romuald photon carbine with adjustable beam width. Matt and Ivor picked heavier Claus-Gewitter Spotshot blasters, Ivanov stunner sidearms, and eighteen-centimetre Beretta serrated skeleton knives. Pumped by his stimulator collar, the kid was also toting an oversized pack with our survival gear and most of the food and water.

When we were ready I programmed the gig's autopilot to bring us to the surface of Pickle Pothole under inertialess drive. The ship would remain topside for ten minutes before returning to the lakebed. I intended to retrieve the little utility buoy and carry it in my pack. Besides its other functions, it was our link to Mimo. And he was the only one able to reprogramme the autopilot of the hidden gig and send it after us ... or summon back-up, using the Open Sesame card I'd left with him. I had already shown Matt and Ivor how to use it, in case something happened to me.

We exited through the cargo bay, which was secure from the rest of the ship and had decon capability, and waited on the ingress-egress platform for pick-up. It was drizzling, but the wind had subsided almost completely and the waves weren't quite big enough to wash us into the drink. I could hear surf pounding against rocks and a distant choral howling of animals. A few odoriferous molecules managed to make it through my ion screen, demonstrating how Pickle Pothole must have got its name: the lake smelled like rotting Kosher dills. Some kind of tiny midge analogues buzzed around us in thick, hopeful clouds. Leechy lifeforms emerged from the water, wriggled across the platform and oozed slowly up our legs.

The ESC-10 descended and hung beside us, humming softly, a colourless ghost craft viewed through nightsight goggles. Bob extruded the hopper's 'airlock' tunnel and it came to rest on the platform.

'You first, Matt,' I said.

She crouched and slipped inside the corrugated tube. The lock closed and performed its decontamination cycle. After a few minutes Ivor followed her, towing his enormous backpack. I used my belt com-unit to summon the utility buoy, secured it, and entered the tunnel myself. A brief zap sterilized my outfit. Then the inner portal of the hopper opened and I went inside.

The others had shed their guns and other cumbersome equipment and pushed back their hoods and eyewear. I did, too. Bob Bascombe was shaking Matt's gloved hand and uttering convivial commonplaces. He was a short man, wearing a slightly different style of envirosuit with a full helmet that tilted back. The four of us and our impedimenta crowded the main cabin of the Vorlon ESC-10, which was fitted out with spartan accommodations – narrow bunks, a compact galley with folding table and benches, storage lockers galore, and overhead racks holding a wide assortment of weaponry and miscellaneous equipment. At the rear were twin doors labelled TOILET and SHOWER.

I introduced myself to Bascombe, who had an overbright smile and a florid complexion. 'Looks like you and your team are all ready for business, Vice President Frost! Are you sure you don't want to wait for morning to do the recon?'

'Call me Helly. I have a question for you, Bob. Does your main dbase back at Dome contain a detailed geological survey of Cravat?'

'I wouldn't call it detailed.' He looked apologetic. 'Our world just isn't all that important. The microcontinents with cratons and igneous formations are pretty well mapped. So's part of the seafloor – for the promethium mining and lutigestoid mariculture projects. But no detailed surveys were made of the limestone lands like Grant. Not much potential for ore bodies or important mineral deposits there, y'see.'

'Too bad . . . I don't suppose this hopper has a rock-reader?'

'Why, sure! Shallow magnetometrics are essential for safe groundside excursion in most parts of Cravat. Grant's not so bad, but some of the other karst micros are really tricky. Place will look solid from the air, shrubs and other vegetation growing, but the soil covers only a thin shell of fragile rock with a whopping big cavern underneath. Set a hopper down – bam! – it can break right through. Can't even depend on trees to indicate firm ground. Some of them send a taproot right through the crumbly rock crust and into the floor of a cave fifty, sixty metres down.'

I gave a nod of satisfaction. 'There's a theory I want to check out right away. Fly us to the place where you found the Haluk remains and hover so we can scope out the terrain.'

We followed him to the cockpit. He seated himself at the controls and the rest of us strapped in. The hopper ascended slowly and headed toward the northern lakeshore. He kept the sky-surveillance scanner going, but there was nothing in the air except a low ceiling of nimbus clouds, flocks of four-winged bat analogues, a zillion insects, and us.

The bubble windows of the hoppercraft and our light-magnifying goggles provided an excellent view. We topped the irregular cliffs and continued inland across a line of pointed crags. Beyond them the ground fell away precipitously into a small blind valley choked with rain-forest.

We slowed and came to hover above the north end of the valley. 'This is it,' Bascombe said. 'I never bothered with a rock survey myself. Big game hunters have been coming to the Pickle Pothole area for years. Everybody knows the limestone strata here are good and strong.'

'Turn on the STP first,' I told him. 'Let's see the lie of the land.'

'You might want to neutralize your nightsights,' he suggested. 'The map's kinda bright.'

I was a little slow flipping the switch, and the luminous stereoscopic terrain projection that sprang into view against the forward windscreen seared my retinas. The valley, roughly cup-shaped with an uneven bottom, was about four kilometres wide. Its walls were extremely steep except on the side farthest inland, where a series of projecting rock ledges formed thickly wooded terraces cleft by a single long ravine.

'I found the alien body here,' Bascombe said. A red X marked the spot on the projection. 'I had my base camp here' – a red square – 'and I was tracking this humpback lacertilian through here' – dotted yellow meanders. 'The humpy was a beaut, biggest crest I've ever seen. Maybe an all-time record! Tracked the big guy this far, crashing and smashing through the bush. Then all of a sudden the critter did a vanishing act. Off the face of the planet. Not a print, not a squeak, not a tickle on the IR targeter. I started casting around – nearly fell on top of the lepido husk. The partly eaten testudo chrysalis was only a couple of metres away. Spent the rest of the day trying to scare up the humpy again, then packed it in. I gave Eve a detailed map of the area.'

'Go to rock-read mode,' I said. 'What's the depth delimitation?'

'About ninety metres in limestone like this.'

He tapped other pads. The 3-D surface projection faded to a flat crimson chart with a complex armature of emerald contour lines superimposed over it, giving details of subterranean geological structure. Even though the scan was difficult to interpret, I found myself holding my breath in sudden excitement. It seemed that what I had hoped to find did, in fact, exist.

Matt saw it, too. I heard her murmur of satisfaction.

'Rotate image to cross-sectional,' I said.

As the glowing diagram clarified, Ivor exclaimed, 'Look! There *is* a cave! You were right, Helly.'

Not just a single cavern, but a whole system. Its multiple levels underlay the entire northern wall of the valley. One branch tunnel extended in a northwesterly direction, off the projection.

Towards Nutmeg-414.

'Well, I'll be jiggered!' said Bob. 'The opening's right on the side of the hill near the ravine. Really well hidden, see? Never suspected it was up there. Damn greenery is so thick you can hardly see beyond arm's length most of the time.' He thought for a moment. 'You know, a cave would explain how the humpy I was gunning for that day managed to disappear so fast without a trace.'

I said, 'It might also explain what happened to Eve.' The deductive threads were coming together. The dead Haluk Bascombe had found might have been part of a group living in an underground facility with access to the caves. Separated accidentally from its alert, gracile-phase companions, the confused lepidodermoid might have wandered through a dark labyrinth for days before reaching the surface. Subterranean thermal scans are impossible. Its friends had failed to find it in time.

I asked Bob Bascombe if the hopper he loaned Eve had a rock-reader. 'Of course. I told you the crate was loaded. You really think she went inside that cave? But why? Your sister's no fool, Helly. She'd know the danger. Why would she risk it?'

'She was looking for proof that a very serious crime had been committed. My associates and I are after the same thing, and I think we'll have to go into the cave, too.'

'Crime? Here on little old Cravat? Explain!'

'It's a mess that we're only beginning to unravel ourselves, Bob,' I said evasively.

'I see.' He bit off the words and glared at me, the breezy good humour transformed to a surprising bitterness. 'One more time, I'm too low-echelon to be trusted by the king-shit Frost family!' Idiot that I was, I thought he was castigating Eve. 'Okay, man, if that's how it is, just tell me what kind of grunt work you want done.'

'You can start,' I said mildly, 'by making us a subterrain geological plot of the region within a fifty-kilometre radius of a place called Nutmeg-414. You know where it is?'

'Yes. It's the closest factory to Pickle. Mothballed, of course.'

'Go to the highest altitude that's practical and simulate a casual flyby.'

He shot me a shrewd look. 'You think somebody's watching us?'

'Could be.'

He programmed an appropriately evasive course that bisected the landmass and eventually took us back out over the sea, where we hovered.

'Is 414 still ex-operational?' I asked.

'Yes. All the Grant facilities have been shut down for five years. They'll reopen when the amount of virus-infected fruit available returns to commercially viable levels. The crop's been really slow to bounce back.'

'How often do your plant biologists visit the site?'

'They don't – unless monitoring equipment sounds an alarm. We've got less than two hundred engineers and biotechs assigned to the Nutmeg project and three hundred and twenty-seven factories going full blast on fourteen other microcontinents. No time to waste visiting sleepers without a good reason. The ten sites on Grant are marginal, anyhow. Almost too far from Dome to be economical.'

There was a chime. The hopper's computer said, *Geological survey complete.*

Bob hit a pad. A long printout rolled out of a slot at the side of the console. It was not nearly so detailed as the low-altitude scan, but it showed clearly enough that the central region of Micro-continent Grant was a frigging Swiss cheese. And most of the caves were interconnected.

One system, complex and multilevelled, led almost directly from an area adjacent to Nutmeg-414 to the site where the Haluk body had been found. The depth limit made its southern extent unclear, but it seemed to continue on almost to Pickle Pothole itself.

I showed the plot to Matt and Ivor. 'Look at this! For all we know, the cave system could underlie the entire landmass. They could be using all the goddamn factories.'

'Who could?' Bob demanded hotly. 'Who's down there? What the fuck's happening on my planet?'

Matt said, 'Helly, I don't see how we can keep him in the dark any longer.'

'I'll decide that,' I said. 'Nothing's really changed.'

'Yes it has,' she contradicted. 'Our tentative plan of action was predicated upon there being only a small clandestine operation going. What if it's not small? What if there's a clusterfuck going on?'

'Perhaps I shouldn't speak up, Helly,' Ivor said solemnly, 'but you did say that I was a full member of this team. In my opinion, you should give consideration to Matt's very legitimate concerns.'

'Eve might very well be dead,' I said, 'but there's a fair chance that she's alive in one of these caves. You know what'll happen if we order Cravat's little SWAT team in there? Your clusterfuck will self-destruct – and take my sister along with it. In a situation like this, a small penetration force has the advantage.'

Bob Bascombe had turned in his command seat to stare at us, and his cerebral processing unit was computing away so fast I could almost smell the ozone. You don't get to be Port Traffic Manager of a Rampart World by being a dummy.

Abruptly, he said, 'Haluk! That's what this thing is basically all about, isn't it? Eve being so anxious to check out my Haluk carcass . . . that rumour about a dead Haluk on board the captured Qastt pirate ship . . . the crazy way the Qastt have been targeting our freighters, when none of the ships carried cargoes the Squeaks usually go after. You think the Haluk are swiping PD32:C2!'

'Yes,' I said, in resignation. 'That's exactly what we think.'

'Why?' he demanded.

'Maybe so they can quit being low-status allomorphs and start playing games with the big boys – the way the Kalleyni and the Joru and the Y'tata do over in the Orion Arm.'

'God almighty,' Bob whispered. 'But the Haluk are so – so –'

'Contrary,' I supplied, appending a smile without humour. 'Right. A change in the Spur balance of power could open a monstrous can of worms. Especially since it seems that the Haluk have been upgrading their offensive technology on the sly.'

He said, 'Oh, shit.'

Matt spoke quietly. 'Perhaps we should ask Bob for his opinion on how this operation should proceed. As he reminded us – this is his planet.'

I gritted my teeth. 'What *do* you think, Bob?'

His reply was a surprise. Without hesitation, he said, 'I think you should go with your original plan, Helly – but modified. Take me along with you. Not into the cave down south by Pickle, though. I don't think Eve got nabbed there. I think they took her when she went to check out Nutmeg-414 after confirming that Luckless Larry the lepido came out of a cave that might have connected to the factory.'

'You could very well be right,' I conceded. 'But we don't want to make the same mistake Eve made. If the Haluk are working at 414 they'll have the place guarded against casual intruders. The cave route is longer, tougher to navigate, but if we went in that way we'd have the element of surprise. And we've got a map to show us the route.'

'It could take a week to reach 414 going underground the way ol' Luckless Larry did. Maybe longer. There's a better way to get inside Nutmeg sites without sounding the alarm.'

'How?' Matt asked.

Bob Bascombe told us.

Chapter 16

They were called yagas – a name originally bestowed by whimsical Russian technicians who thought the bipedal robotic fruit-harvesters resembled the hut on fowl's legs inhabited by the legendary sorceress, Baba Yaga. We'd seen them at work in the orientation holovid, droll-looking machines with bodies about the size of a two-car garage. They strode carefully through trackless jungle on jointed ambulatory propulsion units, their sensors sniffing for the distinctive spicy odour of pseudomyr-nutmeg trees. Eight smaller auxiliary robots, the 'chicks', scurried about gleaning fallen diseased fruit from the forest floor and conveyed their loot to the witch-mother for storage. When the yaga's bin was full, it hauled the chicks aboard for the return journey to the factory. During the off-season, when the harvesting operation was restricted to sampling the quality of the fruit, the forays of the big machines were more infrequent and the loads much smaller.

Bob told us he could reprogramme a yaga to return home to the barn immediately, while each of us hid in an empty chick. Once inside the fully automated receiving and maintenance area, there was a good chance we'd be able to slip out of our hiding places undetected. The idea sounded like a winner to me.

Before we left the hoppercraft I called Mimo, told him what we'd learned, and gave him special instructions. If he didn't hear from us within fifty hours, he was to use the Open Sesame card to alert both Cravat ExSec and Zone Patrol, spilling the entire pot of beans – with the exception of our theory about an alliance between certain Concerns and the Haluk. 'Don't tell anyone about that except Simon,' I said. 'He can decide how to pass it on directly to the Commonwealth Assembly. Maybe through Dan's wife Norma

Palmer. She's got enough political clout to make sure that the charge is taken seriously.'

'Fifty hours,' the old smuggler repeated. 'Two Kedgeree days. Are you certain you want me to wait so long?'

'It'll take time for us to get to the factory in the special ground transport that Bascombe is organizing, and we may have to go into the caves beneath the facility to assess the situation. The minute we find clear proof of Haluk activity or any trace of Eve, we'll contact you.'

'You know that the gig's utility buoy can't communicate from underground.'

'Monitor all of the factory's com frequencies. We'll find a way to get through to you. If another Haluk ship shows up, or you spot anything suspicious approaching our area, do what you can.'

'I understand. *Vaya con Dios*, Helly.'

'You too, *mi capitan*.'

Bob had told us that the local big game hunting crowd were pretty cavalier about landing in the jungle. It was their custom simply to zap a hole in the dense greenery with the ship's blaster and plonk onto scorched earth in convenient proximity to their quarry.

'Let's go down a little more unobtrusively,' I said. 'Maybe the rascals know we're here, maybe they don't. But no sense announcing it with a brass band.'

The rain had stopped and slender mist tendrils were rising from the forest understorey like the smoke of hundreds of small campfires. The hopper descended slowly between towering arboreals that Bob called asparagus trees and landed on the only bare patch of rock within a kilometre of our target yaga. The open space was large enough to accommodate the aircraft but without any room to spare. When I emerged from the corrugated decon tube into the foggy, dripping night I found to my dismay that we were completely surrounded by a tangle of thorn-bearing undergrowth intertwined with stout lianas. The narrow asparagus trees soared a hundred metres high out of the thicket, which looked virtually impenetrable.

Green Hell . . . but through our nightsights it was varying shades of grey.

Bob was the last to exit and seemed unfazed by our situation – even exuberant. His hurt feelings seemed to have mended. Retracting the airlock tube with his belt controller, he gave the secured ship a farewell pat as he grinned at us through his helmet visor.

'Defensive system will keep naughty critters from doing too much damage.' He glanced briefly at his wrist to reconfirm the direction of travel. All of us had primed our personal navigators with the transponder code of Yaga 414 H, the closest one to Nutmeg-414. 'I'll do the bushwhacking, okay? Follow me close and watch your tushies. We should be safe enough, since we're cutting cross-country, not following a game trail. But humpback lacertilians and red orgoglios sometimes follow you quiet and sneaky, then come roaring up from behind like gangbusters. Great sport!'

He wore a wicked-looking Harvey HA–3 blaster in a quick-draw scabbard on his back, and carried a smaller Romuald carbine similar to my own except for its fan-shaped nozzle. Lifting the latter, he hosed the vegetation wall with a swathe of photons. There was a great sizzling sound, accompanied by a cloud of smoke and vapour. The succulent foliage seared away instantly and left a corridor blocked only by brittle burnt stems that we could push through with ease. The hidden animals went crazy, setting up a din of shrieks, howls and ratchety buzzing. Bascombe ignored the noise and strode forward over the waterlogged ground, zapping away.

Matt and Ivor went side by side after him and I came last, keeping an eye out for tailgating monsters.

The route wound through closely growing trees, whose scaly trunks were too tough to be affected much by the beam of coherent light. After the first few minutes the cries of the disturbed wildlife diminished and the jungle became unnaturally quiet except for our crunching, squelching footsteps and the periodic dragon hisses as Bob incinerated the bush. There were oodles of flying insectiles, none exceptionally vicious. Now and then a small animal blundered into the freshly burnt tunnel and then fled. We saw nothing bigger than a housecat.

I had given myself a stimulant dose from the medicuff before leaving the hopper. That, plus the adrenalin flooding my veins in semi-expectation of attack by ravening beasts, left me wired and jumpy. The fact that no large animals of any sort appeared increased my uneasiness. I finally exchanged my carbine for Ivor's more formidable Claus-Gewitter, which had a better targeting scope; but the dense undergrowth and the twists and turns of our course severely limited the spotter's effectiveness. The great lizardlike predators Bob had spoken about with such macho enthusiasm could be trailing us five metres back and we'd never know it.

Most of the ground we covered was soggy but fairly level and our progress was surprisingly swift, no doubt thanks to Bob's wilderness expertise. We left the rank asparagus forest behind after about half an hour and skirted a steep-banked pond where the brush thinned, so that no burning was necessary to clear the way. Beyond the waterhole grew trees of a different variety with jagged-edged leaves and graceful weeping branches that contained both flowers and plummy fruits. Mothlike insectiles winged among them. The scene might have been beautiful viewed naturally, in daylight, but the goggles made it flat and unreal, like an antique 2-D black-and-white screen image.

The rich fragrance of spice suddenly penetrated my ionic screen, inadvertently triggering a memory, as odours will. I found myself recalling a certain winter night at the Sky Ranch in Arizona – sipping a hot cup of wine mulled with nutmeg and cinnamon, a high desert blizzard howling against the bedroom window, Joanna and I sitting naked, side by side on a Navajo rug before a roaring fire of mesquite logs . . .

'Yo!' Bob Bascombe's voice in my hood's intercom brought me crashing back to Cravat. He had come to a halt in a tiny clearing. 'We're almost on top of the yaga. Those are young pseudomyr trees growing all around. Probably a nice grove of mature ones nearby. Ground's rising, getting rockier, kind of territory they favour. You all take a break while I scout ahead. Keep sharp, though. In places like this, open to the sky a little, simurghs can spot you, divebomb you with their poop. Stuff's full of caustic alkali. Splashes right through an ion face-screen.'

He disappeared into the forest and we gathered closer together. The slick surfaces of our envirosuits were smeared with ash, mud and cooked plant sap. Matt had a splatter of dark exotic blood on her hip where she'd casually smacked a long-legged hitchhiker trying to drill through the tough fabric.

I asked Ivor, 'You doing all right in the suit?'

'It's not as uncomfortable as I thought it would be,' he commented, 'except for not being able to scratch where it itches – and forgetting not to touch the ionic screen. I find myself constantly trying to poke my fingers through it and setting off the headphone buzzer.'

'I wonder what a simurgh is?' said I. The travelogue video hadn't mentioned it, probably for good reason.

'In Persian mythology,' Ivor said unexpectedly, 'it's the gigantic, omniscient bird of the ages who has seen the world thrice destroyed.'

Matt murmured, 'Dissolved in its own horrific shit, no doubt,' and the athlete giggled.

I was watching my wrist navigator. Its glowing map showed not only the position of Yaga 414H, concealed in the trees perhaps three hundred and fifty metres away, but also bright numbered dots that represented us. Bascombe, who had modestly chosen transponder Number 4, was approaching the harvester's position.

I tongued the RF intercom. 'Can you see the machine, Bob?'

'Not yet, but I think I hear it,' said his voice in my ear. 'The jungle floor's more open and rocky around here, except for big trees. Tons of nutmegs lying around. Kind of a big surprise. We thought the crop on Grant was –'

Snap.

Silence.

'Hey, Bob?' I said.

There was no answer.

I felt my gut freeze. On the navigator. Number 4 was no longer in motion. Then, as I stared at the display, the dot moved erratically to one side and was still again.

'Let's go,' I said quietly. 'Matt, cover the flanks. Put your C-G on broad beam. Ivor, watch the rear.' We set off at a slow trot.

There was no need to bushwhack. Bascombe had followed a suspiciously wide path through head-high shrubbery. I realized it had to be a trail frequented by large creatures seeking water. The beautiful pseudomyr trees became increasingly larger and formed lacy draperies overhead. A breeze had begun to blow, dissipating the patches of mist and occasionally showering us with flower petals.

I halted. 'Listen!'

We heard a distant animal roar, bird analogues gurgling and tweeting, the sound of wind in the trees, and a purring rumble of machinery.

'Keep close,' I whispered.

The trail suddenly ended in a stony, gently sloping forest glade where the undergrowth was sparse and much larger nutmeg trees grew. Some had trunks four metres wide, with impressive buttresses. Only a few of their branches trailed to the ground.

The purring sound came from a yaga about forty metres away on the glade's uphill side, parked near a low cliff with fallen rock and heavy plant growth at its base. The superstructure of the machine, seeming to crouch on its two massive metal legs, had a conveyor protruding from its rear. A robot chick that looked like a lidded bathtub with an anteater snout and caterpillar treads squatted at the conveyor's lower end and relieved itself of its cargo, which was drawn up into the body of the yaga.

I checked my navigator again. Number 4 had shifted position when I wasn't looking and was now behind the large fruit-harvester in a tumble of rock and brush that extended to the foot of the bluff.

Bob wasn't moving.

We advanced, Matt and Ivor continually sweeping the area with their weapons. The robot chick finished doing its duty and trundled away to find more boodle. Yaga 414H retracted its conveyor and the humming sound intensified. Eerily, the harvester rose from its squatting position so that I was able to see behind it. It loomed over five metres high at full stretch, almost even with the cliff-top.

I switched my nightsights to warm-body capability, and as the scene went green I saw a string of vivid emerald splashes on the ground, together with something else that glowed brightly and was partially hidden behind some rocks. I motioned my companions to halt.

'Bob's back there,' I whispered. 'Cover me. Keep back three meters.'

I approached the shining object, then was brought up short, cursing silently. Just beyond two knee-high boulders, beneath a thorny alien shrub, I spotted a Harvey blaster still gripped by a gloved hand. Bones protruded from the torn flesh of a severed lower arm that glistened falsely green through the goggles.

I started forward again, sick at the thought of what I was going to find hidden in the bushes. There was no movement except for the fluttering of the foliage, no sign of the animal that had attacked Bascombe.

'Helly!' Matt screamed. 'Above you!'

My head snapped up, but I never saw what leapt off the cliff. Matt fired high and the actinic blast from her C-W blinded me. I heard an ear-splitting bellow. At the same time something enormous dropped out of the sky and crushed me to the ground, knocking me senseless.

Struggling in deep water, I tried to hold my breath.

Dumb damn kid, falling out of the canoe right in the middle of Lake Kashagawigamog! Evie was going to kill me. She'd warned me about going out all by myself, me still unable to swim properly even though I was nearly six. Water up my nose and down my windpipe. Chest and head hurting. Can't breathe. Crinkly brightness overhead. The surface, out of reach, and the bubbles of my life's air rising. My eyes wide open and light fading and a last plaintive thought: *Evie, don't be mad at me it wasn't my fault* . . .

A moment later I came to, fighting to draw breath. All I could see was a dazzling blizzard of emerald sparks. The face-screen alarm trilled softly in my earphones. A great weight pinned me from my shoulders to my butt, but it certainly wasn't my teenage sister pressing water from my lungs. Both my arms were immobilized – one beneath my body, the other squeezed against rock. The hideous compression of my ribcage made it impossible to speak. I was lying prone with my head turned to one side. The ionic curtain of my hood fizzed frantically as it tried to protect me from the insistent encroachment of foreign matter.

'I'll have to cut the leg off,' I heard Ivor said. 'No other way to shift the body, I'm afraid.'

No! I screamed silently. No!

'Go ahead,' Matt said in a resigned voice.

No, don't do it! Don't do it! . . .

Chwoik chwoik chwoik.

I felt nothing but increased weight squeezing out my last breath. A discordant horn-bray now seemed to fill my head and the storm of sparks was fading to black. There wasn't really any pain.

'That should do it,' Ivor said. 'I'll give it another try.'

I heard a long-drawn-out Herculean grunt. The pressure eased, then lifted away altogether. A great thud shook the ground. I inhaled raggedly, then let out a moan of relief.

'You're alive! Oh, thank God!'

I was still unable to see anything except dancing green flecks. Somebody fumbled with the ventilator backpack of my envirosuit. A cool blast of air momentarily inflated the coverall before dissipating through the fabric pores and swooshing past my face, blowing away the crud from the vicinity of the ion screen. Most of the sparks vanished. I lay between two large boulders. Matt bent close to me, her face behind its protective ionic veil only faintly visible in infrared mode. The cinnamon skin of her cheeks was transmuted to dusty olive – except for two bright green tears that trickled out from beneath her grotesque goggles.

Tears?

I passed out again. This time the dream was of her. It probably lasted only a few moments, but it was a goodie . . .

When I woke she had gone away. I heard her say, 'Just unclip his backpack and get his gun out of there. Don't try to move him yet. I have to check him with the tomoscanner.'

'Leg?' I whined pathetically. 'You cut off my leg?'

'Don't be stupid,' she said. 'It was the lacertilian's leg Ivor had to remove. That's what landed on you. We thought it had crushed you to death, but the rocks and the soft mud must have saved you.'

She knelt at my head, waving a wand over me with one hand and studying an instrument she held in the other. I heard the *boop-beep* of the small positron scanner attempting to diagnose broken bones, brutalized muscle, squashed internal organs and other *descompuesto* parts of the human anatomy.

I ventured to move fingers and toes, took deeper breaths. 'You know, except for my back starting to hurt a little, I think I'm okay.' I squirmed, groped for the eyewear switch on the side of my hood-frame and went back to normal light-amplification. 'Is the suit torn?'

'No ... You have three cracked ribs, a bruised left kidney, and massive contusions of the upper back and buttocks. You haven't aspirated any exotic lifeforms. Your suit ventilator is functional. The utility buoy you had in your pack doesn't seem to be damaged.'

I said, 'Better me than it.'

With her assistance I crawled out from between the rocks and sat up. The dead monster lay beside us, vaguely lizardlike with a great spiny hump on its back. It was twice the size of an elephant. One of its mighty legs, neatly amputated at the hock, had been thrown to one side. The head, which Matt had blasted to a charred pulp, was as big as a desk and had saw-edged teeth nearly a third of a metre long.

Great sport!

I grinned at my saviour. 'Nice going, Chief Gregoire. You got the skydiving sonuvabitch with one shot.'

'I'll fix you something for the pain.' She put the tomoscanner away and began rooting through the big pack for the meds kit.

'I really don't feel too bad.'

'You're in shock. The pain will come.'

'Thanks for crying when you thought I was a goner.'

She uttered a brief laugh. 'Don't flatter yourself.'

'Admit it. You cared.'

She said nothing, intently studying a small e-book I presumed was a first-aid manual. Not that there was a hell of a lot that could be done for me so long as I was imprisoned within my envirosuit.

Ivor had been prowling about among the boulders and brush at the base of the cliff, carrying the Harvey HA–3. When he returned I asked him to help me to my feet. 'I can't believe you lifted that monster's leg off me. The size of it! My God, it must weigh ... what?'

'At least four hundred kilos,' the kid Hercules said calmly. 'I couldn't have done it without my myostimulator collar. Are you sure you should be standing up, Helly? I could improvise a stretcher –'

'Just let me catch my breath. I'll be okay.'

Matt gave me a plastic pouch containing a mixture of vitamin-laden fruit juice mixed with painkillers from the meds dispenser and I drank it through my hood's sipping tube. Even before the drugs hit home I felt euphoric, overflowing with a goofy and irrational joy. I was alive and she *had* cried for me.

Then I remembered.

'What about Bob?' I asked.

'I'm sorry,' Ivor said. 'He's dead.'

Matt gave a low cry of distress.

'Damn it all to hell. I was afraid of that.'

'I found his remains back in the brush, partially consumed. I think he must have died instantly when the lacertilian attacked him. The later movements displayed on our navigators would have resulted from the animal carrying away his body.'

'We can't be sure that this is the same humpy that got Bob,' Matt said. 'Odds are that we have more than one in the area, unless there's a backstairs way for them to run up that cliff.'

Ivor ported the Harvey. 'This weapon's targeter shows no large lifeforms in the vicinity. Perhaps the other creature was frightened away.'

'Keep alert,' she warned, then said to me, 'Shall we check out the yaga?'

'Might as well.' I looked at the time on my wrist navigator and was surprised to find that only a little over an hour had passed since we left the hoppercraft. With Matt and Ivor following, I limped over to 414H, which was squatting again so that another robot chick could empty its load of sickly looking blotched fruit into the conveyor.

The huge harvesting machine was mud-encrusted, festooned with encroaching vegetation, and hosting a mixed bag of small exotic creepie-crawlies. It had 'arms' as well as legs, two cranes recessed neatly into channels on the sides of the cargo bin that could be extended to pick up the chicks and hook them onto brackets for transport. On the roof was an antenna housing with a small dish and a couple of spiral whips, together with a pair of defensive Kagis and a cylinder that looked as though it might contain gas under pressure. At the front of the bin, metal rungs led to an access hatch about a metre wide. Somewhere inside, I hoped and prayed, was the guidance unit that Bob Bascombe had been confident he could reprogramme, turning the high-tech hut on fowl's legs into a Trojan horse.

'Ivor,' I said. 'Would you please crawl up there and see if you can open that hatch? We need to find a redundant guidance terminal, probably just beneath the antennas. Watch out for the Kagis. If they start to deploy, run like hell.'

But the weaponry must have been taught to recognize human beings as non-threatening. After a few tentative feints produced no adverse reaction from the yaga's defences, the giant youth swarmed safely up one of the jointed propulsion units and onto the machine's roof. The hatch wasn't locked and he had it open almost at once and slithered inside. A few moments later his head popped up.

'It's filled nearly to the top with fruit. No instrumentation is visible. Devices resembling sprinkler heads are mounted on the interior roof framing, and on the upper bulkheads are four small perforated boxes labelled ROVULO–12. I believe they may be fumigation units. The number of insectiles and other small organisms skulking about in the fruit is astonishing.'

My heart plummeted. I didn't even have the heart to cuss.

So Bob had planned to access the yaga's guidance electronically – no doubt through the elaborate control-unit he'd worn on his belt. He'd either known the override sequence, or he could have called it up easily enough from the main computer at Dome via satellite link.

We couldn't. Without the entry code, we'd set off an alarm that would warn Cravat Datasys of our unauthorized presence.

I looked at Matt and she shook her head. She'd figured it out, too.

'Any ideas?' I inquired dolefully. To give her credit, she sounded neither relieved nor triumphant. 'We'll have to abort, Helly. It's the only realistic course of action. We can't simply call for a Cravat Fleet Security assault team. The message might be intercepted by Galapharma moles. We'll have to return to the gig, fly to Cravat Dome, and wave the red card. I'll assemble the best force possible and penetrate the factory. You're in no shape to lead a Boy Scout troop.'

She paused, daring me to deny it. I gave her a plucky, noncommital smile.

'We ought to call Mimo first and get Plan B rolling,' she added. 'Just in case we don't make it. We'll have to contact him anyway to rescind the deadline . . . What about Bob's body?'

I shook my head. 'It would be a magnet for predators even if we wrapped –'

'Helly! Matt! Look!' Ivor called out to us, still sitting on top of the harvester.

We'd ignored the robot chick, never noticing that it had remained stationary beside the yaga instead of going away to gather a fresh haul. Now seven more of the collectors had emerged from the grove of pseudomyr trees and chugged toward us in single file. The first arrived, deposited its fruit, and rolled aside to wait. The next one took its place.

'Jesus!' I whispered reverently. 'You don't suppose . . .'

She stared incredulously. 'Ivor did say that the fruit bin was nearly full.'

All three of us watched, transfixed, as the rest of the chicks transferred their loads to the yaga and lined up, four on either side. Then the large machine's arms unfolded and it slowly began to pick up the auxiliary robots. The workshift was over. Yaga 414H and her little ones were going home.

'All aboard!' I cried, stumbling to one of the waiting chicks. I raised its lid and crawled awkwardly into it.

197

Ivor slammed shut the yaga's hatch and slid down to the ground. He and Matt retrieved our scattered equipment, then found chicks for themselves. Like passengers in some outrageous amusement-park ride, we were hoisted and secured to the right flank of the hut on fowl's legs.

Five minutes later the yaga was striding through the green hellish night, and we were on our way to Nutmeg–414.

Chapter 17

The yaga's striding gait was smooth and unexpectedly comfortable. At first, I didn't feel much pain. Riding with the lid partially open and doing my best not to succumb to the urge to sleep, I selectively squeezed three coffee pouches to achieve maximum heat and minimum cream and sugar. One after another I sucked them up while I studied the subterrain chart Bob had made, brushing aside the odd bug or slimy that ambled over the print's surface.

The only excitement on the journey came when a bat analogue the size of a terrier landed on my chick and persistently tried to crawl inside with me. Closing the lid made me feel claustrophobic but nothing else seemed to discourage the damned thing. Finally, feeling guilty, I shot it with a dart from my Ivanov sidearm. The amount of chemical that would only stun a man-weight lifeform for an hour was probably lethal for a smaller creature.

The contour-line cave diagram was convoluted, its multiple hologram levels hard to interpret without more expertise than I possessed. A sizeable cavern certainly did lie a short distance southeast of Nutmeg-414, but the chart gave no positive indication of its total extent and depth, nor where an access tunnel might connect the cave to the factory.

I grumbled in frustration, shifted position in a vain attempt to relieve my increasing discomfort, and wished that my conveyance didn't smell quite so strongly of spice.

Then I forgot the cave problem entirely . . . because once again the nutmeg odour had triggered an extraneous thought. But this time it was not a memory but a shocking realization.

The bin of our yaga was *full*.

It was the first piece of concrete proof that illicit activity of some kind was taking place. The descriptive holovid had clearly shown that off-season sampling operations involved gathering only small amounts of diseased fruit. And Bob Bascombe had expressed surprise at the quantities he'd seen on the ground, since resumption of harvesting on Grant Microcontinent had been postponed because of presumed crop failure.

The conclusion was obvious: data feedback from Nutmeg-414 – if not from all ten Grant sites – had been faked.

I shared the brainstorm with my companions over the intercom. We speculated on how long the Haluk might have been working on Cravat and how much PD 32:C2 they'd managed to churn out. The consensus on the first query was at least two years, maybe as long as four. On the second: maybe a lot, if the fruits had been well and truly virus-infected and the crop a bumper.

I also wondered whether Galapharma had played a role in setting up the operation in the first place. The more we discussed the matter, the more that scenario made sense. In fact, it seemed the only logical way the rip-off could have been accomplished.

I assumed that the aliens had demanded more and more of the genen vector for their alleged planetary modification projects back in the Haluk Cluster. Gala and its partner Concerns could purchase only so much PD 32:C2 on the open market for their impatient client without causing a noticeable blip in the product's sales figures, which might have attracted unwanted scrutiny at Rampart Central. After all, the stuff was supposed to be only of minor use in human biotransform schemes.

If the Haluk had been desperately insistent on obtaining more of the vector – and their unprecedented collusion with the Qastt pirates proved that they were – then Gala and its allies might have been forced into the Nutmeg finagle on pain of having the 'mutually beneficial' arrangement disrupted.

Galapharma agents, with access to information dating back to the Concern's former occupation of Cravat, could have helped the aliens select an appropriate area to plunder. Teaching them how to use the automated production equipment would have been child's play. Gala might have put moles in place to expedite illicit shipments of supplies to the clandestine operation. Its agents would certainly have bribed the Dome engineers in charge of Nutmeg sampling to ensure that the Grant facilities stayed 'inactive' as long as possible.

Sooner or later, of course, an inspection team would come to the remote, marginal microcontinent to do an eyeball evaluation of the crop – at which point the secret operation would be forced to shut down.

Unless Galapharma owned the planet again by then.

Nutmeg-414, identical to other facilities of its type, was constructed of slick polymeroid that discouraged jungle life from growing or roosting on it. Its gated compound, which included a hopper-pad, was ringed by a tall electrified mesh fence and spindly-armed Kagi units on posts. The six hexagonal building modules were put together like a mosaic-tile flower with one fat petal missing. The central ops unit contained the main computer, communications equipment, robotic control, and the refrigerated vector-storage vaults. Its single outer wall also provided the principal 'human' entrance to the facility – the most likely place for setting up an intruder-alert monitor.

The other hex modules were attached at the five sides of central. Four adjoining sections contained the production facilities; the fifth, at the far left, was our initial goal – receiving and maintenance – where all robot equipment entered and exited. Its entrance was undoubtedly monitored to detect larger animals, but we didn't give a damn. No one would see us hidden inside the chicks.

Below the antenna cupola on the central module were three photon guns designed not only to defend the place from larger aggressors but also to perform yardwork and all-around tidying. One of them began zapping away prissily in our wake as the gate swung wide and we passed through onto the paved apron, sterilizing the organic matter our yaga had tracked into the compound. A sweeperbot vacuumed up the leavings.

Ahead of us, the iris door of the decon chamber opened. I called over the intercom to the others, 'Visors down and fastened, nightsights into neutral. Be ready to switch off your ventilator intake and close your eyes when we get inside.'

Bob Bascombe had laughingly called it the carwash from hell – but assured us that a properly suited human would survive it. It was a cramped place barely large enough to hold a standing yaga, and its walls were studded with arcane gadgetry. When the iris-door closed and the lid of my chick-container popped wide open, I hastily shut down my suit's air intake, squinched my eyes, and braced myself. A thundering deluge of chemical solution crashed onto my prostrate form, bouncing me around as though I were in some monstrous Jacuzzi. It was followed by a series of gentler alternating detergent baths and rinses, which washed away the liquefied remains of stowaway lifeforms. The water drained through scuppers in the chick's floor. Banks of brilliant actinic lamps switched on, drying the machinery and us and killing whatever hardy micro-organisms had survived the wash cycle. Then the lids of the chicks closed once again.

I turned on my air, cracked open the container so I could peer out, and unholstered my stun-pistol. The decon chamber was now normally illuminated and it was unnecessary to activate my goggles. I discovered that our yaga was a vivid chartreuse colour, while the chicks were cherry-red.

'Get your Ivanovs ready,' I said softly. 'You spot any aliens, give 'em at least three darts.' That dosage was enough to kill an adult human being. The Haluk were supposedly tougher than us, especially in the lepidodermoid phase, and I wanted to be sure that anybody we hit stayed down for the count.

The inner door opened and our yaga walked through into the main receiving area, a windowless room some thirty metres wide. The floor, walls, and ceiling were aseptic white. Bob had told us that there were no overhead surveillance cams in the fully automated Nutmeg factories. Troubleshooter robots that patrolled the interior, alert for malfunctions, were equipped with sensors that might conceivably have been programmed to detect intruders. Odds were, however, that the Haluk hadn't bothered.

Two other yagas were already inside the receiving module. One, opposite the entry door, was having its fruit unloaded through a rumbling power evacuator sealed to its rear end. The second stood patiently in a bay to the left while blue and gold fixbots made repairs to its leg. Tall shelves flanking the maintenance bay held spare parts in transparent pods, and a myriad of coded supply containers. A flock of inactive chicks were parked to the right of the entry. A sweeper scouted the gleaming floor for litter, and a few other small industrial robots rolled hither and yon on unfathomable errands. Our harvester clanked across the room to wait its turn at the unloader.

When it stopped moving I whispered, 'Seems clear. You two see anything?'

The responses were negative.

'Okay. Everybody out of the tubs. Make it quick. Into the rear of the maintenance bay, behind the bank of blue cabinets. Ivor, give me a hand. I'm stiff as a plank.'

Matt covered both of us, her Ivanov stunner held at the ready, as the powerful young man helped me to alight and half-dragged me into the shadows. Two hours of travel in the chick along with the carwash pummelling hadn't done my injuries any good. The analgesic I'd swallowed earlier had worn off and now every movement was agony.

I stood next to the wall swaying, hands trembling as I retracted my visor, dragged off my hood, and unzipped the front of my suit to get at the medicuff armlet.

'Is that safe?' Ivor asked me anxiously.

'The factory interior is okay,' I told him. 'Nearly sterile. No telling about the caves, though. We'd better keep our suits on, but there's no reason why we can't breathe the ambient air ... *aaah!*' I'd found the cuff's dose pads, hit myself with max painkiller, and experienced blessed relief. For good measure, I added a stimulant jolt.

Matt watched me, frowning. 'You can't just keep taking that stuff. Sooner or later you'll crash.' She had flipped back her hood and headset. The dark curls were damp, the pressure of the goggles had made marks around her nose and eyes, and her cheeks were streaked with sweat. She looked adorable.

'I'll be fine once we get moving,' I told her. 'Stiff muscles are the worst of it.'

'No – your bruised kidney is the worst of it,' she contradicted me. 'You'd better check your urine for blood, and I want to see your back injuries, too.'

'I'm in charge of the Boy Scout troop again, Matt.'

'Only if you're fit! Take off your suit.'

We argued. She won. While she and Ivor sorted through our equipment, deciding what we'd take with us, I retired discreetly behind the bank of parts cabinets and divested.

Underneath our suits we wore polypro turtleneck sweatshirts, pull-on baggy pants, and soc-moc bootees with contour soles. I used one of the sealable defecation pouches to collect some precious bodily fluid and checked it out. There was an abnormal pinkness, but not too much. The dull internal ache of the damaged organ bothered me a lot less than the residual pain in my bashed upper back and rump. Leaving the souvenir for the sweeperbots, I shambled back to join my companions.

'Any blood?' Matt was brisk.

'The vintage was not quite fumé blanc. I'd call it a negligible rosé.'

'Let's see your back,' she ordered. Muttering, I hoicked up my shirt and turned around, and damned if the woman didn't pull open the elasticized band of my pants, sneak a peek at my bruised buns, and let go with a sharp snap. I yelped, and my heart gave a little leap.

Purely clinical . . . or curious?

'Colourful,' she diagnosed, 'but at least the skin is unbroken. There's nothing to be done about your cracked ribs outside of a hospital. The first-aid manual says they'll heal without treatment. You should take an antibiotic for the kidney. Does that armlet thing of yours have any in stock?'

'No.' I was still rapt in speculation over the waistband snap.

'Never mind. We'll get some from the meds box.' She punched the appropriate code on the sealed container and it delivered two little pill-popper units designed to be used with the sippers of envirosuits.

She shot the AB perles directly into my open mouth. I swallowed them, gave her a manly chin-up smile, and started pulling my envirosuit back on.

'Ivor and I have sorted through the equipment,' Matt said. 'His pack is too bulky and conspicuous, so we'll leave most of the survival gear and food behind. The Ivanov stun-guns should be our weapons of choice from here on in. I'll bring one of the Claus-Gewitters on a shoulder-sling and Ivor will take Bob's Harvey. He's also got the utility buoy and its com-unit in his small pack. Your sore back won't tolerate any weight, so we'll hang a canteen and a carry-pouch with rations and TP and a few other small items of equipment on your belt. Is that acceptable?'

'Perfect.' I struggled to get my stiff right arm into the suit sleeve. Ivor silently helped me. I zipped up, fastened the belt and secured the stun-gun holster, and put on the headset with the goggles retracted. 'Where's the subterrain chart?'

'I have it.' She spread it on top of one of the parts cabinets.

'About three hundred metres southeast of the factory is a sizeable cavern that looks promising.' I pointed it out on the map. 'If the Haluk are using it, they'd most likely have cut a connecting tunnel to the closest hex module. Unfortunately, that would be on the opposite side of the building.' I showed them how we would have to pass through the central ops unit to reach the module that housed the end of the vector-production line and the presumed tunnel. 'Any questions?'

They looked at me in silence, Ivor's eyes full of eager excitement, Matt's *ojos negros* sombre and troubled.

I stowed the chart in my belt pouch, drew my Ivanov and selected the three-dart option. 'Let's go. Ivor, you're tail-gunner again. Keep checking our rear. Matt, stay beside me whenever you can. Let's try to move as quickly as possible.'

The door to the ops module was to the right of the unloader. It was a conventional manual slider with a recessed latch. I did a countdown to three, then whipped it open. We discovered a vestibule that was devoid of life. An airlock with EXIT above it obviously led to the compound outside. Two switch-off loaderbots flanked it. There were no surveillance devices visible.

Other doors on our left were labelled CRYOSTORE and OPERA-TIONS. I slid open the first with great caution. When the room proved to be unoccupied I motioned the others to follow me inside.

We checked the cold lockers where packages of PD 32:C2 would ordinarily be kept until collection. Every compartment was empty.

'Funny,' I said. 'They must keep the stuff down in the caves.' We moved on, giving the ops room a miss since it was the most likely place to be infested with supervisory Haluk. The last door at the far end of the vestibule had a sign saying PRODUCTION 4.

'Heads up,' I whispered. 'This could be it. I'm gonna take a peek first. Stand out of range.'

I sat down creakily on the floor beside the door, opened it an exiguous crack and looked in. No human being ever expects to be spied on at knee-level, and I hoped the Haluk were similarly constrained.

At first I saw very little. The room was much more dimly lit than the vestibule, and a bulky piece of orange-painted equipment was parked almost directly in front of the door. I finally identified it as a roboporter, probably intended to carry packages of PD 32:C2 from the end of the production line to the cryostore. It was deactivated. I motioned for Matt and Ivor to wait and crawled into the production room, pistol in hand.

The robot was large enough to hide me from the view of the five Haluk at work out on the factory floor.

They were in the asexual lepidodermoid phase, thick-limbed, barrel-bodied, tridigital, their swollen heads riding neckless on broad shoulders. The leathery skin was a dark indigo colour, having a rough, pebbly texture. The five individuals were in differing stages of the allomorphic cycle. Each one varied in the number of dull golden scutes scattered on its trunk, upper arms and thighs. Those having the fewest dermal plates were most agile, while their more pachydermatous mates toiled in ponderous slow motion. The large eyes beneath sheltering brow ridges were masked by a dark-pigmented protective epithelium and resembled gleaming balls of jet. Their noses were mere horizontal slits and their mouths tightly pursed sphincters. The heads of all five were densely scaled, an evolutionary device that had once been essential, eons ago on their appalling home world, protecting their brains from increasing solar radiation as the planet raced in its elongate orbit toward perilous perihelion.

Four of the alien workers were hauling containers from the terminus of an elaborate packaging machine and clumsily stacking them on two simple wheeled hand trolleys. Low-tech carts for low-mentality porters. The fifth, a minimally scaled being wearing a utility belt whom I took to be the foreman, stood at the machine's manual control panel starting and stopping the flow of containers for the convenience of the others.

I crept back into the vestibule to Matt and Ivor. He helped me to my feet. 'They're in there,' I whispered. 'Five lepidos. Come ahead slowly. There's a big robot just inside the door that we can hide behind.'

We watched for about ten minutes until both trolleys were stacked head-high. Then the foreman shut down the line and spoke a few guttural words in the alien language to the labourers, who clapped their hands listlessly in what must have been a gesture of assent. They paired up and began pushing the two heavily laden carriers toward the far side of the room, where other machines and storage racks loomed in semi-darkness. About three metres from the wall the sluggish procession halted. The leading Haluk spoke again and the others shoved the trolleys close together. All five gathered around them and the foreman touched one of the controls on its belt.

We heard a whirring sound. The aliens and their load of PD 32:C2 began to sink very slowly on a circular platform.

'It's a lift!' I hissed. 'Shoot! Take 'em out right now!'

Matt and Ivor surged past me, firing the nearly silent stun-guns as they ran. The foreman fell first, uttering a faint wail. The others folded apathetically one after another, probably too dull-witted to realize what was happening.

With the descending lift still less than a metre below the floor, we jumped down onto it. Packages of viral vector went flying, some tumbling down the lift-shaft. I landed on top of the foreman's body with a painful jolt and nearly slipped off the unguarded edge of the platform. Ivor seized my arm in a steely grip and hauled me back aboard. I still clutched my Ivanov, even though I hadn't got off a single shot.

An alien moan sounded. It was the most thick-skinned Haluk of the bunch, still moving. Matt clambered over the fallen and I heard *zzzt-zzzt-zzzt* as she fired one last triple-dart burst, then curtly announced, 'All zonked now. Or dead.'

I thrust my pistol back into its holster and knelt beside the foreman, unfastening its utility belt. We were moving down through a roughly cut shaft with walls that gleamed with seeping water, passing nooks and crevices and one big unlit side-tunnel fanged with dripstone.

'This gadget is probably the lift control,' I said, studying the belt. 'Let's see if I can manage an emergency stop.' There were three studs – white, black and green, labelled with alien hieroglyphs. I hit white, since it would be brightest for lepido eyes with built-in sunglasses.

Bingo! The whirring sound cut off and we juddered to a halt. I listened intently, but all I heard was the tinkle of dripping water and a very faint rushing sound.

'Ivor, put on your goggles, go to long-range IR, and see if you can spot anything live moving around down at the bottom.'

He flopped onto his stomach and did a scan. 'No one below, Helly. The remaining depth is one hundred and seventy-two metres, according to my optical rangefinder. Well below the area scanned in the subterrain chart. All I can see is the base of the lift mechanism and several empty hand-carts. There's light coming from a tunnel at the left.'

I had Ivor position the two loaded trolleys to conceal both the Haluk bodies and ourselves from anyone who might be inside the tunnel, and then we resumed our descent. As it happened, the precautions were unnecessary. We alighted into the dank and puddled rock chamber at the bottom of the shaft.

No one was visible in the dripping passage, which doglegged after a few dozen metres, cutting off the line of sight. The tunnel appeared to be a natural formation only slightly modified to accommodate wheeled vehicles. Tiny lamps, glowing pallidly yellow, were affixed to the walls at wide intervals.

The tireless Ivor stacked the Haluk bodies onto one of the empty carts and wheeled them away into a dark alcove opposite the lighted tunnel. The rushing sound, which I presumed to be an underground watercourse, was somewhat louder in that direction.

We started down the twisting corridor, pushing one of the vector-loaded trolleys as a shield. After about fifteen minutes we reached a downgrade and the floor became artificially corrugated to help restrain the rolling stock. We moved slower and slower so as not to lose control of the trolley and finally reached the tunnel's astonishing end. It opened onto a kind of wide natural balcony edged with a rough-hewn parapet, perched in the upper reaches of an immense vaulted cavern. Golden standard-lamps on the floor far below provided soft illumination. Baroquely ribbed pillars of pink, ochre, and white calcite supported a lofty roof hung with countless stalactites and unusual blade-shaped formations resembling frozen curtains. A long ramp led down from one end of the balcony, curving halfway around the cave's perimeter before reaching the floor.

It was a scene of eerie beauty; but the most remarkable part of it was a sparkling transparent force-umbrella thirty metres in diameter that took up the greater part of the colossal chamber, fending off the moisture dripping incessantly from the speleothems. Beneath it was a raised round stage of what looked like black glass. At its centre stood a pedestal surmounted by an irregular cluster of throbbing jewel-coloured spheres – amethyst, tourmaline, amber, and deep garnet. They were pierced and entwined with glowing neon-red tubing that branched into multitudinous filaments in the lower reaches of the fantastic construct and appeared to flow down onto the stage and spread across it in all directions like a network of burning ripples on inky water. Surrounding the light-sculpture were row upon circular row of upright clear cases about two metres high – several hundred of them, lit spookily from below by the scarlet web on the floor.

Each case had a body inside.

'Jesus God,' I murmured, letting my pistol sag.

The three of us peered over the parapet rim. I flipped down my goggles, switching them to distance mode. As I had suspected, the coffin-shaped receptacles were actually dystasis tanks full of life-supportive fluid, similar to the apparatus that had healed my own comet-scorched carcass. Their contoured internal frames held gracile Haluk, humanoid morphs so unlike the clumsy lepidodermoid phase as to seem a completely different species.

Their skulls were well-formed, crowned by manes of straight platinum hair that drifted in the fluid like fine seaweed. The faces were inhuman and hideous, the skin slate-blue with prominent pale ridges on the forehead, cheeks and slender elongated neck. Their wide-open eyes were very large, almond-shaped, and brilliant azure overall. Each body was modestly clad in a long silvery shift that left only the arms and long-toed feet exposed, but the characteristic gracile wasp-waist was discernible in silhouette.

Haluk technicians dressed in white coveralls moved among the genetic engineering subjects, checking the equipment and making notes on magslates.

Matt had donned her goggles, too. 'Helly,' she whispered. 'The innermost ring of tanks. Look carefully, almost directly opposite from us. Maximum magnification.'

I did, and caught my breath in an involuntary gasp of horror as the field of view sharpened.

The hair of one immersed figure wasn't platinum but golden brown, short and curly. Her skin was waxy pale blue, with the pattern of alien ridges only beginning to form on the brow and the lower half of her slender bare arms. Her features . . .

'Oh, Evie,' I said. 'What the hell have they done to you?'

Chwoik!

A sizzling beam of coherent photons flashed above our heads. Behind us, somebody laughed.

The voice was familiar. 'Easy does it, Cap'n Helmut Icicle. Or should I call you Asahel Frost? All of you! Hands up and drop your pistols or you're fried meat.'

I hesitated, then opened my fingers and let the stun-gun fall. I heard the weapons of Matt and Ivor hit the rock a moment later.

'Howya doing, Bron?' I said conversationally, lifting my arms. 'Or should I call *you* Quillan McGrath?'

Chapter 18

He was inside the tunnel and his commands echoed hollowly.

'Helly, turn around very slowly. You other two, don't move. Touch the long guns on your backs and you die.'

I did as he said, my vision hampered by the goggles still in distance mode. They provided me with an extreme close-up of the hit man's blank-eyed unmemorable face and a foreshortened blurry view of the blaster he held shoulder-high. As I shuffled crabwise I swept my eyes over the dim area behind him. The pupillary zoom of the goggles refocused on a quintet of armed guards standing abreast. Two of them were human and three were gracile Haluk. They wore elaborate fighting suits of flexible armour plating with full protective helmets and carried Allenby carbine stunners larger and more powerful than our Ivanovs.

'Who's that with you, Bron?' I called out. 'The Five Musketeers tricked out for Star Wars?'

He said, 'Shut up and move away from that cart.'

'Whatever you say, *hombre.*'

He had us cold, and it was my fault. Then I noticed that his squad of chuckleheads were pointing their guns toward the rocky ceiling because of restricted space in the passage. Only Elgar himself had us in his sights. The peripheral rangefinder in my optics pinpointed him at 6.2 metres away, far enough so he might not hear me whisper into my intercom mike.

He said, 'Here's how it's going to be, Helly. Two of my troops are going to advance and relieve your friends of their other pieces. Then we'll go downstairs and take a brief attitude-adjustment tour –'

As he blabbed away I let my head droop, tongued the headset

switch, and breathed instructions. 'When I say *go* Matt and I hit the deck. Ivor, do a carom body-block and shove the trolley into the tunnel. Matt, try to hose 'em from below with your beamer.'

'– so you can see how your sister's looks have improved. The Haluk are getting very efficient at genetic engineering. But then, they've had some excellent teachers.'

I raised my head and kept my voice steady and casual. 'Whose bright idea was it to transmute Evie into an alien? Yours? Is that supposed to be some kind of ultimate leverage ploy against Simon?'

Bronson Elgar laughed again. 'My idea? Not bloody likely. As a matter of fact, the –'

'*Go!*'

Matt and I took a dive and Ivor moved with unbelievable speed, whirling about and flinging his great mass against the loaded trolley. It went flying toward the assassin while Ivor rolled across the stone floor toward me.

Elgar was caught flatfooted. He did the only thing possible – fired his Harvey at the oncoming juggernaut. There was a deafening clap of sound as the cart and its cargo of PD32:C2 were blasted to expensive molecules. The tunnel-mouth filled with smoke, concealing our assailants and half-blinding us. I ripped off my goggles and groped for the lost Ivanov. If I'd had any sense I'd have switched the eyewear into IR mode, but my only thought was to rid myself of the confusing magnification.

A hail of Allenby magnum stun-flechettes zinged around us, ricocheting off the parapet. I could hear Elgar shouting obscenity-laced orders to his minions, but he made no attempt to blast us. I hoped he wanted to take us alive.

In a half-sitting position and close beside me, Matt struggled to pull her C-G around and bring it to bear on the attackers, but the beamer's sling had snagged on her backpack. I found my pistol, got up on one knee, and let off a wild salvo of darts into the swirling murk. Even fighting armour has chinks.

I got lucky and heard an inhuman shriek doppler into a moan. One down.

Ivor was squirming toward us, unarmed, like a bear swimming

through swamp gas. God knows where his own Harvey had got to. A big dart caught him in the cheek. He grunted, convulsed, and fell motionless.

An instant later another magnum flechette tore through my sleeve, nicking my right arm. I didn't get a full dose of sleepy-juice as the poor kid had, but enough of the drug entered my system to paralyse that entire side of my body. I dropped the Ivanov again, writhing, and blindsided Matt just as she managed to fire her Claus-Gewitter. Its beam shot impotently towards the cave ceiling.

An instant later Bronson Elgar loomed over the two of us. He lifted his blaster and cracked its butt against the side of Matt's head. She collapsed, taking me down with her. I landed on my back, right on top of my pistol. A thunderbolt of agony from my injured ribs lanced through my skull. Somebody screamed and then it was very quiet.

Elgar stared down at us. There were four guards with him, two human and two Haluk, covering us with their Allenby stunners.

'You really are a fucking great nuisance, Cap'n Helly.'

'I do my best,' I mumbled. The right side of my face had gone numb and suddenly I couldn't see properly out of that eye. I twisted my left arm around cautiously, groping for the Ivanov pinned beneath my torso. The smoke was still fairly thick.

Elgar gave a weary curse and kicked me viciously in the spareribs. The world became a whirlpool of excruciating flame and I heard the screaming start up again. It was me. One more kick and I was gone away into the deep dark.

When I came around my wrists were fastened tightly together behind my back and my ankles were also bound with something that felt like wire. I lay on one of the ubiquitous transport trolleys, being taken for a bumpy ride by a Haluk guard. He had his helmet visor open and his weapon slung across his shoulder. Each small jolt down the washboard corrugations of the wall-ramp caused a small explosion of agony in the part of my chest where Bron had given me the boot. Vomit rose in my throat and I began thrashing, gagging and spewing.

The alien stopped the cart and scrutinized me. His electronically translated voice called out in oddly flat accents.

'Commander Elgar. This one regurgitates and coughs violently. It is possible that he will suffocate if the gastric contents are drawn into his respiratory system. Instructions are required.'

Bron, somewhere ahead of us, sounded impatient. 'Sit him up and hold his head. That's a water container on his belt. Splash his face when he quits barfing.'

'Barfing does not translate,' said the alien.

'When he stops throwing up,' said one of the human guards helpfully. He had been following behind us.

The artificial voice said something but I was too consumed by my own misery to hear clearly. The Haluk trooper yanked me roughly into a sitting position. With malice aforethought, I aimed the next round of puke at the polished armour on his legs.

'Go to your incestuous mother's necrotic copulatory orifice,' the alien said, skipping aside too late. His human comrade gave a snort of laughter.

I forced out an anguished bellow that was not entirely fictitious.

'What the hell are you doing to him?' Elgar exclaimed in exasperation. He came striding back up the ramp. Ahead, a second cart pushed by the other two guards had come to a halt. The bodies of Matt and Ivor lay on it in a heap.

'One has done nothing to him,' my Haluk said. 'The prisoner has deliberately filthified this person with gastric ejecta.'

Bron still had the HA–3 tucked under his arm and was wearing a dark blue commando sweater, drab pants with cargo-pockets, and heavy Timberland trail-stompers. He reached down, detached my flexcanteen, and emptied the contents over my head.

I sputtered and retched one last time. 'Thanks. I needed that.'

'Damn straight,' said the assassin. He stayed well out of ralphing range. 'You planning to vomit any more?'

I shrugged one-sidedly. It was a mistake and I flinched from the pain. 'Might. Or maybe die on you. I'm a wreck. Half-paralysed. Got bashed all to hell in the jungle when a humpy fell on me. Your little toe-taps busted something else for sure.'

He patted my dripping, burr-cut head in mock sympathy. 'Too

bad. You just hang in there, Cap'n. I'll have a medic look you over in a short-short. You won't die. Not before your time.'

He addressed the smirking human trooper. 'Chalky, you and Guido go on ahead with Timikak. Put the woman in one of the lockups. I'll decide what to do about her later.'

'What about the gorilla?' Chalky inquired, flipping his thumb at Ivor's motionless form.

Bronson Elgar considered for a moment. 'Superfluous to requirements. Take him to Number Five Sump and throw him in.'

'Sump?' I croaked apprehensively.

The assassin grinned. 'Part of the cavern's drainage system. It flushes into an underground river. Very useful for garbage disposal.'

'You fucking bastard!' I lunged at him feebly.

Nonchalantly, he hit my forehead with the heel of his hand. I fell back onto the trolley, enveloped in pain so extravagant that it almost smothered my fury, frustration, and grief.

'Carry on,' Elgar said to my Haluk guard. 'I'll keep the prisoner covered.'

The wheeled cart began to roll again and Bron walked beside it. I lay half-conscious on my most severely wounded side, unable to turn over, making involuntary noises with each shuddering intake of breath. We moved off the ramp onto the cave's main floor, past the field-shielded enigma of the genetic-engineering complex, and into a side tunnel where bright light shone from an open door.

Another mechanically translated voice spoke loudly. 'Don't bring that unsanitary conveyance in here, you fool.'

My Haluk guard was apologetic. 'Your pardon is besought, Physician Woritak.'

A tall male gracile appeared in the doorway. He wore a green smock and pants, a coif thing that concealed his hair, and a general translator lavaliere. Hung on a cord around his elongate neck was a diagnosticon device identical to the one that had been used on me by Dr Fionnula Batchelder of Manukura Community Hospital.

Physician Woritak said, 'This, presumably, is the expected patient.'

'Yes,' said Elgar. 'Just get rid of the stun-dart drug so we can interrogate him.'

I was so far gone that I hardly cringed.

The physician grunted obscurely. 'What kind of interrogation?'

'Human psychotronic machines, of course,' Elgar snapped. He muttered something under his breath about frigging thumbscrews, red-hot pokers, and iron bloody maidens being more attractive options, unfortunately unavailable.

Old-fashioned torture would have given me at least a faint hope of lying. But nobody lied to the machines.

'Stand aside, Commander Elgar,' said the Haluk doctor, 'so that a preliminary examination can be accomplished.'

'There's no need for that. Just treat the stun paralysis.'

'Not until one assesses the patient's general condition.'

'Sweet shit. Well, be careful. He's dangerous.'

Woritak bent over me and began waving the diagnosticon above my head and body. When he came to my left arm the medicuff emitted a warning squeal. The Haluk gave a start of surprise, palpated the thing through my envirosuit, then spoke into some sort of wrist communicator. 'Scientist Milik, your presence is required in the hospital annexe immediately.'

Two hulking lepidos, also gowned in green, stood respectfully behind Physician Woritak. At a gesture from him they picked me up as gently as they could, considering my bound condition, put me on a gurney cot on my stomach, and took me into a well-lit chamber full of exotic equipment. I presumed it was a Haluk-style emergency room.

The lepido orderlies used old-fashioned vibe knives to cut away my vomit-splattered suit and then my underclothes. Any confidence I might have had in Haluk medicine took a nose-dive when I saw the doctor summon an e-book from a wall terminal and begin tapping through it and reading intently. I hoped the title wasn't *Ten Easy Lessons in Human Repair*.

When I was naked – but still bound at the wrists and ankles – somebody covered me with a warm sheet of quilted plasfoil. Bron watched without expression, his blaster under one arm. He had dismissed the armoured Haluk guard.

A gracile of lesser stature, who looked female to my bleary gaze, entered the room. She wore a white coverall, and around her wasp-waist was a utility belt with important-looking technical gadgetry. When she spoke, her voice was guttural and low-pitched. 'What is it, Physician Woritak?'

'Milik, what in the name of the Life-giving All-Healer is this device on the human patient's arm? It squeaked when the diagnosticon scanned it.'

The female had the lepidos turn me slightly to get a better view of the medicuff. I groaned on general principles.

'It's a measured-dose infusion unit,' she said, 'intended to provide palliatives and other drugs during convalescence. The human is recovering from some serious dysfunction. This tiny screen is a pathognomonic monitor that will indicate the condition being treated.' She prodded one of the armlet pads. Out of the corner of my operational eye, I could see words scrolling.

Milik nodded. 'Yes. He's recovering from whole-body radiation exposure. Apparently ninety-two per cent healed. Colleague, one strongly advises that these wrist restraints be removed at once. They are impeding the human's blood circulation and interfering with the cuff's therapeutic function.'

'Negatory,' Elgar said brusquely.

'The word does not translate,' said Woritak.

'No, goddammit! Frost stays tied up.'

'Frost?' said Scientist Milik. 'Is that his name?'

'Never mind who he is. Just get busy with the treatment.'

The Haluk physician said, 'Technician Avelok, release the patient's arms and legs at once.' With one stride he invaded Bronson Elgar's personal space, seeming to dare him to do anything about it, and pointed a very long middle finger at the hit man's nose. It was a gesture that signified 'fuck you' in any culture, although the translated voice remained level and uninflected. 'Listen well. Nobody countermands the medical orders of this one in this one's own hospital. Do you want the patient treated or do you not?'

Bron took a step backward, glowering, and hefted his Harvey. To my surprise, he gave in. 'All right. But if the ties go off, I'll have to stay and keep an eye on him.'

'You are welcome to do so,' the doctor said, 'provided that you do not impede our work.'

I felt the tight plastic restraints fall away. Soft alien hands belonging to Scientist Milik chafed my numb wrists. I groaned again and smiled at her, attempting a look of piteous gratitude. The ridged exotic face was almost incapable of expression, but her blue lips lifted slightly at the corners.

'This man is in no state to endanger anyone,' Woritak said, tucking the reference book into his smock. 'He is not only partially paralysed from a stun-dart graze, but he also suffers from trauma to his ribs, kidney damage, and massive contusions of the dorsal musculature and dermis.'

'How long to patch him up?' the assassin inquired insolently.

'Two minutes to administer an antidote to the stun-dart. Ten to stabilize the cracked and broken ribs with injectable bonebrace. Embrocation apparatus will dissipate the infusion of blood in the subcutaneous tissue and minimize pain and swelling from the contusions – another ten minutes. His kidney must heal itself, although one can insert an indwelling antibiotic dispenser to preclude infection. One minute to accomplish that. Total treatment time, twenty-three minutes.'

'Then get going,' Elgar found a stool and perched on it, the blaster propped on his crossed legs.

Woritak's assistants collected the appropriate repair gear and he put them to work. Scientist Milik, who didn't seem to be part of the medical establishment, yet was obviously Somebody, fetched a flask of cool water and held it while I sipped through the tube. The medic pumped a shot into my neck artery and the paralysis abated.

'Hang in there, Frost,' Milik said to me. 'You'll feel almost as good as new in a little while.'

I thanked her and she went away.

Woritak stuck needles into my ribs and slowly the acute pain vanished, leaving only leftover aches from my encounters with the lacertilian and Bron's trail-stompers. The hit man watched, looking stone bored, as a lepido painted my bruises bright red, then positioned a longish apparatus like a tanning light above my back and switched it on. I felt the contused flesh tingle.

'Don't move,' Woritak said. 'The machine's ministrations result in an odd sensation, but it will not cause distress. One must now go to procure your antibiotic.' He left the room. The stolid lepidos continued to monitor the bruise eradicator. They hadn't uttered a sound.

I said to Elgar, 'Did you know we were here on Cravat all the time?'

'What do you think?' His voice was contemptuous.

'Which one of the Rampart Board members blew the whistle on me – Cousin Zed? Ollie Schneider? Are Dunne and Rivello in on the Galapharma scam, too?'

'Why should you care? You're finished – whether you live or die.'

'I suppose your boss has to decide whether to deep six me, or do a Haluk refit job and plug me into the same cockamamy game-plan as Eve.'

He gave a noncommittal shrug. His blue eyes were more opaque than ever. 'It'll all be decided after your interrogation. I couldn't care less myself. But after all the trouble you've given me, I don't mind telling you it'd be a giggle to see you turn lepido.'

'You're working for some sick puppies at Galapharma, Bron. And some mighty stupid ones, too. Do you have any idea what could happen to the galactic political situation if the Haluk achieve human-style stability?'

'None of my business. I don't make Concern policy.'

'You just follow orders,' I said archly. 'It's Alistair Drummond and the other Concern CEOs who make secret decisions to sell high technology to a hostile alien race, breaking the laws of the Commonwealth and putting humanity at risk.'

'The Haluk aren't hostile. Not when you know which buttons to push. They can be downright chummy. Generous, too.' He eyed me satirically. 'Why, a man properly full of cosmic brotherhood wouldn't even mind his sister marrying one.'

Before I could decide whether this was more than an insult, Physician Woritak returned.

He folded the lamp apparatus away from my back and did a diagnostic scan. 'Excellent. The contusions are satisfactorily reduced. Please attempt to turn over onto your back.'

I accomplished the manoeuvre gingerly. There was no pain, except for the low-level kidney ache.

'Are you able to sit up?'

I could and did, with only a bit of wooziness, causing the metallic blanket to slide to the floor. 'Hold still for insertion of the renal antibiotic,' the doctor said. He poked me with something. 'The internal dispenser will dissolve when its function is accomplished. Your treatment is now concluded. All of your injuries are ameliorated. After sleeping for a few hours, you should be quite fit.'

'He can sleep after he sings,' Elgar said. 'Get him some clothes. Can he walk?'

'Certainly not. We can provide an antigrav invalid chair, however.'

One of the orderlies dressed me in a set of lightweight green scrubs, similar to those worn by the doctor, while the other fetched the chair. At Elgar's orders, they immobilized my arms and legs with strong padded straps, detached the chair's small control pad, and handed it to the assassin.

Elgar said to Woritak, 'One last thing, Physician. Come to the security rooms in an hour and bring a sedative for the prisoner. By then, he'll need one.'

The Haluk doctor clapped his hands soundlessly in assent. The lepido-style gesture must have conveyed less than wholehearted enthusiasm because Elgar said, 'Your attitude will be reported to your superiors . . . When you come with the sedative, be sure to leave your universal translator behind.'

'As you wish,' said Woritak.

Elgar activated the chair's control pad, turned on his heel, and left the hospital room. I trundled along after him like Mary's little lamb, headed for the slaughter.

Chapter 19

I woke up coughing, with water running out of my mouth, down my chin, and onto my neck. My aching head rested on something soft and warm.

'Stop,' I moaned. 'Choking.'

'I'm sorry. I was trying to wake you. You've been unconscious for a long time.'

I tried desperately to climb to my feet. 'Must help Eve ... get her out of the damn tank ... Ivor! Oh, God, Ivor ... Mimo! Call the Patrol ... send every cruiser in the Zone!'

'Hold still. Don't try to get up. It's all right.'

'I told the bastard everything. Everything ...'

Strong arms held me in a tight embrace. I heard a voice murmur soothing inconsequentialities, saying over and over again that my perfidy wasn't my fault. My frantic, disjointed thoughts melted into a paroxysm of shamed weeping. Objectively, I knew that emotional breakdown is an inevitable post-interrogation syndrome. The knowledge didn't help.

'Easy, Helly. Easy. No one can defeat the machines. It's over now and you're safe. Safe with me.'

Eventually I got hold of myself. The hangover-style headache diminished when I took a pop from the medicuff. After a long quiet time I looked up at Matt Gregoire's face and realized that my pillow was her lap. One of those stiff cheap polyfoam blankets covered me.

I wasn't really safe and the ordeal certainly wasn't over; but when she smiled at me, I grinned back and said, 'Hi.'

'Hello yourself. How do you feel now?'

'Apart from a terminal guilt complex, I'm probably in better shape than I was back on board *Plomazo*. A Haluk doctor did some fast fixes.' I remembered the savage blow Elgar had given her during the fracas. 'How's your head wound?'

'Hurts. There's a goose-egg. But not to worry, the Gregoires have thick Creole skulls. I wasn't out for long. Actually, I regained consciousness as I was being taken here and played possum. One guard was human and the other was a Haluk. The alien wore a translator and said rude things about a certain Commander Elgar. Called him an arrogant odoriferous accumulation of lepido nose-wax. The human guard thought that was very funny.'

'*Nose-wax?*'

'Nose-wax.'

I didn't dare laugh myself. It might have split open my brittle skull. 'Where are we – in the Haluk slammer?'

'An improvised brig, I think. There were containers in here that the guards removed before depositing me. It's a small dead-end cave, walled off and equipped with a heavy locked door. At least it's dry.'

She sat, and I lay, on a narrow rock terrace padded with a strip of polyfoam slightly thicker than the blanket. A tiny wall-lamp like those we'd seen in the tunnel gave wan illumination to the walls of pink and brown limestone. The wedge-shaped cell was about seven metres long and less than three wide at the door, narrowing rapidly to a mere vertical crevice at the innermost extremity. The ceiling was lost in dark shadows.

Besides the mattress, the blanket, and the waterbottle that Matt had set aside, the makeshift lock-up held a covered white plastic bucket, a little red crate containing some amorphous items, and us. I still wore the Haluk scrub garb. No shoes. Matt had on the sweats and bootees she'd worn beneath her envirosuit, which lay neatly folded on the floor.

'Don't suppose there's any food,' I ventured. 'I'm damn near starving.'

'We have bread and some kind of synthocheese. I've already had some. Let me help you.'

She eased me out of her lap, fetched the crate with the food, and I sat up to dine with the blanket hung over my shoulders. The bread was delicious and the Gruyère analogue abominable, but there was plenty of it and I wolfed it down, feeling my strength return.

When I finished eating I told Matt about the interrogation. She listened in silence, her dark eyes huge, as I described how I'd spilled every bean in my brainpan, every single detail of our investigation. By now, the data had been transmitted to Elgar's superiors at Galapharma – and to the Haluk Starfleet.

'You told them about Mimo, too?' she said.

'They asked me the right questions, and I had to answer. They know *Plomazo* is in orbit around Cravat, hidden in a dissimulator field. A good optical sensor device will spot the ship soon enough.'

'Then –'

'I'm afraid we're finished, Matt. And so is any hope of proving a conspiracy. *Plomazo*'s disappearance – with all of us allegedly aboard – can easily be attributed to pirates. Bob Bascombe's death will be called a tragic hunting accident. As for Karl ... he knows nothing about these secret underground facilities and has no proof of Haluk involvement on Cravat. In time, the Gala moles at Rampart Central will find a way to neutralize him and the others.'

She was staring at the cell floor. 'There's still a long chance that the Haluk won't find Mimo before our deadline expires.'

'I doubt it.' My recovering mind began to consider time-frame equations. 'Any idea how long I was unconscious?'

'They took my navigator so it's hard to say. I'd estimate five hours, at least.'

'The only starship able to take out *Plomazo* would be one of those new ball-retractor Haluk jobs. Two of their colonial worlds are well within a three-hour striking distance of Cravat. I think we can presume that poor old Mimo's history.'

She sighed. 'I suppose they'll kill us now as well.'

'Maybe. But Elgar implied that I might be transmuted into a Haluk, just like Eve.'

'You're joking!'

I shook my head. 'Presumably to put more pressure on Simon.'

'But it makes no sense, Helly! I've been thinking about your sister and the possible motive for her transmutation. It can't simply be part of a scheme to force Simon's hand in the Gala take-over.'

'I admit the idea is just a tad Byzantine . . .'

'Threatening Eve's life – and yours – in a straightforward manner would be far more likely to influence your father. Simon would certainly be appalled to discover that two of his children had been changed into Haluk, but he's no fool. One of his advisors would surely tell him that the genen procedure *could be reversed*. So why should Galapharma bother with such a grotesquely complex ploy, when tactics used by ordinary kidnappers would be so much more effective?'

'Well,' I said reluctantly, 'Elgar did drop another nasty hint.' And I told her the one about a Haluk marrying my sister.

She burst out in disbelieving laughter. 'That's even less plausible. If the Haluk covet your precious Frost DNA, they could mince you up and obtain all they wanted through tissue culture. Sorry, Helly. Alien miscegenation doesn't wash as a motive, either.'

'Then damned if I know what the crazy fuckers are up to. The plain fact is, Eve's out there in that tank being transmuted, and I might join her, and maybe you will too. The reason why is immaterial.'

I had drunk a lot of water with my meal, and at least one of my kidneys had been operating efficiently. I took the covered bucket and went to the dark end of our cell and relieved myself. Inspecting the product afterwards, I found no blood and shared the scintillating news with Matt.

'I'm well on the mend, if not mended. The Haluk genetic engineers will have a healthy subject to play with.'

I started prowling about the cave. The sialcrete floor was icy beneath my bare feet. The door, made of impervious ceramalloy and firmly cemented into the stone, had no peephole that might have revealed what lay outside.

My next move was a rather silly attempt to climb the irregular wall above the makeshift bunk-ledge, with a view towards escaping via some natural opening in the lofty, shadowed ceiling. I managed to claw my way up nearly four metres, taking advantage of every crack and protrusion. But above that the rock was eroded slick as a banana peel and I slid down, defeated, with broken fingernails and abraded toes.'So much for the Great Escape.'

'Could have told you that,' she said, chuckling, 'but the exercise was good for you.'

'I don't suppose they left the utility belt on your envirosuit.' I picked up the garment and inspected it. It was scuffed and filthy but otherwise undamaged. The headset was missing. None of its life-support gadgetry seemed useful in our present predicament.

'The belt was gone when the guards tossed me in here. My backpack, too. I don't remember them taking it, but they must have.'

'Figures,' I said glumly.

'I tried tapping on the cell door earlier, hoping that Ivor might hear it and tap back. But there was no response. Do you have any idea where they might have put him?'

I took her hand. 'Matt . . .'

She tensed. 'Oh, no.'

'After the fight, Elgar and his troopers brought us down into the big cavern. He told them to lock you up. But Ivor was to be thrown into a kind of subterranean drain. To drown.'

She began to weep and I held her close, saying nothing, wrapping the blanket around both of us. When she stopped crying and wiped her eyes on her shirt, I tilted her face up and kissed her lips gently. Her mouth softened for a moment and my tongue touched hers. She drew away, but remained nestled in my arms.

'Weird,' I said, 'the way total disaster turns the thoughts to positive things.'

'Yes. Weird.'

Her body was absolutely still. I stroked her hair slowly and felt myself come to life for the first time in God knew how long. It seemed I'd misjudged that Haluk physician with his human repair manual. He'd done a dandy job after all – not that it was going to do me much good.

'Helly.' Matt's voice was low. 'We got off on the wrong foot at the very beginning and I'm sorry about that. Truly.'

'Mm.' Was I imagining things, or had a note of warmth crept into her voice?

'I mean, I'm ... willing to keep an open mind. Give you the benefit of the doubt on the matter of your felony convictions.'

'Oh, good,' I said, a shade too curtly.

'I never gave you a chance to present your case.'

'Chief Gregoire, I presented it three years ago. And lost.'

'Tell me about it.'

'No. It's a sorry tale, and I'd rather think those positive thoughts.'

'You've been thinking them from the first moment we met.'

'Can't deny that. When you walked into the Rampart boardroom, I fell madly in lust with your *ojos negros y piel canela.*'

'What does that mean?'

'Black eyes and cinnamon skin.' I told her about the Nat Cole song, and she insisted that I try to sing it. We both dissolved in laughter at my off-key imitation of a serenading *caballero*, there in the rockbound prison cell underneath the alien jungle, fourteen thousand light-years from old Mexico.

She took my hand again. Hers was cold and calloused. I lifted it and kissed the knuckles, one by one.

'Helly . . .' She didn't pull away as I touched her breast. 'I know. Maybe – just maybe! – you're willing to consider that I might not be a rogue cop. But I sure am a lowlife beach bum. And a reckless hotdogger who insists on leading the Boy Scout troop even when he's incompetent and incapacitated. It's my fault that Mimo and Ivor and Bob are dead and you and I are heading for the last round-up. So I can't blame you if you don't –'

She said, 'Oh, shut up,' and began to pull my clothes off.

No one came to check on Matt and me for a long time, which probably should have raised our suspicions. But we had those positive thoughts – and actions – to occupy us.

Our first coupling was a frenzied race to sexual oblivion. Later, with the overwhelming need satisfied, we settled into a mutual exploration deliberately prolonged, considerate and ingenious. Neither of us spoke of love, but together we found a respite from pain and fear. After the second blazing release, we fell into a postcoital doze.

When we woke we were languorous and disinclined to talk. The past was irrelevant and the future didn't bear worrying about. We ate and drank again, then indulged ourselves to the point of physical exhaustion – and near hypothermia, once the sexual fires diminished. We put our clothes back on and drifted off into sleep, snuggled together spoonwise on the narrow mattress. Her body fitted sweetly against mine.

We were roused almost immediately by the sound of the cell door being unlocked. Both of us sprang to our feet, expecting that it would be Bronson Elgar come to announce our fate.

But when the door opened, Scientist Milik was standing there.

She entered the cell and handed me a bulky sack. 'Here's some sturdier clothing for you. Get dressed, and for God's sake be quick about it.'

The faded blue jeans, snaggy purlaine pullover, and tired athletic shoes and socks had too obviously been recently worn by someone else. I flung them onto the floor. 'Why should I bother?' I snarled. 'You're just going to kill me – or strip me and dip me in the dystasis tank.'

'The situation has changed,' Scientist Milik said. 'Drastically.'

The door was half-open behind her. I couldn't see the guards in the corridor outside. Which meant that they couldn't see me.

I took a chance and jumped her, twisting one arm behind her back and hooking her delicate alien neck in the crook of my elbow. 'Tell your guards to put down their weapons or I'll snap your spine!'

She went limp. 'Don't hurt me . . . no guards . . . I'm alone . . . here to help . . .'

Matt darted forward to check outside the cell. 'She's right. The tunnel's empty.'

'I'm going to let you go,' I told the Haluk. 'Don't scream or try to use your wrist communicator. I'll kill you if you do.'

Big bad Helly Frost. No forty-kilo alien female was going to get the best of *me*. She tottered as I released her. I led her to the bunk-ledge and sat her down. 'Now explain.'

'There's no time. Please! You must hurry and put those clothes on, then come with me.' Her voice still had the grating husky quality that I remembered from our earlier encounter in the hospital, but there was something peculiar about it, apart from her facile use of human idiom.

Suddenly I knew. Scientist Milik was speaking to us with her exotic Haluk vocal organs. She wasn't wearing a translator.

'Who the hell are you?' I grabbed her inhumanly slender wrist and yanked her to her feet. 'What do you want with us?'

She said calmly, 'I am Milik, head of the entire Haluk genetic engineering project. What I want from you is my life . . . and those of all the people in the Nutmeg–414 cavern facility.'

'What the fuck are you talking about!'

'The man called Commander Elgar – do you know who he is?'

'More or less. He works for Galapharma.'

'He's in charge of security for the PD32:C2 operation. About half an hour ago, he received orders via subspace to destroy this installation.'

'*What?*'

'There's some sort of explosive device in the security rooms. None of the Haluk know about this except Woritak and me. Several human troopers were careless speaking in front of us, because neither of us was wearing a universal translator. I seldom wear mine, and Woritak's had been taken away so he could assist during your interrogation –'

'The bomb!' I reminded her.

'It will detonate in less than two hours unless someone can deactivate it. No Haluk has the expertise. I hoped that one of you might know what to do.'

I said, 'Oh, shit.'

Milik went on hurriedly. 'All of the human personnel have left the cavern. Administrator Ru Lokinak was told by Elgar that the Galapharma humans were orchestrating our defence against an imminent incursion by Zone Patrol. But I believe that the commander intends to arrange the destruction of all the other secret facilities on Grant Microcontinent. Elgar's men sealed the lift-shaft and the tunnel-link to the other Nutmeg factories before they left us. They told Ru Lokinak it was a precautionary measure against discovery.'

The explanation hit me like a thunderbolt. I said to Matt, 'My God, Mimo must have got away in *Plomazo* – and now Galapharma's going for damage control!' I scooped up the clothes Milik had brought and began hauling them on over my flimsy scrubs.

'Is that what happened?' Matt asked the alien woman.

'Yes. I overheard Elgar himself say that a Haluk starship was unable to locate your vessel in orbit, nor anywhere in the Cravat system.'

That was a puzzler. I couldn't believe that Mimo had deliberately abandoned us, or violated my orders. But there was no time to worry about it. I finished dressing and the three of us hurried out of the cell and headed down the ill-lit corridor. Matt insisted on bringing her envirosuit, saying its built-in rescue beacon might be useful helping Zone Patrol home in on us, if Elgar's bomb didn't finish us off first.

After we'd gone a short distance, Milik said, 'There are two guards lying unconscious at their post at the end of this tunnel. I subdued them with sedative injectors on the way in. You'll want to don their uniforms. We can't risk being stopped on the way to the security rooms.'

'Good idea,' I said.

'Woritak will be meeting us in security. You need have no fear of him. He's . . . a good person. We are friends because both of us are physicians. Unfortunately, many other Haluk have a deeply ingrained distrust of humanity. Given the premeditated actions of Commander Elgar and his Galapharma superiors, I can hardly call it misplaced.'

After a few hundred metres, past what Milik said were food storerooms, we came upon a startling sight. The tunnel widened, and on either side were scores of shallow rock niches containing objects that resembled dull golden mummy cases. They were of varying sizes, most over two meters high, and covered with intricate ribbing and shallow chased ornamentation.

'They are Haluk people,' Scientist Milik explained, 'resting in the testudinal phase. Before the race colonized the stars, the Big Change occurred simultaneously amongst everyone each year, when the home planet's orbit carried it into the region of intense solar radiation. Later, on other worlds where the allomorphic adaptation no longer served its evolutionary purpose, the cycles of individuals gradually varied in their timing. The synchrony no longer prevails, but the Big Change is still very inconvenient for an intelligent race. A non-mutated Haluk person can still expect to spend one hundred and forty days aestivating in a chrysalis, two hundred days as a gracilomorph, and sixty as a transitional lepidodermoid.'

'Humanity would have helped you cope,' I said, 'if you'd dealt with us in a civilized manner.'

'There was fear,' Milik admitted. 'And an innate racial pride that shrank from altering evolutionary destiny. And above all a stubborn refusal to take the first step. To ask aliens to transmute the Haluk into *others*.'

Matt and I traded glances. We could understand the Haluk dilemma objectively, but not the means they had taken to amend it.

Matt spoke sadly. 'Even if we do manage to save you and your people from Elgar's bomb, you won't escape our justice. The conspiracy between Galapharma and the Haluk has cost human lives and damaged human institutions. You've deliberately violated our laws and you'll pay the price.'

Scientist Milik laughed. It was a rusty, pathetic sound. 'I've been paying the price for years.'

The small guard post was in an alcove just short of the main cavern. It took only a moment for Matt and I to strip the two unconscious graciles of their helmets, uniform jackets, and Allenby stun-guns. We opened the door leading into the cavern and continued on at a fast walk, unchallenged.

A few lepido Haluk were moving about in the huge underground chamber, apparently doing janitorial chores. We saw no other alien troopers, and there was no sign of extraordinary activity or alarm. The genetic engineering complex looked exactly as it had earlier. White-coated gracile technicians continued to hover around the gleaming tanks, tending the immersed subjects. The uncanny central jewel construct throbbed serenely, transmuting allomorphic

Haluk into stable Haluk and turning Eve into one of themselves.

Outside the force-field umbrella the floor was wet from the dripping stalactites and scored with shallow drainage channels. At the far right, below the balcony where the ramp began, was a sort of loading dock. Numerous trolleys loaded with packaged PD32:C2 stood about, but there were no Haluk working at the dock. A small Homerun gravomagnetic truck was partially visible behind banks of storage modules, waiting inside the entrance to an arched passage much larger than the one on the cave's upper level that led to the lift.

'Is that the tunnel leading to the other Nutmeg facilities?' I asked Milik. She said that it was, but it had been rendered impassable.

'Where does the truck usually take those packages of vector? Don't you use all the stuff here in the genen complex?'

'Only a small percentage of the factory output is needed for this special work. Most of the viral vector produced here – and all of it made in the other plants on Grant Microcontinent – is taken through tunnels to a depot on the north shore. Periodically a human shuttle secretly carries it into orbit for transshipment to Haluk worlds.'

'I'm surprised you take the risk of doing any genetic engineering here on Cravat.'

'It was not my decision.'

We had crossed the cavern and were on the verge of entering the large, well-illuminated tunnel leading to the hospital and the security rooms. Abruptly, I stopped the alien female and swung her around so I could see her blue-skinned face. 'Milik – are you a transmuted human being?'

'Of course I'm human!' she said, her voice breaking. Then the words poured out in a rush. 'I've been waiting for a chance to escape ever since I found out the real purpose of the demiclones. I was such an incredible fool! Thinking I'd be the great benefactor of a worthy, misunderstood race. It was all my idea, you see. I was motivated by pure altruism, but the cost of my project made participation by the Concerns necessary –'

'What are you talking about?' I demanded. 'Who the devil are you?'

Scientist Milik said, 'I *was* Emily Blake Konigsberg.'

'But . . . you're dead!' Matt exclaimed.

'My demiclone is dead. The one who would have returned to Earth on a Galapharma starship and –' She caught herself. 'We have no time for this! Follow me.'

She began to run. Matt and I did, too.

Chapter 20

Physician Woritak was sitting in a swivel chair behind a desk that bore a nameplate saying A. H. WHITE, DUTY OFFICER.

Chalky & Co were gone, of course, and in the security office there were definite evidences of a hasty departure: an upset coffee cup on a second desk making a drying mess of some print-outs, a kicked-over wastebasket, a shelf of datadime containers wildly disarranged as if someone had rummaged among them, and a large weapons locker with the door gaping and the racks empty.

The interrogation machines were gone, too. They were probably Bronson Elgar's personal property that he carried along everywhere with him on assignment – like golf clubs.

Woritak once again wore a universal translator. The first thing he did when we burst into the room was ask how I was feeling.

'Scared,' I said. 'My health is excellent. Where's the bomb?'

He pointed economically to the communications room adjacent to the main office. I went in and winced at the smell of ozone. Someone had methodically drilled almost every piece of com equipment with a Kagi blue-ray electron zapper, isolating the facility from the external universe.

The lone untouched unit was smallish, appropriately coloured black, and bore the manufacturer logo of Carnelian Concern. It squatted in a corner, looking neglected, segregated from its defunct and harmless compeers. Its telltales gleamed dully and the screen of its integral computer badly needed a cleaning. Perhaps no one had done more than bump into the infernal machine and curse it as a useless dustcatcher from the time it had been installed.

Until today, when it finally found its use.

The display showed only the countdown: –102:33 minutes. I

removed the handmike and tried to enter the computer in the conventional manner. Access denied. After racking my brains for a moment, I came up with the ICS official override for Carnelian models, tapped a few pads, and recited it.

Tah-dah! I was inside, able to ascertain the device's mode of dedication and read the directories – even though the file contents remained locked away. I studied and I frowned while Matt looked over my shoulder. Physician Woritak found another place to sit down. He ignored us, reading an alien slate and occasionally whispering into his wristcom. The once (and perhaps future) Emily Blake Konigsberg leaned against the doorframe, her bright blue inhuman eyes shuttered and one four-fingered gracile hand pressed tightly against her mouth. Perhaps she was praying.

If so, heaven wasn't listening.

'Well,' I said at length, 'to quote a very ancient cliché, we have good news and bad news. The good news is that there is no bomb.'

Konigsberg's eyes flew open and she uttered a joyous little cry. Woritak only stared at me inscrutably.

'The bad news is that we have something worse. If I read this computer correctly, we are dealing with a contingency demolition set-up called a photon-blast camouflet system. When it's triggered, multiple generating units scattered throughout the underground facility will discharge wide-angle actinic flares, vaporizing or melting down everything inside the caves. The camouflet feature means that surrounding rock strata will not be significantly damaged. Neither will the Nutmeg factory. There won't be any sort of rupture at the surface of the ground. All traces of Haluk occupation will tidily vanish, and so will we.'

'Can you stop it?' Matt asked.

'I've seen a similar system just once before. It was years ago when I was a young field agent, just starting my career in the ICS. We were raiding an underground contraband depot on Gemmula–5 in the Orion Arm that reputedly belonged to a shadow division of Carnelian Concern. They were suspected of trading high-tech equipment illicitly to the Y'tata Empire. Our team had a whiz hacker, but she couldn't disarm the camouflet modules or stop the countdown. We all ran for our lives.'

'You're saying you can't deactivate this system either,' Matt said. 'No way.'

'It was to be feared that a dire outcome would prevail,' said Physician Woritak through his translator. He rose from his seat, making a gesture towards the exit. 'Let us leave this place. This one did not wish to communicate pessimism earlier to Scientist Milik, for which reason she was encouraged to release you two humans. Now, however, you might wish to consider how you will spend the time preceding your imminent death. This one has just now summoned all of the people to the main cavern, adjacent to the genetic engineering complex. After they are informed of the situation, Administrator Ru Lokinak will lead us in the ritual of docile thanatopsis, since there is no Anointed Elder in the company. Perhaps you humans will wish to participate.'

'Thanks. But we're not quite ready to die yet.' I was glad that the translator would extract the sarcasm from my reply. Woritak did seem to be a well-meaning soul.

I turned to Konigsberg. 'You said the lift-shaft and the connecting tunnel leading to the next Nutmeg facility were sealed off. How?'

'Elgar's men used their Harvey blasters to collapse the rock, blocking the way with thousands of tons of rubble.'

'I don't suppose the Haluk troopers have any heavy-duty photon weapons.'

'No. Only humans were allowed to carry those. Our guards are armed with stun-guns.'

Woritak said, 'The blasters and other destructive weapons were kept in the locker in the next room. As you saw, that locker is now empty. Our maintenance engineers have small rock-cutting torches for repair work, but it would take many hours for those tools to burn through either of the blockages.'

So much for that idea, not that I'd thought it would amount to much. 'What model force-field generator forms the umbrella over the genen complex?'

Woritak lifted his wristcom. 'One will consult the appropriate person.' He muttered. The com emitted untranslated alien gibberish.

235

'Maintenance Engineer Til Iminik says that the device bears the designation SHELTOK UF–90.'

Another wash-out. That particular generator was too weak to form a shield against an actinic flare, even if we could figure out how to modify the field projection from umbrella to dome. I had one last notion.

'The tunnel leading to the other Nutmeg site: do either of you know which direction it takes? Does it go south?'

Emily Konigsberg shook her head. 'I have no idea.'

'One is certain.' Woritak said, 'that it trends to the northeast.'

'What,' I asked him, 'did you do with the belt and pouch that your orderlies took off me when I first arrived?'

'It is probably still lying in the nonsterile-materials tray in the hospital annexe. This one forgot to instruct the lepido technicians to dispose of it. Because they are deficient in volition, they would not do so under their own initiative.'

'Great! Emily, how long to get my sister Eve out of dystasis?'

She was taken aback by the abrupt change of subject, and perhaps also by my use of her human name. The harsh voice faltered. 'I think – less than thirty minutes. We – we would have to disconnect the apparatus, check her vital signs, and give necessary medication. But why not let the poor woman pass away peacefully?'

I ignored that, even though it was a valid question. 'What kind of shape will Eve be in when she comes out? Conscious? Able to walk?'

'Semiconscious at best. She may recognize you. But she'll be very weak for several hours, until normal metabolic processes are re-established. Certainly not able to walk. And her immune system won't be up to speed for days. We have no medicuffs available.'

'You and Woritak go get Eve out of that tank. Matt, give them your envirosuit. They can dress Eve in it. At least she can breathe filtered air and stay warm and dry.'

'During *what?*' Matt demanded.

'Our escape. Maybe.' I picked up the Allenby stunner carbine I'd been carrying, in case some of the Haluk troopers weren't yet in a mood to contemplate death with docility. 'Matt, you come

236

along with me to the hospital. We're going to get the subterrain chart in my belt-pouch.'

'What good will it do us?' she asked.

'Remember the half-eaten testudo Bob found? The one he nick-named Luckless Larry? That Haluk came from here – and it didn't use the Nutmeg connector tunnel, which goes in the wrong direction. That means there's got to be another way out. Let's go find it.'

Emily Konigsberg offered her alien wristcom unit to me. 'Here, take this communicator. Press the black button to reach Woritak. I've also programmed it with the countdown timing.'

We went our separate ways.

There were 86:44 minutes left.

The big problem was the depth delimitation of one hundred metres on the chart. The floor of the big cavern was more than eighty metres deeper, and therefore missing from the printout. The chamber's higher reaches *were* shown in rather confusing detail (which had enabled me to locate it in the first place), as was the super-imposed twisting route of the relatively shallow tunnel system heading south towards Pickle Pothole. This, our potential escape route, I dubbed Pothole Passage.

Unfortunately, the navigable portion of the passage seemed to peter out nearly half a kilometre short of our present location. Approaching the cavern, Pothole Passage deteriorated into a labyrinthine braid of impossibly narrow crevices and partially collapsed, dead-end galleries. Somewhere back in the passable section, an unscanned tunnel had to descend to the lower level of our cavern's floor. It was through this uncharted connector that Luckless Larry would have wandered through the dark to meet death.

No matter how Matt and I studied the mystifying chart, we couldn't decide which branch of the maze might contain the link. There was no way to get an accurate fix on its opening into the cavern.

'We'll have to work by guess and by golly,' I said. 'Let's go out into the big cave, turn south, and see what turns up. The passage link can't be too tough to spot if a lepido discovered it.'

I folded up the chart and stuffed it under my sweater. Besides my belt and pouch, which held a few items of useful gadgetry, I also retrieved the wrist navigation unit that had been taken away from me earlier. It wouldn't be able to receive satellite bearings through solid rock, but its distance-travelled system would operate underground as readily as on the surface, as would its inertial compass; and the transponder would serve as another beacon to rescuers if we ever got within range of them.

In the cavern we found Haluk converging on the central genetic complex from all directions. There seemed to be about forty or fifty of them, graciles trotting briskly and lepidodermoids more or less poking along according to their relative proximity to the Big Change. My heart sank at the prospect of trying to herd a mixed mob of frightened aliens up some constricted crack in the rock in time to escape a holocaust.

None of them paid any attention to us as we travelled in the opposite direction toward the chamber's southern perimeter, following one of the floor drainage gutters. The wall-ramp that curved around the cavern had its foot at the southern end. A dozen or so metres left of the ramp we found a dry, well-lit corridor with many doors along its sides, looked into it briefly, and then moved on. The only other opening in that part of the cavern wall was a large culvert some forty metres further along, into which several of the floor gutters drained. An alien ideograph was painted on the rock beside it.

I touched the wrist communicator and Woritak promptly responded.

'This corridor near the base of the ramp,' I asked him. 'Where does it lead?'

'To the sleeping quarters, dining room and kitchens serving the lepido workers. It has no outlet.'

'Do you know whether it's an artificial construct – or does it incorporate any natural caves?'

He told me to wait while he asked one of the others. Then: 'The lepido quarters were carved from solid rock, as were the quarters occupied by graciles and humans, the administrative and hospital rooms, and the principal storage areas. This was done so that the areas would remain dry and geologically stable.'

'Right. How about the big culvert down at this end? Is it completely artificial, too?'

There was a pause. 'Culvert does not translate. Do you mean Sump Number Five?'

I felt a cold chill along my backbone. 'I guess I do.'

'Please wait while one consults.'

I looked at Matt. 'It's the drain where the troopers disposed of Ivor.'

Her eyes widened in horror. 'Oh, dear God.'

Together, we peered into the semicircular opening. The radius was about a metre and a half. It was darker than Satan's asshole and smelled about as appealing. There was no grille or other barrier.

Woritak's voice spoke from the communicator. 'Sump Number Five is an artificial conduit thirteen metres in length that debouches into a natural subterranean stream. It receives water run-off and floor sweepings from the cavern, sewage from the worker quarters, and effluent and garbage from the kitchen.'

'Thank you for the information ... Is Eve Frost safely out of dystasis?'

'We are treating her. She is resting in an invalid chair. This one must tell you that Administrator Ru Lokinak is not persuaded by your hypothesis of another exit from the cavern. He has declined to speak of it to the others, lest it raise false hopes. Shortly he will begin to recite the thanatopsis. Is there any encouraging information you wish conveyed to him?'

'Not yet,' I said, 'but stand by.' I clicked off, then set the navigator's inertial odometer to zero. The countdown was at –69:03.

My belt pouch held a very small torch. Its meagre beam revealed almost nothing when I shone it into Sump Number Five, but my eyes hadn't yet accommodated to the darkness. I stripped off the Haluk uniform jacket and the helmet and tossed them aside. The Allenby stunner, which was waterproof, had a sling and went diagonally across my back. I crouched and stepped down into the water. It came to my knees.

239

'Stay there,' I told Matt, when she would have followed. 'No sense both of us getting soaked. I'll do this faster alone. You'd better go back and see about getting the others organized. Probably best if you ditch your weapon. I'll transmit progress reports to Woritak.'

'I think I'll just wait until you're out of sight. Give a shout if you run into any problem.'

'And then what? You'll come splashing to the rescue?'

'Of course! I'm a terrific swimmer – especially in sewers.' She gave me a lopsided grin. 'Get going, cowboy. Do what you gotta do. But I have my doubts about this culvert being the way out. If the Haluk troopers threw Ivor into it and expected him to drown, how could a lost lepido have gone through safely?'

'Ivor went into the water unconscious. Luckless Larry could have waded . . . I'll give you three blinks with the flashlight if it looks promising. Two plus two if the route taps out and I start back. So long, Mattie babe. You're the best.'

All she did was nod.

I struck off, moving as quickly as I could. The culvert floor was slippery beneath my sneakered feet. The water deepened, then remained consistently at crotch level. It was miserably cold, but there didn't seem to be any sewage in it – yet.

'It's okay so far,' I called out to Matt. She stood silhouetted against the golden light of the cavern. 'There's not much of a current.'

I continued on, staying close to the lefthand side of the culvert and shining my light on the inky waters ahead. I checked the navigator. At thirteen metres traversed, the smooth arch of the culvert ended and the walls became irregular limestone rock. The water deepened by a few centimetres, but I was now able to stand upright in a larger natural tunnel. Pausing, I shone my torch around. Droplets falling from small blunt stalactites sprinkled my hair and shoulders. Ahead on the right I saw a protruding pipe spewing crud into the stream.

On the left there was a very narrow ledge.

It was a miniature ramp, extending underwater. Facing the wall and using my hands to steady myself, I could sidle up into welcome dryness. The ledge continued above the water, widening as the tunnel enlarged. The stench got worse, inspiring me to move along the shelf at a fair clip, playing torchlight on the rock at my feet.

After I'd gone a considerable distance I stopped to call up a course diagram on the navigator. Its tiny display showed I had travelled almost in a straight line, 93.5 metres on a rough southerly bearing of one hundred and eighty degrees. When I turned around I could still see Matt's tiny figure. I blinked the light at her three times. She waved and went away.

So far, so good.

I flashed the beam around. The ceiling was about ten metres high, crowded with thin, pointed stalactites that wept steadily, making a plurping sound on the sluggish stream, which now had nameless things floating on its surface. Wet rock with small protruding ledges rose almost vertically to my left. Ahead, along the wall, I spotted an elongated shadow.

I went to inspect it and discovered an alcove.

It was the size of a room, reasonably dry, accessible through an opening just large enough to admit a man . . . or a Haluk. An alien lantern, unlit, stood on a long, thin slab of rock that formed an improvised table. It also held a few closed canisters and what looked like an alien board-game. On either side of the table were smaller rocks with flat tops that served as stools. Neatly lined up along the inner wall were dozens of transparent alceram flasks, curiously shaped. Each of them held about five litres of colourless liquid.

Unstoppering one, I took a sniff. The unmistakable odour of ethanol flooded my nostrils, cancelling the abominable stink.

I had discovered the secret recreation room and booze stash of the lepido workforce.

Perhaps Luckless Larry and his thick-skinned asexual comrades were accustomed to assuage their boredom here after finishing the scut work. Perhaps, on one ill-starred day, Larry had exited the makeshift groggery after wetting his whistle excessively and turned left instead of right.

Resisting the temptation to sample the exotic elixir myself, I left the alcove and forged deeper into the tunnel. The roof lowered rather quickly after I had gone another fifteen or twenty metres, and simultaneously the route veered off to the right, cutting off all light from the culvert entrance.

With the constriction of the passage I was forced to proceed at an awkward crouch. To make matters worse the ledge, rendered almost as slick as glass by a thin film of watery mud, began to tilt in the direction of the stream, which was flowing much faster (and, I suspected, much deeper) than before. Long stalactites menaced my head, and nasty little spikelike formations underfoot threatened to impale me if I should slip and fall.

There was also a danger of skidding into the river. At best I'd probably get a mouth- and noseful of alien sewage; at worst, climbing out might prove impossible, since the bank now dropped off almost perpendicularly, with the surface of the water over a metre below. The nauseating smell combined with the speleological hazards nearly made me turn back. Cursing, wet to the skin from the drips that fell from the stone daggers, I toiled on – wondering how any lepido, drunk or sober, could have deliberately chosen to come through this fucking Spike Farm.

Maybe none had . . .

The ledge eventually levelled out, becoming a virtual promenade over two metres wide. The pointy-tipped rock formations also disappeared as I came into a drier region. I was grateful for small favours, because the cave roof was getting lower and lower. In fact, the passage was turning from a tunnel into a mere crawlway.

Dropping to my hands and knees I slithered gamely onward, carrying the torch in my teeth. The space between ledge and ceiling decreased to less than sixty centimetres and the carbine on my back rasped against the rock. Eventually, I was forced to squirm on my belly.

Above the river to my right, the clearance was even less. Then the waterway vanished altogether. Happily, so did its stink. I kept crawling.

Until my probing fingers felt empty air ahead.

I squirmed to the edge of what I feared might be a precipice and shone the light down. The bowl-shaped depression was less than a metre deep and about five metres wide. I gave a little yip of exultation when I spotted another of the alien liquor flasks, lacking a stopper, among some boulders at the bottom. On the opposite side of the cavity, a tall, very narrow crevice led deeper into the rocks.

Way to go, Larry!

I crossed the Bowl Chamber and squeezed into the crack, praying I wouldn't get trapped. My own bulk was less than that of a lepido, even though I was considerably taller. If Larry had managed to get through this Needle's Eye, then so could I.

The narrows turned out to be mercifully short. Almost immediately I found myself in an immense subterranean room containing the most beautiful speleothems I'd ever seen, all of the formations gleaming with moisture so that they seemed carved from pale polished gemstone. My flashlight revealed translucent striped draperies and ornate stalactites hanging from the ceiling. Some of the latter extended all the way to the floor, forming elegant columns as wide as tree trunks, adorned with dripstone fringes. They framed looming masses resembling fantastic pipe-organs, huge animals, and the shrouded statues of ogres. Pools of water were everywhere, fed by droplets tinkling into them like music in a goblin's cathedral.

The river also seemed to have reappeared, somewhat less odoriferous due to dilution of its sewage content. I followed both my nose and my ears to locate its rushing course over boulders along the far side of the great chamber. The river finally led me out of the Goblin's Cathedral into a new tunnel that had a muddy bank littered with rocks and large broken stalactites. As I slogged along, avoiding increasing numbers of obstacles, I heard a distant rumbling sound that rapidly increased in volume. I wondered if there might be an underground waterfall ahead.

Belatedly, I remembered to check the countdown. Glowing red numerals on the alien wristcom showed that it had reached −45:12. I had been inside Sump Number Five for twenty-four minutes, but I still had no evidence that this route provided a link to the higher level of Pothole Passage. If I brought the others in here, we might escape the catastrophic photon flare – clean instant death – only to perish in a gorgeous, putrid-smelling abyss.

Perhaps just a little bit farther.

I hurried along the river, only to be brought up short by a rockfall barrier higher than my head. I decided to see what lay on the other side and then turn back.

Holding the flashlight in my mouth again, using the long stun-gun as an alpenstock, I ascended the unsteady heap. Water was flowing in the midst of the tumbled rocks and they were very slippery. I stumbled, barked my shins painfully, and nearly lost the torch. The pile was three or four metres wide. On the far side I found level ground and deeper mud, as thick and clinging as pancake batter.

The sound of rushing water was now extremely loud, and I was suddenly aware that the air was filled with mist. Thinking only of how little time was left, I restored the gun to my back and squished through foot-grabbing grey mire to the edge of the embankment to see if the cascade was visible. The grade steepened unexpectedly. I lost my footing again and began to slide downslope on my butt. Luckily, a large fallen stalactite checked my skid. Cursing a blue streak because I was now coated with mud, I shone my inadequate light out over the river.

And experienced a start of raw terror.

There was no gleam of dark water – only rags of swirling vapour that danced above a great cylindrical chasm.

By straining my eyes I was able to see the waterfall a stone's throw away, pouring off the opposite edge of the pit, into the depths.

Poor Ivor . . .

I scrambled back up the bank and made a hasty inspection of the area surrounding the chasm. My flashlight barely illuminated the bizarre scene. Just beyond the rockfall were tiered formations edged with sparkling dripstone, looking for all the world like a collection of gigantic fossilized wedding cakes. Water seeped down them sluggishly, and also over adjacent terraces that rose stepwise for about fifteen metres to a lumpy wall pierced by a tall opening shaped like a keyhole.

With my heart pounding, I splashed up the terraces. Each one contained a limpid pool a few centimetres deep with a floor of crunchy crystals. At the top, the keyhole opened into a corridor that split almost immediately into two branch tunnels. The stream that bathed the wedding cakes and terraces flowed noisily out of the left one.

The righthand tunnel was completely dry, even dusty. But at some time in the past it had also been a streamway, for the rocks lining it were well worn, forming irregular stairs leading steeply upward. In an expanse of dust at the tunnel entrance, blurred but still distinctive, were tracks made by a single pair of three-toed lepido feet. The footprints were headed inside. No prints came out.

The countdown was at −33:24. My navigator showed that I had come 416 metres from the cavern. The chart, I remembered, indicated Pothole Passage's navigable section at around half a kilometre.

Was this the link I'd been searching for?

Tapping the wrist communicator, I called Woritak and told him that it was.

Chapter 21

'But you are not absolutely certain,' the expressionless voice said, 'that the passage will lead eventually to the surface.'

'It looks very promising. Well worth taking a chance on. Tell your people to hurry –'

'First one must consult with Administrator Ru Lokinak.'

'Physician, you've got to get moving immediately. The blast will go off in thirty minutes and there's no time for palavering!'

'Palavering does not translate.'

I bit back an angry obscenity. The last thing I needed was to antagonize the only Haluk who'd behaved like a *mensch*. 'Okay. You go and do your consulting. Is my human associate Matt Gregoire there with you?'

'She has gone to procure portable lanterns from the storeroom.'

'I see. Please give your communicator to Em – to Scientist Milik so that I can transmit some important instructions.'

'This will be done.'

After what seemed an interminable time (but was probably less than ninety seconds), I heard Konigsberg's grating voice. 'I'm here, Frost.'

'Is Eve all right?'

'Yes. She's groggy but rational. I've dressed her in the envirosuit but I haven't activated the ventilator yet. We're giving oral medication. She knows you're here. I haven't said anything about the – the problem.'

'Okay. Now listen carefully, Emily. The exit through Sump Number Five looks feasible but there's not much time left. Woritak said that Matt was getting torches. That's good. Each person will also need a space blanket. You know – those plasfoil reflective things they have in the hospital.'

'There are some in the genen complex as well.'

'Great. Be sure you and Matt and Eve have large ones. Don't bother with any supplies other than lights and the blankets. Just get going immediately. You'll have to carry Eve once you're inside the tunnel. Do you think you can do it?'

'Your sister's a small person. Matt and I will manage. Tell me what to expect inside the sump. Must we wade in water all the way?'

'No.' I described the conduit, the ledge walk, the lepido sanctum, the perilous Spike Farm section (which was going to be a bitch to get Eve through), the squeezeway, and the Bowl Chamber. If they got that far, they'd probably be safe.

'I'm going to start back right now,' I said, 'but I might not be able to reach you before the blast goes off. You'll have to tell the others how to cope. This next bit is very important: the first ninety metres of the tunnel are virtually a straight shot, so the photon flare will be able to penetrate.'

'I understand.'

'You'll have to get beyond the linear section into the curved part – where you can't see the entrance any longer – in order to be out of range and have any real chance of survival. Even then things could be iffy. Besides the flare there'll be at least two other effects that might be life-threatening. The first is a hurricane. Because of the confined space in the cavern, the great heat of the camouflet will suck air out of the tunnel as the cavern contents flash and burn – as materials oxidize. Then there may be a backblow of hot gases in the opposite direction. Tell the people to monitor the countdown. At minus one minute you should all crouch, wherever you are, cover up with the space blankets, and brace yourselves. The big winds will be over in a few moments. I'm not sure about what'll happen next, but there might be steam.'

'From the heated river?'

'Exactly. The water nearest the cavern will vaporize completely. Steam expansion may collapse the straight part of the tunnel, but the effect ought to diminish the deeper you go into the bedrock. The blankets will help to shield you from the scalding heat, and the hurricane may even suck most of the steam away. The important thing is to be prepared. Tell people it's vital to cover the entire body with the reflective blanket.'

'Very well.'

'There's one last thing. Do what you can to convince the Haluk to come with you immediately, but if they won't listen, then leave them. If they do agree to come, tell them I expect you and Eve and Matt to *lead the way into the tunnel*. Otherwise, I'll make sure that no Haluk gets to the surface alive.'

'I don't think it would be wise to give them such an ultimatum,' Emily Konigsberg said softly. 'I'll do the best I can. Call back in about ten minutes and I'll have a report.'

As I hurried down the terraces, squelched across the mudflat, and cautiously attacked the rockfall, my mind was churning at light-speed. The Haluk doctor hadn't sounded too impressed by the footprints I'd found – much less by the empty liquor bottle in the Bowl Chamber. My careful explanation of directional bearings and propitious odometer distances seemed to go right over his head. God knew what he'd tell his administrator, or what decision the administrator would finally make.

What if the Haluk leader opted for mass annihilation, rather than have his people captured by Commonwealth authorities and compelled to reveal details of the conspiracy?

What if he forced the women to stay behind as well, to protect the secret?

If there was trouble, would I have time to reach the cavern, perform a rescue at stun-gun point, and lead the three safely into the sump before the countdown reached zero?

I could only stew over the matter until I reached the great chamber I'd called the Goblin's Cathedral. The alien wrist unit's read-out said −22:52. I tapped the com button.

There was no reply.

'Emily – Milik! – Are you there? Answer me!'

When nothing happened I examined the communicator under the torch. It was encrusted with mud but seemed otherwise undamaged, and its yellow ON telltale shone properly whenever I touched the activation switch. There were several other controls, covered by a transparent slide so they couldn't be pressed accidentally. I assumed they programmed the device to call other individuals and maybe set the timer; but I hadn't the faintest notion how they worked and didn't dare mess with them.

I pressed the black button again ... and this time a rich, full-bodied sound came from the instrument's tiny speaker. It was unlike anything I'd ever heard before, three wavering notes sounding simultaneously in an eerie harmonic chord, rising and falling in volume like the regular washing of waves against a shore, or some great beast slowly breathing, with each inhalation a racking sob and each discharge of breath a sigh.

It had to be the Haluk thanatopsis – their death meditation.

I think I howled out loud, a wordless cry that combined fury and fear. Then I began to run across the Goblin's Cathedral, waving the weak beam of the torch from side to side in a desperate effort to gain more light and reach the Needle's Eye exit as quickly as possible. The grotesque formations seemed to come alive in the shifting shadows. I tripped over rocks, stumbled through ankle-deep black pools, dodged heedlessly around the dripstone pillars and the looming monstrous shapes.

The Needle's Eye! Where was it?

It should have been easy to find, a slit in the wall almost directly opposite the river tunnel that led to the chasm. I located a crevice, pushed into it, and realized almost at once that the thing was a dead end. I backed out, shone the light to either side, and spotted another opening. Thank God! ...

But that passage turned out to be much too wide to be the right way out and ended in another cul-de-sac. Again I was forced to retreat into the cathedral. With dripping water making a crystal counterpoint to the alien chant that still sounded from my wristcom, I swept the torch's beam along the wall. No other likely crack was visible anywhere.

I stood stock still, paralysed with dread, knowing I'd made the same mistake as Luckless Larry. I was lost.

Dumb damn Cap'n Helly Beach Bum. Mindfucked by an alien

funeral march.

First thing: shut off the music. Second thing: take a long breath. Third thing: consult the navigator on my other wrist.

When a few pads were tapped, its display showed a diagram of my stygian wanderings, ant-tracks against a simple metre-grid that scrolled to show my progress. There were no details of terrain, of course, but I didn't need them – just the distances and the bearings. I found the section representing the Goblin's Cathedral. Helly coming in, Helly crossing over, Helly returning, Helly trying to go out.

Helly deviating by 18.2 metres from his previous course, because he'd taken a wrong turn among the stone pipe-organs and petrified elephants.

I retraced my steps, resisting the temptation to run, reached the point of deviation, bore left instead of right around a certain formation, followed my bearing slowly and cautiously, checking the display every five or six steps, and ended with my nose pointed into the Needle's Eye.

The countdown stood at −14:40.

Now no longer in any danger of losing my way, I was able to concentrate entirely upon speed. Through the crevice. Across the Bowl Chamber, which I decided would make a perfect refuge for four if we could only reach it in time. Down on my belly to wriggle through the squeezeway like a demented python.

When I reached the worst section of the route, the low Spike Farm passage with its perilous long stalactites and tilted, slick floor studded with sharp stalagmites, I nearly blew it. Proceeding at a rapid crouch, scuttling among the close-set stone icicles like a character in a video game, I was suddenly brought up short and hauled backwards. The gun barrel had caught on a stalactite tip.

An instant later the stone rapier broke off near the ceiling. I was doing a stagger-dance, so the thing sliced my right arm instead of stabbing a hole in it. When it hit the slanted ledge it broke into a dozen cylindrical pieces. I managed to step on one and went lurching towards the wall at my right. If I'd fallen, the spiky little stalagmites would have turned me into Swiss cheese. Somehow, I remained upright, but I banged my head smartly against the wall and momentarily visited dreamland.

I came to my senses almost at once, only to discover that one of them – vision – was still off-line.

I'd dropped the torch, and it had rolled down the incline into the fetid river.

All I could see was the alien wristcom display, which Emily Konigsberg had programmed with human numerals. Against a background of unfathomable blackness, the red-glowing countdown stood at –06:23.

Not quite disaster. I still had the navigator, and when I turned the display on, it showed that I was only a short distance from the end of the Spike Farm. What's more, the yellowish screen emitted enough light so that I was no longer completely blind. Shuffling my feet to detect the stalagmites and holding my navigator high to help spot dangerous danglers, I made my way at last into the clear. Then it was a matter of feeling my way along the curving wall until the tunnel straightened.

Someone was coming toward me. I saw two distant golden lights, side by side and very close together, bobbing near the sump entrance. They were lanterns, so brilliant that they drowned out the main cavern's illumination. It was impossible to tell what lay behind them, only that they were moving down the centre of the culvert. Faintly, I heard the sound of the thanatopsis chant.

'Matt?' I yelled, raising a hullabaloo of echoes. 'Emily?'

I heard a frantic voice answer. 'Helly, they're close behind! Haluk – trying to stop us!'

'I'm coming!' I shouted, and skittered along the ledge like a mountain goat.

I must have covered eighty metres in under a minute. The three women were just emerging from the culvert into the wider natural tunnel when I reached them. Matt and Emily had linked their hands to form a seat. Eve, between them and with her arms draped around their necks, had two lamps tied to her chest. Her suited body was limp and her head hung down.

'Keep left,' I cried, pulling the Allenby around and flipping off the safety. 'Against the wall, out of range. And turn off the damned lights!'

Two armed aliens appeared at the sump entrance just as the lanterns were extinguished. I dropped to my knees, with water coming to my armpits, and took aim. A fusillade of stun-flechettes zinged over my head. I heard a grunt and a splash behind me as I squeezed off two careful shots. Both darts hit home and the Haluk troopers convulsed and fell to the cave floor, their weapons clattering.

'Help us,' Matt gasped. 'Emily's hit.' No more troopers appeared. I surged to my feet, thrust my arm back into the Allenby's sling, and splashed toward the women. 'How many were following you?'

'Only the two,' Matt said. 'Others . . . praying.'

Yeah. I could hear the deathsong distinctly now.

Enough light emanated from the cavern for me to see Matt and Eve backed up against the wall. The water came nearly to their waists. Matt had a tight grip on my sister, but Emily's body was floating away facedown, carried into darkness by the slow current.

Cursing, I waded after her, caught the belt of her white coverall, and drew her slight form up into my arms. Her head lolled and her blue-skinned face was wooden. There was a magnum flechette embedded at the base of her alien skull, I said, 'Oh, Jesus.'

The drug had gone directly into her brainstem, paralysing her heart and lungs. She would never awaken.

The countdown on my wrist read −01:55. I let Emily's body fall back into the water and dashed over to Matt and Eve.

'You can't leave her!' Matt cried in horror.

'She's dead. And so will we be in another two minutes.' There was a small Swiss Army knife in my belt pouch. I popped open a blade and sliced the cords holding one of the lamps to Eve's chest. It dropped into the water and floated.

I said, 'Grab that! I've got Eve. Shine the light along the left wall. There's a ledge. Get up there and get going. Our only chance is to reach the groggery.'

'The *what?*' But Matt was moving as well as talking. The lantern flashed on, dazzling me.

'Little side-cave. Ninety metres in. Go, dammit, go!'

She did, and I followed. The only way I could carry Eve along the narrowest part of the ledge was by gripping both her wrists under my chin as her body hung limply down my back. The second lamp pressed painfully into my lumbar region, but it was too late now to cut it away. I shuffled along crabwise in Matt's wake, knowing that if I fell into the stinking water Eve and I were both doomed.

'I think I see the side-cave!' Matt called.

She was far ahead of me by then. Sensibly, she shone her lantern against the opposite wall so that reflected light helped me make my way. The ledge widened. I transferred Eve to a fireman's carry and loped along. With the wristcom out of sight, I had no idea how much time remained; but I was certain that the delays had cost us our safety margin. We weren't going to be able to make it into the curved section of the tunnel where we would be safe from the photon flare. There was only one other place where we'd stand even the ghost of a chance.

Matt stood waiting when I finally reached the entrance to the groggery. 'Do we go on?'

'Can't risk it.' I ducked my head and plunged inside. Matt followed. I dropped Eve like a sack of potatoes. 'Table slab! Help me cover the door.'

Together, we wrestled the thing off its base. It was thin but it still must have weighed more than a hundred kilos. The countdown had reached –00:31.

'Space blankets?' I grunted, as the slab finally slid into position. Matt was on the floor, scrambling towards Eve. The lit lantern was on its side at the far end of the chamber where she'd tossed it. 'All four . . . zipped in . . . brought yours.' Struggling because of the remaining lamp tied to my sister's chest, she opened the front of the envirosuit and pulled out the compressed silvery squares. A shake expanded them into quilted blankets.

I rolled Eve into one like a tamale and folded the open ends beneath her inert body. Fearful of a malfunction that might cause her to smother, I had not switched on the suit ventilator or the ion screen.

'Get as far away from the door as you can,' I said to Matt.

As we wrapped ourselves I heard a peculiar high-pitched warble. By no means did the rock table-top make a tight seal against the cave wall, so the Haluk alarm klaxon was quite audible inside our sanctuary.

'Get ready,' I said. 'Here it comes.'

Before I ducked under cover I saw the tiny open spaces around the rock slab admit slowly brightening beams of white light. Then the rocks around us shuddered, causing bits of debris to patter down on us from the ceiling. I clutched the space blanket around me. A hissing sound began and turned almost at once into a deafening roar. I was briefly aware of intense heat, and then the oxygen in our little shelter was sucked out to fuel the inferno in the main cavern.

Oddly enough, I had no sense of suffocation and felt no pain. There was only a sudden, surprising ending.

Late afternoon in the Arizona desert in July. The temperature stands near 45° Centigrade and every cactus and creosote bush and ocotillo seems to cower under the merciless flood of baking sunlight.

The only things moving in the arid landscape of sand, wind-carved rock, and waterless arroyos are me and my tough old buck-skin gelding, Paco. All of the desert critters – coyotes, kit foxes, kangaroo rats, jackrabbits, even the birds and the rattlesnakes – are in hiding, waiting for nightfall.

Sensible.

But Paco and I keep on going, because the miniature electronic display on my saddle pommel shows just what I had suspected, what the Sky Ranch foreman's aerial search hadn't been able to confirm because of the rugged lay of the land: that there are thirteen head of strayed cattle in a skinny box canyon less than a kilometre further on. The transponders under their hides had commenced to make blips on my saddle display just half an hour ago. Now they appear and disappear as the steers change position, maybe drinking at the canyon's spring. The signals bouncing from them toward the detector satellite are frequently cut off by the steep walls.

My father had laughed at me that morning when I insisted that I knew where the lost cattle probably were, in a remote spot where

Eve and I had gone prospecting last year. Simon said he might get around to doing a land search in the Desert Rover next week, when he has some spare time.

Next week my ass!

I'd filled the biggest canteen, saddled up Paco when nobody was looking, and rode out.

I was eleven, and knew it all.

Now my water was gone. I'd shared the last of it with the horse a couple of hours ago, letting him drink out of my hat. Old Paco moved slower and slower. Maybe he felt dizzy and sick like I did, breathing furnace-hot air that made your head throb and didn't seem to have any *goodness* in it. Maybe his tongue was swollen like mine, and his skin sizzling and starting to feel too small for his body. Maybe he saw crazy little spots swimming before his eyes and felt his pulse banging like an Apache drum.

Maybe he was afraid he wouldn't make it.

Come on, old boy. We're coming around Mesa Empinada. Not far to go now.

The box canyon is an axe-cut in the steep tableland, heavily shadowed now that the terrible sun is finally sinking. I take the oculars out of their hot case, switch them on and look through them. Mesquite trees growing in there, and a few cottonwoods watered by the life-giving spring.

And cows.

Yes!

I was right, Pop. Not you.

A delicious cool breeze wafts out of the canyon depths and my lungs expand. Paco smells the water and his ears prick and he breaks into a clumsy trot. The cattle see us and bawl a welcome.

Grinning, I take the telephone out of the cantle and call the Sky Ranch, ready to crow over my triumph and tell them to send a hopper to pick us all up . . .

I woke, still smiling and breathing cool damp air with a peculiar alcoholic tang to it, and untangled myself from my space blanket.

Miraculously, the alien lantern still glowed. Even more miraculously, the table slab had missed us when it was blown back into the groggery by the hurricane and shattered into a dozen pieces.I crawled to the two silvery bundles lying side by side against the back wall. They were coated with dust – or maybe it was a dried layer of thin mud. All around them were tumbled liquor flasks, their stoppers popped out by the decompression, spilled contents entirely evaporated.

'Matt?' I pulled the plasfoil away from her face. She was breathing and her eyelids fluttered.

Satisfied, I turned with more trepidation to my sister, gently unwrapped her, and looked down at the pale blue, nearly human face inside the framed hood of the envirosuit. I touched her cheek. It was cold, but the partially transmuted flesh was still soft and yielding. When I lifted an eyelid, I saw that the whites of her eyes had already changed to the vivid azure typical of the gracile Haluk morph. Her irises were still green with an inner ring of amber around the enlarged pupil, just like mine.

Her other eye opened and the pupils contracted slowly. She was alive, and looking at me.

She said, 'Asa . . . you?' Her voice was still human.

I caught her up in my arms, crushing her to my chest. 'Evie! Oh, God, Evie.'

'Did . . . we make it?'

I heard Matt moan and say, 'A good question.'

My fierce embrace relaxed and I lowered Eve to the rock floor again.

'Take it easy, you guys. I've got to check things out.'

I took the Swiss Army knife out of my belt pouch and cut the cords binding the second lamp to her chest. To my satisfaction, it also worked.

Matt was sitting up, rubbing her eyes. She still wore the Haluk uniform coat but not the helmet. In spite of the earlier soaking we'd endured, our clothing and our hair were now completely dry. I still had my navigator and the alien wrist unit, and both were functional.

The countdown now read +122:41. We'd been unconscious for two hours.

I went out of the groggery, shone the light around, and exclaimed, 'Holy shit!'

I'd expected that the underground river would be reduced to a trickle. Instead, it was overflowing its channel and had very nearly reached the entrance to our shelter. The vile stench had completely disappeared.

Aiming the lantern in the direction of the main cavern, I discovered that the tunnel had been plugged by a rockfall about fifty metres back. Much closer to us, another section of the wall had partially collapsed, admitting a gushing torrent of water.

I hurried back into the groggery. 'Heads up, ladies! We've got to get out of here pronto. Ol' Man River is knocking at our door.'

Matt grabbed up the other lantern, knotted its cord into a lanyard, and hung the light around Eve's neck. I slung the stun-gun over my shoulder and folded up one of the blankets and stuffed it under my sweater. My own lamp was fastened to my belt.

Between the two of us, Matt and I eased my sister out of the low doorway and half-carried, half-dragged her onto the diminished riverbank. Then I gave the gun to Matt and carried Eve piggy-back until the lowering ceiling, the increasing slant of the ledge, and the presence of the devilish spikes made it impossible.

What followed was nightmarish. With Eve unable to move on her own, I had to drag her through the highest reaches of the Spike Farm. Matt and I used rocks to pound down the sharpest of the stalagmites, after which we padded the nubbins with her uniform coat and moved Eve over them. Our progress was excruciatingly slow, since we didn't want to risk puncturing Eve's envirosuit. I had lowered its visor in order to spare her from the constant drip of water from the ceiling formations, but Matt and I were soaked almost immediately.

It took us nearly an hour to traverse the Spike Farm. At the end of it, as we came into the squeezeway, it was evident that we had ascended above the level of the rising river. I breathed a sigh of relief, not having shared my fear that we might find the constricted tunnel filled with water and impassable.

257

With the rock floor relatively smooth again, I improvised a travois from the coat and the blanket, towing Eve behind me as I wormed through backwards. When we were safe at last in the dry Bowl Chamber, I declared time out for a good long rest.

My arm and shoulder muscles ached from the strain of hauling Eve, but aside from that, my physical condition seemed surprisingly good. There was no pain from my injuries and no other symptoms aside from normal fatigue. I decided not to use the medicuff.

Opening my sister's visor, I asked her how she felt.

'Better,' she whispered. 'Little ... thirsty. Suit reservoir ... empty.'

'We can cut a piece from the space blanket,' Matt suggested, 'and I'll go back to the Spike Farm and catch some drips.'

'No need for that.' I picked up the empty Haluk liquor bottle. 'Handy container right here, and there's nice clean holy water in the Goblin's Cathedral down the hall.'

'Goblin's Cathedral?' Matt was disbelieving.

'You'll see it when we hit the trail again. Back in a short while.'

Taking a lamp, I slipped through the Needle's Eye and filled the flask at a pool in the big room. All of us drank gratefully. Eve insisted she was comfortable in the suit, sitting propped against the Bowl's wall. But I saw that Matt was pale. I'd begun to feel pretty chilly myself now that we were no longer scrambling for our lives. The Haluk lanterns gave plenty of light but no heat. I wished I'd checked the bottles back in the groggery more carefully. All of them might not have blown their tops, and I really would have welcomed a heartwarming snort of exotic booze.

A better idea then occurred to me, and I suggested to Matt that we share body heat. We sat with our arms around each other, shoulders covered with the space blanket.

Eve looked at us with a knowing smile. 'Make ... a lovely couple.'

I groaned. 'Bag it, Sis.'

She gave a sly chuckle, then sobered. 'Thank you, Asa ... Matt. For coming.'

'We're not home free yet,' I said, 'but maybe the worst is over.'

'Did you really find Luckless Larry's route?' Matt asked me. 'Emily didn't give me many details of your message.' She grimaced.

'There was a lot going on at the time.'

I explained to Eve who Larry was and gave a brief recital of my caving expedition. 'It's also my considered opinion that any way Larry went, given his lepido clumsiness, should be a relative piece of cake for two able-bodied humans toting a gracile crip.'

Eve broke into helpless laughter. 'Deserved . . . that.' After a while I got around to asking Matt just what had happened back in the cavern.

'Emily took care of Eve, who was sitting in an mobile invalid chair. Woritak was having a long and involved conversation with a Haluk named Administrator Ru Lokinak, who was the head of the facility. They'd turned off their translators so I couldn't tell what they were saying, but Emily understood and spoke the alien language. She said the two of them were talking about whether to tell the other Haluk about the photon camouflet and try to escape.

'I asked her if there were any hand-torches available, and she sent me off with a lepido storekeeper to fetch them. When I returned with the lights I found the three of them having a fierce argument. I gathered that Ru Lokinak didn't really believe you'd found a way out. He was also unwilling to order his people to participate in an escape attempt because it would mean abandoning the Haluk who were in genen dystasis or sleeping in the testudinal phase – and that was contrary to some ancient racial code of honour.

'When Woritak requested that Eve, Emily, and I be allowed to escape through the sump, the administrator flatly refused. He gave no reason. After that, Woritak just seemed to give up. He went away to join the others. Ru Lokinak called two alien troopers armed with stun-guns to guard us, then started the death-watch prayer.'

I nodded. 'The leader thought you'd expose the plot if you survived. I was afraid of that.'

Matt said, 'Emily had tried very hard to change Ru Lokinak's mind. She really did her best, poor women.'

'She was . . . a deluded, fanatical idealist.' Eve spoke with an awful tranquil certitude. 'If she'd survived . . . Commonwealth would have executed her for treason.'

I protested. 'Emily freed us from the Haluk prison, Evie. Without her help we never would have escaped.'

'Without *Milik*' – Eve emphasized the alien name contemptu-
ously – 'none of this would have happened! And . . . and . . .'

She subsided, coughing. I went to give her water. Finally she
was quiet, resting with her chin on her chest. I rejoined Matt under
the blanket.

'How did you manage to get away?' I asked her, after a long
overdue private interlude that was necessarily limited in scope.

'The praying Haluk were gathered in concentric circles around
Administrator Ru Lokinak, standing quite close to the genen complex. Emily said they were including the tanked Haluk in their
sacred gathering. Those coloured crystal things were glowing, but
almost all of the other lights in the cavern had been shut off. We
and our guards were at the outer edge of the crowd, among the
lepidos.'

The Haluk had hummed their musical mantra, swaying in rhythm
to the wordless song. After a little while, the women noticed that
many of the aliens seemed to be passing into a kind of trance –
including the two troopers detailed to guard them.

The troopers weren't wearing translators, so Matt and Emily
whispered together and came up with a plan. They pretended that
Eve was in distress, and mimed her need for medication and a
blanket. The guards didn't want to interrupt their prayers, and the
treatment station was in plain sight not ten meters distant, so Emily
took Eve away without a trooper accompanying them. Emily managed to get four of the plasfoil blankets, along with two lanterns
and some cord. She hid the extra things in Eve's lap after covering
her and returned to Matt and the troopers.

As the countdown continued and the ritual of docile thanatopsis
became more intense, Matt and Emily began to edge away from
their half-mesmerized guards, pushing Eve in the antigrav chair
and keeping close to the outer ring of lepidos. No one seemed to
notice when they abruptly took off in a mad dash across the cavern.

Their audacious plan seemed to have worked. They'd almost
reached Sump Number Five when one of the graciles gave the
alarm.

'I think it was Physician Woritak himself,' Matt said. 'Someone
in green medical clothing was shouting at the guards. They came

after us. You know what happened after that.'

'Damn,' I said. 'And I thought Woritak was a good guy.'

'Maybe not,' Matt observed, 'when forced to choose between his own race's political ambitions and the lives of three human women.'

Eve spoke up suddenly in a laboured whisper. 'Do you understand . . . why they had a genen facility on Cravat?'

I looked at her in surprise. 'I guess I thought it was a matter of convenience, or something. Close to the source of vector supply.'

'No . . . very dangerous to work here. The principal transmutation facilities, ones that only eliminate allomorphism . . . are located on Haluk planets. This Nutmeg-414 genen operation was unique. Different purpose. Milik told me when I was captured . . . why she was going to change *me* . . . as she herself had been changed.'

Something frigid did a flipflop in my guts at the same time that a comic-strip lightbulb clicked on above my head. 'The other Emily Konigsberg! The one who died in the alien lifeboat accident. She was some sort of Haluk ringer. A duplicate!'

'Proper term is . . . demiclone. Adult alien individual transmuted radically . . . becomes virtually indistinguishable from DNA-donor human. No need to wait years for ordinary clone to grow up. Some alien genes remain, but most common tests would show demiclone was a true human. I'm not sure what was . . . mission of Fake Emily. Perhaps to spy on Galapharma itself.'

'And if they'd made a demiclone of *you*,' I said to Eve grimly, 'the fake would have delivered the Rampart Worlds to Gala on a plate!'

Matt added, 'And Fake Helly and Fake Matt would have helped serve dessert.'

'Six months,' Eve whispered. 'That's how long it would have taken to prepare our . . . doppelgängers. Asa, do you know . . . that Simon wanted me to take over as head of Rampart Starcorp? Become CEO, bump Zed from the presidency?'

'He told me,' I said. 'I thought it was a super idea.'

'I agreed only under protest. I told him the person he really needed . . . was you.'

'Good God, Evie!'

I would have remonstrated with her, but she shut me up with an incisive command. 'Never mind that. We can ... argue it later, with Simon. Now I must tell you everything I know about the Haluk's conspiracy with the Big Seven Concerns. Beginning with my capture.'

Chapter 22

Eve had come to Cravat for the very reasons that I had deduced. For nearly two years she had suspected that there were Galapharma partisans within Rampart, actively working for a takeover. What she could not understand was why Alistair Drummond was so desperate to acquire Rampart that he would risk his Concern's very existence in the attempt; for if Galapharma's sabotage, theft of significant data, and conspiracy to devaluate Rampart were proven, then under ICS regulations Rampart could sue the big Concern and demand all of its assets in compensatory and punitive damages.

The only theory that seemed likely to explain Drummond's audacious actions involved some truly obscene potential for profit.

The niggling little collection of Haluk mysteries was, on the face of it, unrelated to Galapharma's effort to engineer a Rampart takeover. Eve had not even remotely considered a connection until Bob Bascombe told her his odd story and she discovered that Oliver Schneider had never mounted an investigation of the Haluk corpse. Asking herself *Why?* had set off a new, admittedly far-fetched, train of thought.

Eve had never trusted Schneider. For one thing, he was Zed's man and had on more than one occasion obstructed internal investigations of Rampart affairs that she had personally initiated. She had no proof of Schneider's disloyalty; but like me, she had realized that the head of corporate security would have been the ideal person for Gala to suborn. And now he had failed to check out a Haluk corpse on Cravat, a planet producing *something* that greatly interested the aliens.

Eve knew that Simon would have laughed at the notion of a Galapharma-Haluk connection. It was also unthinkable that she report her flimsy suspicions to the Commonwealth authorities. If she tried to gather evidence by mounting a Cravat investigation that bypassed Schneider's Internal Security Force and used Fleet Security personnel reporting to Matt Gregoire, Schneider would undoubtedly find out about it and find a way to throw a monkey wrench into the works. Crafty old Ollie had eyes and ears in every corner of Rampart. That was the way he earned his huge salary and generous stakeholder options.

So Eve decided to check out Cravat herself. She flew to the planet in disguise and swore her friends the Bascombes to secrecy. If her expedition was a wild goose chase, no harm would be done. There was an element of personal danger, but she was an experienced ET wilderness traveller and had visited the planet's boonies before. She intended to go very well armed.

She also believed that any aliens who might have invaded the Nutmeg factories of Grant Microcontinent would not dare to defend the sites overtly against casual human intruders. Bob Bascombe had already told Eve that big-game hunters prowled Grant with impunity. She also knew that the robot defences of the moth-balled factories were programmed not to harm humans, and that their main doors were left unlocked so that they could provide refuge in an emergency.

Her intent was to land in the jungle near Nutmeg-414, pretend to be a curious hunter, and simply wander boldly into the facility to see what she could see.

As she came through the gate and began touring the compound, two male humans wearing envirosuits with Rampart insignia came out the front door of the factory. They hailed her in a friendly fashion. Thinking they were project maintenance personnel, she concealed her disappointment and told them that she was Eve Frost.

Wow! The guys were really impressed that a Rampart VIP was visiting their backwoods establishment. They transmitted the good news to their boss, Chalky White, who was working inside.

Eve agreed to come in for a fatal glass of beer. Chalky and two other Galapharma security agents nabbed her as she stepped out of the airlock, disarmed her, and took her down to the cavern.

She was confined to a cell for four days while subspace messages corkscrewed around the infracosmos and Galapharma decided what to do with its spectacular catch. Someone came up with a diabolically brilliant idea.

Elgar/McGrath rushed to Cravat to make sure that the scheme was properly carried out. He personally told Eve that the process of transmuting her into a Haluk would begin the next day. He couldn't resist teasing her by saying that she'd be very surprised to know who had suggested her bizarre 'punishment'.

Some hours later a female Haluk paid a secret and emotional visit to Eve's prison cell. The alien identified herself as one Emily Blake Konigsberg, who had once been human. She told my appalled sister her own fantastic story.

Six years earlier, Emily Konigsberg said, she had been a well-paid senior researcher at Galapharma AC on Earth. Because she was attractive as well as brilliant in her chosen field of xenobiology, she caught the attention of Gala's debonair Chief Executive Officer, Alistair Drummond. They enjoyed a brief affair, which dissolved amicably. While they were lovers, Emily confided her great dream to Alistair: She wanted to free the Haluk – those highly intelligent, extremely numerous, misunderstood aliens – from the allomorphism that had so tragically hindered their progress. Emily had studied the Haluk for years, admittedly from afar. She was convinced that the allomorphic trait could easily be eradicated through genetic engineering. And they would be so grateful!

She reminded Alistair that Haluk antagonism toward humanity was largely rooted in envy of our stable physiology and fear that we might dominate them with our superior science. No other non-human race of star-travellers, she maintained, had so great a potential as the Haluk.

Emily Konigsberg's motives for helping them were rooted in her deep conviction that the Commonwealth policy denying genen treatment and other high technology to qualified Insap races was immoral. She pointed out to Alistair Drummond that a Concern willing to bypass that shortsighted policy on behalf of the Haluk would not only redress a grave injustice but also glean enormous profits.

Alistair did not need reminding that the Haluk Cluster had abundant resources of valuable transactinide elements, which the aliens lacked the scientific expertise to utilize, yet had perversely refused to trade to humanity.

The Galapharma CEO was intrigued. He agreed to consider Emily's proposal, sent Concern agents disguised as pirates to sound out the Haluk, and was astounded when the previously intractable aliens bought the deal hook, line and sinker.

Emily went to work in a Gala-equipped lab on the Haluk colonial planet Artiuk near the tip of the Perseus Spur. In a gratifyingly short time she demonstrated how allomorphism might be banished from the Haluk genome. It was somewhat disappointing to Alistair Drummond that the only feasible vector for the modification process turned out to be Rampart Starcorp's PD 32:C2. However, he had plans of his own for Rampart, and the Haluk connection could only enhance them in the long run.

Emily Konigsberg laboured on Artiuk and on planets within the distant Haluk Cluster for several years, overjoyed that her dream was being fulfilled. True, the Haluk were slow to show signs of genuine friendliness toward humanity. They largely remained aloof and suspicious, even towards her, and grumbled over commercial realities that forced them to hand over extravagant amounts of valuable elements in exchange for human genetic engineering expertise and relatively paltry quantities of critical viral material.

Later on, however, when other members of the Big Seven Concerns joined Gala in 'mutually beneficial' illicit Haluk trade agreements, the attitude of the aliens improved. They willingly paid even higher prices for starships, computers, high-tech manufacturing equipment, and other marvellous contraband goods; and while they remained stand-offish to Concern agents, they were much nicer to Emily and to the handful of human colleagues who assisted her good work on the Haluk worlds.

Emily Konigsberg's happiest day came in 2229, when she was presented to the paramount leader of the Haluk Union, the Servant of the Servants of Luk, who came to Artiuk specially in order to meet her. The SSL not only conferred a Diadem of Honour upon Emily, acknowledging her noble efforts, but also deplored the continuing lack of genuine *rapprochement* between their races. Would she be interested in hearing his suggestion for a new direction in Haluk-human relations?

Of course!

Was she familiar with the demicloning process, as it was applied to sapient entities?

Well . . . it was illegal in the Commonwealth of Human Worlds, as were cloning and other radical forms of genetic engineering involving intelligent beings. But the technology was well-documented in scientific literature.

The SSL seemed to know that. He airily discounted the criminal aspect by pointing out that both her own great work and Big Seven trade with the Haluk were also technical violations of Commonwealth law.

Yes, said Emily. But why in the world were the Haluk interested in demicloning?

The SSL confessed that he, also, had a great dream. He was positive that if small numbers of Haluk were transmuted into human form, they could become potent envoys for peace among their own people. By making educational tours of Haluk worlds and familiarizing the xenophobic masses with humanity's goals, customs and potential beneficence, the demiclones could defuse longstanding fears and hostility.

Truly? Emily had asked, not quite convinced.

Indubitably, said the SSL, citing obscure aspects of Haluk psychology.

The human-appearing envoys might also address unrest among the lower classes, who were resentful because only privileged Haluk were thus far being stabilized with the expensive $PD32:C2$, while the proles were obliged to keep on morphing.

The demiclone envoys could point out that when the Haluk finally overcame their racial prejudice and proclaimed to the entire Milky Way Galaxy that they were willing to become brothers (and open trading partners) with humanity, then surely the humans would reciprocate the gesture, and find ways to increase supplies of PD 32:C2. A great new era would dawn for both races.

Think of it!

Emily diffidently wondered whether actual human ambassadors might do the ticklish public-relations job better than demiclones.

The SSL thought not. Sadly enough, Haluk dealings with Concern agents remained grudging because of the inescapable constraints of illicit commerce. Each side, to be blunt, was wary of being screwed by the other because of the secrecy angle.

And aside from Concern agents (saving Emily and her colleagues), no humans of stature interacted socially with the Haluk. Nor would they ever do so, until the Commonwealth changed its laws.

Displaying a surprising command of human idiom, the SSL described the paradoxical situation as a Catch-22, wherein the only solution to the problem is denied by inherent circumstances.

The SSL's words pierced Emily Konigsberg's idealistic heart. She agreed to devote her efforts entirely to the new project, and also agreed that it should be kept secret from Galapharma and the other Concerns conducting backstairs business with the Haluk, lest they misunderstand and put obstacles in the project's way due to crass, commercial considerations.

In its final form, Emily's demiclone process required three steps. First, the Haluk subject was rendered nonallomorphic in the usual manner, receiving a small amount of human genetic material via PD 32:C2. This normally required six weeks in dystasis.

The second step, preparing the human DNA-donor, required a longer period of time and more of the vector's wide-spectrum transferase. The human DNA-donor, resting in dystasis, was carefully infused with selected nonallomorphic Haluk genes in order to preclude rejection syndrome in the alien demiclone subject. After twelve weeks in the tank the human donor was ready, having acquired superficial gracile appearance as a reversible side effect.

In the third step, the Haluk subject received an enormous amount of genetic material from the modified human donor. When the transmutation process was complete, in another twelve weeks, a human-appearing replica of the donor emerged from the tank. Only the most sophisticated genetic testing would be able to detect that the individual was an alien.

Becoming the first human demiclone DNA-donor was, to Emily, an act of loving communion. She hoped that her 'offspring' would be a bridge to peace who would inspire trillions of frustrated and truculent aliens in the Haluk Cluster to become friends of the human race and live happily and prosperously ever after.

After a small ceremony of consecration, Fake Emily went away, supposedly to be trained for her delicate task.

The real Emily expected to be restored to human form after the initial experiment's success. But the Servant of the Servants of Luk told her, with profound regret, that she'd have to wait a bit. She was so valuable to them that they could not do without her services for yet another six months while she was treated in dystasis. She was needed to produce more demiclones as quickly as possible. More human DNA-donors were being assembled and transported to Artiuk (never mind how), and numbers of Haluk volunteers were eagerly awaiting transmutation.

And surely Emily didn't think that the Haluk gracile body she wore was repulsive?

. . . Of course not.

With only the smallest seed of misgiving sprouting in her mind, Emily Konigsberg did as the SSL asked and carried on – until Galapharma found out what the Haluk were doing, as a direct result of the death of Fake Emily in a Haluk starship.

It was a loquacious lepido's fault.

After the noteworthy accident, which was reported in the human media, Galapharma's liaison team, led by Alistair Drummond himself, came to Artiuk to discuss a replacement for Emily and do a general assessment of the situation.

A lepidodermoid waitron, who had been until recently a gracile technician in the secret demiclone lab, offered refreshments to the important humans visiting the huge establishment. It wore a translator to facilitate service, but was under strict orders not to chat casually with the humans. (When Haluk change from the gracile to the lepido stage they not only decline in intelligence, but also tend to be obsessed with the thing they miss most.)

As Alistair Drummond expressed condolences to one of the gracile scientists upon Emily Konigsberg's death, the lepido waitron turned to him and said:

'Dead? Oh, no no! This one give Emily breakfast in staff messroom this morning. She is alive. And looking very sexy, too!'

Drummond invited the stunned gracile scientists to explain. They hemmed, hawed, suggested that the waitron was befuddled by the Big Change, and commanded it to stop boring the distinguished guest with ridiculous babble and leave the room.

But Alistair Drummond was not to be put off. He ordered his associates to seize the lepido, and very gently told the terrified creature to lead the way to the real Emily Konigsberg at once. When the other Haluk objected he repeated his request, and suggested that if it was denied, the 'mutually beneficial' arrangement would be summarily cancelled.

The Haluk graciles found themselves in an impossible position. Short of doing violence to Drummond and his associates, who flatly refused to unhand the lepido, there was no way they could avoid letting the cat out of the bag.

Emily, in Haluk form, was duly produced. Then it was the humans' turn to be shocked and appalled – first by her appearance, and later by their guided tour of the demiclone project. During a private interview with Drummond, Emily tried to explain the project's lofty purpose.

In a pig's arse! said Alistair Drummond, and delivered a scathing lecture on interspecies espionage. Haluk spies inside the Commonwealth government were mildly worrying; Haluk spies inside the Hundred Concerns were serious trouble; Haluk spies inside the Big Seven were profoundly deep shit.

Emily implored him not to force the Haluk to halt the project. It would not only imperil Haluk-human *détente*, but it would also be a mortal insult to the Servant of the Servants of Luk, who had conceived the idea. She suggested a way that might eliminate (or at least minimize) the potential problem.

Dismissing Emily, Alistair Drummond conferred with his

associates. After the dust settled, Galapharma and the other Concerns agreed not to cancel the 'mutually beneficial' arrangement, provided that the Haluk demiclone project was transferred to a secure and secret facility on a human world, where Galapharma agents could keep a close eye on it. Gala would also provide all of the necessary human DNA-donors.

Emily was sent to Cravat to supervise the revised operation, feeling sadly betrayed by her erstwhile Haluk friends and ill-used by her ex-lover Alistair Drummond, who had ordered her to find a foolproof way to mark the Haluk ringers, unless she wanted to spend the rest of her life wearing blue skin and a face that would frighten small terrestrial children.

As it happened, she did both.

'What was the marker?' I asked Eve.

'She never told me. I presume it was some sort of redundant DNA sequence. I ... don't know much about genetics.'

'Never mind,' I said. 'Rampart must employ a whole gaggle of other people who do.'

'But the point is moot, isn't it, Asa? We have no demiclone to test! All of the subjects – all that we know of, at any rate – were vaporized back there in the cavern ... along with the donors.'

'The donors?' A fresh frisson of horror swept through me. 'Are you telling me –'

'I thought you knew,' Eve said dully. 'Only about half of the subjects in the dystasis tanks were Haluk. They'd begun their transmutation only ten days before I arrived. The rest were human DNA donors. Milik said they were Throwaways, former employees of the Big Seven who were disenfranchised for some infraction. The poor devils were told that if they co-operated in a special project, they'd get their jobs and their citizenship back ... It was a lie, of course. Milik told me they were kept permanently in dystasis here. Used over and over as sources of modified DNA.'

'That's appalling!' Matt said.

'That's economical,' said Eve.

We were all silent for a long moment. Then I said, 'You know,

I betcha that right this very minute, spies with human bodies and Haluk minds are engaging in skulduggery back on Earth. Gala and its cohorts probably think the Haluk are most interested in stealing scientific data from other Concerns and Starcorps.'

'And what do *you* think?' my sister asked shrewdly.

I climbed to my feet, stretched, and pulled out the subterrain chart. 'I think it's time we got out of this hole.'

Chapter 23

We started off again, and most of the trip proved to be neither dangerous nor even very difficult. The two women admired the Goblin's Cathedral and were awed by the chasm with its infernal cascade. Larry's putative footprints in the dust impressed them as they had impressed me, and we began our ascent of the Staircase with high hearts.

The lower part of the steep tunnel was dry, wide enough so that Matt and I could support Eve together. Nearer the top there were rockfalls and a considerable amount of flowing water, and the way became trickier to negotiate. We finally had to tie Eve to my back with strips cut from the Haluk uniform jacket so I didn't have to worry about her slipping off. Her own strength was still insufficient for her to hang on tightly, although she seemed to be improving.

We had found no more traces of Luckless Larry. Any footprints would have been washed away long ago by water pouring down the narrowing rocky steps, and he hadn't tossed any more dead soldiers.

About ninety minutes after we had left the Bowl Chamber, the navigator's altimeter showed that we had reached the level of Pothole Passage and the moment of truth: had the Staircase led to freedom, or would it open into one of the many blind corridors that the chart had showed, trapping us in a labyrinth with no outlet?

We climbed out of the hole and found ourselves in a stalactite-hung chamber. One end of it contained a pool about twenty metres wide, crowded with islandlike formations. Its spillway was the Staircase we'd just come from.

While Matt and Eve attended to some personal business I found a high place, stood on top of it, and flashed my powerful lantern in all directions, hoping to orient myself. Check cave features. Check chart. Check navigator's compass.

A few minutes later, I let loose with a jubilant '*Yah-hoo!*' that made the stalactites ring and the women call out to me worriedly. Compass bearings taken on the multiple narrow crevices at the north end of the pool and the single larger tunnel trending southward from its opposite shore corresponded exactly with features on the chart.

'It's okay, gals!' I shouted. 'We're in Pothole Passage.'

They cheered.

I returned to the spot where Matt and Eve were resting and accepted congratulations. Now all we had to do – all! – was continue on for roughly eight kilometres until we reached the exit into the Green Hell.

'How long do you think it might take?' Matt's gaze flicked meaningfully toward Eve, who sat propped against a formation with her eyes closed and a slight smile on her face.

I tried to be encouraging. 'If we're lucky, ten hours. Then we set off Eve's suit beacon and the one in my navigator, sit back, and wait until they pick us up.'

Eve murmured, 'Hope . . . no humpies join the party before that.'

And no Bronson Elgar, I thought.

After half an hour's rest, we started again.

Matt and I alternated carrying Eve and breaking trail. The route was serpentine but rarely confusing, occasionally so constricted that we were forced to slither and at other times opening into large rooms or long galleries decorated with dripping speleothems. The water came and went according to the vagaries of the rock strata; but Grant was a humid landmass and almost all of its drainage was underground, so very few parts of Pothole Passage could be classified as 'dry'.

Periodically I'd check our scrolling track on the navigator against the chart, only to be reassured that we were going exactly right. We didn't talk much. Most of the time, like any hikers on a long, long trail, we saved our energies and tried to ignore our aching muscles and growling stomachs.

Now and then the one of us who wasn't carrying Eve would sing. I contributed off-key cowboy laments and Mexican *canciones*. Matt sang bouncy little ditties in Creole patois or Caribbean dialect. She could carry a tune much better than I. The song Eve pronounced to be her favourite was a Calypso ballad called 'Matilda', about a poor jerk whose girlfriend took all his money and ran away to Venezuela.

For some reason, the two women thought it was very funny.

After we'd travelled for six hours through depressingly damp passages we reached a chamber with ledges that were fairly dry. We made camp on one and slept like the dead until our cramping stomachs woke us in misery seven hours later.

There was no more singing after that, only slogging onward like robots in the bobbing lamplight, stumbling across streams, squeezing through the occasional crevice or crawlway, climbing rockfalls, listlessly eyeing formations so beautiful they should have taken our breath away.

But we had none to spare.

We continued on until weakness and exhaustion felled us again, less than two hours later. My sleep this time was fitful, not because of hunger (my stomach had given up and was sulking) but from a belated attack of nerves. When I finally did fall into a doze I kept having petty nightmares – the looping kind where you do some tedious task over and over again and never get it right. In my dream, I was installing a gas-fire cooker (the only kind to have) in the kitchen of my beachfront shack on Kedge-Lockaby, trying to get the damned thing working but never succeeding because stinkmoths kept flying at me, preventing me from seeing straight . . .

I woke up in a cold sweat, pawing at my face. We had left one of the lamps burning at low setting while we slept, and damn me if I didn't spot a bug skittering away from my head on dozens of hair-thin legs! I remained absolutely still with Matt lying zonked beside me. After a few minutes three of the exotic insectiles came tippy-toeing out of a crevice, foraging daintily. They lacked pigment and looked something like glass centipedes. Since they made no attempt to attack either of us (and I felt no bites), I decided they were harmless.

A glow of excitement kindled inside me. Most cave-dwelling animals survive only in areas relatively near to the entrances. The lightless regions deeper underground are sterile unless organic matter is regularly washed in from the outer world to serve as the bottom link in the food chain, seeding the mud and water with bacteria and other tiny edibles.

The glass centipedes signalled that we were nearing trail's end.

Tucking the blanket around Matt, I crept over to check on my sister. Eve was also sound asleep, breathing regularly and with a strong pulse in her slender not-quite-alien neck. The suit's powerpack was less than half discharged and she seemed warm and dry. When we got outside we could turn on her ion screen and she'd be shielded from ambient perils of a minuscule kind, while Matt and I would have to take our chances with noxious bugoids and germies until rescuers arrived.

But the cavalry had better come soon, because if the little monsters didn't get us, the big ones sure as hell would – more sooner than later.

Maybe I could figure some way for us to shelter in the cave while we waited: hang the navigator in a tree with its beacon triggered, leave a message, hope that the Allenby stun-gun would fend off carnivorous bat analogues and other cave-dwelling wildlife.

But the magnum flechettes wouldn't have any more effect on humpbacked lacertilians and their ilk than peashooter ammo . . .

'Helly?'

I turned at Matt's whisper and came back to her. 'Just seeing if Eve was all right. Actually, I think she's doing better than we are.'

'Is it time to start again?' She didn't sound enthusiastic.

'Not if you don't want to. I couldn't sleep.'

'Tummyache?'

'As we say out West, "My pore belly figgers my throat's cut". And the patter of tiny feet didn't help.' I explained the good news about the bugs.

She held the blanket open. We'd been sharing the remnants of the uniform coat for a pillow. 'Maybe I could help you relax. Come and lie down.'

I did. And her prediction came true, sure enough.

*   *   *

We had 1.2 kilometres left to go, and we all woke refreshed and ready to ramble. Eve was able to walk for short distances now. Her voice was steady and her mind seemed nearly as sharp as ever, but I still flinched internally at the sight of her altered features. The Haluk were going to pay for that, and so was Bronson Elgar, who'd been so amused by Eve's transmutation.

For the next hour or so we travelled through a reasonably spacious, very muddy corridor. Its curiously pitted walls, through which only meagre trickles seeped, had a high-water mark about twenty centimetres above the floor, showing that a freshet had flowed through recently – perhaps the surface run-off of a large storm. We saw many more of the glassy insectiles legging among the ceiling formations, along with black and white furry growth on the walls that might have been plant life. Once Eve caught the merest glimpse of an elongated pink little animal resembling a newt, fleeing before us into the dripping darkness.

We moved along without haste, alternately carrying Eve and letting her walk. We were using only a single lantern now, since we had no idea of their power capacity, and cheering each other up by describing the lavish meals we expected to consume after we were rescued. It wouldn't take long for Cravat Fleet Security to find us. Not with two beacons sending out homing signals . . .

But our good luck had nearly run out.

All three of us exclaimed out loud when we emerged from the tunnel and caught sight of the amazing spectacle. The lamp had been focused on the floor and turned low to conserve power, so the enormous subterranean room we entered was dark. Not entirely so, however, because all of the upper nooks and crannies were crowded with uncountable blue-white sparks. When I dimmed the light still further, it seemed as though we had come out into a night strewn with millions of close-set tiny stars. Black voids like galactic dust clouds occasionally interrupted the glowing drifts of luminescence. The sight was magical.

'Are they alive?' Matt whispered, overawed.

'Must be,' I said. 'Kind of a glow-worm, maybe.'

We put Eve down and moved forward, turning on both lanterns to get a better look at the Glow-worm Chamber's interior. The living galaxy winked out as artificial illumination flooded the room. It was perhaps fifty metres across, not very high but enormously wide, its boundaries on either hand lost in darkness. At some time in the past a great rockfall had come down from the ceiling to make an island at our left; some of the broken chunks were house-sized. The ceiling was composed of jagged, irregular formations, festooned with what looked like dense spider webbing. The luminous creatures, whatever they were, were too small to see. Our tunnel had ended at a rock ledge with water dripping minimally from its rim. Below was a slope of tumbled boulders with a slick mudslide down the middle, and at its foot, nine or ten meters below us, lay an open expanse of black water that filled the huge chamber from wall to wall. There wasn't much of a shore anywhere, except for a mud delta at the end of the chute.

No exit tunnel was visible across the lake. The wall was sheer to the water.

I said, 'Well, shit.'

'I'd say we must have made a wrong turn,' Matt murmured. 'Except there weren't any to make.'

We'd sat Eve down away from the lip of the ledge, so she was unable to see the extent of the problem. She began creeping toward Eve and me. 'What's wrong?'

'Dead end,' said Matt.

'This *is* the way. I'm sure of it!' I hauled out the chart and made the correlations with my navigator. We were on course. The chart showed the section of Pothole Passage we'd just traversed, and it showed the Glow-worm Chamber, and it also showed an exit tunnel on the chamber's other side. Squinting in the dazzling lamplight, I turned the chart this way and that to enhance its hologram aspect. The vertical scale was, as always, tough to interpret.

Finally, to my dismay, I thought I had it pegged.

Eve and Matt were sitting side by side on a low rock, silently shining a beam of lamplight along the opposite side of the lake.

'Guess what?' I said.

'The way out is underwater,' said my sister calmly. 'The level of this lake must have risen after a recent rainstorm.'

'You got it. The exit is over there, about two metres under.'

'How long is the pipe?' Matt asked.

'At least seventy metres. If I'm reading the chart correctly, there should be air pockets.'

'There'd better be,' she said. 'I'm a decent enough swimmer, but not *that* good. And what about Eve?'

'We can shut the visor of the suit,' my sister said, 'turn off the ventilator and close the snorkel. Residual air should keep me alive while Asa tows me through.'

I showed them the chart. 'See, the exit is a kind of slot. It's over four metres wide at the beginning, then pinches to less than half that, then widens out again when you're thirty-two metres in. That's where the first air space should be. The second one is here, another eighteen metres along. Then another twenty or so to the third pocket. Beyond that just a little way there should be headroom and air – until you reach here, a corridor that's definitely above the water level. The cave's outer exit is another fifty metres further on.'

Matt studied the printout. 'No stream flows out of the cave?'

I shook my head. 'This body of water is an underground reservoir, filled periodically from run-off through some source inside Pothole Passage. It probably empties very slowly through cracks in the rock strata too small to show on the map. Larry must have passed through the pipe on foot during a low-water period.'

'So there'll be no current to contend with?' Eve asked me.

'Minimal, I'd think.'

'Good. With air in my suit, it's going to be hard enough to keep me from scraping along the top of the pipe. I think we'd better weight me with rocks.'

'You two can make a weight belt while I reconnoitre the pipe,' I said.

They stared at me, fully cognizant of the danger. Finally, Matt nodded. 'Yes, that would be sensible. And since you're a sport-diver, I presume you can hold your breath for a long time.'

'It's not part of my average day's activities,' I said wryly, thinking of the superlative scuba outfit I used when shepherding *turistas* on the Brillig Reef, 'but I've been known to skinny dip for clamoids.'

Free-diving to a depth of fifteen metres or less. But it wouldn't do to mention that. I took off the sneakers and socks, the jeans, the sweater, and the scrub shirt. My trusty Swiss Army knife served to cut off the scrub pants into swim shorts. I wore my utility belt and hung one of the lamps around my neck with a cord. It was going to dangle like a sonuvabitch, but it was too large to tie to my head.

I gave the ladies a spunky grin. 'Well, I'm outa here.'

Eve said, 'Asa . . . give us a hug for luck, Li'l Bro.'

I embraced her suited body. 'It'll be okay, Evie.'

'Of course.' But there were human tears in her partially transmuted eyes.

Matt said, 'Next.'

This time, the squeeze was anything but brotherly, and neither was the kiss that went along with it.

I put my sneakers back on for prudence's sake and clambered down the slimy boulder slope. On the tiny mud delta I ditched the shoes again and waded in.

The bottom dropped off steeply and the water felt like glacier run-off. My family jewels retreated screaming to the shelter of my pelvis. I conjured up thoughts of a giant steaming bowl of chili, my favourite snickerdoodle cookies hot from the oven, and a huge scalding pot of Mimo's contraband New Guinea Peaberry coffee. Soon, Lord.

Then I called out, '¡Hasta la vista!' And dived with a cannonball tuck.

There were critters in the water.

I suppose I should have expected them, but the sight of teeming multitudes of exotic waterlife in the beam of my lantern startled the hell out of me. I'd never done any cave-diving myself, but I'd taken out other sport-divers who had, and they'd regaled me with yarns about blind albino animals encountered during subterranean scuba excursions.

The aquatic denizens of Pothole Passage were mostly plankton-sized, abundant dots of protoplasm that fled the golden light in frantic schools, disappearing into ultramarine shadows. Perhaps they were a larval phase of the glow-worms. Slightly larger creatures that resembled mosquitoes or midges seemed to scull along with winged appendages. I wondered if they could fly as well as swim.

Now and then, as I swam strongly through the twists and turns of the pipe, I encountered pale piscoids and newtlike creatures that must have fed on the small fry. They were mostly finger-length, lacking both eyes and pigment. One larger fish, at least thirty centimetres long, was exceptionally beautiful, pink and silver with long diaphanous fins like trailing scarves. It crouched sullenly in a side grotto as I swam by and bared its needle teeth at me, knowing that an intruder was abroad, despite its blindness, but sensing by my wake that I was too big to mess with.

A thirty-two-metre underwater swim in relatively shallow water is, for technical reasons, more difficult than free-diving to the same depth; but I made the trip without too much difficulty and came up in an air pocket that provided headroom but little else. The ceiling was fractured limestone and hundreds of rice-sized objects resembling cocoons were cemented to it. I detected a very faint scent of the jungle. Fresh air was definitely coming in from the outside.

The next section of the pipe was clogged with broken rock. In some places, there was just enough freeway for a human body to eel through, and I decided I was going to have to put a leash on Eve to get her past it. Fortunately, the next air pocket, eighteen metres further along, turned out to be a room-sized chamber that even had ledges where a weary swimmer could haul out and rest. I did so, noticing that the Green Hell aroma was much stronger. There was also a ranker stench that made the hairs on the back of my neck prickle.

I shone the light about and froze.

Back in a corner was a heap of dead leaves and other composty forest trash, and mixed with it were bones. Some of them still had bits of rotting meat on them and quite a few were at least as large as human armbones. As I crouched motionless, daring to breathe again only when I was certain that the little cave was without a living occupant, I felt a gentle, steady movement of air across my chilled wet skin.

The place had an exit to the outside.

I checked the chart and sure enough, in that direction was a nearly vertical chimney leading to the hillside above the ravine where Larry had emerged. It was at least twenty-seven metres deep and only a creature with wings or monkeylike climbing skills (or both) could have used it. I recalled the terrier-sized bat analogue that had tried to squirm into my yaga-chick. Its conformation fitted the bill; but the size of the bone leftovers hinted that whatever had carried its meals into this cave was considerably larger than my would-be hitchhiker. I decided to move on with no further ado.

Twenty metres further along, after swimming through waters increasingly crowded with tiny aquatic animals, I reached another air pocket, slightly smaller than the lair but also having a small area of dry rock that I gratefully perched on. The cavity was uninhabited except for numbers of pinhead-sized webspinners with a single white spot on their backs, busily consuming tiny prey caught in their meshes. I switched off my lamp. The place became a fairyland of living stars, and one small mystery was solved.

Onward! If I'd read the chart correctly, there was only a short section of flooded pipe left, and then – *gracias a dios* – open air. I swam along for a few metres until lamplight reflecting from the water's surface showed that air again lay overhead. Bracing myself against the rocks, I switched off the lantern, allowed myself to rise without making a splash into a low-ceilinged tunnel, and filled my lungs with air that was both highly perfumed and stinking.

It was dark, even though the passage at this point was relatively straight, the ceiling becoming higher and higher as it led to a sizeable cavern in the vicinity of the mouth. I knew from my navigator's chronograph that it was night on Cravat, so I waited until my eyes accommodated. Slowly, I became aware of a lopsided grey square in the distance: the cavern's mouth. I quietly smacked the sides of my head to dislodge water from my ears and heard faraway howls and chitters and roars similar to those I remembered from my initial foray into the Green Hell. Paddling noiselessly, I headed toward the dry part of the tunnel.

My feet had just touched bottom when a bulky silhouette partially eclipsed the grey square. Something growled softly.

I turned my lamp's beam full on it and saw one of the low-slung bearlike quadrupeds we'd seen attacking Bascombe's hopper on the shore of Pickle Pothole. Its eyes were like saucers and reflected a furious ruby red. The beast's sharp-edged buzzard beak was wide open as it came gallumphing straight at me, the growl escalating into a raspy bellow.

Dive dive dive!

I turned tail and swam for my life into the submerged section of the tunnel. After a few moments, I realized that the buzz-bear wasn't following. I rested in the Star Chamber until my adrenalin level subsided, then cautiously swam back toward the cave entrance and poked my head above the surface. Paws with impressive talons were slashing the shoaling waters to a lather, but the animal showed no inclination to come after me.

Okay, I thought as I retreated once again. Be like that. Next time we meet, I'll have a stun-gun.

Then I went to fetch Matt and Eve.

I found them waiting on the mud delta. They'd made both a weight belt and a short tow-rope, slicing my scrub suit into narrow strips and braiding them. Eve had also decided that Matt and I would need unsoaked clothing at the end of our swim. Her solution was to tuck our damp but not sodden duds into her envirosuit. There was room because she had lost weight during dystasis, but she was left looking like a ragdoll with wadded stuffing.

(Matt, on the other hand, had stripped to a wispy bra and bikini briefs and looked like another kind of doll altogether as she prepared herself by swimming a lap across the lake.)

I closed Eve's visor, deployed the snorkel at the rear of her hood, and helped her into the water. It took a while to adjust the improvised weight belt (stones knotted in exotic fabric), neutralizing the suit's buoyancy without causing her to sink too rapidly. Finally the job was done and we were ready.

I had described the underwater journey in detail, including my encounter with the cave-bear analogue. The first leg would be trickiest because Matt wasn't at all confident that she could hold her breath while swimming thirty-two metres. I decided I'd have to accompany her to be sure she didn't come to grief, then return to fetch Eve.

I tied one end of the cloth rope to Matt's left wrist, wound the remainder around her arm, and fastened the end with a half hitch. That way, the rope would stay out of her way while she swam, but if she faltered I'd be able to unfurl it quickly and tow her.

'Shall I hyperventilate?' she asked me. Both of us had lamps around our necks.

'Safer not to. Just swim as steadily as you can. I'll let you know when we reach the air pocket.'

'Right.' She tucked under neatly and was gone without another word.

I called out to Eve. 'Back for you in a few minutes,' and followed.

Matt started strongly and for the first twenty metres or so had me hard pressed to keep up with her. But then she slowed, clearly running out of puff, as the elapsed time approached two minutes.

I shot forward, pointing in wordless query to her roped arm. She nodded and I whipped the braid free. It was less than three metres long, with a knot at the free end. I took that in my teeth, positioned myself below her, and struck out with all my strength, pulling her along. She continued to flutter-kick with short strokes but kept her free arm close to her body. A few bubbles trailed from her nostrils. Her kicks weakened and mine became more frantic.

Lamplight reflected from the ruffled surface ahead. I surged up beneath her, taking hold of her body, lifting her head into the air. She gave a great gasping inhalation, then coughed while I held her, treading water as she pulled herself together.

'Okay,' she whispered. 'Close, though.'

'Damn,' I murmured. 'I was really looking forward to giving you the kiss of life.'

Lightly, she let me have one of the other kind. Her lips were bloodless, the dark hair was plastered sleekly to her skull, and her cinnamon skin was pallid. 'Thanks for playing tugboat.'

'You're sure you're all right?'

She'd found a rocky projection to cling to. 'Yes. Now go get Eve. It must be horrible for her, waiting all alone.'

'I'll have to rest a bit myself at the other end. Don't worry if I'm gone a while.'

I left her and swam back to my sister, who reassured me when I asked about her state of mind.

'I could see the reflected glow of your lanterns for over a minute,' she told me, smiling. 'The farther away you got, the bluer the underwater light became. With the lightning-bug constellations overhead, the effect was quite striking. Perhaps Cravat should make this place a tourist attraction.' She paused, and the smile faded. 'Poor Bob. He would have loved to see this.'

There was no answer to that. 'Are you ready?'

'I've been practising breathing shallowly with the snorkel closed. I think quite a lot of air gets trapped in the suit.'

'Just relax in the water,' I instructed her. 'Don't try to swim. I'll cup your chin and tow you across the lake on the surface, then close your snorkel and pull you under. Keep your legs together and your arms tight at your sides and your head down against your chest. That'll help me in the towing. Remember: when we reach the first air pocket, I'll deploy your snorkel and turn on the ventilator so you can breathe. Don't open your visor! There's very little head-room in the first space and I don't want to risk water slopping into your suit.'

I sealed her up. She had the Allenby strapped to her back, along with my sneakers, Matt's bootees, and the trusty space blanket. When she was in the water I attached one end of the rope to a suit hang-up ring on the ventilator housing between her shoulder blades. The other was fastened to the rear of my utility belt.

I stroked across the lake, hauling her with a rescue hold. After I prepared her I gave myself a stimulant jolt from the medicuff, then dived into the pipe.

We almost didn't make it.

My sister's flaccid suited body had less water resistance than Matt's, but towing her for such a distance taxed my still-convalescent powers to the limit. Towards the end, when my limbs turned to lead and the lamplight unaccountably began to fade and hypoxia turned my brain to dull grey meat, I almost succumbed and breathed the water. Only a sudden vision of Matt, abandoned in that miserable subterranean slot, inspired me to poke the medic-uff again. The drug boosted my heart and I managed a dozen strong kicks.

They brought me to safety.

I don't know how Matt realized that I was *in extremis*. But I felt a powerful yank on the lamp lanyard around my neck, and a moment later I broke the surface, wheezing and hacking. It was Matt who brought up Eve and opened her snorkel, she who placed my hands firmly on one of the few useful rock projections inside the pocket, she who improvised a float by trapping air in the plasfoil blanket, using it to prevent Eve's weights from carrying her back into the depths.

After a time we went on, not daring to rest any longer for fear that the cold water would fatally weaken Matt and me. This time Matt went forward alone, certain that she could easily cover the eighteen-metre distance. When I saw the dim blue glow blink three times and knew that she'd made it, I laboriously brought Eve through.

On shore in the anonymous beast's lair, I found myself shivering uncontrollably. I tried to start a fire in the twigs and other trash of the bone-nest, using my belt-pouch's permamatch, but the material was too damp to catch. Fortunately, the air temperature in the den was much higher than that of the water, so Matt and I huddled together in the clammy blanket again to recover. She warmed up rather quickly, while it seemed to take for ever for me to stop shivering.

I could tell that the women were worried.

'You're getting hypothermic, Li'l Bro,' Eve declared. 'Your face is almost as blue as mine. And no wonder, doing all that hard work.'

Matt said, 'Let me pull you through the next section, Eve. I've got my second wind.'

I protested in vain. The two of them set off and I waited anxiously, still wrapped in the blanket, until the three faint blue blinks sig-nalled that they had negotiated the twenty metres. My own trip was slow and torturous, nearly as difficult as the first long haul with Eve. I had not dared to take another dose of stimulant. Once again I felt myself blacking out as I neared the end, but this time I saved myself, surfacing in the Star Chamber like a wounded whale and drawing breath in an agonized whoop.

Matt pulled me out of the water. She had taken my sweater from Eve's suit and drew it over my shuddering carcass. The wool was exquisitely warm and smelled of woman. Someone yanked off my dripping shorts, tugged on almost-dry jeans, and encased my icy feet in Matt's stretchy polypro booties.

I could hear them talking over me as I came around, rolled in the space blanket as tightly as one of Mimo's cigars.

'It's just a short distance. Three metres, according to the chart. I know I can swim it.'

'The animal could be waiting.'

'I'll give it a triple magnum flechette. No problem. You've got to take care of Asa or he'll go into shock. I've seen people in this condition before. It's very dangerous.'

'So is going into the outer cave.'

'We've got to get the beacons in place.'

'I'll feel strong enough in a little while.'

'I'm strong enough now, and you're shivering almost as badly as he is. We have no time to waste. Give me his navigator.'

Fumbling at my wrist. Me trying to protest: don't do it, Evie!

No words coming out. All available energy diverted to the damned shivering.

'It shouldn't take more than ten minutes to set the things up. I'll be right back.'

No Evie no! I forbid it absolutely forbid it. Fuck so cold. Mattie darling don't let her go. Here be monsters . . . Splash.

So quiet so cold so very very dark.

Painful light seared my eyelids. I protested, 'For chrissake!' and began to squirm out of the cosy wrappings. Even when I managed to open my eyes, I was blinded by the dazzling torch.

Matt said, 'He's all right now. Warm, steady pulse and respiration.'

'Good,' Eve said. 'We've got suits for both of you. How're you feeling?'

Matt laughed. 'Better by the minute . . . I can't believe this!'

'Can't believe *what?*' I muttered, pulling myself painfully into a sitting position. 'Will you quit shining the damn light in my eyes? Did you set out both beacons and –'

Three lights. Held by three people.

Matt knelt beside me, holding me up. I finally saw the others clearly after they dimmed the torches and lowered the beams to the wet rock ledge of the Star Chamber. A big sealed duffel bag lay at their feet. They wore dripping envirosuits and their hooded heads brushed the webs of the glow-worms that hung from the small cave's ceiling. One by one they lifted their visors.

My sister Eve.

Captain Guillermo Bermudez.

And Ivor Jenkins.

Chapter 24

Overstating the obvious, I said to Ivor, 'You're alive!' and to Mimo, 'You're here!'

Young Hercules shrugged. 'I was very lucky.'

'However you managed it, I'm damned glad to see you.' I gave him an affectionate clout on the shoulder and he ducked his head shyly. I turned to Mimo. 'You, too, you old smuggler. How did you work the miracle?'

'What miracle? There are still forty-two minutes remaining before your fifty-hour deadline expires.'

'But you were gone!' I protested. 'The Haluk searched the Cravat system and found no trace of *Plomazo*.'

Captain Bermudez, that past master of astrogational chicanery, gave a derisive chuckle. 'They couldn't find their *ojetes* with both hands.'

'So how'd you do it?' I asked.

Eve interrupted firmly. 'Later! The most important thing now is to get you and Matt out of here. Ivor, please help my brother with his suit.'

We exited the cave in short order (the snoring two-hundred-kilo buzz-bear lying near the cavern entrance was such an anticlimax that no one even bothered to comment on it), boarded the gig that was waiting just outside, and headed for the starship at maximum velocity.

Ivor told us his story first, in characteristically pedantic fashion.

His first piece of good luck involved the flechette that had struck him in the face. The dart must have ricocheted off the rock floor, losing most of its momentum and dulling its point before hitting him, because it failed to deliver a full dose of sleepy-juice. Ivor was almost completely paralysed but still half-conscious when the troopers loaded him onto the trolley. He pretended to be out cold, while managing to flex his neck muscles and turn on the myostimulator collar.

In another piece of good fortune, his envirosuit hood was pushed back around his head as the troopers wrestled with his huge bulk and tossed him into Number Five Sump. He went under only briefly and ended floating on his back because of the weight of the daypack that he still wore. Only a small amount of relatively uncontaminated water entered his suit, which retained enough air to support him.

He drifted slowly away into the darkness, barely able to move, too confused and fearful to think straight. Now and then he fetched up against some obstruction and came to a stop, which delayed his journey to the chasm and allowed him time to recover further. After a while he regained partial use of his right arm, probably aided by the collar. When he heard the roar of the waterfall and realized what was about to happen, he was able to close his suit visor. The ventilator was already turned off.

The plunge down the shaft was vertical. At the bottom was a deep pool into which he sank, then bobbed to the surface. He managed to deploy his snorkel and turn on the ventilator as he was carried away into the bowels of Grant Microcontinent, borne along a natural streamway two levels beneath Pothole Passage.

Ivor's wrist navigator gave only a wan glow, not really bright enough to show much detail of the underground river's corridor. In most parts it was very narrow and the current was swift. Fortunately, it had no spiky speleothems hanging from its low ceiling.

As he floated through subterranean blackness, Ivor gradually regained full use of his limbs and oriented himself so he would travel feet-first, avoiding knocks on the head when he inevitably bumped into the cave walls. He turned off the collar to conserve its power supply and watched the display of his navigator in bemusement as it tracked his progress along a featureless grid. During much of his journey, he prayed that his dying would not be too painful or prolonged.

After nearly four hours had passed, the navigator showed that he had travelled slightly more than twelve kilometres in a southerly direction. He recalled with increasing excitement that Nutmeg-414 was approximately that distance north of Pickle Pothole, and that the tall limestone cliffs overlooking the lake had numerous caves – some with waterfalls pouring from them.

Was it possible that he wouldn't die after all?

He turned on his collar again when he saw a faint pinkish light ahead. If it marked the end of the tunnel, within a few minutes he would either splash into Pickle Pothole and live, or be dashed to pieces on the rocks along the lakeshore.

Ivor braced himself as the cataract spat him out. He fell three metres into the water.

Afloat in a disbelieving daze, he watched Cravat's G1 sun rise, then swam ashore. He still had the gig's utility buoy; but since he lacked the technical expertise to summon the craft from its underwater hiding place as Matt or I would have done, he simply turned on the emergency beacon of the navigator and waited to be rescued.

Mimo, in orbit in *Plomazo*, received the signal and feared that the mission had been aborted due to some disaster. He could think of no other reason for the ground party to use an open-frequency emergency signal. He activated the submerged gig's autopilot, returned the small orbiter to *Plomazo*, then descended in it to the planetary surface to find out what had gone wrong.

Ivor told him, leaving the old man in a quandary. Mimo's instincts urged him to come to the rescue of Matt and me and Eve, while experience and common sense dictated caution. Two men, no matter how well armed, were no match for Bronson Elgar and a cave full of aliens. The nearest Zone Patrol cruiser turned out to be over two days away.

Mimo had the Rampart Red Card I'd left with him. But he doubted whether anyone at Cravat Dome would accept its authenticity and obey his orders unless he presented it in person. That seemed risky. If there were Galapharma moles inside the sealed enclave, they might find a way to eliminate both Mimo and Ivor while their associates down in the cavern were disposing of Matt and me, leaving no one alive who knew the extent of Haluk involvement in the conspiracy.

Mimo believed there was a long chance that we'd get away from our captors. If we didn't, they would either kill us outright or keep us for hostages, as they had Eve. In either case, prudence seemed to dictate that Mimo wait the designated fifty hours. After that, he could consult with Simon via subspace before taking further action.

On further consideration, knowing men like Bronson Elgar all too well, Mimo deduced that I might be coerced into betraying his position. So he hid *Plomazo* in one of the local asteroid belts and waited to see what would happen.

The huge Haluk ship came roaring into the Cravat solar system not long afterward and began its search. The aliens would certainly have found *Plomazo*, even dissimulated, if Mimo's starship had remained in a Cravat orbit; but their wider sweep of interplanetary space was perfunctory and incompetent.

When the Haluk vessel finally went away, *Plomazo* returned to Cravat and took up its previous position. Mimo and Ivor rode the gig back down to Pickle Pothole and waited, underwater, until Eve activated her emergency beacons. They found her eight minutes later.

'Did Eve mention,' I remarked to Mimo, 'that the secret Haluk facilities beneath all of the factories on Grant Microcontinent were destroyed – vaporized by photon flares? Including the one where we were held captive.'

'*¡Coño, no!*'

Eve said, 'I forgot to tell him. I was too amazed when the gig came hurtling down out of the night. All I could think of was getting you and Matt out of the cave.'

Mimo and I were sitting side by side in the gig's flight deck with the others behind us. He scowled at me. 'If I'd known that the Haluk sites had been destroyed, then I would have had no choice but to call Zone Patrol – believing you had all been killed. How in God's name did you escape?'

'Matt, you'd better tell him.' I got up from my seat and stretched. 'I'm going to take a break and think about what to do next. Our presumed deaths give us a temporary tactical advantage, but the way I spilled my guts under interrogation is bad news in the long run.'

I went aft to the gig's little messroom, got myself some coffee and a nuked raspberry scone (no snickerdoodles, alas), and settled down with a scratchpad and stylus.

I began with the perception that Galapharma now knew about Karl and my Department of Special Projects back on Seriphos, about our suspicion of Cousin Zed and Oliver Schneider, about our probe of the presumed sabotage, and our scrutiny of the lines of communication between the Gala moles within Rampart. Elgar had asked me whether I had told Karl about the Haluk-Galapharma connection. I gave a modified affirmative, saying that I didn't know how much information Mimo had transmitted from Cravat.

Our first priority, then, was to get Karl and his people – and their database – out of harm's way. I only hoped it wasn't already too late.

The only person other than Mimo whom Gala would consider to be an immediate threat was Simon Frost. I was hazy on just exactly what I had told Elgar about my father's knowledge of the Haluk connection. Simon was certainly safe for the time being: the Concern's agents couldn't get at him while he was en route to Earth on *Mogollon Rim*. And when he arrived . . . what proof did he have, apart from his unsupported word, that a Galapharma-Haluk conspiracy existed?

The anomalous Haluk corpse in Tokyo. I'd told Elgar about that.

Simon would have to use every bit of clout he possessed to ensure that the body was safeguarded, along with the test data showing the presence of human DNA and the eradication of the allomorphic trait. Aside from my partially transmuted sister, that corpse was the only concrete evidence of Haluk genetic hanky-panky.

And Eve herself was the only material witness to the demiclone scheme. I presumed that by now, almost all traces of clandestine Haluk activity on Cravat had been obliterated. The tunnels connecting the sites were probably still in place, along with miscellaneous bits and pieces such as the empty alien liquor bottles and lanterns. But those things of themselves wouldn't convince the

Secretariat for Xenoaffairs that a grand conspiracy involving the Haluk and an outlaw human agency existed.

We needed more witnesses.

Such as the Rampart employees at Cravat Dome who had co-operated in the clandestine production of PD32:C2. Perhaps their bribery had been accomplished in such a convoluted manner that tracing the bag-man and his source of funds would be impossible. But Emily Konigsberg had said that Bronson Elgar was in charge of security for the entire PD32:C2 operation. It was possible that he'd done the recruitment work himself, and that one or more of the bribees could finger him.

Candidates: the Nutmeg project engineer who had falsified the Grant sampling figures; the shuttle pilot who had flown the vector shipments to an orbital pick-up point; and the Dome flight control personnel who had turned a blind eye to the unauthorized activity. Perhaps more Dome people had been involved, but those were the obvious targets.

In Elgar's position, I would have wasted the lot. But maybe not in an abrupt wholesale slaughter that might cause more problems than it solved. The assassin might have decided to make the deaths look natural by stringing them out over several days, or even weeks. After all, he still believed that Matt and I were dead, and Mimo and Simon and even Karl Nazarian posed only long-range threats. Bron might think he had plenty of time to tidy up the loose ends. I finished the coffee, licked the raspberry jam off my fingers, and went to tell Mimo to drop me off at Cravat Dome.

'Alone?' Matt exclaimed in exasperation. 'So you're still determined to play cowboy! What if Elgar *is* still there?'

'Then I'll arrest him.'

The black eyes blazed. 'And if you're killed, what happens to our mission?'

'You'll take over, of course, and do the job a damn sight better than I would. My own part of the mission is accomplished.' I tipped a solemn wink to Eve. 'The next CEO and President of Rampart Starcorp is safe and pretty nearly sound. You four know everything about this conspiracy that I do, and it's vital that you stay alive and tell your stories to Karl, Simon, and the truth machines. I'm the only one of the bunch who's expendable, so I'm the one who goes hunting for rascals in Cravat Dome – right now.'

Ivor looked hurt. 'I realize that the others are important witnesses, but there seems to be no compelling reason why I shouldn't accompany you and render assistance where it's needed.'

'There are three reasons,' I contradicted him coldly. '*Uno:* that bod of yours is recognizable at fifty metres. *Dos:* you got flushed down the toilet once already on this mission and it made me feel very guilty. I hate that. *Tres:* I really can do this job faster and better working alone.'

'He's right,' Eve said.

And that put an end to the arguing.

I checked our position. We were about thirty-thousand kilometres out, not quite halfway to *Plomazo*'s orbit. I said, 'Mimo – is it possible that your classy gig has an illicit programmable transponder ID?'

He smiled sweetly at me. 'Do bears shit in the woods? No smuggler could do business without one.'

'Excellent.' I told him the registration number I wanted. He tapped it in. 'Now turn us around and then cut off the signal that hides us from Cravat's scanner satellite.'

When the manoeuvre was accomplished and the disguise in place, I keyed Cravat Starport Flight Control.

'Cravat Control, this is gig RA-733B Light, inbound from orbit. Please activate lander lock for a touch-and-go with passenger discharge.'

'Affirm, RA Light, you are locked to land . . . We do not scan your primary.'

I said, 'Primary vessel *Blue Rambler* ex Seriphos is performing routine solar evaluation. I request surface transport for one passenger.'

The bored voice said, 'Understood, RA Light.'

'Please patch me through on a video channel to Port Traffic Manager Robert Bascombe. My priority code: Alpha three one one.'

There was a beat of silence. When the flight controller spoke again, he no longer sounded bored. 'Uh ... RA Light, we will transfer you to Port Traffic Office. Stand by.'

The Cravat Port logo bloomed on our flight deck viewscreen, along with a canned musical theme that might have been 'It's Not Easy Bein' Green'.

I frowned. 'Sounds like they know Bob's dead. It's too early for Cravat Fleet Security to have started a routine search. He told his people he'd be gone for at least two days and we're only a couple of hours over the line. Elgar must have set off the ESC-10's emergency beacon.'

Cravat Starport was hardly a beehive of activity. The gig's terrain scan showed only a single big ship on the ground. Its transponder ID matched *Rampion Sentinel,* one of the fast, heavily armed freighters Matt had assigned to the Cravat run. The three other ULD vessels parked on the pad were small fry: the lone ExSec cop-cutter assigned to the remote world, a passenger ferry from Nogawa-Krupp, and a Rampart Starcorp mobile hospital, probably doing its scheduled planet-to-planet circuit with expensive diagnostic gear unavailable to the local pillrollers. Two SLD orbiters for satellite maintenance and shuttle service stood at a respectful distance from the starships. All of the other vehicles in port were aircraft.

'Which one is it, *mi capitan?*' I asked Mimo. 'Old Bron sure brought his own mount to the barn dance. Has to be one of the three down there.'

He studied the collection. 'I vote for the travelling hospital. Those things go everywhere, and they have no hard and fast schedule.'

I gave a short nod. 'I agree. When you're back aboard *Plomazo,* keep an eye out for it trying to sneak away. Give it the pirate's stand-and-deliver challenge. If it stops, disable its drive. If it runs, kill it.'

'Gotcha.'

A middle-aged man with emaciated features, prominent front teeth, and a testy expression appeared onscreen.

'Terence Hoy, Assistant Port Traffic Manager. To whom am I speaking?'

I kept the voice-only channel open. 'Please turn on your communication encrypt.'

Grimace. 'Very well. Encrypt activated.'

I showed him my freshly scrubbed, debearded face. I was wearing one of Mimo's violet designer sweatsuits, comfy garb favoured by travellers, and I had a handy alias and cover story all prepared.

But Terence Hoy gave a violent start as he caught sight of me, and I knew my infamy had once again blown the gaff.

'Do you recognize me, Citizen Hoy?'

'I thought,' he blurted, 'you were Thrown Away three years ago! What the devil are you doing in *Blue Rambler*'s gig?'

Unless he was a Golden Galaxy Best Actor candidate, Terence Hoy hadn't heard about Asahel Frost from Bronson Elgar, Ollie Schneider, or any of the other villains in the piece. So I had an honest man to deal with.

'Look at this thing carefully.' I held the Red Card up to the viewer's eye. 'It authorizes me, Asahel Frost, brand-new Rampart Vice President, to co-opt your body and soul on pain of your dismissal and disenfranchisement. The signature and code are Simon's. You can have your people check its authenticity with Central, but if you value your ass you'd better not make me wait while you do . . . Are you in charge of the planet now that Bascombe's dead?'

His affronted expression melted into perplexity. 'Yes. But – but how did you –'

'Never mind. I want you to meet my gig at the starport *now*. Come out to the pad on a transport van. Bring a computer with Cravat full-system access.'

'Very well.'

'My business here is extremely confidential. You will tell no one my true identity.'

'I understand. I'll be waiting.'

It was full daylight on this side of the planet, and the fifteen-hundred-metre forcefield that covered the enclave was a faintly sparkling hemisphere, The buildings inside, separated by wide swathes of parkland, were clearly visible. The landing pad immediately adjacent to Cravat Dome was fused native soil hemmed in by poisonously green forest. An electrified fence and guard pylons with zappers surrounded the pad, but it was otherwise open to the elements. Maintenance vehicles, ground transports, and industrial robots trundled about in the vicinity of the big freighter. We saw a few humans in full envirogarb among the hoppercraft.

Flight control set the gig down on the small X in the Light Spacecraft section. There was no ship conveyor, so after landing, we obediently trailed a FOLLOW ME bot to a parking space next to the two orbiters. A van that looked like a big blue jellybean rolled up to us and extruded an airlock passage.

I tucked a Kagi pistol into the waistband of my sweatpants and bloused the top to conceal it. 'Take care,' I said to my sister and my friends, and went off to do what I had to do.

Terence Hoy was waiting in the van, which was some sort of VIP robolimo with leather seats, tables (one holding the computer), and a lavishly appointed bar. By the time that we shook hands and sat down together at the computer table, the gig was already on the move, heading back to the X for lift-off.

'Where would you like to go?' Hoy asked me. His smile was not reflected in his eyes.

'Can we get into the Dome without passing through the passenger or freight terminals?'

'Certainly.' He addressed the van's robot. 'Driver: enter Aperture Three.' As we rolled away smoothly I studied the two parked orbiters. They were identical, with big cargo bays capable of carrying sizeable satellites – or a respectable load of contraband viral vector.

'The green decon module labelled _1_ leads to the passenger terminal,' Terence Hoy said. Only the unnatural rapidity of his speech betrayed his unease. 'The yellow module at Aperture Two is for freight. Aperture Three, the red decon module, serves emergency vehicles, fullers, supply loaders and maintenance bots. The Dome has a total of twelve apertures at ground level. Its Sheltok DF-1500 forcefield projector is state-of-the-art, able to deflect half-ton meteorites. Not that we have to worry much about hazards like that on Cravat.'

'Only man-eating humpies and birds with corrosive shit,' I muttered.

He gave a forced laugh. 'So you're acquainted with our colourful wildlife. Are you a big-game hunter, Vice President?'

'In a manner of speaking.'

Our van entered the red decon chamber and was zapped to sterility. We continued through an airlock into a short, featureless tunnel ending in a semicircular portal four metres in diameter, apparently curtained by dancing sparks. Heavy equipment and moving human figures were visible beyond the aperture arch.

'I've never had any experience with such a powerful forcefield,' I said. 'Is it harmless to the touch, like the lesser ones?'

'Certainly. It feels very solid, like greasy glass.'

Interrupter units stood on either side of the portal interface. Our van triggered the interrupter and the sparkling curtain vanished. Rotating cherry-beacons on top of both units began to flash a warning and a loud mechanical voice said: *Forcefield aperture now open. Please proceed. Do not stop in the zebra-stripe interface area. Please proceed. Do not stop –'*

We rolled through into a hangarlike building.

I said, 'What happens if you stop on the stripes and the field turns on?' The zebra area, about twenty centimetres wide, transected the portal. 'Do you get shocked, like with the smaller generators?'

'No.' Terence gave me a superior smirk. 'Any object remaining on the interface area when a Sheltok DF-1500 field reactivates is sliced in two. There are safeguards in place to prevent such accidents, of course. Only in the event of an emergency dome lockdown or the unlikely physical destruction of an interrupter unit would there be any real danger.'

The sparkles reappeared behind us, the cherry-beacons turned off, and the admonitory voice shut up. We had arrived inside Cravat Dome.

'Is there any reason,' I asked, 'why we can't pull into a quiet corner and stay here for a few minutes?'

'No problem. Driver: return to van parking station.' A fleeting trace of hospitality crossed his austere face. 'I hope you'll allow me to give you a short tour of the enclave when you can spare the time. Rampart Starcorp did an outstanding job on Cravat, creating an attractive oasis for our nine thousand residents. Employee turnover is very small.'

'I'm here to discuss employee attrition, not turnover,' I said baldly. 'Tell me about any sudden deaths that have occurred here within the past thirty-six hours.'

His fingers tightened on armrests of his comfortable seat. 'We only found out about Bob –'

'Besides Bascombe.'

'There have been two, neither of which were in any way suspicious. Jeremy Malvern, a shuttle pilot, died late yesterday of a drug overdose: yoxostiline, an autoerotic stimulant.' He scowled in disapproval. 'It's illegal, but there's always plenty of it available for a price.'

The poor bastard wouldn't be toting any more contraband PD32:C2 to Haluk ships in orbit, but maybe he'd died happy. 'And the other casualty?'

'Costanzia Vacco, a project engineer. She suffered a heart attack while jogging and was found on the Ring Promenade about two hours ago. I'd just learned about it when you called me. Very sad. Connie was only thirty-eight.'

'What project did she work on?' I asked. The answer would tell me whether or not I'd come on a wild goose chase.

'Nutmeg. She was chief crop futures analyst.'

I let out a slow exhalation. Gotcha, Bron . . .

If I was good enough.

'Please get on your computer and see whether anyone besides this Connie had regular access to crop sampling data from mothballed Nutmeg sites.'

'Mothballed?' he repeated.

'Yes. Anyone who might have been able to alter the feedback from the inactive sites to your Nutmeg-1 office here in Dome.'

Hoy picked up the little mike and whispered into it. Names began to scroll down the monitor screen. None were highlighted.

'It looks like Connie was the only one.' He eyed me resentfully. 'Are you going to tell me what this is about?'

Instead of answering, I asked, 'How many flight controllers do you have?'

'Twelve are all we need – plus the robotics, of course.'

'Regular shifts?'

'For the eight senior controllers. There are always two on duty for six-and-a-half-hour stints, round the clock, twenty-six-hour planetary day. Four juniors do fill-in on days off, sick days, and so on.'

'Did the pilot Jeremy Malvern have a regular flight schedule?'

'Let me check.' After a few moments he pointed to the screen. 'We only have three shuttle drivers. Their schedules are pretty flexible, depending on satellite maintenance needs and the schedules of nonlander starships – Rampart couriers and express shipping outfits like StelEx that deliver and pick up from our orbiting dump-station. Here's a record of Jeremy's hours over the past eight weeks.'

I studied the screen. Most of his flights lasted two hours or less. But once he had stayed up above the world so high for nearly five hours. 'What was he doing this time?' I asked.

Terence consulted the computer. 'Weather satellite maintenance. One of our Carnie W5's is a lemon, always needing to be babied along.'

'Let me see Jerry's flight time for the past year.'

There were seven more of the long tours, at wide intervals. They would have been convenient for periodic transshipments from the secret Haluk dock on Grant.

I said, 'Please see which flight controllers were on duty during those eight time periods.'

Just two names popped onto the screen: Anders Foss and Franek Odnowski. Terence Hoy anticipated me by asking the computer another question, then said, 'Andy and Frank are on duty right now.'

'Take me to them. Fast.'

Chapter 25

The jellybean van's top speed was fifteen kph, but we didn't have far to go.

Flight Control was in a tower on top of the passenger terminal module less than two hundred metres from the equipment hangar.

We pulled up at an entrance flanked by a small garden and a parking lot full of go-carts, which seemed to be Cravat's ground conveyance of choice. One of them stood at the terminal door. A woman in an envirosuit with the hood down was kissing its driver goodbye.

I jumped out of the van. 'Make it snappy,' I said to Terence, who gave me another look. But he led the way with alacrity. I followed him across the uncrowded concourse to a cylindrical central structure with a ring-mezzanine restaurant and a spiral staircase. At its base was the tower elevator.

When the doors slid shut on us and we began to rise slowly, I pulled the Kagi pistol out of my waistband and clicked off the safety.

'For God's sake!' Terence cried. 'What –'

'Only a precaution. Does this lift open directly into Flight Control ops?'

'Of course not. There are other offices in the tower as well. Access to operations is restricted.'

'How many people normally working in ops?'

'Just the two controllers, Andy and Frank. Traffic is normally very light ... But, look here! Red Card or no Red Card, I've a right to know just what you intend to do.'

The lift doors opened on an empty corridor. I tried to calm him. 'I intend to take the controllers into custody, under authority granted by Simon Frost himself. I have strong reason to believe that the two of them and the dead shuttle pilot accepted bribes from a Rampart rival. Their scheme involved carrying contraband vector into orbit. The stuff was picked up later from the dump-station.'

He goggled at me in astonishment. 'Christ! You don't mean to tell me that Connie's death was connected –'

'And Bob's,' I affirmed grimly. 'She was involved. Bob was an innocent victim. I can't say anything more about it now. Where's the door to ops?'

'It won't open without the day code.' He looked embarrassed. 'I can't recall it, but I can get it easily enough from the computer in this office.' He nodded at a door marked PLANETARY MET.

'Do it,' I said. 'And order your security personnel to seal the entrances to the passenger terminal. Quick and quiet. Nobody comes in or out.'

I remained in the hall and he left the door open. I glimpsed a big viewscreen showing atmospheric plots of both hemispheres and other paraphernalia of weather prediction. A couple of meteorologists went about their business after murmuring greetings to the Assistant Port Manager.

Terence returned almost immediately. 'The day code is 34B–6LQ. The precaution is really only *pro forma*, you understand, intended to keep out curious passengers and –'

'Stay in the met room,' I told him curtly. 'If Andy and Frank surrender quietly, I'll be back with them in a few minutes. If you hear a ruckus, get a special-weapons assault team here on the double. Be sure to tell them not to shoot the guy in the purple sweats.' I closed the door in his face and trotted down the hall to flight operations. The electronic lock was a travesty that a bright child could have hacked into. I tapped in the code, opened the door a crack, then kicked it open the rest of the way and burst inside, yelling 'Freeze!'

The room was about twelve metres deep. Its polarizing picture-window filtered out the sparks of the forcefield and had a striking overview of the starport and the forested mountains in the distance.

It smelled of ozone and scorched meat.

A voice drawled, 'What *does* it take to kill you, Cap'n Helly?'

He was standing sideways before the big double control console, motionless, as ordered. He still wore the navy-blue commando sweater, olive cargo pants, and Timberland boots. His Kagi was pointed at the head of a tow-headed man in the lefthand control seat. A body was slumped in the other one.

'Drop it, Bron,' I said.

'I'll finish him first,' the assassin told me calmly.

'No,' the controller moaned. 'Please. Oh, God! Poor Frankie –'

'Shut up, Andy,' said Elgar. He entwined his fingers in the toffee-coloured hair and gave a cruel yank. 'Rotate your chair to face the man in the door. Stand up slowly.'

'You can't get out of here, Bron,' I said. 'Fleet Security has the terminal sealed.'

'Then you'll have to tell them to go away.'

He prodded the back of his captive's neck with the gun muzzle, still gripping the man's hair as he rose. Bad luck for me. The controller was a lot taller and bulkier than Elgar and made a perfect shield. 'Start walking, Andy. To the door. The guy'll get out of our way.'

With only had a second to decide what to do, I drilled the controller in the foot with a blue ray. He screamed and lurched back against the hit man. The pair of them tumbled to the floor. Before I could sort them out and take aim again, Elgar fired twice. The first blast went through Andy's neck. The second missed my head by less than a centimetre.

I dived out of the door.

Chwoik chwoik.

Elgar fired two more shots while I was in mid-air. They scorched the ceramalloy bulkhead of the corridor and I rolled aside, out of range. He sent a couple of shots past the doorframe, ankle-high and knee-high. I waited. Our Kagi pistols weren't powerful enough to pierce the wall.

Silence. Not a peep out of Andy. If I wanted a live hostile witness to interrogate, it looked like I'd have to settle for Bron.

The silence lengthened.

I raised my pistol high above my head and took a blind shot

inside the control room. Some kind of equipment gave up the ghost with a soft tinkling explosion. There was no other response.

As rapidly as I could, I fired three more blind blasts at different levels. More flight-control gear perished. I ripped off one of my sneakers and poked the toe around the doorframe. Bait refused. Shoe back on. Deep breath. Crouch. Jump out firing.

The flight control room was empty except for the two dead men.

Cursing, I dashed to an unmarked door on the right side of the room. It opened into a stairwell. I galloped down to the ring-mezzanine level, flung open the door, and came out with the pistol steadied in both hands.

I'd arrived in a vestibule just outside the restaurant. An elderly woman wearing a smart apple-green velveteen cloak emerged from the adjacent ladies' room and screeched at the sight of me and my gun. She turned and fled back into the john. I quickly checked the men's toilet and found nothing. An adjacent maintenance closet was locked.

Pulling down the sleeve of my sweatsuit to conceal the Kagi, I scanned the dining area. There were a few patrons sitting at the tables and a single open-mouthed server. No sign of Bron. I looked into the kitchen. None of the workers had seen a fleeing man.

He might have circled to the external stairway on the cylinder's opposite side. I started around, simultaneously looking over the railing. My vantage point was excellent, affording a view of the entire open concourse. The persons below were peaceably going about their business, apparently not having heard the old woman's startled cry. There were so few people in the terminal that I easily ascertained that Bronson Elgar was not among them. It hardly seemed possible that he had managed to reach the baggage area or hide behind one of the counters without being spotted by a port employee.

The only ExSec guard in sight stood beside the archway that led to Aperture 1. A sign above it read: TO ALL FLIGHTS. The guard was keeping an alert eye on the people moving around the concourse. He wore only a sidearm.

I cursed Terence Hoy. Hadn't the idiot heard the fire-fight going on in the corridor outside Planetary Met? Where was the goddam SWAT team?

I came full circle on the mezzanine. Outside the restaurant was a port phone with a notice telling me to press O in an emergency. I did, and got a live human being.

'Connect me to Planetary Meteorology,' I said.

'Sir, this phone is for internal and emergency use only. If you –'

I let loose a scorching storm of profanity and threats of dire retribution, but it was only after I evoked the magical name of Terence Hoy that the scandalized operator put me through.

Terence averred that he was just about to call the special-weapons assault team. I told him to get a fucking move on and described the fugitive. Then: 'The internal stairway that leads from Flight Control to the restaurant on the mezzanine. Does it continue down below the concourse?'

'Why, no. It ends on the main floor.'

'The central elevator. Does it go to the basement?'

'The only lower-level access is through Baggage Handling and Maintenance. I had guards posted there, per your orders.'

'Good! Then we may have the bastard penned. Tell the SWAT team to meet me on the main floor.'

I hung up the phone and went down the inner stairway. It opened on the side opposite the passenger elevator, facing the terminal entrance. I slipped out onto the concourse as casually as I could. Clutching both hands to my belly and holding the cuff of my purple suit over the pistol, I began a slow circumambulation of the central cylinder.

Where would I go if I was Bronson Elgar?

I hadn't the faintest idea. Maybe he'd dodged me and gone back up to the tower offices, looking for another hostage. Maybe he'd frightened the kitchen staff into lying about his presence. Maybe –

Twenty metres away, the cylinder's elevator door opened. Out came the little old lady in the apple-green cloak, holding tight to the arm of another woman with white hair. The pair of them started for Aperture 1, moving with surprising speed.

Oh, shit.

I yelled, 'Elgar! Stop where you are!'

The figure in the apple-green cloak whirled around and took a shot at me. The blue ray lanced past my shoulder and nailed a flight-bulletin kiosk. Several bystanders screamed and shouted.

Elgar was running, dragging the woman along. The cloak fluttered around both of them, making it impossible for me to get a decent bead on him. There was too much danger of hitting the woman – and besides, I needed him alive.

'Guard!' I shouted. 'Stop him! Don't let him get out the aperture!' There had to be passenger-transport vehicles in the green decon module beyond the forcefield interface. If Bron managed to reach one, he'd be clear and away. His fake hospital ship was waiting.

The security man at the aperture drew his sidearm, but before he could fire, Elgar shot him in the chest. The guard fell. Elgar turned around and sent another beam at me. He missed and I hit the deck.

Then pandemonium broke out. Frightened people started running in all directions. One or two smart ones dived to the floor, like me. A six-man SWAT team, armed to the teeth, came rushing in through Baggage Handling on my left, bellowing 'Halt!' through helmet amplifiers.

Bron didn't. And he didn't let the old woman go, either.

I howled, 'Rampart Security! Don't shoot!' Then I got to my feet again and started to run, praying that Terence had told the team about my purple sweatsuit.

The SWAT team was firing deliberately high above the fugitives in a futile attempt to intimidate Elgar. I saw the woman start to sag, either swooning from terror or suffering a heart attack at the sight of the criss-crossing beams of blue death just over her head. She must have tripped up the assassin as she collapsed. He staggered and fell to his hands and knees, the cloak billowing around both of them.

The apple-green fabric settled around one figure. The other crawled toward the interrupter unit.

Bronson Elgar had unfastened the cloak and dropped it onto the woman.

The SWAT team, thrown for a loss by the switch, held its fire. So did I, until I realized that the creeper was Elgar. If he got through the aperture, he'd be able to turn the forcefield back on from the other side. It was undoubtedly blasterproof, and by the time we reached the interrupter and re-opened it, he'd be behind the decon airlock.

Elgar hit the manual control of the interrupter unit. The field winked out, the cherry-beacon began to rotate, and the canned voice recited its warning.

What had Terence said about the field safeguards? '*Only in the event of an emergency dome lock-down or the unlikely physical destruction of an interrupter unit would there be any real danger.*'

The aperture would close if either interrupter was destroyed.

Elgar continued his frantic scramble across the floor. I stopped, gripped my Kagi in both hands, and took aim.

Chwoik.

The nearest interrupter emitted a puff of smoke and its flashing red beacon died. The sparkling curtain rematerialized inside the aperture arch. I saw the old woman stir and lift her head, but the other figure at the field interface lay unmoving.

Both halves of it.

Chapter 26

It was pleasant on the open porch of my new beach house. A gentle breeze blew off the sea and kept the bugs away, and now that the sun was down the elvis-birds were humming mellowly in the mint palms. As the tropical sky faded quickly to indigo, stars popped out and a hundred comets gleamed like slashes of silvery chalk.

'I love it,' Matt said.

'Told you so. Stay here with me for ever. Or three weeks, anyway. It'll take Simon that long to get back to the Spur after setting off his fireworks in Toronto. The Haluk will deny everything, of course. Interesting times upcoming, babe.'

'Mmm. And a million things to do, now that I'm VP Con Services.'

'Us Vice Presidents have to stick together. Promise you'll stay on K-L for three weeks. I'll take you to the Isle of Rum-ti-Foo and we'll listen to my great old Jimmy Buffet songs: "Volcano". "Stars on the Water". "Cheeseburger in Paradise".'

We were lying together in a hammock built for two. I nuzzled her *piel canela*. Quite a lot of it was available, since she still wore her bikini. Our first trip together in the yellow submarine had been a tremendous success.

'Three weeks,' she said dreamily. 'I think we deserve that much – unless the hot lead Karl has on Ollie Schneider's whereabouts pans out. I want to hook that bastard to the machines and interrogate him myself. He's probably the only mole who can implicate any of the Rampart directors in the conspiracy. Of course, they may all be innocent . . .'

I nipped her ear. 'Tell you what: let's kidnap Zed and wring the truth out of him. To hell with law and order.'

'Idiot! No wonder they threw you out of ICS. You know we have no proof whatsoever that he's disloyal. Or the others, either. And with every director stonewalling as a matter of principle, we're stymied. There'll be no more voluntary interrogation sessions of Rampart bigwigs.'

I kissed the side of her neck. 'Our own confessions were block-busters. And Eve's was supernova class. They'll do.'

She uttered a sceptical little grunt. 'Hold the cheering until we're certain that they're held admissible in our suit against Galapharma. Alistair Drummond's lawyers have already filed twenty-three objections.'

'Piffle.'

'The objections could be upheld,' she insisted. 'Of course, if we manage to track down Schneider and add his confession to our own evidence, it would be a different matter ... Pity about Bronson Elgar. Just think of the tales he could have told.'

'So I goofed,' said I. '*C'est la guerre.*'

'I'm glad he's dead,' she admitted. 'What kind of a human monster would deliberately maroon a man on a comet?'

'It's right there, you know.' I pointed. 'The big one, just above the western horizon.'

'Really? Helly's Comet?' She laughed, bounced up out of the hammock, and pulled me out after her. 'Let's get a telescope! I want to see it in close-up.'

'I found it to be just a trifle disappointing. But whatever you say.'

She paused, looking up at me, her black eyes gleaming. 'On second thought, I have a better idea.'

'Let's hope,' I said, 'it's the same as mine. There should be just enough time before we're due to pick up Ivor at the hopper pad and go to Mimo's for the party.'

We turned our backs on the comet and went into the house, hand in hand.